Ghosts
Of The Soon
Departed

Published in the State of North Carolina

The United States of America

Imagician Press 2012, 2015

Cover Art: Oil on canvas *Ghosts of the Soon Departed* by Alvin Ward.

Back cover photo of T.A. Epley courtesy of Allison Moe.

Graphic Design by Sonji Noodles

Imagician Press

Greensboro, North Carolina

Autumn 2015

Ghosts Of The Soon Departed

A Novel by

T.A. Epley

Acknowledgements:

For Support: my family, particularly Lucy, Sam, Alma, Yakov, &
  Matisyahu.

For Loyalty: my friends, particularly Chris G.

For inspiration: Roho

DEDICATION:

Oh, sister

backslider, fare you well
backslider, fare you well
if I never see you anymore
oh sinner, fare thee well
oh sinner, fare thee well
I will meet you on kingdom's shore

~traditional~

Ghosts Of The Soon Departed

Ghosts of the Soon Departed

Dixie, he tried to remember it.

He couldn't recall the tune. Maybe a few bars of "Shall we gather at the river?" A forest of emerald green leaves and loamy black earth receded behind the child as he ran. He panted in the August heat, his blonde hair clinging to the sweat on his brow. His bare feet, tough and calloused, impacted the moist leafy ground and pushed it behind. Fear followed on his heels. Had they followed? Am I pursued? Lacking the presence of mind to recollect the melody, he abandoned the idea of a soothing cadence. Breaking through a line of trees, he stumbled across a small stream, dispersing a flock of midges hovering above the surface of the crystal water. A second later the midges resumed their dance above the current. The brambles tore at his arms and scratched his face. Will they catch me? Will they shoot me? Crawling to avoid the toughest tangles and branches, he emerged from the other side of a thicket. In front of him loomed the ridgeline. He assaulted the mountainside while exhaustion threatened to disable his limbs. As the slope became severe, the boy's legs grew weak. Eventually it became too steep to walk up the ridge and, occasionally backsliding, he had to crawl the last leg of the ascent. He looked back over the terrain he had just crossed. "Damn... shit... hellfire...," he gasped in short cotton-mouthed breaths. He turned and scanned the valley below for his destination. Past the foot of the mountain, fields stretched out, church steeples punctuated the wilderness, and off in the distance, some four miles away, a small, muddy town glimmered. The bare-foot knave shielded his eyes from the sun's glamour with the salute of his right hand. Pinching his side to relieve a cramp, he finally spotted a chimney poking above some hardwoods in the valley...

Ghosts of the Soon Departed

Caleb

Ghosts of the Soon Departed

1864

"Caleb, they ain't no sense in you getting rid of that cook-stove. You're going to miss it come winter." The tall, horse-faced man spit into a receptacle on the floor as if to punctuate his exclamation.

"I won't live that long without the money it'll fetch. I still got the fireplace in the other room," Caleb replied. The dark haired, severe looking man was driving in the final nails. He stepped back and looked at their work. The chimney that once came all the way down through the floor was now held up on a small platform, six feet up the wall.

"I'm telling you J.D., this will make for a lot more room in here." J.D. examined their handiwork, before saying, "We should have just bit the bullet and tore that thing out of there. Wait till a goose-drowner comes and you'll have a waterfall in here." He walked around to the other side, studiously examining it. "Even if it don't leak, cold air's going to pour down it all winter. Might as well sleep in the holler with the deer."

Caleb walked up and pulled on the supports. The collection of stone sat on the shelf impervious. "That's why we fill it up with old newspapers and sich, then seal off the top."

J.D. started to gather up the tools. He was extremely tall compared to most of the folks in the area, six-foot one to be exact. His face was long and drawn downward with large chapped lips and puffy bags under his eyes.

Despite this, his every move was determined and resolute. His arrogance and self-reliance poured through everything he did. He never thought it was a good idea to plant squash this year- he knew it was a good idea, and if the crop didn't come in- it was because his nephew shirked the weeding or planted the rows too close together. In any event, he was right and his plans did not reach fruition because of the incompetence of others.

Caleb found a broom in the corner, although it was worn down almost to the nub, he was determined to sweep all of the sawdust and dirt out of the shack. So he leaned into it, looking much like the devil at his bellows. Caleb's eyes were set close together. With his appetite for whiskey they were almost always blood-shot and his black, oily, hair kept his forehead completely hidden. "If you don't mind eatin' at odd hours and cleanin' up after yourselves," J.D. proclaimed, "feel free to use my kitchen I got set up in the backyard."

"I might have to do that until we get ar'n set up. Much obliged." With the tools back in the wooden box, J.D. took a step to leave. Suddenly a ten-year old boy stumbled in through the open door.

The two men stared at their nephew, awaiting an explanation for his sudden calamitous entrance. He was soaked with sweat; his feet caked in the black moist earth of the forest. He leaned forward with his hands on his knees. Forest debris was tangled in his hair and red lines traced the cutting paths of briars he had stumbled through. After panting and coughing for a few moments he looked up, and for the first time realized that anyone else was in the shack.

The boy looked back down and after a couple of deep gasps said, "Yankees." The men turned and looked each other in the eye.

* * *

The wagon rocked and jerked over the creek-bed, disrupting some midges at play. "Least it ain't been no wet season. Rivers are all perty low. I mean if we'd ah had a really rainy season like last year, why we'd be lucky to have made it across half

6

the streams we've come up on so far."

The soldier was sitting holding on to the wagon with one hand, and with the other, the barrel of a carbine whose stock rested on the toe of his right shoe. Beside him at the reigns sat his companion, guiding the mules onto the opposite creek-bank.

They were both young men. From a mile away one could tell they were officers if only by their hygiene, going so far as being clean-shaven. The fabric on their backs stood crisp, clean, and deep blue in the slanting rays of the afternoon sun.

"What makes for a rainy season anyhow? I mean looks like one season would be the same as the next, but they ain't. You got you're droughts and you're floods and all manner of gradation between. People say they ain't no rhyme nor reason to it, but mark my words they's a science in everthang and just cause they ain't figured it out yet, don't mean it ain't the case that there's more to it thern luck.

"See, the world's just openin' up for young folks like us. Hell, when this here war's over who do you think's gonna be runnin the show? You don't need King Solomon to tell you ther ain't no further to look thern me and you. Hell, my paw always said…"

As the officer with the carbine in his hand continued to drone on about science and the future, his companion indulged in his recent acquirement, that is: his ability to tune his partner's voice out completely. It was a proficiency that they both valued. The driver could go about his business without being driven mad by the constant jabbering, and the jabberer could continue his orations without fear of interruptions.

They made a strange sight in this ramshackle war. Their mules were well fed, groomed, and shod. The officers, like their livestock, practically glowed with good health. The wagon itself looked like it had just rolled out of the Cartwright's shop.

The team swam through the humid air of the foothills. As the officer continued his monologue, beads of sweat rolled down the back of his neck, and he swatted away a cloud of gnats.

"We shouldn't ought to stopped, I think that put us behind." He took up the carbine and cradled it in his lap. "How far do you think Morganton is anyway? Bet we don't make it afore dark." He looked up at the sun's position. "No, ain't no way in hell. Did you ever think you'd git roped into doin this?

"I mean what'll they have us doin next, walkin' some general's dog." He began to mimic a general's guttural voice, "Now see here, Cumberland is not to shit anywhere but within the confines of the enlisted men's camp." The officer laughed, then a bullet passed through his chest.

The blood began to soak into the cotton undershirt of the officer. He felt a sharp pain, a weakness, and then nothing. When he slumped over on the seat there was no one to catch him.

The moment the other officer heard the gunshot, he leaped from the wagon to the side of the dirt path that served as a road. The mules halted dead in their tracks when they felt the reigns go dead. About fifteen yards ahead there was a small cloud of dense white smoke lingering in the air.

The officer took out his service revolver, then reached up and pulled his dead companions revolver out of its holster. Concentrating his fire on the tree next to the large puff of white gun smoke, he fired and walked forward. Shooting one revolver, then the other, into the smoke. Creating not a small amount of smoke himself, he advanced.

* * *

Caleb felt the slugs digging into the tree. His back was leaned against the bark, and every round that impacted the tree trunk sent a vibration through his body. He was trying to reload his musket. The charge didn't want to go down the barrel. When he finally got it rammed down, he spilled all of his percussion caps onto the leafy ground.

The gunshots were getting closer and Caleb was shaking uncontrollably as he tried to retrieve one of the caps. Suddenly the firing stopped, and Caleb closed his eyes and held his breath. A moment later he let out a weak cough and streaming tears. In his right ear he heard the hammer of a pistol being pulled back.

Caleb released the grasp on his gun and it tumbled onto the ground. He gazed up at the officer's determined, set countenance. Suddenly the officer's grim look softened. He opened his non-aiming eye, and looked the sniper over. "You, you're, a rebel?" He said with a strong inflection of bewilderment.

Suddenly a bullet erupted from underneath the officer's chin and the pistol wavered, then fired, grazing the back of Caleb's lower leg. With the two reports still reverberating through the hollow behind him, the officer slumped onto Caleb.

"What in the hell took so long, you God damned horse's ass?" Caleb said as he pushed the dead body off of him.

"He jumped off the wagon and put it between us! I had to slip up on him." J.D. dragged the body back up onto the road, the heels leaving two little parallel tracks in the earth.

"Well, the bastard shot me, sure as hell." Caleb lifted his leg and exposed a blood soaked area.

"Ah hell, you're bleeding like a stuck pig. Is the ball still in you?"

"No it just cut a little ditch in my flesh," Caleb said, pushing himself up and clinging to the tree for support. He felt the warm blood run down the leg of his trousers.

"Hold up and I'll give you a hand." J.D. helped him into the back of the buckboard wagon. In a minute he reappeared with some linen from one of the officer's packs.

"Here, tie it off best you can so it stops bleeding. You're turning into a ghost." J.D. stood up in the back of the wagon and examined the road in the direction of the wagon's origin.

"Well shoot. Where's the rest of them? What the hell are two Yankees doing here buy themselves, driving a buckboard wagon with hardly a thing in it no less?" J.D. walked to the front of the wagon and looked over the heads of the mules. Then he reached down and pulled the carbine out of the dead officer's hand. He pulled a lever and the small rifle ejected a shiny cartridge. "What in the hell is this?"

"That's one of those new guns, everthangs in that cartridge, slug, powder, wadding, primer. You load it through the back," Caleb said as he finished tying off his bandage.

"I swear this is awful peculiar. Not only are they on the wrong side of the Mason/Dixon Line by hundreds of miles, but they got the best looking mules I ever seen and these fancy guns I ain't never even heard of.

"Hell, that one acted shocked that I was even a Confederate. How the hell do you get way out here without knowing... I mean, damn, talk about getting lost." Caleb said as he waved away a yellow jacket attracted by the smell of blood.

"Well it's damn curious." J.D. jumped off the wagon and pulled the officer down onto the road. He dragged the one body over to the other, and started going through their clothes. "They got some nice pistols and I think this pair of boots just might... I'll be damned!" Caleb leaned up, trying to look over the edge of the wagon, "What is it? What did you find?"

J.D. ran over to his brother waving some bills over his head, "We're rich! There's gotta be fifty greenback dollars here."

"Is that right? Fifty? They can shoot me again if there's fifty dollars, federal in it!" They yelled and howled with delight. They kissed the money, folded it a hundred different ways, and counted it back and forth to each other several times.

"Fifty-eight dollars J.D., Fifty-eight! That's Twenty-nine dollars apiece. Our troubles are over." Caleb leaned out so he could see the dead bodies, "Best get them boys in the ground. If another yellow jacket lights on that'n- they'll be enough to carry him off! There's a shovel on the side of the wagon."

"S'pose it's the least I can do, see'n as how they've made me rich." J.D. buried them at the foot of a big boulder off the side of the road, interring them and most of their gear wholesale. He covered their shallow grave with rocks. The two men feared the onset of more troops, and made haste to depart.

Gathering the guns, J.D. threw them in the back of the wagon with Caleb and snapped the reigns. As the mules marched forward, their vigor renewed from the short rest, the two guerillas laughed and sang songs. Cicadas joined in the revelry, but everything else was still and quiet. The forest was sleeping through the stifling heat of the day, awaiting nightfall when it would spring back into life.

"It's going to take a while to get to the pass, I think we can take the high road and save some time."

Caleb was lying back with his head in his hands. He responded without opening his eyes, "These mules ain't gonna make it up that hill with this wagon, I don't care what condition they're in."

J.D. looked the wagon over. "I'll strip it down, then they can handle it pretty easy. Once they're up top I'll carry the rest of the stuff, including you, up the hill."

"Much obliged. Your own flesh and blood, and you treat me like baggage."

"My pleasure."

The mules wound their way through the hilly countryside until late afternoon, while Caleb slept an impossible sleep in the stifling heat. Finally the team halted at the foot of a steep grade and J.D. shook his slumbering brother. "Wake up. I'm going to take the wagon up over the pass."

A few minutes later Caleb sat on the forest floor with the supplies from the wagon. J.D. had the reigns in his hands and he drove the team forward while he walked beside the front left wheel. Though the grade was steep, J.D. puzzled at how the mules struggled with it. When the mules finally reached the top of the ridge they were frothed and absolutely exhausted.

J.D. looked down over the now visible valley. His sleeves were pulled up, and his tanned forearms shined in the sunlight with a sheen of sweat. He took his hat in his hand and wiped his right arm across his brow. By the time his brother and all the gear had been hauled to the top, he was sorely fatigued.

"I'm telling you Caleb, they's gotta be somethin wrong with this wagon. I damn near killed them animals getting it up here, and look at them, they're as strong and healthy as any I've ever laid eyes on."

"They're spoiled," Caleb replied. "Look at them! Ain't never pulled a plowshare in their good for nothing lives. You're mistaking laziness for a virtue. Find me an old nag with a back so bent its belly drags in the turnip patch. It'll pull this wagon to the top of Table Rock all on its own. You keep bragging about them two damn halfbreeds, but I say their full of nothing but sloth."

J.D. seized one of the mules by the muzzle and peered into its mouth. Caleb laughed, "You can't spot all worthlessness in their teeth. Matter of fact, the better them teeth look, the more evidence you got for soft livin'." J.D. forsook his inspection and spat some tobacco juice. "How's your wound?" asked J.D., examining the bandage.

"The bleeding musta stopped a long time ago," replied his brother. "I still feel a little weak, but once it scabs up nice and proper I should be as good for nothing as ever I was."

J.D. helped him up into the back of the wagon. "You'll have a hell of a scar." Caleb pulled his hat down over his eyes and laid back in the wagon, "Won't be the first I've got, won't be the last I get."

The wagon resumed its course. Working its way through hollows and fields, across small streams, and past dirt floor cabins. Women and children, all of them white, inhabited the fields. The brothers had never known anyone with enough wealth to own slaves.

In fact, practically the only time they ever saw black folks was when runaway slaves took to the hills to hide out. Sooner or later they would be found out and sent back to their masters. Word spread quickly through the sparsely populated area, and people would gather by the roadside to watch the slaves marched back to a plantation somewhere. They would have stocks or heavy iron collars bolted around their necks with a chain connected to the back of a wagon.

People gathered out of curiosity, but also because of the fear Nat Turner had put into them. Renegade slaves like Turner might yet again kill white people in their beds, and seeing a slave at large, returned to the plantation from whence he came, slaked many people's fears.

They finally pulled into their neighborhood with a few buzzing horseflies trailing the smell of Caleb's injured leg. J.D. pulled back on the reigns beside Caleb's house, and looked back at his brother lounging on the wagon. "Why do you get the wagon?" He asked.

"Hell, you're getting them two show-ponies. What do you got to complain about?" Caleb replied.

J.D. came around the wagon to help him. He took one of Caleb's arms over his shoulder and helped him to the shack. "Suits me. That wagon's going to need some work. Them wheels ain't swinging freely."

"Just let's sit me on the stoop," Caleb said. J.D. sat him down on one of the rough rock steps leading up to the front door.

"I still say it's them spoilt mules of your'n." He pointed over to the two fatigued animals.

J.D. went over to un-harness the mules and tend to them. After they were well settled under a shed, he came back to the muddy, wore out area they called Caleb's yard. His brother was nowhere in sight. J.D. admired Caleb's shack for a few moments.

It was the only one in the neighborhood with a plank floor elevated up off the ground. Before winter they planned to do likewise with J.D.'s cabin next door. There was laundry drying on the line in the back yard.

A sheet, caught by a puff of wind would come into view at the edge of the house, and then recede back out of sight. It looked like a strange apparition disappearing and reappearing. The ghost's message was simple: Caleb's wife was back from her mother's. J.D. turned to go, but Sally saw him through the open door of the cabin and ran out to confront him.

"Look here you shiftless, good-for-nothing scoundrel. What's the meaning of you running off and getting my Caleb half killed?" She had the knuckles of her left hand dug into her hip and was shaking a finger on her other hand as if it were a whip she lashed at her adversary.

"Now look here Sally, we got responsibilities to the government. Hell, they're liable to conscript us back into service at any time, we're supposed to report for duty soon as we's built our strength up. If we don't, and they find us out, we's likely to end up in front of a firing squad."

Sally folded her arms in front of her and gave J.D. the evil eye. "Now you listen here, General Lee, when the twos of you come back from that federal prison you wouldn't nothing but bones. If it'd been a week later you'd of been dead for sure.

"For a while I thought Caleb might die regardless, now it's took me I-don't-know-how-long to get you boys back into some kind of shape, and just when I've got my husband back into the pink, you get him shot. I hope you hear me real good when I tell you the war's over. It's over for the two of you anyhow.

"I don't care how much longer all these other fools kill each other, but I love this man I got in here and I love his family, yes even a no account mule-skinner like you. Now so help me God, if you ever report back for duty, they'll come looking for Caleb too, and if that happens you better just not come back."

J.D. had been taking small steps backward as Sally advanced, now his heel caught a rock and he fell backward onto his flank. Sally had the aspect of a gorgon, her stringy hair hanging into the hard orb of the sun. Sally's features were obscured and all he could see was a dark silhouette as he winced into the blinding light. "In fact, you best not ever cross my path again, or you'll cross swords with the devil inside of me."

She turned and walked back into the cabin, leaving J.D. sitting on the ground. He rubbed the bags under his eyes and lay back in the dirt.

* * *

The next day, while J.D. was trying to figure out the carbine they had captured, there came a knock at his door. Wondering if the main body of Yankees had finally caught up with them, he put a pistol to the door of the cabin with his left hand and opened it a crack with his right. Sally was standing there with a steaming pie held up at shoulder level. J.D. tucked the pistol into his belt behind his back and opened the door.

"What you got there?"

Sally blushed, "Why surely it hasn't been that long since you've seen a blackberry pie. I felt bad about yesterday and the need for repentance. It's nice to have the money to buy flour again, what flour there is to be had at any rate. Why don't you come over and help Caleb with that wagon?"

"Thank you kindly." He took the pie and set it on a small table next to the carbine.

"You know, I've been studying on what you said yesterday and I think you're right. If they want us back as soldiers well they can just come and find us. We'll just lay low till this whole thing blows over."

Sally spread an open hand across her wishbone in relief. "You don't know how happy that makes me." She started to cry slightly. "I couldn't survive seeing the two of you coming back like scarecrows again... or not coming back at all." She wiped the tears away, and smiled timidly.

"Well, tell Caleb I'm going to help myself to this pie and I'll be out there to lend a hand in a minute. And don't you fret none, the only thing worth fighting for, as far

* * *

Caleb had three of the buckboard's wheels up on rocks. The loose corner was supported by a log, so that the remaining wheel could float freely. He was studying the hub when a hand clapped down on his shoulder. "Well brother, what's the verdict?" J.D. leaned in and looked at the wheel. Caleb grabbed a spoke and said, "Watch this." He gave the wheel a spin and it turned freely, spinning and spinning with no sign of binding.

J.D. gave the wagon an appraising look. "It must be one of them others." Caleb shrugged, "I've tried the others. They're all as good as this one. It's got to be them mules."

"Hell, if it is! Early this morning I plowed with one, then the other, just to see what they're capable of, and I'm telling you they're as strong as... well, mules."

Caleb took off his hat and ran his forearm across his brow. "Hell, this don't make no kind of sense, they should have handled that hill easily. It'd be different if they looked wore out afore hand." Caleb got up and circled the wagon; he had a pronounced limp, but seemed to be doing well, all things considered. J.D. got up on top of the wagon and walked back and forth, looking down on it. He stomped with the heel of an officer's boot. "Hey, what's this?"

"What'd you find J.D.?" Caleb peered down at his brother's feet.

"There's another compartment under here, go get that pry bar out of the toolbox!"

J.D. found a crack and insinuated the bar into place. He leaned on it, but the façade wouldn't budge. He stood up, placed his right foot on the bar, shifted his weight to it, and kicked. There was a loud pop, as if a tree were breaking loose from its stump. A piece of plank popped up in the air, spinning. It settled beside J.D.'s foot and sunlight poured through the hole in the wagon, reflecting off coins of gold.

They both gasped. J.D. reached in and ran his fingers across the discs, half expecting them to vanish. "I'll be God damned." He took the large wooden toolbox from Caleb and placed it over the hole. Caleb looked up at J.D.

"We've got to get this thing out of sight!"

* * *

A couple of hours later they walked away from an old barn and back across the fields toward their homes. J.D. was grinning uncontrollably as he led the mules. As Caleb limped forth, he gave one last paranoid look back at the wagon.

J.D. gave a short laugh, "Don't worry about the wagon, it'll be fine. This is the best thing that ever could have happened to us." He was practically exploding with joy.

Caleb stopped and grabbed his brother by the collar, "Listen, you fool, there's a whole pile of gold back there in that barn."

J.D. gave him a calm smile, "Don't worry, nobody's going to find...

But Caleb cut him off, "I'm telling you right now, people don't loose something like that without they come looking for it. Soon this place will be crawling with Yankees; they'll want that gold back!"

J.D. put his hand on Caleb's shoulder, "Relax, remember when we were in that hell of a prison? Sick as death, starving, eating a rat when we were lucky, living in our own filth?"

"I remember it well enough that I don't want to go back, I'd sooner go to hell, the good and proper one!" Caleb was on the verge of a breakdown, with the image of the prison brought so vividly before his eyes.

J.D. turned his brother back towards home and started walking with one arm around him, talking in a reassuring tone of voice, as one might talk to a frightened child, "This is God's way of paying us back for all our hardships. I remember a preacher told me that after Job persevered through all his afflictions the good Lord made it so all his friends brought him earrings of gold, and that feller had a lot of friends."

Caleb rubbed some feeble tears from his eyes and gave a small chuckle. "See? You're feeling spry again," J.D. continued, "but you're right about the blue-bellies, they'll be wanting the gold back. We'll need to cover our tracks. Is Sally going to be home tomorrow?"

"No, I think she's going over to her mom's house to gather Polk-salad."

"Fine, that'll be a good time to take care of things. Just tell her we got some work to do on your shack, and she needs to stay a couple of days. Then we'll take these mules up on the mountain, shoot them, and let the wolves and panthers eat the carcasses. We'll burn the wagon, and the gold we'll put beneath the floor in your shack. We'll get us a mess of bricks and close in the under-side of your place, Sally'll get a kick out of that."

Caleb was back inside himself. Soberly he asked, "How long do you think we'll have to sit on the gold?"

"Well, definitely till the war ends, and if the Yankees win, and don't be too damned surprised when they do, we'll probably have to keep it hid a lot longer."

Caleb's old confidence was returning, "I'm glad you're my brother, I don't know how I'd get along with out you. Just imagine when we get our hands on that money. I wonder how much it'll fetch?"

"A king's ransom, I would imagine. Until we collect on it though, best not to let it go no further than me and you. We don't want to put anybody in danger needlessly."

The two small hovels were coming into view. "Caleb, how long you had that plot signed over to you from old man Johnson?"

Caleb contemplated the question, "About five years I reckon."

"Best get that deed down to the courthouse before somebody tries to snatch it out from under you. I wouldn't trust Johnson as far as I could throw him."

"I'll get it down there sooner or later."

"You said that five years ago."

"I reckon I did."

They parted ways and J.D. took the mules back to his stable, already he was mourning their loss, but a mere transitory thought of the gold wiped away all of his concerns, and left him in an opiate like delirium. Caleb got back and told Sally about the work he was about to commence on the domicile. She responded enthusiastically and left that same afternoon, that her groom might get an early start.

* * *

The next morning they took a wheelbarrow out to the old barn. After a few minutes they pulled the buckboard out into a green field and set fire to it. The varnished wood was soon consumed and they went back to the barn. J.D. took up the wheelbarrow and Caleb limped along beside him, back out into the harsh sunlight. A voice from behind them suddenly broke the timid silence. "What are you doing?"

Caleb's heart almost seized. He turned around and there stood his sister's boy: Marshall. Caleb reproached him scornfully, "What are you doing here, trying to scare somebody to death?"

It was Marshall's turn to look startled now. "But uncle Caleb, I saw smoke from the knob over there," he indicated a hill with his finger, "and I come running thinking the old barn was on fire."

J.D. set the wheelbarrow down, "Well now you can see that it ain't, so you just get on back to what you's a doin'."

"Well I wouldn't doing nothing important. Maybe I can help yuns with your chores." He stepped up to the wheelbarrow and looked down into it. "What you got in here anyways?" Marshall felt a hand grab him by the collar and toss him back away from the wheelbarrow. He wobbled a few forced steps, trying to keep his feet under him. "I don't get it. Where are yuns taking a load of red dirt to?"

Caleb was growing angrier by the minute. He shouted at the boy, "If you ain't the most disrespectful youngun I ever seed, I'm going to tan your hide good if you don't get your big nose out of our business right now!"

Marshall's eyes opened wide, "God almighty, I've never seen you so tore up over something, much less nothing."

J.D. finally stepped in to smooth things over. "Look Marshall, you can help us by taking this here quarter-dollar down to the dry goods store and fetching us a trowel. Get yourself a candy while you're down there too. I'll come by your momma's house to fetch it in a little while. Just leave us be for a couple of days, Caleb had a dream about that prison camp last night and it's got him all riled up."

Marshall looked embarrassed for Caleb and promised to do what J.D. advised. He ran off happy as a lark, with the thought of candy hastening his steps.

As soon as their nephew was out of ear shot Caleb beseeched his brother frantically, "Why did you have to make me out a crackpot just to get rid of him. I'll be lucky if it don't spread over the whole countryside. By the time it gets back to me they'll be saying I piss the bed every night."

J.D. reassured him with a calm voice, saying, "Don't worry, Marshall thinks the world of you. He ain't going to say nothing to nobody. Besides, I had to smooth things over one way or t'other."

Later on, while J.D. bricked in the shack's under pinning, Caleb built a crate that would be affixed under the plank floor. Late that afternoon Caleb took a sack of gold from out of the dirt in the wheelbarrow, and entombed it under the floor of his cabin. After J.D. set the last brick, they fell back and stared up at the red sky.

"When are you going to take care of the mules?"

"Don't worry Caleb, I'll take care of it in the morning." He swatted a mosquito.

The sun was sinking behind the mountain, setting fire to the lingering clouds overhead. Their fortune was secure, the evidence was passing from the world, and in the valley a strange tranquility descended.

Yet nearby an insect deliberated, "Katy did, Katy didn't?"

1865

It was a warm spring, with the money spent and the well run dry, when the war finally began to wind down. For the better part of a year the brothers had "paced the floor" so to speak: that same floor which concealed the cause of their paranoia. Sally associated their restless, distracted behavior with the fear that they might, yet again, find themselves conscripted and pressed into service in the Confederate ranks. Often times Caleb would wake in a sweat with terror gripping his very soul, or pass the night as he had the previous eve: without any sleep at all.

Sally and her family, particularly her mother, looked to the Union as a means to put the wealthy gentry of the county in their place. Much of the South Mountain community, in fact, were Unionists, so much so that Sally could see her husband and brother-in-law as becoming part of an ever-dwindling minority. Caleb and J.D. were often met with contempt, if not outright hostility by their neighbors. In the past one could have counted on help digging a well. Now the brothers didn't even bother asking for it. They knew their place in the community; they harbored no delusions.

* * *

Thus it was on a beautiful April morning, after a sleepless night, that Caleb put his foot in the bucket and was lowered into the well. He and his brother worked in shifts until well after dark- hoping to accomplish their task in one day's effort. They were stained from head to toe with red mud, drenched with sweat, and thoroughly exhausted. The only help they received that day was in hauling the dirt to the edge of the woods, and so, while they labored in the bottom of the shaft, Caleb's nephew and wife labored on the surface.

In the dark night someone came by the well, which was odd considering the family's ostracism. Caleb was swinging a mattock in the bottom of the well by the dim light of a small lantern when he heard an excited exchange between his kin and a neighbor. The voices resounded and distorted down the shaft of the well until their meaning was completely obscured, but the frantic nature of the conversation could not be disguised.

Finally his brother leaned over the opening and shouted through cupped hands, "You better git up hyear, we got trouble!" Caleb rode the bucket back to the world he knew. Twenty minutes later he, his brother, and the messenger were marching along the cool deserted country lanes toward the township of Morganton. Sally had been obstinate to the last, threatening all of them with varying degrees of bodily harm if they, "...persist in defending a *nation* -that has been your *ruination*- by bearing arms against the only power able to effect your *salvation.*"

Caleb kept running the words through his head and wondering what high minded, uppity, Unionist, alderman she had pilfered them from. She stomped and stormed as they walked away, with her insults and colorful metaphors reverberating in the air long after she was out of sight. Finally they could here nothing but their footfalls and the low drone of a bullfrog harem.

A blonde haired youth of thirteen years had been enlisted to, "Go up into the South Mountain area and round up who so ever you can to assist in defending Morganton from Federal troops." The boy had spent the entire day doing just that, to return with only two men. In spite of such adversity the young patriot was exploding with optimism.

"Don't you worry, General McCown's put together a regiment to head the blue-coats off down at Rocky Ford. They ain't about to make it across the river, we got an Honest-to-God General, two Colonels, artillery, and a congregation of the finest sharpshooters ever lived to our name. It'll be a cold day in hell when the Union takes Morganton!"

J.D. was scared to death, he didn't want to fight, but he didn't want the Yankees to have free reign in looting the countryside. He had a deathly fear that the Union soldiers were coming to Morganton to find their missing shipment of gold. He reacted with animosity to the boy's comments, "What in the hell are we suppose to do?"

The lad's zeal was not about to be deflated, "Hell sir, don't fret none, all ther waontin' you to do is to find some high ground in town and keep a look out for any Yankee 'might sneak by our lines and try lootin' the town. They's people up ever tree and on ever roof with squirrel rifles. I just hope they's still a perch left when we git there. Any blue-bellies walk up the street we'll leave 'em with more holes thern a flour sieve."

Caleb felt tired beyond his years and wondered if the gold was worth the burden he felt. In a hollar beyond the dirt road a whip-poor-will called it's ghost like cry. "D'gya herethat? That there's a good omen. I only feel sorry fer us a missin all the real fightin. If we're lucky we might git into a little scrap in town but I wouldn't count on it." He picked a stone up off the ground and threw it into the black forest, as if he hoped to pelt a Yankee.

* * *

The moon was high when they got in sight of town. They could make out the vague outline of some of the larger buildings, but there wasn't a single candle or lamp to be seen.

Caleb's anxiety intensified. "Pert near deserted." He whispered.

"Naw, they just don't want to present any targets. It's a cavalry they say's ah comin' in from Lenoir, but they's talk some might sneak in on foot tonight, so they ain't nobody lightin' so much as a match."

Sweat was forming between Caleb's palms and the stock of his musket. With a dry throat he choked out a question, "Where should we go?"

The boy pointed to the silhouette of one of the buildings. "They said they was gonna post some folks with pistols up on the courthouse, but when I left they said they hadn't fount nobody yit. Ya'll got pistols, maybe that's yer roost."

The brothers said nothing else; they simply stole off into the dark deserted streets wondering if a trigger-happy sniper would mistake them for Yankees in the night. When they got to the courthouse they realized that the doors were locked. They huddled in the shrubs and scratched their heads while their hearts pounded louder and louder. Finally J.D. boosted Caleb up and he clamored onto a second story landing.

Caleb reached down, "Give me your hand and I'll haul you up."

J.D. answered back in a hoarse whisper, "They'll blind side us if we're both up there. I'm going to try to get up on the landing on the other side. If I cayn't git myself set up over yonder I'll be back in five minutes." With that, J.D. disappeared around the corner of the building.

Caleb took the revolver out of the front of his belt and tucked it into the belt-line at the small of his back. He lay down on his stomach and looked toward the river. Ten minutes elapsed and Caleb abandoned the idea of passing the night with the company of his brother. Somewhere out there, maybe a couple of miles away, was Rocky Ford.

Caleb had little doubt that the Union would try to cross there. If the General's troops were going to stop the Federals, they would do it at the river crossing. He wondered how big the command actually was, Caleb imagined the "regiment" at around a score of withered old men. Then he wondered if perhaps there was a contingent at all.

He sighted down the barrel of his musket and tried to decide which avenues he could command from the cold stone that caressed his belly. He kept his rifle pointed down the most likely approach from the river and listened to the soft chirp of the crickets. He kept his eyes peeled as the slow hours of night passed by.

Occasionally he would detect a small movement at the end of a street. He would take a bead on the shadow as it flittered closer to his position. Then the shape would wander into the streaming moonlight and Caleb would release a long held lung-full of air, as the hound dog lifted its leg on a tree in the courtyard.

Gradually the sky began to change hue, from black, to dark smoke, confederate gray, pale soft pink, and finally the crimson predecessor of dawn. Caleb listened with heavy eyelids, as roosters heralded the coming dawn. Sleep had been trying to grasp the sniper for hours, and Caleb was losing the battle for consciousness. The sun ascended above the horizon, casting its dull rays upon him. He looked, with eyelids at half-mast, toward the friendly glowing orb, a train engine and a line of cars moved lethargically at the edge of town.

Suddenly the report of a canon crawled across town to Caleb. His body tensed with adrenalin. The soft crackle of distant small arms fire could be heard with some strain of the ear. He could feel a renewed sense of alertness, quickly he darted his view from street to street, but saw not a soul. The echoing sound of a howitzer reached his ears yet again.

He listened to the reports and scanned the second story windows of the town hoping for a signal from a fellow sniper. He saw nothing. The report of a different piece of artillery reverberated through town. Then a similar report rolled across the courtyard. It was definitely a different piece with a lower, louder tone. In the battles he endured during the first year of the war, Caleb never learned to recognize which artillery piece made which report; the battlefield was simply too crowded with them. He could tell though, that this was a new piece, and that the original report never returned.

After "sounding-off" several more times the canon fire dissipated and the soft, distant crackle waned, then ceased. Silence reigned in the street for a moment. Then Caleb saw a figure come around a corner and start walking through an alley toward the square. The barrel of his rifle spun down the alley and his dull, weary vision blurred across the bead of his musket and tried to bring the figure into a recognizable contrast. It was a bearded man in suspenders and wool pants; he wore a white cotton shirt and walked on a wooden leg with the help of a cane.

Caleb laid his head down on the cold stone, still wet with morning dew. He felt like crying, but conceded only a moment of despair. The old man made it to the corner and pulled a crate from under a store window, dragging it to the edge of the street. He sat down on the crate and leaned out, looking down the dirt road toward the river.

* * *

Caleb woke to the sound of horse hooves. He could feel the stone of the landing against his left cheek. With a sudden realization he jerked up and tried to lift his rifle and fire at the nearest horseman. His musket, however, remained firmly planted on the landing. It took what would later seem like ages for the sniper to realize that a U.S. cavalry boot was standing firmly on the barrel.

He looked, from the boot, up to the blue clad body attached to it, just before the other half of the pair crashed into his jaw-line. Sparks exploded in the overhanging roof above him, and as he lay on his back the world dimmed from view.

It was a cold day in hell.

* * *

Caleb came back to himself. His head ached. There was a numb, dull, throbbing sensation in the right side of his face. He could taste the coppery flavor of blood on his tongue. Something quivered beneath him. When he tried to open his eyes only one of his eyelids peeled back. He could see the upside down flank of a dark brown horse. The tale swished into view, then disappeared again.

He could see the Courthouse and it's crabgrass lawns. It was at the other end of a long street. The one legged man was talking to a mounted Yankee, while others milled around the square with pistols drawn. Some were on horseback, some on foot, and others were dismounted leading their horses along with their free hand.

They seemed to concentrate their wary eyes on the second story windows, but the town was silent, almost serene. Caleb counted not more than a dozen troopers. He had expected to see many more. He knew that his left eye had swollen shut, so he tried to reach up with his right hand to examine it.

His hand stayed where it was and he felt something tug on his boot. The Union soldier who captured him must have tied his hands and feet together under the horse. He could feel the hard saddle pressing against his ribs. The morning dew was gone and the road below him looked like dry powdery silt. The dust had a few stains where blood drops had fell. He worked his mouth and felt dried blood flake on his upper lip. He spit a mixture of saliva and blood, then turned his head toward the direction the horse was facing.

The horse shook its head and sent waves through the reign to the hand of the Yankee. He was standing to the right of the mount, in the shade of a dry goods store looking away from Caleb and down the ruts of the highway. He wore a short cape that extended to his elbows and a feathered hat with a full brim. Caleb imagined that he must be a low ranking officer. Caleb heard the strange tap and shuffle of the one-legged veteran behind him.

"What are you damn sons-of-Cain fixin to do with this hyere boy!"

The Yankee turned with a start, "What? Go back to your home Grandpa. This fella's took up arms against his own country. He'll be dealt with according to the statutes of the Articles of War."

The feisty old man poked the young officer in the shoulder with the tip of his cane. "He's already took a beatin' by the looks of him. Why don't you just confiscate his guns and send him home to his momma in one piece?"

The Yankee grabbed the cane and jerked it out of the old man's hand. He then broke it against the wall of the store and shook the splintered end left in his hand at the old man. "Damn it! You miserable coot, get the hell off the street and back home where you belong. There's plenty of beatings to go around."

Having thusly threatened the old man, he started leading the horse down the street toward the edge of town in what Caleb amusingly perceived as an organized retreat. Presently he stopped and looked back toward town. The old man was now out of sight. The retreat had been a success.

Unlike the South Mountains, the Morganton area hosted a few small plantations and it seemed as if every slave within five miles of the township had congregated to catch the snow. They were of all ages and both sexes, sitting perched on a rail fence at the edge of the road and milling about, barefoot and smiling, in the grass lawn behind it. One of the boldest walked up and tried to engage the Yankee in conversation.

"Is it the gospel truth that old man Lincoln done said we's free men now su'?"

"Seems like I heard something to that effect boy." He kept his eyes peeled down the road, obviously anticipating some arrival.

"If'n ya don't mind me ah askin' su', who you is?"

"I'm Lieutenant Kelly with the Eighth Tennessee Cavalry. That's all you need now." The young slave looked confused, "So, you not a Yank?"

Finally he turned to the man, "I'm going to Yank a knot in your hide if you don't shut your damn mouth and leave me be."

The slave shied back to the grass lawn where his friends had overheard the proceedings. He kept mumbling in a conciliatory tone, "Yes su', sorry su', I'm powful sorry su'."

Caleb watched the black men sitting on the rail, upside down in his vision, as they pointed down the highway and elbowed each other. Their excitement grew and they began to cheer and wave their straw hats in the air with the approach of troops.

The road was low around the far bend and at first all Caleb could see was the guide-on and U.S. flag. Occasionally the top of a hat would bob into view; then two columns came into full view. The horsemen held their bridles with their left hands and gripped their carbines with their right. Their blue uniforms shone intensely in the bright April sunshine.

The foremost ranks were stained wet up to their armpits, with mud caked up to their knees. As they came closer he could see that some of the ones in the main body of the formation were dry. They were miserable, to a man, and the soggy ones had taken on a coating of fine ochre colored dust. They rode forth grimly, like a lynch mob without the enthusiasm.

The former slaves, now exultant in their newfound freedom, cheered and whistled with fingers in their mouths. The smaller children threw hundreds of freshly picked dandelions between the rails of the fence, trying to lace the rutted out highway with floral gold. As the first ranks reached the cheering entourage, and the horses began to trample the delicate yellow blooms, a greasy rider with a five day beard spit a great gob of tobacco juice into their midst.

The black glob hit one of the women in the face. The jubilation faltered. The soldier cried out, "Hail Columbia, Happy Land! If I don't shoot a nigger, I'll be damned!" He then raised his rifle and shot a freeman sitting on a fencepost not three feet away. He was hit directly in the chest and blown off the fence.

By the time his back impacted the earth, the entire hoard were fleeing for their lives among screams of panic. As they fled, some dragging small crying children by one arm through torn dandelion stems, the troops laughed and shouted their approval. As smoke trickled out of his barrel, the shooter grinned wide with his newfound celebrity.

An officer with a gray mustache that ran down to his chin broke off from the main body and rode up to Lieutenant Kelly. The Lieutenant saluted and his superior returned the salute.

The Lieutenant said, "Sir, the square is secure. We captured two rebels; we think they fell back from the river. They were positioned on the landings of the courthouse with revolvers and rifles."

The ranking officer took off his hat and ran his sleeve across his forehead, and then he leaned over his mounts neck to examine Caleb. "Looks like this one's seen happier days. Where's the other one?"

"He's hurt pretty bad when we took him prisoner. So we just took him into the courtroom and left a guard with him. Should I take the prisoners to the rear?"

The commander stared at Caleb with his pale blue eyes, deliberating. "No, put this one in the courtroom with his friend, it's been a while since I cross examined a witness," his horse made a nervous movement and he gave it a calming caress along its neck, "maybe they can tell us where their friends retreated to."

"Yes sir."

He waved his hand, and in this gesture, he tried to encompass the town, saying, "It's our responsibility to secure the town proper while other units rove the surrounding country looking for food, supplies, and production centers. I've ordered the men to work their way out from the square to the edge of town and then report back. Take me to this courthouse."

"Right this way sir." He turned the horse around and led it briskly to the foot of the landing.

Lieutenant Kelly started to untie Caleb's feet and hands. The other officer dismounted and handed his reigns to an enlisted man who led the horse away. "Can he walk?" he asked the Lieutenant. "Certainly sir." He put Caleb on his feet and tied his hands behind his back.

A Sergeant came around the building and exchanged salutes. "Sir, we thought you might want to remove the enemy flag from the grounds."

"Excellent Sergeant, lead the way."

There was a small bonfire started on the lawn, and after the banner was brought down they threw it into the flames. "You'd think I'd get tired of that but I never do."

They led Caleb up the spiraling rock steps and onto the landing, where J.D. posted himself the past night. He felt a nauseating horror when he saw the vast amounts of blood pooled on the cut stone. As they stepped onto the landing, flies dispersed from their feeding.

"Damn boys, looks like somebody stuck a pig."

They opened a door and walked into the courtroom. Caleb had never seen so many chairs, there must have been a couple of dozen. They all faced the same direction except the ones gathered around the judge's bench. The windows were open and a scarlet cardinal fluttered around overhead trying to find an exit. J.D. was the color of salt and sat in a chair with his hands tied behind him. There was a small puddle of blood under his right foot. The guard on duty came to attention behind J.D.

"As you were, soldier."

He retired back into his chair and cradled his carbine.

"Sit this one in a chair beside his friend."

They did so. "Sir, my brother needs a doctor," Caleb pleaded.

The ranking officer calmly removed his gloves. "So he's your brother, is he?" He looked at the Lieutenant, "I can see the family resemblance."

"Sir I'm begging you. Can't you see he needs help?" Caleb looked over at his brother. J.D. was panting in a tired lethargic rhythm with his tongue resting on his lower lip.

"Hell yes, son! I can see that; but we all need things. And what I need right now is to know where your friends went to."

"What friends?"

"Don't get smart with me son, your brother's ah dyin'."

A frantic alarm rose in Caleb's voice, "I ain't getting' smart sir, me and J.D., we was all alone all night. A boy come got us at our place, it's a good ways off. Said Yanks was comin', get up in the courthouse, that's all we know. Now please get the doctor."

His interrogator stared into his face for a few seconds, "What's your name son?"

"Walker, my names Caleb Walker."

"And your brother?"

"J. D., I mean James Darin, James Darin Walker."

The officer turned to his subordinate, "Bring up the surgeon. Oh, and my gear as well." He looked around the large room, "Looks like I'll need a table up here, and a bed from one of the nearby houses."

"Yes sir," Lieutenant Kelly said. He left the room.

The officer started pacing around the room, his boots tapped softly on the wooden floor as the red songbird fluttered from wall to wall near the high, tiled ceiling. He pulled back the curtain at one of the windows and looked out. Without looking away from some unknown object outside, he asked the guard if he new the nature of J.D.'s injury.

"Saber wound to the right leg below the knee. The bone stopped it sir."

After a moment he gave the cloth back to the breeze and started walking back towards the brothers. "This Jeffersonian architecture is pitiful. That's what's wrong with you hillbillies: you've got no taste. At least the honest to God seccesh' on the plantations have a little class. If it wasn't for…"

His boot steps ceased, and he looked down at a chair in front of him. It was a simple wooden chair, varnished and tarnished beyond years. It had arms and across those arms laid two rifles. In the seat of the chair lay two revolvers.

The officer picked up one of the rifles. He examined it, turning it over several times then finally grinning with what seemed like satisfaction. Suddenly the door burst open and a number of blue clad soldiers entered. They carried a trunk, a long table, and a bed in pieces. While they set up the bed, the officer sat down in an empty chair and fondled the rifle. Finally the crowd left by the same door through-which they'd entered.

"Where did this carbine come from?" The officer asked as he continued to stare at it.

"Sir, those are the arms we took off the prisoners." As he answered, he motioned with the barrel of his own carbine, indicating J.D. and Caleb. Suddenly the door burst open and a man with huge sideburns rushed in. He carried a large, black, leather bag. When he saw J.D. he hurried to the side of his chair and opened the bag.

Suddenly the commander stood up and burst forth with violent condemnation, "What in the hell do you think you're doing?" The man looked up at him in dismay, motioning toward J.D. with his palm up, "This man needs help."

"So you're going to lend aid and comfort to our enemy."

"But he's a prisoner and he's in a frightful…"

The officer cut him off, "We've got our own wounded to tend to."

"I've already treated our men, I've been attending them all morning."

The officer's face tensed, he took a couple of steps toward the doctor then paused. After a moment of agitated silence he took on a sinister tone, "I heard one of our boys, just this morning, said he had a splinter in his hand." The surgeon's forehead wrinkled with further confusion as the officer continued. "Now you get the hell out of here and go man to man until you find and treat that soldier. You'll not touch a prisoner until you've taken care of every bunion, blister, and sunburn to be found in the entire command."

"But sir I thought…"

"Get out I say!" and the doctor quickly evacuated as the officer advanced toward him. The physician tripped as he stepped out onto the landing, falling on his hands and knees over the dried bloodstain. The guard chuckled to himself, this put the officer into an even grimmer mood.

"What the hell are you laughing at?"

"Nothing sir." He took on an immediate poker face.

His superior pointed to the door with an extended finger. "Leave at once. You are dismissed."

The soldier was flabbergasted. "Yes sir," he said in an uncertain tone. The soldier closed the door behind him. Caleb was angry and perplexed, "What are you doing? We had a deal!" The officer pulled a chair, and facing Caleb, sat down. He grinned in a relaxed confident manner, as if his recent agitation had never occurred.

Caleb grew more frantic; he shrieked hysterically with a shaky voice, "We had an agreement! You said if I answered your questions you'd get a doctor for my brother."

"I did say that, and I'm a man of my word. The hell of it is: I just thought of a new question." As he said this he held the rifle out in his hands and smiled at it. He looked at the weapon with the same affection a man might emote when gazing upon his newly delivered, firstborn son.

At last Caleb recognized the carbine. He felt a cold sweat break out on his back, as if a noose was around his neck. "It's a simple question, shouldn't take up too much of your time." He laid the gun across his knees and looked Caleb dead in the eye, "Where did you get this gun?"

"I found it."

"Where'd you find it, in a corn crib, a hollow log, maybe a pig's ass?" Caleb felt the bottom drop out of his stomach, "Bull Run."

"You found this rifle at Bull Run?"

"Yes sir, after the battle was over. I took it off a dead soldier."

The officer smiled and stood up. He began to pace around the room randomly. "You found it at Bull Run. You know it's interesting… the history of certain firearms." He opened the bolt on the rifle, removed the cartridge, studied the breach, then restored the brass cartridge, and closed the action.

"This carbine for instance, it's a British model, manufactured and first exported in 1863. It's really a beauty, really a couple of years ahead of it's time to tell you the truth. Now, here's the most curious aspect of this particular piece, that is: the history of it: how you found it on a battlefield a full year before it came out of the factory."

"Did I say Bull Run, I meant Gettysburg, sure as hell."

"No son, I think you said what you meant." The officer turned back toward him, "Where abouts do you boys live?" Caleb looked over at his brother. He was as pale as a ghost with his head hanging down limply over his chest. J.D. pulled in his swollen tongue and shook his head slightly. Tears pooled in Caleb's eyes, "I cayn't say." The officer went over to the table and pulled a pen and a leaf of paper from a small leather satchel. He wrote something down; then he grinned, walked over to the door and knocked. A Sergeant walked in, "Yes sir."

"I want you to put together a detachment of twenty men who can read. Then set up a couple of tables in front of the bonfire and go through every document in the court files." He handed the piece of paper to the Sergeant, "If you find any paper with one of these names on it bring it up immediately. Burn everything else."

"Yes sir." The soldier took the sheet of paper and disappeared down the stairs.

The officer closed the door slowly enough that it squeaked loudly. He walked casually over to his gear and pulled a small tin drum out. He took the lid off the drum and emptied the contents, and then he walked back to the landing with the empty drum. He opened the door a crack and leaned his torso through it, mumbling something. He closed the door and walked back to the table where he left the carbine.

Picking up the carbine, he said, "You boys are ridiculous. You're fighting for a country that doesn't even exist. This morning at the river... Americans murdered Americans, that's all."

"We're not killing our countrymen, we're defending our country. I fight for the Confederate states of America, more importantly, I fight for North Carolina."

The Cardinal that had been flying around the ceiling landed on a windowsill exhausted, it looked out the open window and saw the free open skies; then its body was torn apart violently as a piece of lead ripped through it.

What remained of its body fell out the window; only an explosion of crimson feathers remained, floating in the bright sunshine that poured through the window. The officer opened the breach of the carbine and blew a plume of smoke out the end of the barrel, as Caleb watched the feathers settle on the windowsill. The door flew open and a gust of air poured through the room, scattering the feathers across the floor.

Yankee soldiers ran in with their rifles at the ready, one spoke, "Sir, is everything…"

The officer started toward them as if he might kill them, "Get the hell out of here damn it, you sorry bastards. If I need your help, then I'll damn well call for it." They bid a hasty retreat. The officer locked the door behind them, and then he went across the room and locked the door to the other landing. He looked at Caleb with contempt, "Your not fighting for your country."

"The hell I ain't! I'm fighting for the Confederate States of…"

The officer swung the rifle down against the table. He held it by the barrel and swung it down like an axe. The stock broke in two and clattered to the floor. He stepped around the table and came within a few feet of Caleb. He leaned down so that their faces were level, "Lee capitulated last week."

"He what?"

"He surrendered, you damn backwoods fool. You ain't fighting for the Confederacy, there's no such thing. North Carolina is part of the United States." Caleb watched as a small eddy of wind in the corner of the room raised a handful of downy red feathers into the air then dispersed them on the wooden floor. He was dumbfounded and helpless, even more so than before.

J.D. moaned softly. They both looked over at the wounded man, one with sudden concern, and the other with bemusement. "That's right Jed, it's over. Only people fighting now are buffoons. You've lost everything and gained nothing." He paused and looked back at Caleb, "Or have you?" Caleb looked away. The officer chuckled to himself and went over to the table.

He picked through the material dumped out of the tin until he found a straight razor and a strop. He walked back over to Caleb and threw one end of the sharpening strap over a post on the back of his chair. He began to run the blade back and forth. "I think you know exactly where that carbine came from." Caleb felt his stomach sickening and his throat preparing to convulse. The hiss of the blade sliding across the strap filled his left ear. "The war's over, I wonder what you have to gain by keeping this information from me?"

He dropped the strop and let it hang off the chair. Someone knocked at the door. The officer walked over, unlocked the door and leaned out. In a moment he returned to the table with the tin drum. Steam was rising out of it softly. He sat the drum in the windowsill at the far end of the room, came back to the table, gathered some more items, and then returned once again to the far window.

He took a framed photo of Jefferson Davis off the wall, looked at it for a moment, and then threw it out the window. He hung a small round mirror on the nail and shaved a few flakes of soap into a mug with the razor. He walked back toward Caleb as he stirred a brush in the mug to make some foam.

"A buckboard wagon left one of the bordering states some time ago. It carried two officers and a fortune in gold." He paused to let the words take full effect. As he turned and walked back to the open window, he continued, "I questioned the last officer to see them alive. I looked over their orders. They were headed for the gulf coast of Florida."

The officer spread the foam over his face with the brush and began to shave. His voice took on strange tones as he tried to hold his face in a certain posture for shaving, and talked without moving his lips very much. "They never made it. The officer

I questioned said that one of them carried a very unique rifle."

The commander made eye contact through the mirror. "It was an 1863 model British Carbine." He finished shaving and looked at Caleb in the mirror. "Now let me tell you something. I'll have that gold." He said so with menace.

He began to examine something else in the mirror. Taking it off the wall, he crossed the room and held it up to J.D.'s face. He turned and went to the door. Caleb looked over at his brother, his head hung limply from his neck, and his hands, no longer clenched, lay open and relaxed behind the chair.

Caleb began to cry and kick with his feet until the chair fell over in the floor. "You bastard!" he screamed. "You no good bastard, whyyyy…" he wailed loudly, "why? You son-of-a-bitch!" He began to sob with anger, some of it directed at the officer, some at himself for his helplessness. The commander walked up and set Caleb's chair upright.

"You know damn well why." The officer laughed to himself and crossed the room to the open window. He took a small white towel and dipped it in the hot water. He wiped the excess foam off his face and started speaking in a casual tone. "Look at you. You must really enjoy drama. Hell, I'll admit to having a weakness for it myself. But I don't guess you get much theatre around these parts. Hot damn, I saw a good one in Philadelphia one time.

"It was about this fella', he had to kill his best friend, his leader, the one person he loved and respected more than any man on Earth." The officer examined his face in the mirror, dumped the water out the window, filled the receptacle with shaving implements, and deposited them on the table as he walked toward Caleb. "But he killed him all the same, he had to, because it was for the good of his country.

"Now if that man had to kill this person who had been like a father to him," The officer drew his revolver and pressed the barrel painfully to Caleb's forehead, "what chance, in hell, does a little piss ant like you have?" His voice took on a menace outside the bounds of sanity, "I could blow you away like a feather, with no more significance. You're going to tell me right now you little shit, what's went with that gold?" His thumb slowly drew the hammer back.

Caleb looked up at him with bloodshot eyes, "Do you think, I'll let my brother's death be for nothing?"

A tense moment passed then a knock came at the door. The officer didn't move, a few seconds later the rapping repeated. The commander slowly uncocked the pistol and walked to the door. He spoke for a moment with a soldier at the landing, then the man was invited in and they walked over to the desk.

The soldier carried a piece of paper and the officer seemed to have forgotten about Caleb. At the desk the officer produced a rolled up map. He unrolled it on the table and laid his revolver on one end to keep it from rolling back up. They examined the sheet of paper, and then consulted the map. As they continued to compare the two documents the doctor burst through the doorway. The commander let go the map and it contracted back into a roll and came to rest over his pistol.

As the doctor frantically checked for J.D.'s pulse the officer stormed around the table toward him. "Where the hell have you been?" He roared.

"Sir I was only following your…"

"We've waited here for God knows how long, and where were you? You're tardiness has cost this man his life." The doctor looked frightened and on the verge of a nervous breakdown. "You God damned quack! I've got a good mind to have you flogged." The doctor stammered, "But you told me to…"

"Don't try to pass the buck, you slimy little worm. The only thing worse than a quack is a coward! What do you have to say for yourself?" The doctor only trembled silently, kneeling with one knee in a pool of blood at the foot of J.D.'s chair.

The officer drew his saber and took a step toward the physician, his face full of bitter condemnation. Once again the doctor made a clumsy but hasty retreat out the nearest door. "And stay out of my sight!" The commander yelled after him.

As he passed Caleb on his way back to the table he sheathed his sword and stopped to turn toward the prisoner. He kneeled down toward him and spoke softly, "That's one thing you have to get use to in the military," he grinned widely, "incompetence."

He went over to the table, "I do have some good news though. We have your address now, and I hate to think of you walking all the way home, so we're going to take you back ourselves. Maybe you can show us around the place when we get there; I know there's one sight in particular I would like to see."

When Caleb was walked out of the courthouse and onto the grounds with a pistol in his back he looked up at the spring skies. The sun still cast it's rays down on the small town, but clouds were growing larger, banding together with their brothers, and threatening to form a dark federation of downpours.

He could see the reflection of the courthouse in the large storefront window across the street. The bonfire was burning larger than ever. A table was set up on the lawn. Various Union soldiers, some officers-some enlisted, glanced over documents then tossed the papers into the fire. Caleb imagined they were looking for his name. He was led to a patch of earth in the shadow of the great column of smoke rising from the fire.

Caleb and his guard waited while four soldiers carried their burden out from the courthouse steps. They had used the Confederate flag in the courtroom as a stretcher, each holding a corner. J.D.'s body bulged down in the center the soldiers were exerting themselves strenuously to avoid letting that bulge drag on the ground. Despite their efforts, the flag made jarring contact with the earth more than once, and J.D.'s boot heels caught clumps of weeds constantly.

The flag was too short for his legs, which hung off the back edge below the knee. When the ground contacted his feet it caused them to jolt forward in a disturbing marionette-like kick. They finally reached Caleb and dropped the flag clad body to the ground with exclamations of relief.

An officer then walked around the bonfire with a short-handle shovel and threw it at Caleb's feet. He turned to the guard, "Six foot deep and not an inch less." Then he jerked the bloodstained banner from beneath the brother like a magician with a tablecloth and returned to the fire to cast his offering.

With his teeth clenched in hatred and disgust, Caleb took off his shirt and set to work digging the grave. His hands were blistered and tender from the digging he had engaged in on the previous day, but he had little choice. As his sorrow, anger, and indignation soared, he could feel numbness spread through his limbs.

He concentrated on the revenge he would take upon the sadistic murderer with the close shave. As long as he channeled his passions into his labor he proceeded vigorously. When his anger waned however, and despair welled up inside him, he could feel the intense pain of the, now split, blisters in his palms, the dizziness of sleep deprivation, and the crippling self-pity of his position and circumstance.

By the time the sun reached its zenith it had been lost behind the mass of clouds gathering into a storm front overhead. Flies had been conducting brotherhood meetings upon J.D.'s corpse and now ants were beginning to discover the body. The day continued to wear on as Caleb endured the bites of a persistent, bloated horsefly.

His back was red and sweaty; it must have been very attractive to the horsefly that would land on the tense salty flesh every few minutes. Caleb felt the sensation of a needle piercing his left shoulder and finally brought his hand down on the insect oppressor. He looked with satisfaction at the remnants of the parasite on the torn flesh of his palm, then the focus of his eyes adjusted with his hand becoming fuzzy and the bottom of the grave he stood in coming into sharp relief. He looked at the dirt wall on his right. It was all he could do to climb out of the hole; his trembling, fatigued limbs were failing.

Finally he rolled out onto the lawn and stared up at the sky, wide-eyed and oblivious to the dead body that lay beside him. A moment later the murderer himself was leaning over Caleb. He examined the exhausted gravedigger for a moment. Caleb saw the villain silhouetted against the darkening clouds in the sky, and for a moment he wondered if he were hallucinating.

"I got half a mind to roll you off in this hole with your brother, but I've got need of you yet," and with that he dragged the dazed man away. Caleb could see the protestations of the flies when a soldier rolled the dead body into the grave and started to fill it in with earth. "Only the flies to mourn him," he dimly thought before blacking out.

* * *

Caleb awoke to the large drops of rain that precede torrential showers. They were great obese drops and fell at lengthy intervals. He was in the back of a wagon. He leaned up and saw a trail of dust behind him. He turned and looked at the coachman, who paid no attention.

Caleb thought of jumping down and heading for the wilderness where he could hide till things simmered down, but when he first moved his legs he heard the chains rattle. The driver looked back at him, it was the same horse faced soldier that had guarded him in the courtroom.

"Don't get a wild hair back there. I won't hesitate to shoot you. I'm tempted to go ahead and do it on any account, just to save us this headache." There was a great degree of agitation in the man's voice and Caleb felt he had better not test him. Looking at the scenery he could tell they were on there way back to his home. They must have found a piece of paper at the courthouse with his address on it.

Hopefully Sally was at her mother's, that's all the comfort he could find. Soon the officer who interrogated him would have the gold. He had dismissed everyone from the room when the questioning turned toward the gold. Caleb felt he knew why. The officer wanted the gold for himself, that seemed obvious.

He held no scruple in trying to retrieve the treasure, and in light of that, Caleb felt a great concern for Sally. Like so many who do not pray, Caleb turned toward this as a last resort and knelt into it fervently in his moment of dire need.

He saw no one better to turn to than God, for this officer seemed to be the very embodiment of Satan and it would be quite natural for beings with a shared enemy to form an alliance to thwart the common foe. He could hear a distant thunder rolling across the landscape, and as if the sound had let loose a cork in the skies; water began to fall in soft cold sheets.

The rain was much softer and lighter than he had anticipated. When he ceased his water sodden supplications the trail of dust was gone and the road was damp. They were in his neighborhood now and he watched in astonishment as they passed his shack.

Then he realized they must have found the deed to J.D.'s spread. He had never gotten around to filing the title to his land at the courthouse, so perhaps they thought he and his brother both lived at J.D.'s dirt floor cabin. Caleb could see a couple of men in the doorway of the cabin as the wagon rolled up, one disappeared inside, then a moment later the commander emerged from the dark interior and strode up to the wagon.

"It's about time you got here with the prisoner, we've got our orders. We can't lollygag around here forever…" A minute later when he had ran out of things to berate the driver about, he addressed Caleb, "Alright boy where is it?"

Caleb pointed at J.D.'s cabin; "You don't think I'd keep it in my house do you?"

The officer put his hand around Caleb's neck and drove the back of his head into the wet wood of the wagon. He leaned closely over Caleb and whispered venomously, "I don't give a damn, I just want you to tell me where the gold is or I'll kill you, then tear this place apart, and by God I will find it."

Caleb tried to tear his assailant's hands loose. He felt the blood pooling in his head and the horrible sensations that signal the impending collapse of your trachea. Finally he released his grasp and Caleb gulped down air ravenously. The officer withdrew, and a couple of soldiers unshackled Caleb, and brought him out into the muddy, bare, dirt lawn.

They carried him, one under each arm, to the edge of the well and placed him on his feet looking down into the hole. The cold rain trickled down his bare back and he shivered weakly. The bucket was at the bottom of the dry well and he could see the rope disappearing into darkness.

Suddenly he felt his hand brought up between his shoulder blades and a flash of pain swept over him. The officer leaned his head over Caleb's shoulder, "last chance," he said. He inched Caleb up to the very rim of the hole. "Where is it?"

Caleb's toes were hanging over the edge of the hole. He found it almost impossible to utter the necessary words. "I won't say." Escaped his lips without any defiance or vitriol, only with the pitiful whisper of a man on the gallows, frightened out of his wits, and attempting to trick his tongue into bravery.

Then came the push and the visible surface world flew away. It was replaced with the dark subterranean world in which only recently his brother had been interred. With frantic instinct Caleb's hands shot out in front of him, and gripped tightly the rope. His arms gave a jerk, which jarred them to the sockets and the rough fabric of the rope burned through the palms of Caleb's hands. He held on as long as he could, then released the rope leaving blood and small chunks of flesh imbedded in the braided hemp.

He hit the bottom almost as soon as his hands left the rope. He felt the bones in his legs would shatter from the force, but somehow the joints bent in all the right directions as he buckled to the bottom of the pit and felt the hollowness one endures when the wind is knocked out of him.

The pain beneath his ribs, along with that of his hands, left him dazed and wallowing in self-pity. He was in the fetal position, crying and cursing, with hot, sticky-faced anger, until he could once again breathe easily. He could feel his pulse throbbing in his wounded palms, the pain growing dull, and his hands stiffening.

He looked up and saw a soldier looking down the well. The soldier was lit by the soft flickering glow of a fire, but Caleb couldn't imagine how they might have started a bonfire in the rain. The soldier disappeared and Caleb was left to himself.

He sat in the mud, exhausted and ready to sleep. He had such a need for slumber that circumstance was meaningless. His brother was dead. He would be dead very soon. His wife would then starve to death. These things meant nothing, only one thing had any significance for Caleb now: sleep.

He sat with his back against the wall of the shaft, closed his eyes and immediately slept. His eyes jerked open and he began coughing reflexively, and gagging convulsively. He pushed himself up off the ground, and then jerked his hands back from the intense pain the effort caused his forgotten hand injuries. The rain was coming in a torrential downpour, what his father would have called "a real goose-drowner." He coughed and gagged for a couple of minutes then regained his senses. He wondered how long he had been asleep and found it difficult to believe it was anything more than two minutes. He pulled one of his suspenders back up on a shoulder.

He must have fell asleep and rolled onto the floor. He figured the water to be about three inches deep, and set his mind to devising a way to sleep. If he were to sit up, he'd fall over after he passed out, if he were to lie on his side or stomach he would draw water, and if he slept on his back he'd choke on the descending rainwater.

Finally, he sobbed, cursed, and gnashed his teeth before resigning himself to the tortures of the damned. A crack of thunder wallowed itself down the reverberating shaft. The electrical activity continued and soon the shaft was lit with flashes of brilliance. Lightning from cloud to cloud sometimes provided a split second of broad daylight at the bottom of the well, while the shafts that struck the ground provided only residual light, reflected from the lip of the hole.

The night passed slowly and the water rose little. The rain was frigid and Caleb began to tremble as the cold penetrated to his core. Occasionally he nodded off and awakened a moment later to the horrible drowning sensation. Fear had flown far away from him, sorrow, pain, and even the cold abated, leaving him only the weariness.

His need for sleep hijacked his senses to the point of making him delusional. His mind floated far a field. He heard the voices of the dead. He saw angels and devils. He tasted strange foods on his tongue. He felt his eyelids crawl across his pupils like two bloated slugs. He coughed small amounts of water out of his lungs and sinuses. The cycle began a new.

A flash of lightning overhead cast the interior of his tomb in the light of sharpened quicksilver. Within that interval he saw his brother, sitting as his mirror image, with his back against the far wall. Caleb put his scalp against the earthen wall and looked straight up the shaft gasping.

He saw the circular opening of blue sky and the wispy cloud-cover, high above. The almost translucent clouds floated past the opening on a spring breeze. It was morning and Caleb couldn't decide from whence it came. The windless dissected his view of the sky and the bucket swung softly overhead in the new rays of the morning sun.

As it swung, it released drops of water to freefall in soft arching paths down the shaft, finally sending ripples through the puddle at the bottom. Suddenly a hand reached from out of view and turned the bucket upside-down. More than a gallon of water poured into Caleb's face. He leaned over at the waist, coughing and retching, when suddenly the bucket landed on the back of his head painfully.

A familiar voice poured down, "Put your foot in the pail, polecat." Slowly he was raised to the surface and blinded in the daylight. He felt hands grabbing him from various directions and throwing him down in the mud. Immediately he began to succumb to the sleep that had been eating away at him all night.

A boot in his ribs had the effect of chasing away that which he desired. The pain in his side coupled with the pump knot on his head dragged him, unwillingly, into the land of the living. First his eyes opened a crack, then they slid back until he could see a blurry strange world take shape.

The shack was gone, leaving only two charred walls and the stone chimney standing. Everything else was burned down, the two walls surviving because of the rain. The yards as far as he could see had been plowed to depth. Hazily he thought what a task it must have been in that rocky terrain.

As if in answer he heard the report of a pistol and turned to see a fallen mare with gun smoke caressing it's head. An officer was walking away from the body while he returned his revolver to its holster. The terrain around him was pockmarked with holes, some three foot deep, others filled with cloudy red water.

The soldiers milling around seemed as miserable as he felt. They watched him with a grim hatred, and fear finally overcame his exhaustion as he wondered what was to become of him at their hands. The gray-haired officer leaned over his prostrate body. "Where the hell is it?" He asked.

"Where is what?" Was the reply, and oddly enough a genuine reply. In his delirium Caleb couldn't remember what the cause of all this might have been. The officer looked around nervously at his troops, then addressed Caleb for a second time, "You know damn well what!"

Caleb's mind locked into position as if some teeth in the gears finally met.

He wanted to lead them to the gold, he wanted to desperately, and he no longer cared about anything as abstract as dishonoring his brother's memory. He feared however that he might find Sally at home, and he wasn't about to lead this angry mob right up her petticoat. His thoughts attached themselves to the first feeble lie he could formulate. "I buried it."

"I'll be damned! You did no such thing." The exasperated commander encompassed the dug up land about him with a sweep of his arm.

"Not here. Up in the mountains."

The officer took off his hat and rubbed the stubble on his face with his fingertips. After a moment's contemplation he began issuing orders to his subordinates. He gave command of the detachment to a junior officer and ordered them to proceed to the next objective, rendezvousing with the main body of troops as soon as possible.

Only the Commander and Lieutenant Kelly stayed behind. Watching after the departing men as they disappeared down the muddy lane, the commander said, "Boy, I've lost all patience with you. If you're trying to play me for a fool…" He turned and looked down at the prisoner, "Either we come back to our horses with what we're looking for, or we'll skin you alive and tie you up in a tree by your ankles for the wolves."

He grabbed Caleb by the arm and set him up on his feet forcefully. The officer put his hat back on and cut deep into Caleb with his blood shot eyes, "I mean no exaggeration, mark well my words." He gave Caleb a bitter shove, "Take us to it!" Thus began their march.

Caleb began walking. He had said "the mountains" so he knew he would eventually have to make his way uphill, but otherwise had no idea where to go. He simply put one foot in front of another without a single thought of navigation.

His mind was consumed with everything except his destination. He was oblivious to those who held him in their charge, as well as the terrain he traversed. He thought of his brother, and wondered what he was doing right now. He thought of Sally and wondered when dinner would be ready.

He imagined what it might feel like to be skinned alive and couldn't quite remember what put the question in his head. He felt one of his suspenders fall of his shoulder and as he put it back he realized he was bear-chested. He couldn't believe he had left the house that morning without a shirt, how foolish.

He trudged along like a zombie, for hours without knowing why, or with whom. He climbed ridges and descended valleys, operating on some instinctual sense of navigation. Eventually he felt an urgent pressure on his bowels. Without any preparatory rituals at all he let his suspenders fall and dropped his trousers to his knees. As he did so and squatted with one swift motion, the officers were startled out of their own private reveries and nearly shot the man.

"What the hell… Damn son, if you've got to take a shit, is it really worth dieing for?" They circled in front of him and his eyes grew large. Lieutenant Kelly remarked to his superior, "Good Lord, these backwoods boys got worse manners than any nigger I've ever seen!"

They stepped to one side and turned toward the forest as if to express their sense of etiquette in the absence of Caleb's. Seeing the two blue clad figures in front of him had awoken his feverish mind to reality. He looked up and saw that the sun was very high.

He listened to the officer's mumble to each other a few steps away. He tried to make out what they were saying. He thought they were coming to the determination that he would never have buried the gold this far away and were debating whether to go ahead and kill him. He thought maybe his fear was feeding his imagination, but looking at the position of the sun again he new they had been hiking through the wilderness a long time.

For just a moment he calculated the odds of coming up behind them for a death struggle, but there was two of them and he would be killed. Still, he thought, better to be killed outright than skinned alive, and he had no doubt the threat would be carried out.

Suddenly he realized where he was. His father had taken him by this route to fish for trout, perhaps a hundred times in his youth. It had been years since he had been here, but his body had brought him along that circuit without the assistance of his conscious mind. The river lay just ahead.

He studied the terrain, examining every nuance, comparing it to images tucked away in the nostalgia of childhood. About thirty feet ahead there was a thicket of vegetation. It was the kind of dense growth that occurs along the banks of a river. As best his memory could provide: behind that veil of muskadine, Virginia creeper, and honey suckle, was a drop off to a pool in the river. If he could cover the distance and let the river carry him down stream, perhaps they would consider it too much trouble to find him and kill him. Perhaps they would simply give up and leave.

Suddenly he realized he had been sitting there several minutes and at any moment his captors would turn around and drag him to his feet. There was no time to contemplate the merit of his plan. He jerked up from his squatting position while simultaneously hoisting his pants to his waist with both hands. In the same motion he leaned forward into his sprint.

Never in his life had he put so much strength into a lightning dash, as he now did. And never before had it seemed to take so long to run ten yards. What lasted only a second seemed like hours, hours spent waiting on a bullet to crash through the back of your skull. The last couple of steps, he heard angry shouts, and then he planted both feet on the bare rock inches in front of the curtain of foliage and dove through to the sound of gunshots.

When he let go his trousers to dive through the vines his pants fell again around his ankles. He felt himself pass through wall of leaves, and then he was lost in space. He had thought the river right in front of him, but he fell for what seemed like ages. He was more scared than he had ever been in his life when he didn't collapse into the water immediately.

Every second he fell, his terror increased, still, it seemed as if he would never get wherever he was going. He felt the air rushing across his naked body with the souls of his boots pointed skyward and his hands stretched out like a dart falling from heaven.

At last he broke the water like a meteor and tried to use his forward momentum to make a horseshoe turn back toward the surface. Before he could stop his submerged descent, he struck the bottom.

He crashed his ribs along the bottom. The rocks in the riverbed had the effect of a biblical stoning upon his body. He was ground into the river-bottom with a terrible force, stars appeared before his closed eyes, much of the skin was torn away from the front half of his body, the air in his lungs burst out of his mouth in huge bubbles, and he felt his ribcage threaten collapse.

With neither air in his lungs, nor the strength to draw air into them, he slowly floated to the surface. Returned to the surface, all the sounds of the river suddenly crashed out of their silence and into his ears. The pain of his body dissipated and left only a hollow throbbing. His senses were quickened, he heard the roar of an upstream waterfall, felt the icy cold of the water, tasted the blood in his mouth, and saw the noonday sun reflecting brilliantly off the rapid dappled stream.

He waddled weakly into a cove behind him and dragged himself onto a cold rock that had never been touched by the sun. He could see only directly across the stream where another cliff rose to heights unknown. The top of that cliff as well as all things up and down stream were not visible inside Caleb's sheltered bay.

He took stock of himself as he choked breath back into his sore lungs. He was lying on his back and his body, as much of it as he could see, was covered with blood. Much of the skin around his knees, upper chest, and the tops of his feet had been sheered away. His elbows and the area around his triceps were in rough shape as well.

The blood in his mouth was coming from his fleshy inner lips, as if he had been punched. He imagined the force of breaking the surface of the water caused that. He felt the color drain out of his face when he saw how his genitals suffered the fall. They seemed horribly mutilated, but with so much blood it was difficult to tell how badly. He was somewhat relieved when after a moment's examination he counted two testicles.

He wondered for a moment why his boots had not protected his feet, then realized the water had forced his boots and pants off with the force of his entry. His clothes were out of sight now, and, he imagined, already well down stream. So, for a moment he lay there, bloody and naked on the dark cool stone. Then his head lolled back, embroiled with involuntary slumber, and the midges began to feast upon his body.

1875

Caleb sat in a wooden chair with his head in his hands. He stared down at a section of flooring between his feet. Though he was only in his early thirties, his hair was predominantly gray. Nearby Sally was boiling oatmeal in a small pot on the wood-burning stove. It was early winter and a small cauldron rested in the hearth of the fireplace. Inside the cauldron was a beautiful dress of Parisian design, her church-going dress as a matter of fact. The dress steamed in the water while, hopefully, a small stain dissolved.

"Caleb, there's honestly no sense in brooding over it. The doctor's just going to come have a look, I don't think amputation will be necessary," she mockingly told him.

"Ain't brooding, woman. Thinking." It wasn't much, but she couldn't remember the last time he said more.

"Call it what you will, I'm weary of it." She crossed the room hurriedly to stir her dress with a wooden spoon and examine its progress. "All you do is think, you never talk to me, you hardly help at all with the crop. What's going to become of us?" His only answer to the question was to stare down at the plank floor and grin mysteriously.

"It's the war," she said emphatically. "The war ruined you like every other man we know. You've been like a lost child ever since. You walk around scared of your own shadow. We go to town- you ask every Tom, Dick, and Harry if there's been any strangers arrive." She crossed the room in exasperation and reached behind him, pulled out a small pistol.

Disgusted, she threw the gun down on the table beside him. "When's the last time you took two steps without a gun?" She waited for a reply, "Huh..." Her foot tapped anxiously until, all of a sudden, her emotions pivoted and an intense look of concern invested her features. She kneeled down on the floor in front of him trying to enter the downward slant of his field of vision.

He gazed up into her face weakly. He seemed to be looking at her from a million miles away. Her eyes were watery with unshed tears as she spoke, "The war is over! Its gone and done with. The Armies disbanded years ago. I don't know what to do, every day you get worse. Think for a minute. You can't kill memories with a pistol."

Unconsciously, she was wringing the front of her apron in her fists, while she tried to think of the perfect utterance to dispel the curse, "Can you think of one good, logical reason... I mean anything, that would be worth somebody coming back from ten years ago and tracking you down?"

The color drained out of Caleb's face and he looked back down at the floor as if death just knocked from underneath. But the only knocking came from the front door and Sally quickly erased any sign that she was distraught, straightened her apron, and crossed the room to let the doctor in.

"Well, now Missus Walker, and I thought lilies never bloomed in the winter." The doctor's cheeks were scarlet form the cold, but his bedside manner seemed unaffected.

"Why doc, you could charm a weevil right out of its cotton." She blushed for the desired effect.

Most of the doctor's visits were free, or seemed that way. For a bushel of moldy, bruised apples the physician would ride all the way out from his office in Morganton and examine Caleb to determine his recovery from old wounds or to succor him in his frequent spells of illness.

Caleb rose from his chair in solemn recognition of the doctor's arrival. He limped across the floor without any attempt to hide the pain it caused him. The doctor, moved to pity, crossed the room and met the veteran half way.

"Poor fellow, I see the left knee is causing you some pain as yet," he consoled the man as they shook hands.

"A mite," Caleb grunted.

"What's that you say, dear boy?"

Sally stepped in to dispel the doctor's confusion, "He said the wound still haunts him."

"Oh," the doctor laughed drolly, "I see."

The doctor had moved to Morganton only a few years before and originally haled from Philadelphia. A few of the more colloquial expressions still eluded him. Doctor Eden had been extremely kind to the Walkers and never lacked a platitude for Sally in particular.

On this visit, while Sally tended to her dress and her cereal, Dr. Eden examined Caleb's troublesome knee. This he had been doing on a regular basis since his arrival in Morganton. The prognosis was always the same, "If it's changed at all, it's gotten slightly worse."

"Doctor, I wondered if you might enquire of my groom that which we discussed so recently." It was her pet way of talking to the doctor, as if she too were college educated.

The doctor looked puzzled, "Perhaps, you might jar my memory."

"It's," she hesitated, "of a delicate nature."

"Ah yes, we did converse about such a matter." He escorted her to the door, "It is quite frigid outside my dear, but we must think of the protection of your modesty."

The latch closed on the door behind her and her breath began to blossom into frosty steam. The sky held a gray, stern sea above her, and the terrain underneath her feet was hard and solemn. In the past ten years Sally had come to the conclusion that Caleb could not father a child. He could seldom perform the duties of a husband's office at all, and when he could, the efforts were literally fruitless.

When the doctor first came to town she had been thoroughly impressed with his manner of speech, flattering banter, and chivalrous attitude. She had imposed upon his kindness, that perhaps he could lend aid to her ailing spouse, and he had taken it as a sacred duty to do so. Sally had very little with which to pay the good doctor and would stop at short of nothing to show her gratitude.

One of the first things the physician did was to examine Caleb and confirm her suspicions that he was completely sterile. She took the news with what dignity she could muster and considered it her lot in life to persevere. Now years later she found herself in the family way and felt that only a second opinion could salvage her reputation. As the minutes passed she grew more nervous, but finally the door opened and the doctor emerged.

"Remarkable, simply remarkable!" He proclaimed.

"What is it Jerry?"

"Ma'am, your husbands loins have the regenerative powers of a lizards tail!" He checked himself and blushed shamefully. "Pardon me madam, my off color metaphor, but suffice it to say: it would not at all surprise me if this time next year you were nursing his first-born son."

So it was that she danced for joy and cried not a few tears while her husband sat in a chair and stared at the floor.

* * *

That night as husband and wife crawled into bed and blew out the oil lamps Sally told Caleb of the coming of a child. Caleb's response was negligible, as if she had told him the weather was going to take a turn. Night folded its wings about them and they submitted to slumber's soft caress.

Sally dreamed she was walking through a spring meadow, it was a beautiful, sunny day, and the field was crowded in daisies. Slowly she became aware of a faint, ghostly cry. It seemed the cry of an infant. She followed the sound toward the crest of the meadow.

Beyond lay a homestead. Much like the house she shared with Caleb, only larger, finer, in better repair. She knew it for home. The cries of a baby came from within. She knew well that it was her child. She rushed to the front door, a broad smile on her face. It was locked. She rushed around the house for the back door. Passing a window, she could hear the baby within chortling. The shutters were chained, but they were rather slack. She cracked the shutters open a few inches to gaze within.

There, on a fine brass bed, atop a quilt of her knitting (though she couldn't remember its creation), was a plump, healthy baby. Sally had never felt such unbridled joy. It welled up from deep in her soul. She called to the baby (though there were no words), and the child rewarded her with an ecstatic smile.

A cloth diaper hid the gender of her offspring, and she bolted for the back door to remedy the situation. She found this door locked as well. She began knocking and calling for Caleb to open the door. She couldn't hear her own voice.

Suddenly, she felt desperate. She screamed silently for her husband to open the door. She stepped back from the door she had been wrapping on. Her hands had left bloody marks on the wood, and they tingled softly at her sides. If he wasn't inside, perhaps he was somewhere in the surrounding fields. She turned her back on the house suddenly, and shouted into the endless daisies.

No one answered her calls, but how could they, when even she could not hear them. A fear seized her, and she whipped around. The house was gone. There wasn't a blemish to mark where it had stood a moment ago. She walked foreword, feeling the air with her hands. It simply wasn't there.

She looked behind her. There it was. She took a deep breath and exhaled in relief. It was behind her all along. She knew that. How silly. She went from window to window, looking for a way in. She paused to watch the baby crawl a foot or two, on the beautiful bed, in the simple room.

Passing the front door twice, she stopped to meditate on her problem. Something slammed loudly. Something behind that door. It sent a tremor through the whole structure, casting Sally off the front stoop. The sound thumped again. It was incredibly loud, and recurred like the beat of a leviathan's heart.

Sally hurried around to the window. The child seemed calm, but the sound came from beneath the floor of its room. She hurried back to the front door and pulled and pushed on it until the brass doorknob came off in her hand. There was a loud crash within.

She ran back to the window and saw that the floor at the foot of the child's bed had erupted. It was busted out from beneath, as if a great beast had burst up into the room from unknown depths. An inch closer and the foot of the bed might have fallen in.

Black-faced hornets clouded out of the rupture, in a swarm. They flew irregular circuits, in and out of the fissure. The air was filled with their buzzing. She noticed a window at the head of the bed. The headboard was dead against the window casing. Why hadn't she discovered that window before. She ran around to it, and found it chained as well. However, these shutters did open wide enough to pull the baby through. From this window, the floor was blocked from her view. What she could see, were the hornets wheeling through the air below the bed.

The baby watched, with amusement, it seemed, as its mother's arms reached through the window. Sally called to the child, beckoning with frustratingly silent words. Come to me. She tried to act as if it were a game, something jolly, to amuse the baby. The child laughed and clapped its hands.

Sally noticed the edge of the quilt. She stretched as far as she could. The more she pressed in with her shoulder, the more the shutters tried to close, and pinch her arm off. She could see her fingertips pat the very edge of the quilt. The quilt, and everything on it, slid slowly, but unmistakably, away from her hand.

The woman screamed without sound. The quilt was sliding toward the foot of the bed. Slowly it slithered from her. The baby was nearing the foot of the bed. She tore herself away from one window and ran to the other, fearing her child would be gone with her next glimpse.

The view from the other window sent her into a raving panic. The quilt extended down into the hole in the floor, and it was being pulled, ever so gradually down into it. She ran back to the previous window and tore at the shutters with all her might. At last, her heart withering inside her, a hinge broke.

She grabbed the headboard and started pulling herself though, but the aperture was very nearly too small. As she felt the flesh peeling off her body, she forced her way through. The baby was at the foot of the bed, and it laughed as its mother slowly dragged herself into the room.

Suddenly a board snapped loudly, as Sally found herself on the bed. She looked up to see the baby go over the edge. She scrambled, hand and knee, to the bottom of the bed. Looking down, she could see the floor solid again, as if never a thing had happened.

From beneath the floorboards, a baby's cries could be heard.

She gasped and jerked up into a sitting position in bed. She was nauseous, frightened, and gasping for air. Her nightgown was soaked through with sweat and she was sitting in a puddle of urine. She whipped her head around the room several times and slowly realized where she was. She tried in vain to calm herself, but her heart was pounding like never before. Suddenly the piercing sound of an infant crying came from beneath the floorboards of the shack. Sally began to shriek like a madwoman. Her cheeks were already stained with bitter tears, but now they poured forth yet again.

She fell out of bed, nearly breaking her arm, and crawled across the room while the incessant crying continued. She pushed the door of the cabin open and tumbled down the stoop and out into the yard. The dampness of her nightgown began to freeze her, so she disrobed. A moment later Caleb appeared in the open doorway to witness his wife, naked as the day she was born, sitting in the front yard at two in the morning screaming hysterically. He imagined the temperature to be no more than thirty degrees.

"What in the hell's gotten into you woman, its cold as Canada out here." The commotion seemed to have broken him out of his psychological stupor.

"I ain't never setting foot in there again, its haynted! There's a spirit in there and its set to curse our baby."

"Stop talking foolishness, you old hen. You had a nightmare is all!"

"Well, I ain't dreaming that sound, listen."

Caleb heard the distinct sound of a baby crying, and it was coming from beneath the floor. "Ah, that could be anything, or more likely: nothing."

"That ain't nothing, it's a baby crying if I've ever heard one." She looked around, wide-eyed and frantic. "I bet our house is over a baby's grave, I bet that's what it is."

"Don't be ridiculous."

"I'm not being anything, I'm just telling you I won't stay in there."

She was serious too, no matter how long he argued with her, he could not persuade her to come back in, and she ended the conversation by making an oath to sleep at her mother's house until the house was moved off "the grave sight of that poor child". Then she turned around with what dignity she could gather, and marched off in the direction of her mother's house, shivering and nude.

Caleb walked back into the house, cursed, and punched the wall. Then he looked down at the floor, through the floor, at the gold. A baby cried loudly in his ear. "Shut-up!" He screamed. He knew how superstitious his wife could be, and he wondered what he could do. The house would be moved across the street, and the gold hidden elsewhere.

He went to the door and looked across the rutted out drive, he owned that lot and a strip of land beside it. The land was cleared, except for a gigantic oak. He decided to move the shack across the road as soon as possible. He looked back down at the floor, and then went outside to the shed to get his toolbox.

He pried loose some boards in the floor and reached down into the darkness. A pale object cut up across his body leaving bloody scratches in its trail. It screamed loudly, shot across the room and disappeared out the open door.

Caleb lay back on the floor and tried to calm himself. His heart was beating like a sledgehammer. He gritted his teeth and dug his fists into his face. He grunted, and cursed through his teeth. "A cat, a damn cat," he said. He collected himself and reached back down through the floorboard.

Long streaks of blood shown on his bare torso where the cat had clawed its way up his chest and over his shoulder. Finally he emerged with a burlap sack, sat it on the floor and went back out to the shed. He came back with a shovel and a pick. He leaned the tools against the wall and picked up the heavy burlap sack. He poured the contents out on the table and watched the gold glow in the light of his oil lamp.

He looked around the room searchingly, until finally his eyes came to rest on the cauldron hanging in the hearth. A moment later he was silhouetted in the open doorway of the shack with the pick and shovel resting on his right shoulder and the cauldron held by its wire handle in his left hand. The heavy iron pot rubbed his left calf softly as he stepped out into the moonlight.

* * *

Caleb was already busting up the brick around the bottom of the shack when his nephew Marshall came by to help the next day. Marshall was a young man of twenty-two now and stood tall, proud, and erect. His hair was light and wavy, a trait he must have acquired from his father. The way he carried himself, you could tell at a distance this was a well-contented man. "Howdy uncle, come out to give you a hand." He proceeded then, to give him his hand in friendship.

They exchanged some brief pleasantries and Marshall was saddened to smell hard liquor on Caleb's breath at such an early hour. Marshall was a fairly successful mason and had to reprove his uncle for busting out the bricks in such a destructive manner.He showed him how to take down the wall while leaving the individual bricks intact for second hand use.

They worked side by side all day and exchanged good news. Connie, a girl from town, had agreed to marry Caleb, and now Caleb found out that Sally was expecting. Marshall hoped that the whiskey Caleb was drinking was of a celebratory nature, but his uncle seemed as grim as ever. Caleb's hands were shaking and he was perspiring noticeably, though it couldn't have been more than forty-five degrees.

A couple of days later the house was sitting in its new position. Marshall had agreed to brick up the undercarriage of the shack, even though Caleb had curiously said it was no longer necessary. He finished tapping the final brick in place and cleaned off his trowel. Caleb was leaning against the oak tree in the lot beside the house.

Marshall walked over to wish his uncle well. The lot was directly across the street from where J.D.'s old cabin use to be. Now there was only an old stone chimney standing lone sentinel where J.D. had lived. When Marshall was within a few feet of his uncle, Caleb pointed across the street, "What are you going to do with J.D.'s old place?" It was about the most that Caleb had said to him the whole time they worked together. He figured he should give the matter a little thought before answering.

Finally he said, "I'm not sure what J.D. had in mind when he left it to me, I've already got the spread my Daddy left us." He paused, "I figure I'll let it set a while, I ain't got much need of it right now."

"Probably for the best," Caleb said.

Marshall felt at ease now, knowing he had answered in the way his uncle had hoped. He knew how dearly Caleb treasured his privacy and was happy to provide for it. Marshall took a cursory look around the meadow in which they stood. The huge oak tree would provide ample shade in the summer.

On one edge of the field Caleb's house now stood, bordering the other side was a small stream they simply called "the branch". The water flowed quietly next to the idyllic meadow. It would be a great setting for a Sunday school picnic. The past spring he had seen an ocean of daisies crowding the field. He couldn't imagine anything bad ever happening here.

1890

The intervening years passed for Caleb as though a watch in the night. He worked when his wits allowed him to pursue the labors available, but much of the time his mind was on other things. The field beside his house seemed to be a source of soothing pride and his rocking chair slowly wore the finish off the plank porch he built on the front of the old shack. The old hickory rocker eroded two rough lines on the porch, both of which pointed out into the meadow. He would sit there rocking, cradling a shotgun, watching the grass grow, counting the leaves on the old oak tree, as they changed a startling Autumn crimson and fell, one by one, as if the tree were hemorrhaging.

The old shack went through a few modifications to adjust to the birth of the twins. In addition to the new porch, two additional rooms were added on, one for Caleb and Sally, one for the boys. They were given the names of Dale and Graham and they were identical. Until they grew old enough to learn their names it was decided that one would have his hair cut short, while the other's hair would grow wild, in this way they could be told apart.

The boy with the long hair was Dale, his brother of the short hair, Graham. It was five years before Sally built up the nerve to cut Dale's beautiful hair, which by then, he had become quite use to. She was only too happy when he begged her not to cut it all off. It was decided from that time to keep his hair cut at the point of his shoulder blades, exactly where it remained until his fourteenth year.

He had been criticized heavily for having the hair of a girl in the local schoolhouse; it was something that always got his goat. He managed to hold his own when the other boys in his class ganged up on him with a pair of scissors, their intentions were obvious, but the split lip and black eye, Dale gave to the first two assailants, were even more obvious. There brewed around school many schemes and conspiracies to take the strength from this contemporary Samson. It seemed only a matter of time until the forces plotting against him were successful in their endeavors.

That all changed in a matter of a few weeks. Dale happened to get hold of a trashy western novel romanticizing the supposed exploits of "Wild" Bill Hickok. Dale read the outlandish propaganda printed therein, whereupon he circulated the small tome amongst his classmates. The book told of the gunman's run-ins with armed bandits whom he always dispatched with the help of his trusty Schofield model revolver, usually while protecting the honor of a beautiful flower of the west. It extolled the Lawman's bravery, integrity, skill, honor, and (above all else) his handsome good looks.

It was more than an antidote. Dale was the undisputable picture of a fourteen-year-old Hickok. Soon all of the girls at the school were swooning over him. It did not take long for some of the other boy's hair to grow noticeably longer. Their fathers stopped all of his competitor's cold in their tracks. No one else had a mother who worshipped her son's long hair, or a father who took so little notice of his children that, despite the hair, he still couldn't get their names right.

Dale was benevolent and kind, a boy scout before boy scouts. He excelled at school and, when he could fool himself into believing his family could afford it, looked forward to a higher education. Graham was a different matter. Graham quit school when he was twelve, which, of course, was not unusual at all. What were unusual were his motives.

Most children quit school as soon as they could read and handle basic mathematics, many even before. They would quit so they could join the rest of their family in the field. Sharecroppers and tenant farmers were the norm.

It was by manual labor, the sweat of the brow- that a boy became a man, and most boys became men very early. Once they became men in the fields, they would take a girl for their wife, and turn that girl into a woman, not in the fields, but in the matrimonial bed where girls had been transformed into women since time immemorial. Once the boy and girl became man and woman they wasted no time creating more boys and girls. Why? Because they needed help in the fields. It may not seem a philosophy of the highest order, but at least the fields were fields, and not the horrible, crushing, soul-flaying work of the sweatshops, no the sweatshops were for their urban counterparts.

Graham didn't leave school to help his parents out in the fields. Neither did he quit school to move west looking for opportunity, join the Army, or move to the city for a factory job. Graham left so he could cheat at cards, fight roosters, and stay drunk. He told his mother quite plainly that he "didn't give a damn" what she thought of him and it was obvious, as well, that Caleb didn't give a thought to what he damned.

Lest we make any mistake: they were born, they grew, they were loved, thrashed, ignored, sheltered, fed, churched, schooled, scolded, praised, and accepted to lesser and greater degrees, just as all children before had been, and as all future children shall be.

Most of their physical characteristics came from their mother or thin air. They neither had Caleb's dark, straight hair, nor his smooth complexion. The roman profile, the bold nose and high cheeks of Caleb Walker were absent. The twins had round faces with small pug noses, strawberry blonde hair, and ruddy faces. It was just as well that Caleb took little notice of them. It was questionable if he could have picked them out in a lineup.

The patriarch of the family had a way of looking at someone without ever seeing them. He was someone for whom the world held no immediate concern, and he, in turn, never concerned himself with the world. He had no friends and the only family that ever visited him was his nephew Marshall. His wife treated him respect-

66

fully, but not lovingly, almost as if he were an honored houseguest whom she knew only by reputation.

His employers praised his abilities in the fields, because he never worked as if it pained him to be out in the 110 degree weather bringing in someone else's crop, making a rich man richer while he received enough pay to keep him alive for tomorrow's work, but not enough money to make him anything but poor.

The other workers resented their employers. They never vocalized their contempt, but it was evident in their eyes. For every single worker, two evil eyes, and two hands guaranteed to go no faster than necessary to keep their job. It was thus with all the laborers, except Caleb.

He acted as if there was nothing backbreaking, or heartbreaking, going on. He behaved as if he were still at home relaxing in his Rocking chair, as if that magical meadow still floated before his eyes. Then there were other days, when he was terrified. Of what no one could say, but he feared something. People said it was his brother's ghost, his wife claimed it was the baby that screamed under their floor (and swore it still kept her up nights), while other folks said it was an enemy he made during the war.

Whatever it was, it kept him home, armed, and sweating bullets. On the day in question he was watching a couple of squirrels wrestle for acorns in the uppermost boughs of the old oak tree. It was early morning and he was trying to decide whether to have squirrel for breakfast.

Sally was inside putting on her fancy dress for the Sunday meeting and the two boys were in the branch looking for spring-lizards. Most of the spring-lizards were far down stream, as the twins long ago played out the muddy banks closest to home. With about half a dozen in a mason jar they could be seen walking back toward the house bare foot, with their Church-going pants rolled up above their knees.

Sally walked out on the porch and leaned out around the corner of the house to see the boys making their approach. "I want you to look... If those young-uns have messed up their pants I'm going to skin them alive." She walked back toward the front door and stopped when something crunched under her shoes. She looked down, "Hickory nut shells, I declare…" She reached inside and produced a broom. She began to sweep the hulls off the front porch with noticeable irritation.

"I'm thinking of inviting the pastor for dinner tonight," she told her husband. "The boys are planning on going fishing, so it would just be the three of us." Their backs were to each other as she swept and talked. "I know you've been feeling peculiar of late, maybe it would help if you talked about it." He did not respond. "I swear them boys better hurry up or I'm going to skin'em." She paused for a moment, then the movements of the broom reasserted itself, this time with a slow deliberate cadence. "Last chance to go with us," she said in her most soothing affectation.

A shotgun blast answered her. She spun around with her hands on her chest just in time to see the limp body of a squirrel hit the ground below the oak. Before the broomstick tapped the porch floor the other barrel of the shotgun was emptied. First came the thunderous report, then the light tap of the broom falling to the floor, then the other squirrel wobbled around on its bough, tried to crawl along a limb, fell off clumsily, grabbed at twigs as it fell through the tree, and hit the ground. The two boys ran to the foot of the oak. The shorthaired boy picked up the wounded squirrel by the tail. It twitched, sneezed, and barked. He swung the animal over his head by the tail, then swung it into the tree trunk. It resounded with a dull thump, and then each boy carried a squirrel up to the porch.

A bit of the color had come back to Sally's cheeks. It took quite an effort for her to behave as though she weren't shaken. "Graham can you, skin and gut them critters? I'll put them on a skillet for you Caleb, but you'll have to take them off when they're done frying. Gene, get me a fire going in the woodstove, honey."

"But ma, ain't it about to hot to cook inside?"

"Nonsense. Your pa's going to be out on the porch all morning and we've got Sunday school now don't we?"

"Yes'm," he said without enthusiasm.

With the squirrel-meat in quarters and sizzling in a pan of fatback, the three of them left the house to Caleb that morning and walked the mile and half to the Church building. The only thing Caleb said all morning was, "Ain't talking 'no preacher." Now he took the empties out of his sixteen gauge and loaded it with two fresh, paper, shotgun shells. He leaned the firearm up against the house and went inside.

A soft breeze was passing through the open windows of the kitchen as he stepped up to the wood-burning stove. The squirrel was about finished frying, the flesh had taken on the gray-blue pallor associated with cooked small game. He set the skillet off the burner and collected the meat on a plate. Carefully, he poured the hot sputtering grease into a coffee can. Despite his best efforts a little grease spit up and burned his knuckles.

He sat the plate on his rocking chair with a handkerchief over it to keep the flies off. Then he went round to the back of the house where the pump was. A quart size bell jar hung from the pump by a piece of wire. The pump had been a gift from his nephew Marshall. Caleb had developed an irrational fear of open wells and Sally grew exasperated with the limitations this posed.

When she had asked Marshall's advise he proposed a pump and proceeded to pay for it and install it himself. Marshall was quite generous and equally, quite unpopular. Since he became one of the most trusted masons in the region and his bank account began to reflect the fact, it had been tough to stay on good relations with his kin. As far as he knew, every relation of Marshall was dirt poor, and they all begrudged him his success. They acted as if there was something unseemly about a Walker or a Lackey having any money. They resented his success, and though they never told him in so many words, they made it clear by their treatment of him.

Back on the porch, the man, old beyond his years, tore bits of flesh off the bone and washed the greasy meat down with cool clear water out of the quart jar. He took a bite off a hind leg then stiffened; he heard something on the other side of the house. He sat the plate down at his feet silently and took up the shotgun.

Marshall loped around the corner of the building to find the barrels of the sixteen gauge a few inches from his chest. He didn't seem surprised at all. He simply pushed the tip of the barrel away from his body calmly, and slowly. He was wearing a nice suit. His jacket was hanging over one arm, exposing his pen-striped vest and gold fob. In his left hand he held a pie of some sort with a white cloth over the top and in his right hand he held a white sphere, somewhere between the size of a baseball and softball.

"Howdy uncle." He sized Caleb up as the older man put the dish back in his lap.

"Squirrel makes a good breakfast." He paused again uncertainly, "Missus baked yuns a pie, apple cobbler matter of fact. You wouldn't believe it but our trees come in pretty good this year." Caleb was eating his breakfast spitting an occasional peace of shot onto the plate, with a pert "tink".

Marshall noticed that the head had been fried up as well. It sat there on the plate with its acorn sharpened incisors and its dull blue eyes staring out at them. "I bet this here pie would compliment that varmint quite nicely. Why don't I just take it in the kitchen and cut you a slab?" He knew better than to wait for a reply that wouldn't come, so he went to it.

A moment later he came back out the door with a wedge of apple cobbler. He sat the small dish at Caleb's right foot, and then took a bite out of the white ball in his hand as if it were an apple. "Hope you don't mind; I helped myself to your garden." Caleb could smell the turnip in the air.

Marshall watched his uncle's nostrils examining the smell of the vegetable. "Couldn't help myself, I can't stand the greens but I'm quite fond of one right up out of the ground." Caleb stopped eating and looked out toward the oak tree.

"That woman wants me to talk to doctors, wants me to talk to preachers."

It was the first time Caleb had said anything to him in months. Even though his uncle kept staring out at the meadow, almost as if he were talking to himself, Marshall still felt as though he had been singled out for some great platitude. "Well, I mean, maybe you should. I don't see what harm it could do: you talking to a feller that might be able to... You know, maybe a little advice is all you need to help you relax and get more work done."

He felt like he had hit on the right path in his monologue, "We all know you're never happier than when you're working. I know how it is; I'm the same way. I never feel more satisfied than after a hard days labor. It gives a man a since of pride to live by the industry of his own two hands. No sir, a man that makes an honest living by the sweat of his brow need not be ashamed before God nor man."

Marshall felt quite satisfied with his sermon, until he noticed a foreboding scowl on Caleb's face. "What's the matter uncle? You think they got something else in mind?" Marshall asked in a worried voice, "Just what do you think their intentions are?" His uncle didn't say anything, he just picked up the squirrel's head and cracked open the cranium like a walnut. He took out the small tan brain and popped it in his mouth. He ground the pasty tissue between his molars then washed it down with the crisp, quick water.

* * *

When he and his wife sat down to eat the last meal of the day, it was not with the preacher, but with Doctor Eden. The physician was in his usual high-spirits, discussing the ins and outs of his office back in town. Sally listened attentively, smiling rapturously, and giggling like a precocious little girl whenever an anecdote took an amusing turn. Caleb was his morose, silent self. He rarely looked up from his plate, simply sitting stooped over his food, grinding a mouthful between his molars with a strange, subtle movement of his jaw.

Finally the good doctor leaned back and pulled the cloth handkerchief from his collar. "Mighty fine cooking, ma'am. The best, I swear I've ever had." Sally got up out of her chair and began clearing his place while she spoke. "Now you go right on with that. I swear if you ain't the snake-oil salesman." She walked over to the stove. "Would you like some coffee doctor?"

Doctor Eden blew the steam off the top of his cup and stared at Caleb over the dark pool of Java. "Missus Walker, did you hear about Darin Mobley?" She stopped clearing the table long enough to commiserate, "Oh yes, that poor unfortunate man. Has his family been able to take care of him?"

"The actual truth of it is this: it's Darin that's providing for his family." Sally tried in her clumsy way to seem shocked, "Why! How on earth could he provide for them? Since the war he hasn't been able to tie his own shoe."

"Well ma'am it's this new hospital…"

"Broughten?" Though they conversed facing each other, they both stared out the corner of their eyes at Caleb.

"That's right. They have doctors over there who understand the trauma of war better than any others in the country."

"You don't say." Caleb dragged a biscuit through some gravy on his plate.

"I most certainly do. These are not the dark ages my dear lady. Medical science is slowly eradicating all pestilence and contagion, whether it be of mind or limb. It's a great time to be alive. In this day and age there is no set back that could be called permanent. We can't cure every ailment, but sickness that resists our efforts today, fall tomorrow."

"Well I am most impressed. I would have thought Mr. Mobley's case too far gone for relief."

"The medical field is rapidly approaching the day when we can retire that antiquated adage, 'too far gone'."

"Why, if it brought an invalid back to his prime imagine what it could do for Caleb!" The doctor's face now turned to point in the same direction his eyes had been pointing all along. "Why that's true."

He continued in a rehearsed tone, "I would hardly even call your husband's difficulties debilitating. His condition is simply an unfortunate inconvenience. What is needed, and this is simply my opinion Mr. Walker, is something to grease the wheels of communication. A new outlook, that's what these associates of mine can give you. Perhaps you may yet again greet the dawn with a smile, converse with your beloved wife at length, take your children fishing... live the good life in a sense. I would hate to think of you robbed of the bosom of your family, existing like a hermit in a multitude."

Sally walked across the room and placed her hands on Caleb's shoulders, "Think of it, you could be well again. Let's do it. We can go to the hospital first thing in the morning."

"Why certainly Ma'am. I can make all the necessary arrangements and by this time next week your husband will be talking so much we won't be able to get a word in edge-ways. What do you say Mr. Walker? Of course we'll need your complete cooperation, but going in for treatment is a big decision and I'm sure your wife and I would both like you to do right by yourself as opposed to others making the tough decisions. So I leave it up to you. Tell me exactly how you would wish to proceed."

There was a long pause while Caleb stared blankly down at the half-cleared table. Doctor Eden cleared his throat and said, "Well, let's have it." There was another minute of silence in which the doctor and wife grew visibly impatient, "For God's sake man, say something."

Caleb leaned back in the chair, gazed at the ceiling, and then looked back down at his plate. The veteran licked his lips and said, "Pass the potatoes."

1920

Thirty years of staring at a wall. Thirty years of listening to the shrieks, wails, screams, and laughter of the madhouse. Thirty years smelling the urine and feces. Three decades worth of lunatics babbling obscenities in your ear. Thirty years of men in white suits and the husks of men in green pajamas. Walls made out of mattresses. Blood stains on the mattresses. Endless, sleepless nights strapped down in a bed. Thirty years for eyes to grow dim. Thirty years for ears to grow dull. Thirty years for memory to erode. Thirty years for rust and cobwebs. Three decades for spines to curl. Thirty calendars in the trash. Limitless time to wonder if a world still exists beyond the walls.

A lot can happen.

In thirty years.

* * *

Softly, slowly, a form takes focus. A nurse, waving her hand in front of his face. A voice, speaks from a thousand miles away. It's an endless refrain, with each stanza that much closer to audibility.

"Mr. Walker? I said, 'Do you want to see your visitor?'"

The old man's head rises and falls in an almost imperceptible nod.

The woman disappears and the wheelchair begins to roll. The chair gobbles up the clean white tiles of the hallway. A black man in a white suit marches in front staying a few feet ahead of the wheelchair as it chases him through doorways. Some how the black man always unlocks and opens the door just before the chair catches him. The old man has witnessed the pursuit many times, but has never seen the chair eat him. Finally he's pushed into a room with two large windows full of sunlight. The windows are sandblasted so the light can't pass through. The sunlight can only pool up against the glass like water against a ship's porthole.

"Here he is Mr. Lackey. He just got up from his nap, so he might be a little groggy."

The nurse, somehow as starched as her own uniform, sat down in a corner to read a copy of "Life". Marshall had been visiting his uncle every other week since he was committed. The change had been gradual and was easy to accept. The strong young soldier of the Civil War had become a bent, feeble, toothless, and senile old man. Caleb was seventy-seven, but he hardly looked a day under one hundred and seven. No one would have guessed the old man was only ten years Marshall's senior. Marshall still had all of his hair and even at this late date it was salt and pepper, not gray.

The nephew stood tall and erect, his strength and bearing seemed to be all it once was. He didn't wear glasses, walk with a cane, or have dentures. He wore a stately suit, and told time with a gold watch. Somehow, he confronted the looming specter of infirmity twice a month. Twenty-four times a year he came and made idle, one sided conversation with fate: exemplified in the person of his uncle. This would be the last time he came to the hospital however. He found himself the bearer of significant tidings.

Marshall tried to explain things as simply as he knew how. He wasn't even sure how much Caleb remembered concerning his current circumstances. "Do you understand?" The old man nodded. "She's dead. You do understand that?" Once again Caleb nodded.

"Sally put you in here thirty years ago. She's dead now. Dale is coming next week to get you and take you home."

Between each sentence Marshall paused for a few moments, hoping the extra processing time would do Caleb some good. "Sally sold all of your clothes a long time ago. I'm going to go buy you some clothes. What kind would you like?" The old man nodded. "How about a nice suit like the one I've got on? A few pairs of dungarees and some shirts would probably be good for around the house." He continued on, talking about trivial matters in a happy manner while his thoughts drifted to darker realities.

After Caleb had been committed Sally moved in with Doctor Eden, leaving the children to scratch for themselves at the old house. The new couple told everyone that it had been necessary for her to divorce her husband because of his hopeless, chronic ailment. The truth of the matter was, she had never divorced him. If their marriage dissolved it would become impossible for her to exercise control over Caleb's continued residence at the mental hospital.

According to the good doctor he had wed his bride in Raleigh and honeymooned there a week. The fact of the matter was that they honeymooned without the usual formality of getting married. For thirty years the doctor's wife had been the envy of privileged society in and around the township. The cultured upper crust accepted her despite, or perhaps because of her poor relations and the scandalous background from which she emerged.

It must have given her new peers a since of melodrama and intrigue. In the thirty years that she reigned as hostess and lady of the most unquestionable character, she never visited Caleb. Marshall and Dale begged her just to look in on him. They felt if she saw the state he had been reduced to, she would feel remorse and sign the papers for his release, but it was not to be. Dale took up work at the post office and married one of the many girls that chased after his good looks in school. Unfortunately she died during a vain attempt to bring his firstborn into the world, and Dale had been too heartbroken to remarry. He still lived in the same old house beside the meadow.

Graham was quite a different matter. His demeanor soon put locals on the watch for him. At his convenience, the town's Sheriff kept tabs on him and soon no one would gamble with him because his reputation as a cheater spread quickly. It wasn't long before Graham decided his luck had run out in the one horse town. He hopped in a boxcar and disappeared down the rails one day, even he couldn't have told you where to. Most people said "Good riddance," and washed their hands of him. He would breeze back into town once or twice a year and hit his family up for money. With a fist full of bills to buy beans and some new patches on his old clothes he'd vamoose, much to the relief of some people.

Doctor Eden made countless attempts to befriend the two boys, and it didn't seem to matter to him that their mother's attachment had cooled. He begged Dale to come live in their home (a mansion compared to the old converted shack), but he refused. It was an easy matter to detect Dr. Eden's sincerity in the invitation. It was equally simple to pick up on Sally's lack of sincerity when rendering the same offer.

Every time Graham came into town Sally avoided him like the plague, but Dr. Eden slipped him twenty dollars. Graham had shown Marshall the bill. For some reason the doctor sincerely liked the boys, never considering them the embarrassment Sally held them for. This visit, like every other visit was spent trying to impress these facts on the old man, and just the same as always Caleb nodded politely without understanding a word.

Since he was committed, Caleb had met with only two visitors. One week Dale would bring him a sarsaparilla and sit to talk with him and the next week he would receive a visit from Marshall. This had been going on for thirty years. The visits had become ritualistic and Marshall was just finishing the litany. Instead of crossing himself he kissed his uncle's forehead and stepped out into the July heat.

Caleb missed the Independence Day celebrations, the festivities that toasted the futility of Caleb's most patriotic and life shattering youthful crusades. As the Post Office's Model-T curved along the dusty red roads Dale told him all about the fireworks display, the lemonade, and the straw hats with red white and blue bands on them.

Even now some of the homes flew the stars and stripes off their porches with the flagpole at a cant. An image broke in Caleb's mind of a large field, smelly with gunsmoke and littered with dead bodies. A line of blue men stood a hundred yards away and he was running toward it with the heavy feel of wood and iron in his hands, all around him a chorus like the whaling of a thousand Indian braves assaulted his ears. Suddenly he felt a jolt and flew up in the air. His behind slammed back down in the seat of the ford.

"Sorry paw. You all right?" The old man looked around at his surroundings as if for the first time. "I keep forgettin' to dodge that there hole in the road."

"I saved somethin' for ya'." Dale pulled a straw hat from behind his seat and threw it on his father's head. "How do you like that paw?" He rubbed his nose and continued, "I had me a slew of 'em left over from Teddy's Bull Moose campaign. I told everbody, 'cayn't go wrong with Roosevelt,' but it was like talkin' to a post. I'm still a Bull Moose Republican from way back. Hell farr, the man got shot ah campaignin'. Think that stopped old Teddy?" The old man nodded. "Well then you don't know Roosevelt. He just left the bullet in him and went ahead and delivered his campaign speech. It was the speech what slowed up the slug. If the damn fool weren't so long winded… not that I care, mind ya'. Why, I could listen to the feller talk all day. 'I talk softly, but I carry a big stick!'" Dale shook his fist as if it were the stick.

An awkward silence fell upon the father and son, punctuated only by backfires from the smelly engine of the automobile. The Bull Moose Republican finally spoke in an apologetic tone, "Sorry paw, I guess I got carried away and went to runnin' off at the mouth. I get caught up sometimes and…" His mind fumbled around for a fresh topic and finally caught hold. Excitedly once again, he said, "Hot damn, wait till Graham gets word you're out. Boy now, you'll be excited to see him after so many years, and lest you're fooled don't go to thankin' just cause he ain't seed ya at the Looney Bi… Hospital these payst years that he ain't missed ya. Truth is- he

78

don't come to town much and when he does- he's here one minute, gone the next. If it don't happen to be visitin' day... I'll tell you what- I bet he's about due to breeze back into town. If'n the soles of his feet ain't ah itchin' too bad we might talk him into stayin' ah spell this time. What do yah say?" The old man nodded. "Hell yes! I thought you'd like that. We'll be home soon and I'll bet burlap to silk it's just the same as you recollect. Course maw, God rest her soul, she's in her grave; but I got this here colored lady to come in and cook and I cayn't say as you'll have any complaints."

They pulled up beside the old house and Caleb stumbled out of the Ford. His limp was quite pronounced now, but he could still walk. The rocking chair sat in the same place it had occupied thirty years before. Dale helped him into the seat and the old man's eyes gazed again at the lovely field.

There was something quite profound in that meadow, the way the tall grass changed it's bearing with the wind, the way a cicada called loudly from the top of the old oak, the shadows of passing clouds dimming and brightening the scene, it was all very poignant, but it signified something. "See paw, it's just like you remembered it," Dale sat down on a new porch railing, "except for the Poison Ivy." The tree trunk was now engulfed by green, oily foliage; no bark could be seen.

"If you can just wait right here, I've got to get the Ford back to the Post Office. I'll be back on my horse in a few minutes." He returned to the idling vehicle and left, dragging a cloud of dust behind him. Caleb was left alone, feeling much like a ghost in a graveyard. He looked around and, though everything seemed familiar, nothing specific could be remembered.

The south was reconstructed, for that was the purpose of the reconstruction. It had been woven out of the broken refuse of misdirected patriotism. Caleb took the straw hat off his head and stared at the red, white, and blue hatband. He felt as if he had stepped through the looking glass. Not walls, but only forests and fields surrounded him. There were no screams or cackles, only the chirping of birds and the humming of insects. It was the first time he had been alone in ages. He cried a little bit behind the shield of his privacy, he couldn't have said why.

He dried his eyes and looked across the country lane. There was a cleared area where a house once stood. Polk-salad and honeysuckle were reclaiming the area for an encroaching forest. Only the stone chimney stood sentry over the long gone threshold. The old Veteran stared at the chimney, so much like a tombstone, and wondered who use to live there.

A form came over the hill. It was a black woman carrying a large basket. She walked along the ditch line of the road, and soon crossed the edge of the meadow as she marched up to the old man. "How do, Mistah Walkah?" She smiled brightly at Caleb. "I'ze come for the cookin', and I'd juss like to say how happy I am that tu goot lode seen fit to bestow you to ya family." The old man nodded. "Well… ah 'spect ah bes' git to ut!" She carried the basket into the house and reappeared a few minutes later. "Here's you some iced lemonade.

"Mahshall brought a block of ice in from town dis mounin'. He's a good man dattin'. You muss be awful proud. With the ice and all, he's pullin' out all de stops."

She disappeared back inside and Caleb drank some of the iced lemonade. He'd never had ice. He'd never seen a lemon. It was heavenly, even better than the sarsaparilla, and he smiled for the first time in thirty years.

Twenty minutes past, and Caleb drank the lemonade, but never quicker than the cook could fill it back up. Then he heard hoof beats in the distance, coming from the same direction where the cook had originated. Over the hill a dapple-gray mare trotted.

Marshall sat on the saddle with a small boy sitting right in front of him. He let the boy down off the horse, then got off and tied a lead to the porch railing. "Uncle Caleb!" He took the old man's hand in his and clamped his other hand around it as well.

His eyes looked moist. "I wanted you to meet my grandson." He put a hand

on the child's shoulder. "Gene, this is my uncle Caleb. He fought in the Confederate Army and he's been away for a long time… Strictly on account of a misunder-
standing, you see… And, well, now he's back with his family where he belongs." He
turned the lad around and kneeled down to look him eye to eye. "Now Uncle Caleb
here has been feeling awful poorly so I don't want you to grieve him none. Just show
him your respect and love."

"Yes sir," the boy Gene answered back.

"Alright skeedaddle, you can go play in the branch till supper time, just don't get
out of hearing." Marshall watched after his grandson as he ran across the meadow.
"Things sure were different when I was his age…" He turned around and slid back
out of his nostalgia, "or were they?" He chuckled softly. "I guess that's what we say
when we get old, huh uncle?" The old man nodded.

The dinner was huge, much like thanksgiving, with the notable exception of the
turkey. There was fried chicken livers, catfish, hominy, fried okra, cornbread, black-
eyed peas, and for desert canned peaches and sweet-potato pie. It was like a real
homecoming. The cook couldn't serve the food fast enough.

Marshall had borrowed a pair of dentures from a dentist in town. They were
only a display model and not fitted to Caleb's mouth, so from time to time they would
come out with his fork or fall to his plate with a loud "chink" if he chewed with his
mouth open. Despite living on borrowed teeth, he ate voraciously. "Why Mistah
Walkah, ah believe you could eat a whole row of okrey straight out the garden." She
heaped another big helping on his plate. "Yah'ont some mo' ah dat lemonade?" The
old man nodded.

Dale cleared his throat and all eyes fell upon him, except the eyes of his father,
still intent as they were upon the feast. "I'd just like to say how happy I am… well, we
all are, to have paw back with us." Everyone nodded and mumbled their agreement.

"Furthermore," he said, "when I was down at the post office, I friend of mine
brought in a load of mail from the three-eighteen out of Raleigh, told me Graham

has been in Statesville living out of the hobo jungle for a few days now, and when this friend of mine goes back to Statesville in the morning, he's going to present Graham with a train ticket I bought for him.

"So I beg all of you, and ask Miss Dempsey," he looked over at the black girl, "if you all might be right here again tomorrow for a repeat performance of tonight's entertainment… this time with an expanded cast!" The dinner party received the news with much fanfare. Caleb wondered who this "Graham" person might be, hopefully not a doctor.

The next day Caleb was once again in his rocking chair when an approaching cloud of dust announced the arrival of the Model-T Ford. Dale got out, still looking like the dashing western gunfighter after all these years, his hair was anointed with scented oils and he used only the finest mustache wax.

He stood tall and erect in the bold sunlight. He looked as if he could tame an earthquake. Then from around the automobile and out of the cloud of dust that had piled up on the Ford when it stopped, walked the dried out hulk of one who was once Dale's twin. It was like comparing a mighty redwood to its rotting stump.

Graham's back was hunched over and he had yellow skin. His hair was cut in a flattop style and he wore a four-day, unkempt, growth of hair on his face. Caleb could see his toes through one of his shoes and noticed that there were bloodstains on his old worn out overalls. As the prodigal son came closer Caleb noticed a distinct odor, as if his son had been sleeping in a can of sardines. The shabby apparition walked up to the porch, crossed his hands on the railing and smiled a great, fool-hearty smile. Sun reflected off a gold tooth and dazzled the patriarch.

"He still knows the look of gold," the hobo said, "look at him." Graham kept grinning and maneuvered his head from side to side. Caleb followed with his head and eyes, like some cobra entranced by the bulbous tip of the snake-charmers flute. "So, he cayn't understand anything I say?"

"Shut the hell up Graham!" Dale's anger was rising.

"Settle down, Wild Bill."

"And don't call me that. My name's Dale."

"Is that so?" Graham looked at him mockingly, "You look a lot like a feller got shot in the back, died with aces and eights in his hand, under other circumstances a winning hand."

"And you look a lot like something the cat dragged in… or coughed up."

Graham laughed loudly, which only increased Dale's tension, then he tried to look his father in the eyes. It was impossible. The old man was looking his gift son in the mouth and wouldn't take his eyes off the tooth. "Old man… they tell me all you can do is nod your head up and down. Is that true? Have you forgotten everything?"

The aged veteran stared intently at the gold, pursed his lips, and shook his head back and forth.

* * *

That night they sat around the table once again. A gloom had settled over the dinner. From time to time the borrowed dentures would fall out of Caleb's head and Graham would laugh hysterically until the heel of Marshall's boot came down on Graham's toes.

Finally Graham spoke, "Much obliged for the tooth, cousin. Maybe your friend could set paw up with somethin'."

Marshall smiled graciously, "Sure Graham, I've been thinking the same thing myself. In fact, we might get your Daddy an appointment for next week if that suits everbody." They all nodded and mumbled in agreement. "What do you think about that uncle? Maybe get you some new grinders?"

Everyone seemed pleased with the prospect and Graham laughed at the idea. He had went to bathe in the branch where some stones had been used to damn it up for a crawdad hole. Afterwards Marshall took him into Morganton and bought him a pinstriped suit, a bowler hat, and new shoes. After supper he excused himself and borrowed ten dollars from Marshall. As he went out the front door he met Dale leaning against a post on the porch.

"Where do you think you're going?"

"I'm taking the car into town. I want to shoot some billiards, show my ass to some floozy's… with any luck maybe they'll show me theirs!"

"That vehicle belongs to the post office, I cayn't let you take it to go rabblerousing."

"Stop teaching Sunday school and stand aside, I'm a man on a mission."

"You can take a horse!"

"In my new suit, I think not."

"Listen here Mister Vanderbuilt, put a monkey in a suit and it's still a monkey, you ain't fooling nobody."

"Dale, you ain't my Lord and master, you won't be my brother, the least you can be is a gracious host."

"Listen Graham, you ain't gonna' walk all over me. That Ford is my responsibility, if you get drunk and wreck it or…"

Marshall stepped out onto the porch, "Keep it down for God's sake, your paw is trying to get to sleep. Let him take the Ford, I'll take complete responsibility." With that, Graham jumped over the porch rail and ran out to the automobile while Dale threw up his hands in a show of futility and retreated back into the house.

Caleb was lying in his bed staring up past the ceiling connecting the dots of his mind. The gold of the tooth melted into a cauldron, the face of the Bull-moose Republican devolved into the face of a newborn child, Marshall shrank into an out of breath, frightened, ten-year-old child. The years in the hospital melted away and the events beforehand began to materialize in his brain.

He could remember now, the Cavalry Officer who had tormented him. He had been a major player in some rather intense dreams. In those nightmares the Officer had horns, hoofs, and a pointy tale. Finally he knew the devil to have a human counterpart, a man of flesh and blood who had bedeviled him in his waking hours. He thought of his wife for the first time in decades, he remembered her tender kisses, how she had cared for him when he was ill, how she had nurtured their children, and that she was now dead.

Dead. How could she be dead? Where was she buried? What had she died of? His brother too… dead! Yet he remembered the details of his brother's death, and as he did, he cried. He cried bitterly, his face grew hot and he imagined the tears that ran out the corners of his eyes and wetted his earlobes as sliding across a griddle, sizzling and evaporating. They were tears of anger. He felt cheated, as if the deck had been stacked against him. He cursed and gritted his teeth.

He tried to run through everything in his mind, fishing trips with his father, barn dances, and Sunday school picnics… working with the meager crops his family raised. They were nostalgic, if not epic memories. Then came his enlistment in the Confederate Army, from that point his mind proceeded from degradation to degradation. The battles, murderous nauseating victories, worse defeats, eventual capture, hellish prison, immoral escape, brotherly betrayal… At the thought of his brother's body, rotted away under the courthouse lawn, while he lay in a comfortable bed with a stomach full of tater-cakes, it became too much to bear and he began sobbing feverish tears yet again.

After his brother's demise things grew very foggy, there was his escape from the two Yankees… and the gold, yes he remembered the gold, so rich his entire life, yet living the life of a destitute, slovenly hillbilly. After the gold, time was lost, literally lost.

What had happened to the last thirty years, where had it gone? What had become of the world, at dinner his family had talked of "the war to end all wars" and "aeroplanes"; they had tried to give him some idea of what had happened in the world over the past three decades, but he could make neither heads nor tails out of it. They had tried to update him during their visits, but they had been talking to an empty husk.

Now he felt his spirit re-entering his body. His body? What had happened to it in the last thirty years? He rose out of bed and lit a kerosene lamp. He adjusted the wick and in the soft light of the flame he examined himself in the mirror of his bureau. An old, stooped, wrinkled, bald, toothless, liver spotted geezer stared back out of the glass. It seemed too sudden. The spirit that filled the decaying body was not an old decrepit soul; it was vital and filled with resolve. It was a young soul, a soul evicted some fifty years before. It had returned to it's former home to find it condemned and on the verge of collapse.

* * *

Dale was sitting on the front steps when he saw a trail of dust rising some distance away. It was past 2PM and he had been sitting there waiting since dawn. Caleb sat in his chair slowly rocking. His eyes traced the movements of an extremely large and brilliantly hued dragonfly. The Model-T came to a skidding stop in front of the house. Graham's upper lip had been split in two, but it had been made one again with a few stitches. His jacket had been cut clean through in an eight-inch slash below the left shoulder. Dale walked right past his brother and examined the automobile. There was dried blood to be found throughout much of the interior.

In anger he questioned Graham, "What did you hit?"

Graham placed his hand on his brother's shoulder, "Nothing, something hit me." He grinned widely and there was an empty space where the gold tooth had been.

"Oh! So you got into a fight. Where's your tooth?"

"I'll be digging it out of the outhouse soon enough." Graham started walking toward the front door.

Dale talked as he walked after him, "Not here you won't, I've been putting away

86

some money and I think I can cover another train ticket; how's Oregon sound?" Graham turned back at the doorway, "I'll damn well stay here as long as I want. It's just as much my home as it is yourn."

Dale straightened up and stretched his shoulders forward and back. "It's time for me to finish what somebody else started." He cracked his knuckles and closed in on Graham.

"You don't need to go digging in shit to find gold."

The would-be pugilists lowered their fists and looked at the back of the old man's head. Something changed in their faces, years drained out of their countenances and their faces took on the wondrous expression of curious children. They both walked down the steps and around the porch to face their father. They each put a hand on the railing and looked into the weathered eyes, clear, cold, and blue, as the two orbs focused on a point somewhere beyond the twins.

"Ages ago I was fool enough to try and get myself killed over a rich man's slave. I went through trials no man should ever have to face. I thought I was doing it so I could help protect our kin and our acreage. I was wrong.

"I remember one time I got caught out in a snowstorm. I tried to walk home but my feet was gettin' awful cold and I was startin' to worry. I come up to this plantation house and asked the feller lived there if I could hold up in his barn till the weather broke and my shoes dried out. He said, 'Son, I'd be happy to oblige, but I worry that you might give my horse fleas.' I walked the rest of the way home and bit a leather strap while my father took off a couple of my toes.

"You see boys, I fought a war on eight toes to make sure that plantation owner would never have to do a lick of work in his life. I've been beat, froze, starved, and betrayed as fare back as I can remember. I suffered everything without complaint because during the rich man's war, I became a rich man."

Graham arched his eyebrows, "But Paw, we ain't rich."

"Yes we are son. We're the wealthiest family for a hundred miles. You see, one fateful day, me and your uncle, God rest his soul, we bushwhacked a couple of Yankees and what do you think they were carrying but enough gold to damn a river. Neither of us knew why they had so much gold, but we did know that they was likely to be bluecoats a comin' to find out what happened to it… and come they did. They killed your uncle and damn near killed me trying to get the gold back from us.

"When they left they were convinced that the both of us were dead. I couldn't spend the gold cause that would bring them right back down on my head. So I decided to hide it and guard that hiding place until I was fifty, then I'd retrieve it and retire in wealth and luxury with my family. I was three years shy of that retirement when I became the victim of treachery.

"I lost thirty years of my retirement, every bit of it locked away in the loony bin while we all could have been livin' high on the hog. Now that I'm free and I've got my wits about me: I don't plan to loose any more time. I may not live long enough to reap the full fruits of my vigilance, but at least I can die knowing that the two of you will live in the lap of luxury for the rest of your days."

The twins just stared at the old veteran in disbelief. "Well stop your lollygaggin' go down to the bank and rent out a half-dozen or so of them safe deposit boxes and get back up here so's we can bring in the harvest. I'll be waiting right here."

Without a word they went to the Model-T and drove it slowly out of sight. The old man rocked back and forth slowly while he watched the ruby colored dragonfly buzz along in a rough figure-eight above the meadow. He felt a strong tingling numbness in his left hand but couldn't remember hitting his funny bone.

He held the hand in front of his face and flexed his fingers slowly. He laughed resignedly and felt the tingle rise up his left arm and into his shoulder. He sat back and gazed on the beautiful green meadow as it grew paler and paler, slowly washing out into the whiteness of an overexposed photograph. At last the world was colorless, dimensionless, and evacuated.

1st Marshall

Ghosts of the Soon Departed

1864

Spanish time-keeping figured the year at 1540 Anno Domini. Hernando de Soto led his horse along the banks of the Catawba River, and the local tribesmen felt ill at ease. Another twenty-seven years passed, before the Spanish built Fort San Juan on the outskirts of their village. The following year, the villagers in the settlement of Joara burned the fort to the ground, and killed the soldiers who dwelled within. They had endured all of the outrages they could stomach. European settlement had begun.

It was more than thirty years since the Trail of Tears had put an end to this first chapter in the persecution of the natives. One of perhaps a hundred Cherokee to evade the U.S. Army, and the effects of the Indian Removal Act, now lived in a small hut, where, so long before, a Conquistador had trod.

He was a squatter, and was driven off whenever he made camp. As he awaited his latest exile, a child befriended him. The small boy would never forget the redskin he had "tamed", and would always treasure a longbow the gentle savage had crafted for him. Often, in the coming years, he would fabricate an arrow, in the way he had been taught, and stalk the forests for unwary game. The young boy notched his arrow and made his way out to the road. It was a loamy, bracken highway creeping and winding through an uninhabited side of the nearby ridgeline. Marshall, as the child was named, had ranged quite far a field. He heard a creek murmuring beyond the next gentle rise of the road and followed the sound. There was tall grass growing in the middle of the lane, between worn areas where wagon wheels scarred the earth. He reached the river and walked out into the shallow ford. The cold water felt good on his bare feet.

A bird, about the size of a crow, swooped along at treetop level and landed on the side of a large hardwood. The tree was on the opposite bank of the stream. The bird was an enormous and reclusive woodpecker known locally as a wood-hen. The archer drew back his bow and sighted along the feathers. The bowstring snapped and the missile bit into the bark of the tree with a satisfying vibrato. It missed the bird by less than a foot and the startled creature beat an alarmed retreat. As his prey disappeared out of sight, Marshall turned his attention back to the arrow. It was now driven into the bark of an Elm, and at an extremely inconvenient altitude.

The lad placed his bow over his sun burnt shoulder and climbed the tree with greater ease than most people climb stairs. Reaching an area some thirty feet into the upper reaches of the elm, he plucked the arrow out and sat a moment, perched on a stout bough. He heard faint hoof beats and the unmistakable clatter of a wagon approaching the ford.

"They must be on their way to Morganton," he thought to himself. The tangle of leaf and limb left the approaching pilgrims mysteriously cloaked. He could catch only glimpses as they momentarily appeared in the tiny windows of his field of view.

As best he could tell, two figures, both on the driving bench, were approaching on a mule drawn, buckboard wagon. It was only when the two mules splashed out into the ford that Marshall was taken aback. The two young men, one holding the reigns and the other riding shotgun, were both dressed in the deep blue of Yankee troops.

The wagon halted in the middle of the stream and the two mules drank from the rippling stream. The man on the shotgun side took off his boots and rolled his pants up above the knees. He waded upstream and filled a few canteens while his partner tied off the reins and fanned his face with his hat, exposing short blond curls.

"Look at this," the man in the water said. He splashed happily up to the water's edge where plump blackberries bowed the stems of a briar. In one or two places the fruit of the plant actually touched the waters surface, carving a faint "V" in the slow current. He took his hat off and started filling it with berries. The soldier on the wagon placed his hat on the seat next to him, dipped a coffee cup in the current, and poured the contents over his head.

"Hurry up with those berries, we ain't got all day."

"Hold up, we got plenty of time."

The one on the wagon groaned, "Listen, I want to sleep in a bed tonight, that ain't going to happen if we're still here picking blackberries. By God, I'll buy you a blackberry pie when we get to Morganton, let's go!"

His partner made no motion that he was ready to leave, although he began picking a little faster and cursing a little louder with every thorn. Marshall couldn't believe the Yankees were moving on Morganton, he wondered where the rest of the troops were. His heart was like a hammer beating against the anvil of his throat, and his hands trembled as he tried to ready his arrow in the advent of his discovery.

The soldier wading in the river heard a faint noise. It was the sound of an arrow falling through the tangled limbs of a tree, glancing off boughs as they redirected its trajectory.He turned and saw an arrow planted firmly in the road. The plumes in its shaft pointed toward a young boy wrestling with the bark of a tree, trying to regain his balance.

"Hell's bells partner! Looky what the squirrels grow to around here." The driver turned half around in his seat, "My-my, that's a big one all right. Say, what you doing up there boy?"

Marshall screwed up his courage and shouted, "Yankee, go home," as loud as he could. The audacity of the cry frightned even himself as it reverberated.

Enraged at the boy, the soldier wading in the stream, stepped resolutely toward him as if to give him a thrashing.

"Who do you think you're..?"

Suddenly, he stepped on a slick rock and lost his balance. He stumbled around for a moment, and then collapsed into the water. His cohort laughed as he watched the plump blackberries float under the bunkboard and down stream. The soldier worked his way back onto his feet and put his hat on. He was drenched and cursing. He started marching toward Marshall's tree with marked agitation.

"Damn you for distractin' me, you little piss-ant, I ought to ring your neck." Marshall started crying and hugged the tree tight. "Come down out of there you damned spy! Don't make me drag you!"

The blonde Officer sighed and then scolded his comrade, "It's your own damn fault you fell, peckerwood. We're leaving right now, there ain't no time for monkeyshines." His partner just stood staring up at the boy gritting his teeth. "I said 'lets go' damn it!" Finally the Officer turned back to get on the wagon, but seeing the arrow beside him he snatched it up out of the ground.

"You think you're a damn Cherokee or something?" He broke the arrow in two and threw it in the river. Marshall watched as the wagon lumbered off over the crest of a small rise and disappeared.

Thirty minutes later Marshall was in a dirt floor shack and exhausted, gasping for breath and trying to tell his uncles what he had seen and heard. His uncles grabbed their muskets and ran out the door. The young boy collapsed on the ground and felt a tense nervousness pour through his body, his head swam, his guts churned, and his limbs trembled. For almost twenty minutes he felt as if he might die- not from anything in particular, just from an hour of frightening, exciting activity in what had otherwise been a tedious, dull, and disappointing existence. When he had finally reached a tranquil state, his Aunt Sally walked in.

"How do Marshall? I see them good for nothing uncles of yours got that chimney shelved in place. Any one-man worth his salt would have took the whole chimney out, then patched the roof, but not the good-for-nothing scallywags in your clan. Ain't nothing they won't stoop to, if it means less work." She looked around the bare room as if it were possible for someone to hide behind nothing. "Where are the shiftless bastards anyway?"

"Ma'am, they went to head off some Yankees that's marching on Morganton."

"What? I'm going to kill that son-of-a-bitch myself! Them Yankees better not lay a hand on him, he's mine."

"But aunt Sally... I thought you'd be proud, they're protecting us from the Northern aggressors!"

Sally looked down at her nephew and the stern mask of indignation was lifted, exposing a tender façade of pity. "Marshall, you've always been wiser than your age, and I think maybe, maybe you're old enough to understand the truth. It took me a long time to learn the truth, and I'm afraid some people, like your uncles, will never discover it." There was a great deal of mercy in Sally's voice; a commodity Marshall never would have suspected her of having. She led him out to an apple tree in the front yard, they sat under its shade and she spoke to him. "Marshall, there is no northern aggression."

"But, they killed my Daddy. They shot him, in a field somewhere. I'll never see that place. I'm forgetting him. I didn't know he'd be gone for good, I would have paid him more mind."

"Now listen to me Marshall, cause I'm preachin' the gospel, and ain't no truth other'n what I'm tellin'. They just plain ain't no northern aggression. A few years ago some rich folks, folks with big farms, big mansions, and big feather beds got scared. They got scared that this here feller that got elected president was going to take their niggers away from them. They wanted to keep their niggers because it was them niggers what made them rich.

"They figured the only way to keep them would be to form their own nigger-keepin' country with their own nigger-keepin' president. Them rich people was a lot of things, but they wouldn't stupid. They knew if they formed their own country there would be a war. There wouldn't enough of them rich bastards to fight no war, and if there had been, they still wouldn't ah wanted to, so they had to get the poor folks like us to fight it for them.

"They lied to us, plain and simple. They said, 'The north's coming down on us like a swarm of locusts cause they don't like the way we conduct business. They hate the southern man and his way of life so they're trying to destroy it. Grab your guns and fight for what you believe in.' They couldn't concoct a good lie about what we ought to be believing in, so they say we're fighting for 'the cause'. Ask any blame fool what they're a fighting for and they'll say, 'cause'. It's so damn foolish you have to laugh. You're daddy died so a rich man could stay rich, but look around here... not a pot to piss in."

"I got a pot to piss in, gotta share it with my sister, but it's still mine."

"Now hush up a minute and take what I'm about to tell you to heart! The Yankees are coming. They're coming to save us from the rich slave-holders that are thowing they're weight around Raleigh and Richmond- getting your daddy killed and trying their damndest to get my Caleb killed. The sooner the Federals get here and end this war the sooner we'll be out from under the heel of these rich planters. God-willing they'll hang everyone of them when they get here, but their not going to hurt us.

"No sonny, they're coming to save us. We can't let on that we're waiting for them, if we do- those rich bastards will be on us like a pack of wolves. But you just wait for them the way you wait for Christmas and welcome them the way you do Christmas morning, because that's going to be the happiest day of your life."

Marshall sat there in silence for a little while, he had just been told the exact opposite of everything he had heard in his short lifetime. Sally looked him evenly in his eyes, "Do you believe me?" He cleared his throat, "Yes ma'am", and for some reason he did. "Good boy! Now run along and think about what I've told you. Think, but don't talk, understand?" But Marshall had already taken to his heels... he ran a long way without understanding why.

* * *

The next day there came a knock on his uncle's door. J.D. opened the door cautiously, "Yeah?"

"It's me J.D."

"Ah hell, little man! Come on in." J.D. seemed happy as a lark to see his nephew. "I thought it was Sally again. That woman's crazier than a shit-house rat."

The smell of freshly baked pastry filled the shack. "What smells so good J.D.?"

"Blackberry pie my boy, that crazy heifer chewed me out, then baked me a pie!"

"Smells good!"

"Don't know anybody who'd like a piece do you?"

"Met a feller yesterday fancied some." Marshall's eyes fell on a strange new rifle, half assembled and lying on a worktable beside the fragrant cobbler.

"Hell Marshall, I was hinting maybe you wanted a taste."

"Much obliged uncle. I'd rather starve thern eat anymore Polk-salad."

A fierce look came into J.D.'s eyes, "Listen son, you don't mean no harm, but never talk about something you don't know nothing about."

An image of the emaciated state his uncles were in flooded back into Marshall's mind. They had indeed starved in federal prison and he was sorry for saying something so stupid. J.D. set out a piece of cheesecloth on the table and carved out a large crumbling section of pie, placing it on the cloth in front of his nephew. After a short blessing Marshall tore into the pie ravenously. A minute later he was licking the cloth. Then for a moment all was silent as J.D. studied his new rifle.

"Uncle, what can you tell me about my daddy?"

J.D. sat the gun down on the table, "Well… I'll tell you, my sister couldn't have picked a better feller to marry. He was kind, devout, full of humor, generous, honest, everybody thought the world of your paw and that's the gospel truth."

"What went with him?" J.D. had imagined his father dying in a heroic charge toward a superior enemy, a death befitting his character.

"It's true, the three of us, Caleb, your paw, and me, fought side by side against them Godless bastards. Let me tell you son, I saw things that would curdle milk. If ever you took that blue uniform off a Yankee… you'd find horns, hoofs, and tail, and I'd be the only one what wouldn't be surprised. I won't bother telling you which battles we were in. Seems like we can't agree with the Union on anything, even call the battles by different names. Until we can at least agree on that I don't see no sense in naming names. We were in some humdingers as far as fighting goes, I will tell you that."

"Did paw fight bravely?"

"The honest truth is, we were all scared shitless, but some more than others. Your daddy was the least scared of all of us. That being said, he was so scared you wouldn't have known him if you saw him, during the fighting I mean. When you're running under that flag towards a big line of cannons and men, the fellers beside you are catching pumpkin-balls or getting ground into sausage with grape-shot, and there's a big line of bayonets rushing up into your face, and you know, if you stop, the guys running behind you'll get you with their bayonets or trample you, maybe not on propose, but dead is dead, with or without the malice… well you don't know what limit mortal terror can come to, unless you've been there.

"When your ass puckers up so's you couldn't drive a ten-penny nail into it with a sledgehammer, when the piss is running down your leg and you don't give a damn, when your heart's beating so loud you can't hear the cannons over it, that's when you find out what scared is. Then, when it's all over and by some trick of fate your not trying to scoop your guts back up out of the grass and stuff them back in your belly, when somehow you've cheated every chance allotted to man, and you stand sound of life and limb, that's when your nerves give way and you feel like your going to die from surviving.

"We was, all three of us, sitting in a ditch, after a scrape one day, weak as day old kittens. Enough bedlam for us, says we. The next big push we'd take French leave. Then it happened, out along the coast. One night we stole out, the three of us. We left in the middle of the night, abandoned the picket line. They said we'd get help from the navy, but we hadn't had a victory since I don't know when. We thought surely to be killed. There had been a lot of massacres by that time.

"Well, hell, we got our signals all crossed up, lost in the dunes, and ended up inside the Yankee pickets, soon as we realized it, we found some Yankee Uniforms, won't tell you how. We gussied ourselves up as Yankee Artillery men, thinking to slink off in disguise. Damned if the Union pickets didn't up and capture themselves three "Yankee deserters."

They took us back to their base, and they's making an awful fuss, court martial this, and hanging that. They were about to flog us for starters, when the attack come.

"It wouldn't no damn time until the fort surrendered, and there we was prisoners of our own troops. Our boys was mean as hell to us, and we couldn't tell them nothing, for fear we'd be found out as deserters. One of our guards could tell right from the way we talked, where we was from. He was intent on bashing our brains out and tossing us in a river before we ever made it to prison.

"Your daddy saved our hides though, he got up the gumption to talk to a Navy officer, come to drop off some sailor prisoners. He was real careful in his asking. Guards, knowing where we were from, would kill us for traitors to the cause, our fellow Yankee prisoners might well kill us for spies, if they knew we were rebels in federal uniform, and we might meet a firing squad if we were returned to the officers of our company, being deserters as we were.

"This sessech Navy officer took pity on us, and had a little talk with the guard. It was a fine line to walk, and from that point on we were mute as could be. When we had to talk, we tried to mimic the feds. They took us down to Andersonville in Georgia, we thought hell, least ways we won't die now. Looked like we would have got smart by then, but it took a might more time."

"So daddy died in an escape attempt?"

"Marshall, if I was anybody but who I am, I'd be telling you stories of bravery and sacrifice. Death for the sake of glory: it would be a noble tribute laid on the alter of freedom, a blow against tyranny benefiting free men everywhere." J.D. was staring blankly toward the table now, not at it, but through it, as if he could see the pits of hell raging miles below their feet. "You're daddy ate a rat." He paused for a moment.

He looked at his nephew suddenly and imploringly, "We was starving, dying, they were letting us starve to death and they were happy as rutting goats when they found one of us stiff in the mud. It was one less for them to keep track of. Your daddy caught this rat and it had big scab marks all over, like the smallpox, only for vermin, we called them scabs wufs.

"Everybody knows you don't eat a squirrel with wuf marks on it, but we were starving, he 'spected to die if he didn't eat this here rat, wuf marks and all. Don't you do it, say's I, but he thought I was covetous of the varmint. Thought if he tossed it away I'd gobble it up my own self." There was a subtle, desperate edge in his voice. "He thought I was trying to trick him and take his food... his rat... and I was. I was hungry. I wanted the rat, I didn't care if it had leprosy; I was starving." Marshall's uncle seemed very matter-of-fact all of the sudden, not detached, or solemn, just quietly honest.

"There's a point when desperation takes over; there ain't no loyalty no more, not really. You can be loyal only so far as it benefits you. We had all reached that place where, if friendship was a boon- so be it, but if having friends meant going hungry one more day than you had to... He ate the rat. Mostly he ate so nobody else would, but he was a good man, and you should store that away, only good and bad don't exist in places like that. There ain't no good and evil, it's replaced with living and dead. Your paw got dysentery from eating that diseased rat."

"What's dysentery?"

"He shit himself to death. It didn't take long, there wouldn't much of us left at that point." Marshall wasn't crying, he just looked confused and scared, as if he could no longer trust the world around him to be what he thought it was. As if the water might catch on fire, or the clouds fall out of the sky and crush him under their weight.

"You've never told me…" Marshall faltered, then timidly resumed, "how'd you and uncle Caleb manage to get out of prison and back here?"

Caleb worked his jaw back and forth for a moment, then clearing his throat, he said, "Well, a Yankee Sergeant Major, he was dying of some kind of a hurt he got before his capture. It turned septic and he got the fever. He was dying for sure and there wouldn't a damn thing nobody could do for him. He had this real nice jacket and I knew there would come a time when I'd be in need of one.. I reckoned he wouldn't long for this world anyhow, so I took his jacket.

"Couple of days later this feller, looked like a mayor or a judge or something, real clean and proper and all, he went pilferin' through the prison yard with a couple of guards. They was asking people questions, turning over dead bodies and staring at them. They finally come to me, all laid up in a corner where I was sitting in the fleas and the mud."

"The fancy feller looks at me and says, 'Sergeant Major Miller?'

'Yes?' I says.

'Thank God we've found you sir! I've been hired by your kin in order to restore you to your family and rescue you from your depravity.'

"I must have stared at the feller like a looney-bird for two minutes solid, without saying a damn thing. Then I just started balling, and the feller hugged me. He hugged me, my mud, my lice, and my fleas!

'I'm pastor Evans' says he, 'and I've been charged by your parents with the task of retrieving Sergeant Major Eugene Miller from the Confederate Prison Camp in which he was unjustly interred.'

"At this moment some poor wretch behind me started ah moaning, and I mean to beat the band! All eyes turned toward the son-of-a-bitch, cause he was raising one hell of a fuss. I turned around like everybody else and saw lying in the mud ten feet away, none other than Sergeant Major Eugene Miller, the same bastard I stole the coat off of.

"Before anybody could do anything, I ran up and kicked him in the face as hard as I could. That shut him up. I turned around and you should have seen the looks everybody was handin' me. There couldn't have been a drop of blood left in the pastor's face. Finally I pointed down at the poor sod and said, 'son-of-a-bitch stole my rat!'"

"The pastor come up and put a blanket over my shoulders. Told me the depravity I had been subjected to had made me feeble minded. He felt more sorry for me after I kicked an invalid in the face than he did before! He started leading me away when I come to think of Caleb. I made up some cock and bull story about how an enlisted man saved my life in combat and how I wouldn't leave without him.

"I really got the old pastor's goat; he was in tears over my loyalty. It was all horseshit though; I would have left Caleb in a pit of ants before I stayed another day in that hellhole. My bluff did the trick, and they found Caleb on the other side of the camp, laying in the mud just staring up into the sky.

"I was worried he might call me his brother and bring the roof down on our heads, but he didn't take no notice. As delirious as he was, he let us lead him around without any complaints, and after the good pastor paid the guards off, we were on our way. He was taking us to Baltimore, but we locked him inside an outhouse somewhere near Elkin and skedaddled back here."

Marshall had probably imagined a thousand different scenarios that encapsulated his uncles' experiences before coming back home. Never had he come anywhere near to the truth. J.D. was quiet now, picking at the little flakes of piecrust and nibbling at the crumbs. "Uncle Marshall, I can't wait till the Union soldiers come and put an end to all this. It don't make no sense. Everybody's suffering, everybody's worse off than they've ever been. Killing, dying, and you can't even tell me why."

J.D. didn't say anything. Outside the blinding sun stared down on the country-side relentlessly. Inside, J.D.'s shack was all gloom and the smell of gun oil, a few blinding rays of sunlight squirmed through the cracks and spotlighted sections of the dirt floor.

"They had this thing they called the dead-line down yonder. It was a little fence inside the stockade wall. It was about two foot high, and nothing to step over, but if you did, the guards shot you dead as hell. I saw many men cut down by bullets, bleedin'-out right in the cracked red dirt."

"Trying to escape?"

"Not in the way you're thinking."

Quiet descended. Finally J.D. spoke, "There's one thing I haven't told you yet. I vowed to your paw that if I ever made it back home I'd look after you as long as I live. I gave him my word and my word didn't mean a damn thing back there. But I ain't back there no more; I'm home now. Anything I have is yours, anything I can do for you, I will. I've started by telling you the truth about where I've been and what I've done. I ain't told nobody else and I never will, Caleb don't even know the whole of it. I ain't your paw, I could never be the kind of a man your paw was… but if you'll let me, I'll look after you like a feller looks after his own younguns."

Marshall was thoughtful, he had felt lost for a long time, but now he felt found. He wanted to purge himself of every misery his body had been stockpiling for the past year. He finally knew the answer to every question he had ever felt worth asking.

J.D. eventually felt a little embarrassed and told the child to go out and find a quiet place where he could be alone and peaceful. Marshall took his advice and ran out the door and into the forest. Running felt good. Watching the trees zoom past on either side of him and feeling the leaves beneath his bare feet, it was a far cry from the terror filled sprint of the previous day.

A little winded, he broke out of the tree line and into a meadow far behind the line of shacks and cabins where his kinfolk lived. He made for the old barn and climbed into the loft. There was a cool breeze passing through the loft and the cushion of the straw felt good on his back. He fought down the urge to weep. He tried to take a nap, but kept having to wave away a turquoise colored horsefly. It was a great day in his young life and he looked forward to the next great day- the day when the Union troops would march into Morganton and liberate the town from the evil, rich landholders.

The jarring sound of the barn door closing jerked Marshall out of a hazy dream about his father. The afternoon had grown late and there was someone in the bottom of the barn.

"Let's just leave it here tonight. We'll come back for it in the morning and decide what to do with it."

"How much do you think there is?"

"It's hard to say, more than the both of us could spend in a lifetime, I suspect."

"Will it be safe in here?"

"It will for one night. Now let's get going, I'm hungry."

It was the voice of Marshall's uncles. He heard the door open and close and he quickly climbed down to the ground. The buckboard wagon was parked in the barn. Bloodstains still marked the spot where one of the Yankees had been gunned down. He heard the muffled voices of his uncles outside the door. He stole up to the door and peaked through the crack. He could see Caleb and part of J.D. through the narrow slit.

J.D. said, "Let's go then," and they started to walk away. Suddenly Caleb turned around and before Marshall knew what was happening his uncle was swinging the door back into the barn. As Caleb walked in, Marshall tried to remain hidden behind the opened door. Caleb walked around the front of the wagon, apparently looking for something. He craned his neck for a moment, and then with a look of relief, he scooped up his hat and slapped a cloud of dust off of it.

Suddenly the hinges on the barn door groaned loudly and the door moved a couple of slow inches. Caleb squinted over the wagon and slowly circled around toward the door. He wrapped his fingers around the edge of the door and swung it closed. There was nothing behind it. He exited the building waving his hat in the air, "I found it!" Marshall's head popped out of a haystack in the corner and he crawled to the nearest wall, watching his uncles walk away through a knothole.

He then turned his attention to the wagon. It had sounded as if his uncles were talking about money, but where was it? Did they take it with them? "Anything I have is yours," the words came back to him. But what exactly did J.D. have? What did he have that he couldn't spend in a lifetime?

Marshall turned his attention to the buckboard. It didn't take any time at all to determine that there was some unaccountable girth associated with the wagon. Soon he discovered the access to the false bottom. Inside was a mixture of cotton and gold coins. It was impossible to determine the amount of gold without upsetting the elaborate system of fluff and metal, and Marshall had no intention of betraying his investigation.

Looking at the gold he suddenly felt very nervous for some reason. An awful temptation arose in his mind, causing him to wonder if just one of the coins could possibly be missed. He reached in and stroked one of the discs with his fingertips. He noticed then, what looked like the edge of a Bible sticking out from beneath the wood. He started and his heart began to beat fiercely; just for a moment he thought he knew some of the terror Cain felt, all those centuries ago.

Timidly he pulled the book out and found that it contained a couple of letters. He cursed for not having learned to read and vowed that by the same time next year he would be literate. Marshall returned the book and set everything back the way he had found it. The future looked bright.

1865

It was a fine spring morning and Marshall was sitting under a chestnut tree reading a bible. It was the only book his family owned and thanks to the help of a neighbor he could now fumble through the words at a slow pace. The day was pleasant and a soft breeze was blowing through the new leaves overhead. He read aloud, "...I will bring evil from the north, and a great destruction. The lion is come up from the thicket..."

"Marshall," J.D. said as he came around the tree, "we're going to need your help." His pants were covered in mud.

"What's the matter?" Marshall said as he laid the book in his lap.

"Well's run dry. We're going to have to go down a few feet at least, if we're going draw water."

They walked back toward J.D.'s shack. It had been a rather cold, dry spring until the previous week, when the sun finally shook off it's wintry dullness. The ground was now thawed and soft, but the big rains had yet to come. The south was in turmoil; everywhere there was upheaval as Northern Armies quashed the feeble remnants of once proud Brigades. At least, that was the news from points afar. To look at the never-changing mountains and the ever-starving people as Marshall saw them every day, one could only believe the world was in an eternal stasis.

When they arrived at the well Caleb and Sally were dragging the wooden font that capped it off to one side so that only the open hole and the winch remained. Soon operations were under way, and as sack after sack of red dirt was lifted to the surface, Marshall loaded a wheelbarrow and took the load to the tree-line for dumping. Sally helped her nephew, while Marshall's uncles took turns at the bottom of the well with a pick and short-handle shovel.

The young lad enjoyed helping them out; they seemed more like his real family than his own mother who had lapsed into despair since she was widowed. Of course Caleb displayed some of the same despondency as Marshall's own mother, but J.D. seemed to be a soothing balm for his shaken brother. Caleb seemed to depend on J.D. almost the same way a dog depends on its master. It was a matter of course then that Sally didn't always get along with J.D.

J.D. and Sally would go through extreme and regular cycles: from what seemed to be familial fondness, to complete animosity, and then back again. They seemed to share a good comradery during the work at the well, but when the job proved more than anyone bargained for, everyone became increasingly grim and tight-lipped. What was initially estimated to take a few hours was now stretching on endlessly. There was an unspoken determination to finish the work in one go, but it was beginning to become uncertain as to whether anyone had the stamina to meet the goal. The sun set and the blackness of night crept in so that a lantern was now needed both for the well digger and the surface workers.

Well into the night, after a chill had entered the air, Marshall saw a dim shadow appear on the moonlit road. He watched as the figure drew closer; it appeared to be a boy about his age. The figure homed in on the lanterns like a moth. When the stranger's face reflected the soft glow of the wick, Marshall could see that it was a boy not much older than himself. They examined each other for a moment, and then the stranger cleared his throat.

"Evening. Who lives up this way? Is this 'Walker Town'?" Before Marshall could say a word Sally spoke up, "Depends on which Walkers you're looking for and why." The young man removed his hat when Sally appeared and answered her resolutely, "Stoneman's Cavalry is on the march from Lenoir. The General's moved on to fry other fish, but his troops, they'll be here by morning."

"Praise God," Sally cried, "they're here at last, 'saviors shall come up on mount Zion!" In the dull light of the lantern Marshall could see the messenger's countenance assume an aspect of shock. "Damned if I ain't met up with some Yankee's harlot", the boy gasped.

At this, Sally grabbed the boy by the ear and damn near picked him up off the ground. She began to shake his head around violently. He, in turn, began screeching like a scalded pig.

Sally howled during the assault, "You listen to me, you little rat pecker, I'm a flower of the south, a southern belle, a genuine lady of the first water!" To emphasize her daintiness she smacked him loudly and violently every so often with her free hand. "A woman of my station is always chaste and pure. Never do we sully ourselves with unrefined behavior, neither does anything course nor vulgar ever cross our lips, you no good little chicken fucker!"

As the poor trapped boy used both hands to try and free himself from her grasp, J.D. finally awoke and separated them. He had been napping nearby waiting for his turn to dig. The boy rubbed the side of his head mournfully, "Holy hell sir, she damn near took my ear off!"

"Maybe next time the runt will respect his elders," proclaimed Sally. J.D. cast a suspicious eye on the boy, "Just what are you doing up this way at this time of night anyhow? You some kind of chicken thief?"

"No sir, I ain't stealing 'em," he gave Sally a sidelong glance, " nor doing anything else with them. I'm raising the alarm! Yankees will be pouring into Morganton by first light, if not sooner."

"Union troops?"

"Yes sir, cavalry, like a plague of locust, them. They tore through Lenoir yesterday, killing, looting, and raping. Ain't got no respect for nothing. The town's putting some folks together so's we can force them to take the long way around."

"They really think the Yankees will bypass the town if we put up a fight?"

"We ain't got nothing here that's worth a Blue-belly getting himself killed for. They figure the Yanks will take the hint and give us a wide berth."

"Holy shit." J.D. drawled the two words out slowly, then reluctantly he leaned his head over the well, "Caleb, we better get your hind-quarters up here."

Sally's knuckles went straight to her hips; "His hind-end can stay in the center of the earth where it belongs."

J.D. replied grimly, "Now Sally, I know we had an agreement, but this is different, you know what happened in Lenoir."

"I know the lies this little whipper-snapper's been spreading." She gave him a sideways glance, "Ain't worth nothing but fertilizer."

"Woman," J.D. said dismissively, "you don't know what you're talking about, we ain't got much, but what little we do have, I aim for us to keep." He then enlisted the two boy's help in hoisting Caleb out of the well, while he officially ignored every aspect of Sally's ensuing tantrum.

Caleb followed J.D.'s lead as if he were sleepwalking. Since Caleb had returned from the war, Marshall had never known him to act resolutely concerning anything, but even he was amazed when he followed J.D. down the road and out of sight, almost as if he were a bull and his brother was leading him by the brass ring.

Sally continued to shriek and oath curses even after the trio had long disappeared into the night. Marshall told his hysterical aunt that he needed to go use the bathroom and excused himself. Half an hour later he had caught up with Morganton's would-be Paul Revere and his uncles, though he followed them at a respectable distance. He knew if he betrayed his presence, he'd be sent back home straight-away, yet his sense of curiosity spurred him on. Finally his quarry halted behind a little mud bank just on the edge of a town blacked out. He tried to eaves drop, but they whispered too softly and soon his uncles vanished into the streets.

As the other boy stepped down from the edge of the mud bank Marshall arrested him with a loud, "Psst!" The boy just about jumped out of his skin, but when he recognized Marshall in the pale moonlight he breathed a sigh of relief. They talked for a few moments and in their adolescent excitement it was decided that the boy from town would show Marshall where the makeshift militia had dug in.

It was at a crossing known as "Rocky Ford" where the two boys spied the hasty earthen works of the town's defenders. "I'm sitting right here and watch the fireworks. Them Yankees don't know the stomping there in for." Marshall wanted to watch as well, but he felt the ridge where they were sitting was too exposed. He wished the boy luck and skirted down stream where he swam across with the ease of a duck, and climbed up onto the opposite bank. He hid out in a stand of trees at the water's edge until the dull light of morning began to creep into the river-valley.

With the growing light Marshall could finally see how the stage had been set. The road coming in from Lenoir led to a bridge that had been tore up and partially dismantled by General McCown's men. The General's troops were occupying a couple of rows of shallow trenches on the high ground across the river and they had one small, brass canon trained on the approach from Lenoir. There was no noise and little movement visible from the trenches some 250 yards distant.

Marshall wondered what could be going through the minds of the dirt farmers and pig breeders as they prepared to train their squirrel rifles on human beings for the first, and probably last time in their lives. It seemed unlikely that the cavalry would try to cross at the only point of the river where troops were dug in. The young man thought on the other hand that if they did choose to cross here, that they would have canons much larger than the tiny artillery piece the defenders wielded. He pictured the Union troops routing the General's men from a distance at which the defenders could not hope to reach with their weapons. Yet the fools sat waiting for a huge onslaught which would outnumber them by ten to one and outgun them at a similar ratio.

With the sun just struggling to climb up from the blood red horizon Marshall heard the sounds of a great mass of horsemen and wagons approaching. In a few moments they appeared, four columns of cavalrymen approaching the river. They halted approximately twenty-five yards from the remains of the bridge. A horseman with a drawn saber and a large red plume in his hat galloped to the front rank and spoke to the men. A moment later a couple of dozen riders trotted forward into the muddy water on the downstream side of the bridge.

As the horsemen waded to the halfway point, gunfire and thick white smoke erupted from the trenches atop the far hill. Men spilled off their horses, horses collapsed into the water, and in a few seconds horses and men began to scramble back toward the muddy banks from which they entered the river. The troops still waiting to cross finally began to return fire in sporadic bursts, but before the group could return from their fording attempt the brass howitzer on the ridgeline sent it's dull thunder resounding through the valley. The shell exploded on the muddy bank, throwing dirt into the air and leaving more casualties in its wake.

With horses and men lying on the bank and drowning in the water, the Union Troops finally shook off their shock and started peppering the earth works across the river with carbine fire. The musket fire on the hill died down, but the small canon roared again, this time missing its mark and felling a small tree beside the highway. At this point a group of fifty or so soldiers galloped away, skirting up river. Hoorays, howls, and cheers erupted from the troops dug in up on the hill. Suddenly the celebration was cut short when a large piece of field artillery fired from somewhere in the rear of the mass of blue uniforms and horse flesh. The round exploded to the rear of the trenches and the crew manning the howitzer ran and dove into a nearby hole.

Marshall couldn't see the Union cannon so he stepped out into the current where some overhanging tree boughs would keep him hidden. The water still had the chill of winter and he shivered as he pushed a leafy, low hanging limb down and peeked over it at the battle. The Union cannon fired a second time and when the smoke cleared the barrel, the Confederate howitzer was found to be pointing down in the dirt. Marshall could now see that dismounted troops had moved up into a small stand of trees near the bridge where they continued to fire on the embankment.

As the canon and small arms fire waxed, the vigor of the men in the rifle pits waned. If at first the three hundred odd men on the ridge had fought as if they numbered a thousand, now they fought as if they were fifty. The Union troops continued to pepper the hillside until Union Cavalry could be seen approaching the Confederates on their own bank. Apparently the detachment sent upstream had forded the river and were now flanking the Rebels. With the sight of this, troops charged out of the trees and crossed the river on the runners of the bridge, which were still intact. The rebels fled in mass and many were shot in the back, falling face first onto the earth.

Marshall felt something collide softly against his knees. He lifted up the leafy bow and saw a Union soldier floating on his back, with his mouth gaped open and full of blood. Marshall fell back into the water startled, and anxiously backed away from the body. The corpse ended up right on top of him, and he struggled to regain his footing. As he calmed down, he decided to pull the body to shore so it could be recovered.

He dragged the body up to the bank by the epaulettes of his jacket. When it rested half out of the water, with its eyes staring blankly into the sky, he stopped. There was a deep hole in the top right corner of the man's forehead, it wasn't filled with blood and one could see into his skull a couple of inches.

Suddenly the man coughed out the blood and moaned hoarsely. Marshall scrambled out of arms reach and felt the color drain from his own face. The soldier's eyes closed, then opened again. He clawed a handful of clay out of the water's edge, squeezed it in his fist, and expired. Marshall leaned back over him. The trooper was as white as a bleached sheet; with his coal black hair in loose wet curls he looked the picture of a martyr.

Marshall noticed he was wearing a holster. He undid the flap and removed a colt's revolver. He stuffed it into the back of his belt and took another look at the area around the bridge. About fifty of the town's defenders were sitting in the open with dismounted troops standing guard around them. A couple of Yankees were trying to repair the howitzer while the vast majority swarmed the bridge trying to reassemble it. Horses and men were being fished out of the river and dragged up on shore. A couple of mounted troops were working their way down river, scanning the current and the banks. Marshall took one last look at the dead body. As he disappeared into the forest the boy knew that although the living differentiate between a corpse and a martyr, to the dead there is but one death.

He found, some ways from the river, a toppled tree that had brought up roots and earth when it fell. Curling up in the hollow the tree left in the ground, he took a much-needed nap. When he awoke the sun was high in the sky. Upon arriving back at the river he could see guards posted on either side of the bridge, with a few soldiers cooking something over a small campfire nearby. The muddy road was marked by the passage of a small army.

Marshall walked down stream until the bridge was out of sight, and then swam across the slow tranquil river. As he proceeded back toward the courthouse, he connected with the highway and followed it to the edge of town. As he approached the town square there was a small grassy field to the left with a rail fence butted up against the ditch-line of the road. In the road itself were hundreds of trampled dandelions. As he came within a rock's throw of some of the town's buildings he found half a dozen slaves stooped on the other side of the fence. As he approached they started gathering up a prostrate body. Marshall greeted them with, "What happened to him?" pointing at the slave they were carting off in a wheelbarrow.

"Fell off du' fence suh'."

"He fell off the fence?"

"Yes suh', dis' moanin'."

Flies were buzzing around the body and where it had lain the grass was slick with blood. There was a large store between Marshall and the courthouse so he decided to go in through the back door and spy what was going on in town through the glass window in the storefront. There had been a glassmaker in town before the war and the owner of the general store had commissioned him to put in a huge window.

When the window was completed it was found that on a sunny day, people outside the store could see nothing but their own reflection in the window. The storeowner had the incompetent artisan ran out of town on a rail, but the impracticality of his window remained. As Marshall walked into the store he could see that most of the stock was gone. The place did not look like it had been ransacked however; more likely, the owner hid most of the contents the day before in an attempt to prevent its theft.

The building smelled of whiskey, broken bottles of which decorated the floor. A few shelves held stubbornly to their collections of balms and snake oils. A cracker barrel was spilled out in the floor and the only light in the place was spilling through the huge front window.

Marshall could see a column of smoke ascending into the sky from the lawn of the courthouse across the street. The loitering cavalrymen and the foot traffic in front of the store prevented the boy from discerning what was going on across the way.

Suddenly the door burst open and a soldier walked in holding his jaw. He noticed Marshall standing in the center of the room dumbfounded and shouted, "Hey boy! You Unionist or are you still kissing General Lee's ass like some of the rest of these fools?"

"No sir," said Marshall, "God bless Lincoln! I'm only glad ya'll are finally hear to put an end to this big mess."

The soldier stared at him intently for a moment, and then a grin crept across his face. As he grinned wider a chuckle forced its way out, finally giving way to loud laughter. Suddenly the laughter was cut short, as if the soldier had been hit by a bolt out of the blue. He cupped his jaws with both hands now and grimaced in pain. He lowered himself onto the floor and rested his face in his hands for a few tense minutes.

"What's wrong?"

"My tooth." He hissed through his hands. He stood up and staggered past Marshall, over to the few untouched shelves. He picked up vials and bottles, scanning them for some hope of salvation. He swooned and leaned his head into his arm, and his arm onto the wall. Marshall watched a couple of drops of perspiration run down his neck.

"Ain't there no tooth powders up there?"

"Hell if I know, I can't read!"

"I can read."

"You can?"

With a nod of affirmation from Marshall, the soldier took down every box and bottle on the shelf and laid them at his feet. "Go through these and find me something." He dug through the pile for a couple of seconds then held up a small brown bottle with a chewed up cork in it.

"What's that one say?"

"Burnett's Cocaine."

"Yeah, that ought to do the trick."

He snatched the bottle away greedily, but he didn't unstop it right away. He just stared at the medicine; this seemed to have some therapeutic value in itself. He smiled and seemed to forget all about the pain that had him nearly crippled just a moment before. He turned and walked toward the front door. He was reaching for the doorknob when he suddenly dropped his hand and turned back toward Marshall.

"Much obliged for your help." He rested his hand on the hilt of his saber, smiling. "Don't like the war, huh?"

"I hate it. My daddy got killed early on. I know the only way it'll end is ya'll comingdown here and putting an end to it."

"I'm glad you see it that way, boy." The soldier sighed and looked out the window, "what people don't know is that the war's already over. The ink's dry on the surrender paper and we're just working our way around trying to tell everybody, only sometimes they start shooting at us before we have a chance to tell them anything."

"So the war's over already?"

The Yankee nodded gravely, "Sorry about you're paw."

"Ain't your fault."

"Maybe not, but I'm sorry."

"I'll be alright. My uncle's sworn to look after me like I was his own boy."

"Sounds like a good man. Keep working on your letters and you'll make him proud."

Marshall looked across the street and saw what looked like a man digging in the courthouse lawn with a short-handle shovel.

"What's going on over there?" He pointed toward the courthouse.

"They're burning the town records."

"What about the feller digging?"

"Oh… well that's a nasty business. When we rode into town this morning, I was with the advance party, there were a couple of hold-outs guarding the courthouse from the terraces on either side." The Yankee picked up the edge of a torn white curtain hanging from the window. "The one digging we caught asleep, but the other one, his brother…" he took a short breath and exhaled audibly, "well, he turned on us after we snuck our way up the stairs." The soldier unsheathed his saber and wiped the blade along the fabric of the curtain. "I was the second man up the stairs and when I got there my Sergeant was trying to wrestle the reb's rifle out of his hands. The reb had him backed up to the iron railing when I come up behind him and struck his leg with my saber. He fell back and we was able to disarm him."

Marshall's eyes were wide and he felt as if his tongue had swollen in his mouth, finally he stammered. "Is, is he… alright?"

The Yankee sheathed his sword. "Bled to death more than an hour ago." He turned and walked back out into the sunlight. Marshall turned and as the swordsman pushed his way through the crowd in front of the window he managed an unobstructed view of the gravedigger across the street. Caleb held the shovel like a cane under one palm while he wiped away the sweat from his forehead with the back of his other hand, then he turned away and began digging.

The Yankee walked out of the storefront feeling low, after telling the young boy such a gritty story. At least he left before he could say anything truly disturbing, or so he thought to himself. "Has anyone got a shaving mirror?" The congregation on the sidewalk continued to mill around with no reply. The picture window in the storefront was reflecting the brilliant scene in front of it with great clarity and the soldier forced his way through the small mob. Kneeling down, he stationed himself directly in front of its mirror-like surface.

He took a large, tarnished spoon out of his pocket and carefully shook a little white powder onto it. Sitting down the bottle of Burnett's Cocaine, he wet his finger and began rubbing the powder on his gums. When the medicine had been consumed, he stowed away the bottle and the spoon. He sat there for a moment staring at his own reflection, then leaned forward and pulled back at his lip and cheek with his finger, peering into the maw of his reflection.

Marshall's face was hot, and his eyes were burning, though he did not yet cry. There was a roaring in his ears like a train barreling through his head. His molars were clenched and a rage began to pulse through his limbs like nothing he had ever known before. With nervous, shaky respirations he looked through the storefront window as the Yankee knelt in front of it. He stared at the soldier's open mouth and gazed into the open black pit of a huge cavity that had dissolved a great portion of one of the horseman's molars. All other images disassociated themselves from his mind, as he looked deeper and deeper into the dark void.

He drew out the pistol he had taken from the dead soldier that morning and held it so that the barrel nearly touched the pane of glass. The Yankee continued to examine his tooth decay as the revolver hovered a few inches away, its sights trained on his face. Marshall drew back the hammer and the cylinder revolved. An eternity passed in a moment, then pressure began to intensify on the trigger.

A dry snap resounded in the barren room and the boy choked back his tears. Again the hammer went back and again the pull of the trigger signified nothing in the realm of retribution. The ritual repeated itself another five times with the same results. Finally the heavy barrel swung down to the floor where Marshall came to rest after the buckling of his knees. He leaned forward into his hands and mourned for second chances that never had a chance.

Marshall was practically sitting on the pistol. His sweaty face trembled in his palms. From time to time a soldier would come in to see if there had been anything of value left for the taking. They didn't take any notice of the young man crumpled in the floor, after five years of war they had seen much worse. When finally he decided to make his way home, it had begun to rain softly, and from the looks of the darkening sky, it would get much worse before it got better.

When he stepped out onto the street, there were no other civilians in sight, only Yankees. The bonfire of court papers was smoldering, producing the thick, white, foggy smoke one often sees when burning wet leaves. Caleb was lying limp on the ground. At first Marshall thought he was dead, but when the Yankees loaded him into the back of a wagon, instead of the grave, he thought better of it. A bluecoat rolled J.D. into the grave, disturbing a great swarm of flies that had congregated on his body. Dirt began to rain down on his dead uncle and Marshall took a moment to look down into the hole.

"Move along there son, this ain't none of your affair."

If only the soldier were right, if only it wasn't his affair. He walked away from the earthen tomb and onto the long road home. He could see a wagon at the end of a long straightaway, and then it disappeared around a corner. The soft rain had ceased, staying just long enough to bed down the fine dust on the highway. The sky was now building to a massive thunderhead. He would be drenched before he got home.

* * *

It was dark when his weary legs turned onto the lane where his family lived. The torrential rains had come and drowned the ditch lines with red water long before darkness had engulfed the lands. Now he could smell smoke in the air. As he got closer he could see Marshall's shack burning from the inside out. Uniformed soldiers were stationed in the yard, visible in the prime-evil glow of the flames.

Many of the bluecoats were digging holes in the ground, while a couple of horses were yoked to a plow and pulled it back and forth across the muddy ground. A sudden thunderclap would set the horses into a slight panic, and the corresponding flash of lightning would set the hellish scene into sharp contrast, then the strange ritual would continue.

Not withstanding the flashes of lightning, Marshall managed to crawl through the swamped ditch-line and pass without detection. Soon he would be back home in the heart of Walkertown. His mother would probably pray a psalm of thanksgiving for his safe return, then thrash him to within an inch of his life for his foolhardy excursion.

* * *

His prophecy had come to pass. All the next damp and dreary day his mother watched him like a hawk, never once letting him out of her sight. Marshall could only wonder what was happening in Morganton. There was also a great curiosity building in him as to what had become of his surviving uncle. His curiosity would not be satiated that day, as he was kept under house arrest and they received no visitors. The next morning before his mother had awoken, Marshall stole out of the house determined to find out what had become of the world he had, until recently, known so well.

J.D.'s shack had been razed and his yard was a torn and blistered landscape. The Yankees had been looking for something: Marshall knew what it was. The brick skirting was still intact at Caleb's cabin and the boy suspected that the gold was safely behind that short brick wall. He knocked on Caleb's door. For a long time he waited. Finally he pushed the door open. There were no holes in the floor.

For whatever reason, the Yanks hadn't searched Caleb's home, only Marshall's. The only unusual sight was a pile of things in the middle of the room. There were jars of strange preserves, silverware, drapes torn right out of windows, and various other trinkets assembled into a small mound. Marshall left the cabin and headed back toward town. The sun was just coming up and the sky was cloudless and filled with color.

The highway had seen a lot of traffic since the rainstorm, more, in fact, than it had ever known, according to the tracks. As he continued to walk toward Morganton he met more and more people coming from town with big armfuls of various goods. Marshall thought for a moment that perhaps the Union troops had been plundering as they marched, as it was rumored Sherman's men did.

Perhaps they had left their train of stolen goods unguarded and the people were reappropriating them. Soon it became obvious that this was not the case. When two shoeless old men passed him carrying a mahogany door with linen and shoes piled high upon it, Marshall knew that the door couldn't have come from the Union wagons.

In town there wasn't much of a Federal presence. Here and there a Union soldier could be seen patrolling the streets on foot, but for the most part the square was crowded with civilians. Some were dancing and singing and a great many seemed to be drunk. Still, there were others screaming oaths at the other townspeople and shaking their fists while nearby their wives and daughters had tears running down their faces.

The owner of the general store was standing before his front door with a two by four in his hands threatening a group of hooligans across the street. As the mob taunted him Marshall could see nar'd'wells come in through the backdoor of the store and carry off the cracker-barrel. The large front window had now been completely busted out; whether by the crowd or the Yankees there was no way to tell.

Someone in the crowd clocked the storeowner in the face with a rotten potato, almost knocking him off his feet. A soldier saw the potato being pitched across the street right in front of him, but continued walking as if nothing had happened. Disgusted, Marshall turned to leave town. Just on the outskirts of town he heard two women screaming at each other. One backed out of a doorway in front of him pulling on half of a large thick book. She eventually dragged her opponent out onto the wooden walkway in front of the building where they continued their tug of war.

"Let go of the damned thing."

"I will not, you animal. This was a gift from my grandfather."

"Your grandfather was a bastard."

"Hush your vulgar mouth and give me my book. You can't even read!"

The book, which had been open, suddenly split at the spine and they each fell with a thud onto their posteriors. With the woman's profile now in relief, he could see that it was aunt Sally.

She dropped her half of the book, and clutching a dress she had been carrying over her shoulder, started walking briskly back toward Walkertown.

"Come back, I had that dress specially commissioned in Paris," she pleaded.

"Don't you worry, the good Lord looks after thieves! You'll have him to reckon with some day!" After swearing thusly in her genteel and cultured accent, the lady took what dignity she had left back in to the building and closed the door.

Marshall saw that the book was called "Don Quixote", whatever that meant. He was tempted to take it, but walked on back home, he'd had enough. He was still about half a mile from Walkertown when he spied a form lying prostrate in the ditch. It was a man completely naked and apparently dead. There were sores and scratches all over his back and the soles of his feet were bloody with gnats swarming to get at the blood.

Marshall turned him over and found that it was his uncle Caleb. It looked as if he had been disrobed and dragged up and down the road. His face was black and blue with one eye swollen shut. The palms of his hands had lost huge chunks of flesh, but worst of all was his chest and upper arms, where there was no skin to be seen. His ribs in a few places made contact with the air. It looked as if the flesh had been ground off of his body, and what wasn't gone bore large bruises and welts. Insects had obviously been feeding on him, a few of which had been caught in the blood as it dried and grew tacky. Their feet were immobile but their wings still buzzed hoping to free themselves.

A moan broke through the dry bloody lips and Marshall realized his uncle wasn't yet dead. It seemed hopeless to move him, as the ensuing infection would surely finish the work his injuries had begun. The boy thought of the pistol he had left in the General Store, if only he could shoot his uncle and end his misery now. Instead, he started picking off the little yellow eggs flies had been laying on his body. Undoubtedly there would still be tiny maggots to fish out of his wounds in the upcoming days, but at least he could get rid of a great many now. He wondered who he could get to help him carry Caleb the last half mile back to his home. He could see a few people approaching on the highway from Morganton, their arms filled with booty. Sally must have walked right by her husband, face down in the ditch; no Samaritan was she.

One of Caleb's scabby eyes cracked open, "Marshall?" He croaked softly. "Caleb, what happened? Looks like you've been skinned alive."

1875

It was a cool February day as Marshall cut across the courthouse lawn with a roll of string from the dry goods store. He paused at a small section of grass, only slightly greener than the surrounding blades, and then hurried back to the construction site nearby.

"It's about time you got back; now run me a plumb-line on that load-bearing-wall!"

The young man hurried back to the wall he had been working on and tied the string to a lead weight. He had been apprenticed to Mr. Colbert ever since the war ended. Reconstruction had been good to the masonry workers. For the past few years he had worked side by side with his mentor and was his most valuable worker. Marshall wasn't content however, and knew that within the next few years he would be competing with Mr. Colbert for new jobs. He was twenty-two now, and had grown into a well-respected man. Many people hadn't prospered as he had.

With the ending of the war many men had never come home, and of those that did, few returned whole. Women greatly outnumbered men and Marshall was now the object of many matrimonial schemes, but with his mother's recent passing he was afraid to love a woman whom the grave could rob him of. He now had more family below ground than above. The only kin left to him was his uncle Caleb and his aunt Sally.

* * *

After a long day shivering in the frigid wind with rough bricks in his numb, pale hands, he left the work-sight and took the short stroll across town for some cider and ham at a local provender. On his way there, a door opened onto the street in front of him and who should step out but his Aunt Sally crying into a handkerchief. A shingle above the door read, "George M. Eden, MD." The doctor stepped out onto the front step still holding one of Sally's hands in a comforting embrace.

"Now, my dear, fret not, for I will do all in my power to assist you in your travail." She turned and rushed down the street away from Marshall, who was left staring at the back of the doctor's head.

"Excuse me." The Doctor wheeled around as if he were a wanted criminal. "Oh my, Mr. Lackey, how you startled me." A look of relief came over his face.

"What's wrong with aunt Sally?" The nephew pointed down the street at the fleeting image.

"The poor woman is distraught at the prospect of never producing an heir for her husband."

"She can't have children? Why not?"

"Please, keep your voice down. This matter is highly sensitive. In fact, a may have said too much already. I have the confidence of my patient to think of you know."

"That's alright, I couldn't expect a Doctor to give me the time of day without putting a dollar bill in his hand."

An affected look of shock and disdain swept over the portly doctor's face, "Why, I never heard of such…"

Marshall brushed by him saying, "Oh, just crawl back in your hole," and continued walking.

After supper he collected his horse and headed back out to his family home. Since the demise of his parents he had made many improvements to the land and the structure. He was well liked and respected among his community, though there was the odd whisper concerning the fact that he didn't attend church. His home sat on the leveled out face of a hill and overlooked quite a bit of countryside. He could sit on his front porch and see the smoke from Caleb's chimney, if not the chimney itself. A small garden lay in ruins in front of his home. Marshall mourned the neglect, but with his long hours at work, there was simply no time for tending to it. What he needed was a wife; he knew it as well as every tongue that wagged in and out of town.

There was no end of matrimonial prospects, but finding a bride that wouldn't preach to him and try to drag him to Sunday meetings every week, that was something else entirely. It was early Sunday morning and he could hear bells ringing in the distance. Nearly everyone would be at church. He sat on the steps of his porch and enjoyed the first rays of the sun as they warmed his rested limbs. He drank the last gulp of coffee from a tin cup and stood up to stretch. He felt content, but knew it would be a lonesome day. Then the thought occurred to him that he might visit his uncle Caleb.

He decided to walk the old lane back down to Caleb's shack. Since the war, Caleb hadn't been much use to anybody. Mostly he trapped rabbits and worked other folk's fields. Marshall watched the ditch-line; as he walked he stared at the hoarfrost shining white in the morning sunlight, another five minutes and it would be gone. He thought about the ditch he found Caleb in, after the Federal raid. Soon he had reached the front door of Caleb's home and although he knocked, he could get no response. He cracked the door open and stuck his head in, "Caleb, you in there?"

He started checking the wood line, knowing Sally was too embarrassed of Caleb to have ever taken him to church with her. Soon he found his uncle inspecting a rabbit-gum, the trap was roughly built, from a hollow log.

"Howdy, uncle. Any luck?" Caleb nodded his salutations at his nephew then shook his head regarding his luck. He dumped the bait out of the rabbit-gum and carried it under his arm as they walked toward the rest of his string of traps.

126

After a long silence Caleb finally said, "Cold snap."

Marshall brightened at this, "Sure is uncle. It's tough on a man, working with his hands, outside and in this kind of weather. You're playing it smart if you asked me, staying hole up next to a fire." He took a couple of traps in his arms as Caleb kept collecting them.

"Say uncle, why are you bringing in your string of traps?"

"Moving the shack across the lane."

"I'll be glad to help you. You know I worry about you sometimes." They stopped at another rabbit-gum and Caleb leaned down to inspect it. "I wonder sometimes, with all you've been through, if there's anybody could ever know how you feel." Inside the trap a small rabbit ran from one end to the other, panicked and mad with fear.

1890

The undiluted dream is something we rarely wake to. Marshall found his bride, and in answer to his prayers- she never made him pray. Their children however, enjoyed no such immunity, and by the fall of 1890 they had quite a string of offspring. Three boys (seven, five, and three) followed their mother on the way to a small Baptist church.

"Now Marshall, don't worry about me, I'll be fine. The baby isn't due for another month and I'm getting to be an old hand at this motherhood business, so quit your fretting."

"I can't help but worry. What does that old carpetbagger know anyhow, probably stole that diploma off a real Doctor's wall before he hotfooted it out of Philadelphia. For all we know that baby could be due tonight."

"Momma do we have to go to church," the oldest of the boys said, "can't I go with Paw-paw over to Caleb's?"

"That's a fine idea, couldn't he come with me, sweetie?"

"I ain't going to let him miss Sunday school; one heathen in the family is quite enough, I'm sure. Besides, there ain't no sense in it- your cousins are going to be at church too." She handed off a pie she had been carrying. Strings that ran under the pan suspended it and it was wrapped in a white cloth. Caleb accepted the article, holding it as one might hold a parcel. "Don't mislay that pie, it's for uncle Caleb."

They stopped for a moment in the yard of the church and Marshall watched as his wife Connie straightened the children's sharp little suits. There were a dozen other mothers on the lawn doing the same thing, the preacher stood in the doorway of the building. The pastor's soft lily-white hands shook the calloused hard working hand of one of his neighbors while Marshall turned his back to the establishment in hopes that he wouldn't be recognized as that good for nothing heretic of a father who never goes to church with his children.

"Now, Jim, Luke, Seth… I want you boys to be good for your mother. There'll be time for horseplay later, but the moment you step onto church grounds you need to mind your manners."

"Why Marshall Lackey, I can't believe Connie's finally got you out to the Lord's house. We thought you were forever lost."

"Well don't count me found yet Aunt Sally." Sally had the preacher's right shoulder under her left hand. "Pastor Douglas, you remember Marshall don't you, he's been to three Baptisms," Sally looked down at Connie's ripe belly, "and has made an appointment for a fourth."

Mr. Douglas transferred his little black bible with the red ribbon from his right to his left hand so that salutations might be exchanged. "It's a pleasure to see you back among us Mr. Lackey. I do hope you can stay for the sermon; you might be surprised to see how a little guidance can benefit a man. We're all in need of God's blessings."

"That's funny, I feel pretty blessed as is. I mean, I have plenty of business, I work for myself so I'm not beholding to any boss man, my family enjoys great health, and my Sundays are free. In contrast take old Lyle and his kin over there- works his fingers to the bone as a sharecropper, in debt up to his neck to the land owner, consumptive, lost one child to smallpox, another during a birth that killed his wife as well, and he's attended church every Sunday since birth."

"Well brother, not all of our blessings will be found on this side of the grave."

"I reckon you're right preacher, Lyle ain't found none of his yet."

"Can't I persuade you to enjoy our hospitality just this once?"

"Nah preacher, the pressure of Connie's right heel on my left foot tells me it's time I moved on, besides, you'll be seeing me at the baby's baptism."

Sally took the Pastor's right arm in her right hand, "You'll have to excuse my Nephew Mr. Douglass, he can't be reconciled. He's just like Caleb that'a way. It's a peculiar family, seeing as how we get two black sheep for the price of one."

Marshall took a step back and gave Sally a head to heel appraisal. "Why! Aunt Sally, that dress must have cost a fortune, wherever did you get it?"

The normal pre-service bustle died away within earshot of the question as many waited with bated breath for the answer to the conversation they had never dared ask. Sally blushed under their gaze and after a long and awkward moment, squeaked out "a friend of the family."

"You must have friends in high places. I know the Mayor and I don't think his wife could afford anything along those lines. Well, my hat's off to you all the same." And with his hat in his hand he took a few bowed steps back, wheeled around, and happily walked up the road in the direction of Caleb's house.

Sometimes eternity can stop for a moment, and sometimes a moment can stop for an eternity. Somewhere along the line Caleb's life had stopped, it had yet to end, but it had long since stopped. Marshall knew very well that Sally intended to sweep him under the rug. That sort of thing was considered quite respectable; it might even be looked upon as a social grace. The poor were forced to look after the infirm, while the wealthy and affluent could usually gain (or buy) an appointment at some clinic or sanitarium thereby gaining freedom from a relation's embarrassing presence. This new Hospital of Broughton's was supposed to change all that, but Marshall had his doubts.

He wondered how the twins would cope with their father's disappearance, and then he wondered if they would even notice. It was a beautiful morning as he veered off the road and started to cut across the fields toward Caleb's home.

Soon he came in sight of an ancient barn and took a moment to peer inside. Sunlight was pouring in through a trap door in the loft and doodlebugs had pocked the dirt floor with their funnel shaped homes. Every time Marshall passed the barn he couldn't help looking inside and wondering if he had actually seen a buckboard wagon laden with gold, or if it was just a fragment of some dream. Dream and reality are easily discernable, each with their own characteristics. Yet time blurs their features just as distance obscures objects.

If there had been gold, where was it, lost in J.D.'s unmarked grave or hiding in the depths of Caleb's tortured mind? If there ever was any gold, it was probably taken back by the Union troops who burned J.D.'s cabin down. Marshall could see the gold now, just some nameless stack of ingots piled on the floor of some vault in Fort Knox. It was better to think of it stacked in some hollow tree, just waiting for the wood to rot away and the sunlight to pour in, or maybe it's at the bottom of an old well, or in a fifty-five gallon barrel of axle grease and at any moment, with it's simple discovery, a person's world could change forever.

He walked through the barn, leaving disaster in his wake for the doodlebugs, and walked out the far door and through the autumn fields. A chicken hawk passed overhead with a couple of catbirds harrying it, as it retreated. He shooed a few flies off the linen wrapped pie he was carrying and marched toward the small plume of smoke rising from the Walker's wood burning stove. He stopped at the edge of their garden, took off his jacket and hung it on their clothesline. He sat the pie down and pulled up a turnip, which he peeled with a pocketknife before retrieving his articles.

* * *

"How was your visit with Caleb?" Connie asked.

"Worrisome, I don't know what's going to become of him."

They sat in a couple of rocking chairs on their front porch as their sons and the Walker children played in the front yard. Graham sat on the edge of the porch with his feet hanging down, while his brother Dale engaged in Cowboy and Indian games on the lawn. Marshall cleared his throat and addressed Graham, "Why don't you go play with your brother Dale?"

"He don't want nobody calling him Dale, he only wants people calling him Wild Bill." Marshall looked down at the back of Graham's ruddy neck and said reproachfully,

"Graham, don't you like your brother?"

"I hate him."

Connie turned to her husband, "Let's go get that tea."

They left the porch and walked down a well-worn path to a small spring in which a jug of tea was submerged. Marshall leaned down and pulled the jug out of the chilly water.

"Is it cold?" Connie asked.

He uncorked the jug and took a draught from its lip. "Cold enough, I suppose." He put the stopper back in the jug and watched a crayfish wander about on the sandy bottom of the spring. It had been hiding under the jug and now it looked for a new refuge. "That boy of Caleb's worries me, honey."

"What, Dale?" she asked.

"No, Graham. He certainly doesn't like the attention his brother is getting."

She put her hand on his shoulder, "Maybe it goes deeper than that. Anyhow, is sibling rivalry that unusual?"

"It's not a rivalry. It takes competitors to have a rivalry. Graham doesn't try to compete with his brother; he just sits back... brooding, maybe plotting, hell I don't know. Maybe that's what's bothering me- just not knowing." He stood up and turned around to find Graham standing in the middle of the path, not three feet away.

"Got any spring lizards in there?" the boy asked.

"Oh, Graham, I didn't know you were coming with us. Uh, spring lizards... oh, I don't know if you'll find many this time of year, but there's a big crawdad right yonder if you can get it before it climbs under a rock." The boy kneeled down at the edge of the water and a few seconds later came up with the dripping, writhing crustacean. He held it pinched firmly by its back while the struggling crayfish reached back with its claws for something it could never grasp. In the sunlight its carapace gleamed a brilliant blue.

When they got back to the yard they found Dale with his back against an oak tree reading to the Lackey children from a dime novel with the words, "Thunder From His Guns" on the spine. He would stop reading from time to time and turn the book around in order to display an illustration to the enthralled crowd. Marshall started pouring the tea while Graham held his ear to Connie's stomach.

"What are you going to call him?" the boy asked.

"We haven't decided on a boys name yet," she answered.

"What if it's a girl?"

"Julia."

Ghosts of the Soon Departed

Julia

Ghosts of the Soon Departed

1909

The key slipped into the lock with its faint metallic sound. It turned counter-clockwise one complete revolution, and then slipped out of the keyhole. A slim body entered the room, closing and locking the door, leaving the key in the lock. A young woman with strawberry blonde hair leaned with her back against the door. She wore a loose fitting calico dress and riding boots. Her skin was slightly freckled, but no one would say blemished.

She crossed the hardwood floor as if it were a sandy beach: with no noise whatsoever. She drew the curtains and removed a bulbous ornament from the headboard of her brass bed. She reached in the hollow brass tube and removed a number of papers, all folded in the same meticulous way. She lay across the bed on the flat of her stomach with her feet bobbing in the air behind her head. She wet her lips as her eyes ran across the handwriting in front of her. She whispered a fragment of the words scrawled therein, "Ask me a secret and I'll tell you a promise." Suddenly a loud knock on the door stirred her out of the trance. Alarmed, she stuffed the papers under the mattress and unlocked her door.

"What the hell are you doing in here with the door locked in the middle of the day?"

"I was just going to change out of my riding clothes," she said.

A look of exasperation crossed her father's face. "And to do that you need to lock the door?"

"I'm not a little girl anymore, Daddy. A woman needs her privacy."

"Well, even a woman needs to clean up the mud she tracks into her father's house. As spoiled as you are, anybody ought to know better than that."

"Oh, did I leave tracks? I'll clean those up in a jiffy"

They walked down the short hallway and into a rather well appointed living space where a fire crackled in the hearth. The girl went outside and came back in with a small pail of water and while she cleaned the mud from the floor with a towel, her father cleaned the same from his work boots by the fire.

"Julia?" he called.

She was just putting the red stained towel into the pail and turning said, "Yes, Father?"

"Could you bring me the tin of shoe polish from my shoeshine kit?" She stood and straightened her dress before retrieving the small can and presenting it to her father. She offered it to him in her outstretched arm, but he only stared her dead in the face until the hesitation grew absurd and slightly disturbing. He just sat there with a boot on one hand and a dingy cloth in the other, boring a hole through her with his eyes. Finally she let her hand fall to her waist and gave him a puzzled look.

"Open it," he said.

She popped the top on the small tin drum, and looking inside she blushed scarlet.

"What's wrong?" he said sarcastically.

"This isn't your can of Shinola, you took it from my room. You did this on purpose."

"Why, my darling you sound hurt. What could be in that little old tin to make you turn all them colors?"

"You know *exactly* what's in it. You're just trying to humiliate me."

"You damn well better be humiliated," he said, raising his voice to a slightly hysterical register, "if you ain't sorry, the least you can be is ashamed."

"Why do you insist on embarrassing me?" she said in a bitter tone.

"To teach you a lesson; and not from any malice as you would like to dramatize it. Now tell me what's in the can."

"You know good and well what's in the can."

"I want to hear you say it."

"False eyelashes," she squeaked out with a sniffle.

A smug look crossed Marshall's face. "Hand them here," he said.

He examined the contents of the can. All of the shoe polish had been carefully removed and not even the scent of the Shinola could be detected. The two eyelashes lay in the silvered innards of the container like strange insects in some collection. He shook them out onto the embers of the fire. He gave his daughter a troubled glance as she sat down in an armchair on the opposite side of the hearth.

"I *ran out* of Shinola today," He said sarcastically. "Honestly, you must have thought that was the most ingenious hiding place didn't you? Thought you were really getting one over on your old man, didn't you? It's not as if I searched your room, you put them in the one thing I might want out of your room." She stared into the fire avoiding his glance.

"Go ahead and sulk, you might think you're too old for a hickory stick, or maybe you think I'm getting too old to properly apply one. I can assure you that neither is the case, and if you need proof, I'm prepared to perform a practical demonstration."

"Daddy, I'm eighteen years old and…"

"And I don't care if you're eighty," he interrupted, "are you trying to scandalize the family?" An unanswered pause filled the room. "Them's the trappings of a harlot and you know that, you're no fool." He stood up and started pacing in front of the fire saying, "When your mother died I swore I'd bring you up right, and with no more of that foolishness that they teach down at the First Baptist Church. I've tried to mold you into an intelligent, cultured, ethical person, and without any 'heaven and hell' mumbo jumbo. There's no reason why a person can't do the right thing simply because it's the right thing. We're not animals. We don't need carrots dangling in front of us to keep us moving forward, But you know what they all told me. 'Why,

Mister Lackey, *raise a child without the Bible?* She'll run wild on you sure as the world.'

"I can't believe you'd listen to a single word that knitting circle had to say."

"Well it looks like you're trying to fulfill all their prophecies just as quick as you can.

"What use do you have for false eyelashes in the first place? Show your face with adornments such as those and they'll be screaming 'brazen hussy' from the mountaintops. I know I raised you better than that. We're not some ignorant, cousin marrying, hillbillies. I've worked hard to provide you with the kind of upbringing we dared not dream of in the days of the Confederacy. I lifted myself up by my own bootstraps and brought my family right up with me. We're better than this and we're better than them," he said, pointing to an unseen demographic whose presence he never the less felt in the room. With a huff and a scowl, he sat back in his rocking chair and awaited a response from his sobbing daughter.

"When are you leaving?" she said.

"First thing in the morning. I have to be in Baltimore by the fourteenth to help your brother negotiate his loan." He smiled lovingly until she grinned and giggled. "Are you sure you won't come with me? I hate the thought of you all alone in this house."

"I'll be fine Daddy, I'm not a little girl anymore."

"Well just stop trying to prove it with false eyelashes and we'll all be fine."

* * *

A marble colored sphere lay on a green felt cloth. The pool cue struck it like a piston and the sphere shot two feet across the felt, collided with a black orb bearing the insignia of an eight. The impact produced a sharp crack audible even to people walking by the pool hall on the sidewalk outside. The eight ball ran down the corner pocket like a frightened rabbit.

A ruddy-faced man, somewhere in his thirties, stood up from the pool table and started chalking his cue. His hair was trimmed into a tight crew cut and he wore dungarees and a white cotton shirt.

"So, double-or-nothing…" he ran his hand over his scalp while he contemplated, "…means, you owe me, three dollars and seventy-four cents."

A bearded man threw his cue down on the table and thrust his hand into the pocket of his overalls. He withdrew a handful of change and crumpled up greenbacks. "This is the last time, do you hear me Graham? The last time! That there shot wouldn't nothin' but a snowbird, plain and simple. Always putting me behind the eight ball… it ain't right and it ain't fitting."

"There's no rule against it," Graham said.

"Damn it Graham, don't insult me! I never said you were a cheater. If I thought you were cheating I'd tell you to your God Damned face. It's not about that. There's a certain thing called dirty pool and that's exactly what you play. You ever hear that phrase?" he asked as he threw the assortment of legal tender on the table.

"There ain't nothing dirty about winning," Graham said with a sly grin. His opponent stormed to the door, and turning, shouted from the open doorway, "It's the last time!"

Graham's brother squeezed in through the doorway as the angry man left. Graham collected the money from the table, while his brother approached him. Dale's hair was still reminiscent of "Wild" Bill Hickok and the resemblance had only increased since Dale had grown the distinctive facial hair of the once great (now dead) gunfighter. He wore a suede brown jacket with fringe and cowboy style boots on his feet.

"Hey, guess what?" Graham asked his brother.

"What?"

"It's the last time."

"Who have you pissed off now?"

"Just a loser."

Dale looked back at the door as if he expected the ruffian to still be looming. "Well, it doesn't take a winner to put a bullet in you."

"Let 'em try." Graham said as he began unscrewing the two halves of his pool cue. He looked Dale from head to toe while he put the stick away in a leather case. "What the hell do you want with me anyhow?"

"Maw wants us down at the drugstore. I think she wants to talk to you."

"Well, I don't want to talk to her", Graham hissed.

"Listen, she wants you to come work for Doctor Eden," Dale said as he followed his brother out on to the cold sidewalk and up the lonely street.

"And that's probably exactly what she called him too, 'Doctor Eden'. She flaunts him around like he's some kind of show pony. She throws him right in everybody's face, "my husband: the doctor. Does he even have a first name? Does she know?"

"Of course he's got a first name, everybody's got a first name."

"Then what the hell is it!" Graham demanded, "if he really has a first name, tell it to me, or is it blasphemous to invoke his name out loud?"

"Okay, I don't know his first name, is that what you want to hear? Still, he's got one."

"People have first names, bullfrogs don't," cried Graham.

"Don't give me that bullfrog bullshit, it's disrespectful."

"Well, just let me take stock," demanded Graham, "lazy man's gut, at least five chins, bald, warts, skin the color of a rotten apple, smell- not much better…"

"Shut the hell up," stormed Dale, "I won't have you running him down in the middle of a public street for the whole world to hear. And stop walking so fast, for somebody that don't want to go to the drugstore, you're sure in a hurry to get there."

"Maybe if I get there while I'm all riled up, I'll have the guts to punch him right in the middle of his puffed-up face."

Dale jerked Graham around by his shoulder, "Now you listen to me! We're tired of cleaning up after your messes. Who do you think keeps the sheriff off your back? That's a pool hall back there, not a gambling den. And you might as well advertise your poker games in the News Herald for all the secrecy you manage. We've done everything we can to try to help you; all you do is throw it right back at us like we're abusing you or something. You've got to be the most hateful feller I've ever seen. You ain't got one ounce of gratitude for what we go through, trying to keep you out of jail, trying to line you up with some work, and we've tried no end to drag you into a church where you might learn something that would do you some good, but you, you'd rather breathe somebody else's cigar smoke, live off whiskey, and run through loose women. Well, we're about fed up. So, if you want cut loose into the world and marked for life, we'll be happy to oblige you, and you can live out the rest of your days like Cain."

Graham looked his brother coldly in the eye, "Don't I have to kill my brother first."

A look of alarm swept over Dale's face, "Now what in the hell do you mean by that?"

For the first time in their conversation, a big toothy grin appeared on Graham's face, "Nothing, just a little biblical humor," he laughed quietly, "don't be so gullible."

"Well I've noticed that your gallows humor always revolves around my scaffold, not yours."

"Relax, you win, I'm going to turn over a new leaf."

"You are?" Dale asked with raised eyebrows.

"Well, it is winter, hard to find a new leaf. But I'll try to behave myself a little better until the Spring, when there's millions of new leaves just waiting for somebody to turn them over."

"That sounds too good to be true, but I'll take you at your word," Dale said reluctantly as they sauntered, yet again, up the desolate street and toward the R/X sign that was now in view.

Doctor Eden was just putting some instruments into his black alligator bag when the two brothers walked into his medical office. The bell affixed above his entry-way gave sharp little cries as the door opened and closed. "Gentlemen, gentlemen... just the fellows I hoped to see this evening. Please have a seat just a moment," he made an expansive gesture to include the couch and leather chairs in his small, well appointed waiting room, "and I'll be right with you. I just have to settle the affairs of my desk."

With that said, he started shuffling papers and opening and closing drawers in a desk that sat in a room off to the side.

"Just a show for our benefit, he doesn't have to do a damn thing to his desk," Graham whispered as Dale gave him a harsh look and tried to silence him with a finger touching his lips and pointing up at his nose.

The doctor stepped back into the waiting room and motioned with his hand, "Please boys, step in here a moment." They followed him as he unlocked a door and stepped into a long narrow room with a teller's window facing out to the waiting room. The walls of the room were lined with all types of pharmaceuticals. There was a cornucopia of pills, syrups, powders, and spirits occupying all variety of bottles, boxes, and vials. A brown bottle with the lid off sat on a counter beside the window. Graham picked it up and pulled the cotton from its neck. He sniffed the bottle then put the cotton back in. The doctor snatched it out of his hand. "If you're going to be helping me, you have to remember never to do that," he snapped. "You didn't even check the label. If it had been chloroform you'd be stretched out on the floor right now."

"Well, you've told me what it ain't, maybe now you can tell me what it is," Graham said with dry sarcasm.

"It's laudanum," Doctor Eden said as he pointed at the label held in front of Graham's eyes, "but it's too potent. I need to water it down some before I can take some over to widow Nelson." He took the bottle, poured a little into a bigger bottle, then filled the bigger bottle up with a solution he took down off a shelf. "She's been

144

having trouble getting to sleep nights. A tablespoon mixed with this solution ought to help her doze off. A table spoon of the undiluted stuff would knock her out cold, maybe for eighteen hours or more."

Dale picked up the bottle, "Is that right?"

"Oh, don't give me any of your grief, Dale. The "Food and Drug" act is one of the most heinous injustices in the history of medicine. Your precious Theodore Roosevelt has set back the science of physicians, such as myself, a hundred years or more. Since that piece of foolishness breezed through the oval office, it's become more and more difficult to get people the medicines they want. It's become an exasperating business; I can't even get Burnett's Cocaine anymore. I have to use an off brand that has no name recognition. Some of my customers have stopped using cocaine altogether. And after years of loyalty, can you imagine?" The old frog shook his head thoughtfully.

"Sir," Dale began feebly, "I think you wanted to see Graham here for a reason?"

"Oh," the doctor came back to himself, "I did as a matter of fact." He turned to Graham "Son, and I call you son because I want the both of you to think of me as your own father, I thought I might be able to help you out," he said, smiling magnanimously. "I could use someone around here to deliver prescriptions and whatnot. Thought you might be interested in some good honest work. If you've got outstanding debts, I might also be able to clear those up for you. You could start fresh, with a blank slate so-to-speak, forget about all the embarrassing and foolish mistakes you've made over the years. What d'ya say? Can I count on you?"

Graham stared coldly right into the old doctor's eyes, "The only thing that's foolish and embarrassing in my life is you." Graham turned and a few steps later the bell above the door rang, "Good luck Doctor rubber-neck." The bell above the door rang again and Graham was gone.

The doctor turned to Dale, "Can you go talk to him?"

Dale could see that Doctor Eden was truly troubled, "Sure Doc, but…"

"Father," the doctor interjected.

"Uh, okay father… the only thing is that I've got to be at choir practice in five minutes. I can try to…"

"Apologize for me," the doctor said, interrupting once again.

Dale gave the doctor a curious look, "Don't you think he should be the one to…"

"Just do it, please."

"I will sir, I most certainly will," and Dale walked back out into the street.

With his arms folded in front of his chest, the old doctor stared down at the floor of the drug room, his eyes were watery and he seemed lost in some reverie. He finally came to himself all at once and put the solution back up on its shelf. Then he looked down at the counter-top quizzically. "Now what the hell have I done with that Laudanum," he mumbled to himself.

* * *

Graham walked the long trek back to the old home place in Walkertown. With his father in Broughton Hospital and his mother living in Morganton now, he and Dale divided the house between them. With a light coating of powdery dust on his shirt, shoes, and trousers, he pumped a little water out and drank down a couple of mason jars full. Then he heard what sounded like the call of a mourning dove out behind where his uncle J.D.'s house had once stood. He walked out past the old stone chimney and into the area just at the edge of the woods. Julia sat on the roof of an old pigsty with her bare feet dangling over the side. She was wearing a loose, white cotton dress and the wind was playing with her soft feathery hair.

Graham's eyes narrowed as he walked up to the old abandoned pen. Taking one of her tiny pale feet in his right hand, he kissed it as if it were the hand of Maid Marion. She laughed and pulled her foot out of his hand. He hoisted himself up onto the edge of the roof beside her and put his arm around her waist. She let her head rest upon his shoulder and they sat silently for a few minutes. A mourning dove landed in a nearby tree and began to coo, they both laughed, scaring the bird away in a noisy, frantic beat of wings. "I've been waiting quite a while for you, I'd almost given you up", she said in a swoon.

"My brother came and dragged me over to Doctor Eden's so the good doctor could insult me with his snobbish job offers."

"How is your brother?" She asked.

"Oh, Dale still thinks he's a gunfighter or something even grander, maybe a prophet or a politician, or something. I don't know." Graham sighed, "He even talks about joining the Army, says he's going to leave any day now."

"Really, how long has he been saying that?"

"About two years now." They both laughed for a few moments then kissed softly in the fading light.

"It's going to be a cold one tonight," she said. "I need to get home and start a fire."

He held her close, "Won't you marry me Julia? You know how much I love you."

She glared at him and said, "Now you just look here Graham Walker: I've done told you one too many times that you're barking up the wrong tree if matrimony's your heart's desire. Paw would never let me marry my own kin, he wants me to be a cultured sensible lady and not one of these old hillbillies what weds their first cousins." "But I ain't your first cousin I'm your…"

She cut him off in mid-sentence, "I know exactly what you are Graham: a hustler and a pool shark. What kind of life is that for an honest decent woman like me?" She broke free of his embrace and hopped to the ground. "I can't marry you. No matter how much you love me… no matter how much I love you. I couldn't hurt paw like that, not after he's lost maw and spent the greater part of his life heart-broke. I can't add on to his suffering on your account."

"Well, maybe if I just talked to him darling… what matters most to him is your happiness. It's just foolishness that you can't see that," Graham pleaded.

"Don't you dare," she scolded. In another moment a look of tenderness crossed her face. She walked up to Graham, who remained perched atop the roof. He leaned his face down and she held it between her soft, trembling hands. Her eyes were moist with emotion and she spoke in a soft quavering voice, "Paw's left for Baltimore. Come up to the house tonight. If I can't give be your wife, perhaps I can at least give you what's a husband's right." With that, she pressed her lips softly to his and slipped away up to the road, her feet making no sound at all.

* * *

As she had insisted the night did grow cold, with a sharp wind scouring the surface of the hillside where a pair of boots trudged. The form silhouetted in the chiseled moonlight marched up the road, past a garden where the plow had yet to touch the waiting earth, and toward the quaint little home up on the hill. The soft light of a kerosene lamp beckoned him toward the window from which it glowed. The door to the house opened and the door to the house closed.

Julia was sitting on the cook-stove across from the front door. She looked up when he entered the room and a wide grin spread across her face. She looked down toward her lap and pursed her lips to try and suppress her joy at seeing him. She had an afghan brought up around her shoulders; it was white with small, light blue floral patterns here and there. She wore it like a shawl and it hung loose down to her calves as her feet fidgeted in the air.

"I thought maybe you weren't coming," she said. "This house is a bit drafty when there's a wind gusting up." She stopped for a second and a little color flushed to her cheeks, "I cooked dinner earlier and the stove's still warm. Since I was a youngun' I've been sitting on it for warmth."

She batted her false eyelashes and let the afghan fall from off her shoulders, revealing her small rounded breasts. The knitted cloth fell in a loose pile around her hips. She leaned back and stretched her arms across the cupboards that lined the top of the stove behind her shoulders. The warm cast iron she leaned back against was embossed with the word "MAJESTIC", but with her body concealing the middle syllable from view it read "MAJ IC".

The ruddy faced, shorthaired lover she had dreamed about on so many long lonesome nights crossed the room suddenly, leaning into his steps. His lips met hers with a force that betrayed none of the tenderness she had grown so accustom to. He kissed her roughly, with a primitive quality she had not prepared herself for. She knew then that she had teased him too long.

He fumbled with his suspenders as he bit at her neck, more than playfully. His trousers fell to the floor and his rough icy hands were dragging their way across her back almost immediately. He licked her breasts and pulled her knees apart. She held onto the outside edges of the cupboards with a death-grip, laying her chin on his right shoulder. She stared blankly at the wall opposite her as he dragged her buttocks across the stovetop toward him.

He dug his fingertips into the flesh of her flanks and made fumbling and aggressive attempts at penetration. Her eyes began to well up and one of her false eyelashes came loose and dangled from her eyelid. Through the obscuring veil of that eyelash her eyes came to rest on a fixture hanging on the opposite wall. It was a crucifix with a small effigy of Jesus upon it.

She hung there, her arms spread out, hands clasping an immovable object, naked from the waste up, a loose cloth girding her hips, her body stretched out, and she looked at the form on the cross, mirroring her posture as his emaciated body hung on his cross.

Suddenly she let go of the stove and shoved her assailant blindly from her. She gathered her afghan up over her shoulders and ran to her bed sobbing. Her face had been buried in her pillow for a minute or two when she felt someone sit down beside her.

Slowly, she sat up. She put her hand on his cheek and said, "Oh Graham, it's not that I don't want to, it's nothing of the kind but... I have to get married, if not now, someday." She let her hand drop down into her lap limply and looked down at the floor. A couple of seconds passed and in a hollow voice she said, "When I do get married, if I'm not a virgin... I do love you."

He held a silver flask out to her. She giggled a little, brushed her nose with her arm and took a long cool draught from it. "Where did you ever find gin?" He shrugged and lay back on the bed with a morbid look on his face. He didn't have much color. She drank a little more of the gin then lay down beside him. She draped an arm across him and held the cool metal of the flask to her warm tear-swollen cheek. "Maybe we could elope," she said solemnly, as if it were a prayer. "Maybe we could elope and move to Savannah, maybe we could do that." They lay together silently for a time, just staring at the ceiling. She hoped the dream of Savannah would come true. She began to feel groggy. She watched the room revolve around her slowly a few times, then she drifted away from Graham.

2nd Marshall

Ghosts of the Soon Departed

1920

It was clear to everyone at the funeral that the dress the old woman had requested to be buried in was hopelessly worn out. She lay in a hospital bed with influenza for over a week while her strength wore down. Finally, with her "husband" taking a nap in the chair beside her bed, she waved the nurse over to her bed side and said softly, but distinctly, "Burry me in that Sunday dress, you know, the one I use to wear when Caleb would…" Then she went pale and looked beyond everything in the room, at something beyond everything we know. The nurse woke the Doctor, but she was dead.

Now she was lying in the most expensive coffin Doctor Eden could find, dressed in the most faded, worn out dress anyone had ever seen. As people leaned over the casket, their handkerchiefs went reflexively from eyes to nose as they were overwhelmed by the smell of mothballs. Doctor Eden, Marshall, and Dale shook people's hands as they filed under the canopy to pay their last respects.

"Doctor," Marshall said after the line dissipated, "now that the formalities are taken care of, I hope you don't mind if I take a few moments with Dale. We have some important matters to discuss."

"Actually, I do need a few moments alone. So please, by all means," the Doctor said in a shaky voice that had lost its bed-side-manner.

Dale gave the old man a hug and Marshall shook his hand, wrapping his left hand around the back of Doctor Eden's hand for extra warmth. As they walked away Dale whispered, "Not hearing her last words has really bore down on him." Marshall nodded gravely as they walked out of the graveyard and back toward town.

They were both sweating gallons in their heavy dark suits. It didn't take long for them to shed their jackets and carry them folded over their left arms.

As they passed Broughten Hospital, Marshall spoke softly, "You do realize the significance of Sally's passing don't you?" Dale nodded and Marshall continued, "It's my turn to visit Caleb tomorrow. I'll tell him that you'll be coming to collect him next week. That should give us enough time to make the necessary arrangements." The tap of Marshall's cane on the sidewalk echoed through the quiet streets. "There's something else I want you to do, if you can."

"You know I'll try to do whatever you tell me uncle, just you name it."

His uncle motioned at a bench sitting on the sidewalk and they both sat down. Marshall took out a small glass bottle and offered it to Dale. They passed the bottle back and forth in silence. At length Marshall cleared his throat and pitched the bottle into the tall weeds of a vacant lot.

"I want you to try and find out where your brother is and get him back here," Marshall said suddenly, surprising even himself by practically shouting.

"After what he did to Julia?" Dale gasped.

"He'll want to pay his respects to Sally," Marshall said.

"If he does, it'll be the first time. A man like that has no respect. You can't pay for something if you don't have the necessary currency!" Dale was clearly agitated, but Marshall kept talking to him in a soothing voice, saying, "Dale, this feud can't last forever. You've not been hurt nearly as bad as I have by all this, and I've decided to let bygones be bygones."

"Well I hold people to a higher standard. I tend to believe a man should live with integrity. It would be different if he would just admit to his error and try to make up for it." As Dale's face grew redder he looked away from his uncle saying, "I can't do it, not after what he's done."

"It's been over ten years Dale. His mother's dead, and his father's going to be released from the mental hospital after thirty years. It's his right to be here after

154

all." He waited for his nephew's response, but it didn't seem to be forthcoming. A Cicada buzzed from a tree nearby with its loud, sustained call. Minutes passed by and Marshall's head began to reel with the heat and the alcohol. He tried to think of something else to say about the subject, but he faltered.

"He raped your daughter," Dale said finally and without warning. "Most men would have killed him for that. I don't know why you didn't kill him." He stood up, "Let's go, Gene's waiting on us." They started walking up the sidewalk, Dale carrying both of their jackets.

"If he was in so much need of shooting, why didn't you do it?" Marshall asked abruptly.

"Because when I got the letter telling me what had happened I was already in the service, hundreds of miles away."

"Well, you've seen him since and he still walks the earth," Marshall said as he wiped sweat from his brow.

"Well, he can just continue to walk it far from here. I don't want him around Gene."

"Maybe he'll take a liking to Gene, the boy needs his father, I'm not much of a substitute."

Dale took a harsh tone with his uncle, "Don't be foolish, that boy's had it tough and you're the only one who's ever stuck by him. His mother was drugged and raped by her own cousin, nine months later when he's born there ain't nobody for him to call daddy. Wouldn't nobody have nothing to do with him or his Momma for a year. Finally she finds somebody to marry her, but after they have a few kids together he won't have nothing to do with Gene and sends him to live with you." They both stopped under a canvas canopy in front of the pharmacy, "Who could that boy ever count on if it weren't for you?"

"I pity anybody needs to count on an old man like me."

"Well uncle, I ain't never stopped counting on you," Dale said and nudged his shoulder with the top of his fist.

Marshall leaned in through the door of the pharmacy and called to a young boy sitting at the counter, "Get your hind end out her Gene, we've got to get back home." He turned to his nephew; "You owe it to me to do as I ask. So I'm asking you as a personal favor to bring Graham home."

Dale sighed painfully as Gene came out of the drugstore with a bouquet of flowers in his hands, "Okay, I'll see what I can do."

Gene looked up at his Grandfather, "I got them flowers you wanted grandpa."

"Good boy," he said as he rubbed the boy's head. "Now say goodbye to Dale."

They exchanged farewells and Dale asked if he could take the flowers to Sally's grave for them, since he was going back. They told him the flowers were for something else, and that they had already sent flowers to her grave. He watched as the two of them crossed the street and stopped to linger at one corner of the courthouse lawn. They both got down on their knees and prayed, and then they walked away, leaving the flowers lying in the grass. Dale was dumbfounded; he had never seen his uncle pray before.

* * *

The 2:15 was running behind schedule and Dale hoped it was lying in the bottom of a ravine somewhere. Before his pocket-watch read 2:20 however, he heard the distant calamity that announces the arrival of a train. The sun was high overhead and there was no shade to be found on the platform. Underneath his hat, Dale's scalp was soaked with sweat. He carried a folded newspaper under his left arm and within its depths he could feel the outline of a revolver.

The train slowed to a noisy, steamy stop and in a moment a form stood at the top of a small set of steps in the car directly in front of Dale. A dried out husk of someone he once knew stood there. Life of late had not been kind to his brother, he

156

was such a shell of his former self that it was difficult to believe this was Dale's twin. Graham walked down on to the platform and looked his brother in the eye.

A porter appeared in his red hat and walked down the steps with a five-gallon bucket. He handed it to Graham saying, "you're bags sir." Graham took it without a word and Dale gave the porter a penny. The porter disappeared and the train left without further ado. The two brothers still stared at each other in silence.

Suddenly Dale leaned forward and embraced his brother, who did not return the provocation. Quickly Dale took Graham by the arm and began escorting him across the platform to where the Model T was parked. He spoke in a brisk, jovial tone, saying, "Graham, its such a relief that I could finally talk Marshall into welcoming you back, I'm only sorry it has to be during such a time of misery, what with the passing of our Mother and all."

The bucket slipped out of Graham's hand and the contents spilled at their feet. Dale scanned around the platform quickly to see if anyone was visible. Reassured that they were alone, he got down on his knees and began refilling the bucket while he said, "I'm so sorry I have to be rushing you this way Dale. Only they've prepared a fish-fry for you up at the river and we need to hurry or we're going to be late."

"It's a surprise; so don't tell anyone I've told you about it or they'll skin me," he said as he handed him the bucket. He pointed at a car just off the platform, "That's the car I'm using. I'll run ahead and get it started so's you can just hop in and we'll be at the river before you can say 'Thomas Edison'!" He made good on his word, leaping from the platform and hand cranking the car into caliginous life. He jumped up into the driver's seat, but when he turned around he saw that Graham hadn't moved an inch and was simply staring at the car.

Worse still, Dale saw one of the black men who hung around down at the station walking toward his brother with his hand out. Dale left the newspaper in the seat and rushed to intervene, but before he got there they were shaking hands, and as he ran up, he heard the black man saying, "so good to have you back Mister Walker, we've missed you something fierce and I can't wait to tell all them folks that's been asking about you that you've been restored to us."

Dale didn't slow down, but grabbed the man by his other arm and dragged him out of Graham's earshot. He made a few contemptuous, but indecipherable remarks then grabbed the man by the back of the neck and shoved him away. The black man barely kept his feet under him and when he recovered from the shove, continued in the same direction, rubbing the back of his neck. Graham finally spoke, saying, "What the hell was that all about?"

Dale looked at him sternly, "You'd think somebody's been giving away watermelons down here, the way this station's become infested." He took the bucket out of Graham's hand, "And the way you take up with niggers, you'll have them eating at your table before long."

"I ain't got no table and I've been lucky enough to be a guest at theirs in times where I wouldn't have had food otherwise."

"Some day you'll have to decide between your pride and your appetite."

"That's an easy decision. Why did you shove him anyway? There's more to it than that."

"He said the fish-fry was cancelled and I blew my stack a little bit. I've put in a lot of work and planning to make that come off."

"Somehow I doubt that." They we're just getting to the car and Graham walked around to the back bumper to examine a large wooden barrel. "Hey Dale," he said over the sputtering noises of the engine, "what have you got a barrel in the rumble seat for?" Graham waited until Dale was in the passenger seat to respond, "It's a cracker barrel. The fellow down at the General Store knew I was headed down here and he asked me to bring it in to town for him."

On the way through town Dale stopped at the General Store and told Graham to wait in the car. He went in the store and a few seconds later he emerged with a teenager in a heavy apron; they took the barrel down off the rumble seat and sat it beside the building. Dale climbed back in and said, "Okay, you ready to see your Daddy?"

* * *

After a brief introduction and reunion, mostly one-sided, Graham took a walk around the old shack to give it the once-over. A few modifications had been stitched on to the old hulking shanty, but it certainly hadn't changed its character. He walked past a small garden, where the few rows of corn were already growing tall. At the creek, he noticed that a section had been damned up with stones from downstream. He walked up behind a ten-year-old boy in short pants. The child was sitting on his haunches leaning over the cloudy water. He held out his hand to try and make a shadow on the surface.

"Hey old man, what are you up to?" Graham asked.

The boy kept trying to look through the silt-clouded water. "I need bait for the river."

"Spring lizards?" Graham asked.

"Or crawdads, I don't give a care which," answered the lad.

"They'll never bite, at least not this time a year. What you need is grasshoppers," Graham offered.

"Uncle Dale," the boy said in a plaintiff tone, "you don't even fish anymore."

"Actually, it's uncle Graham, and if I didn't fish every day I'd starve to death." The boy turned around and looked at his uncle for the first time. "I'm sorry uncle but you sound just like…"

"…the devil?" Graham interrupted, "Yeah, I get that a lot."

Graham took a fly-swat off the nail where it hung on the porch of the old shack. The boy took up a cane fishing rod and together they headed out across the fields of hay that butted up against the Walker property. As they walked, Graham smacked the occasional locust with the fly swat, stunning it long enough to get it in to a bait-jar. "Uncle Graham, what you going to do while you're back in town?" Graham took off his ratty old hat and wiped the sweat off his forehead. "Well sir", he said, "think I'll get cleaned up and go shoot some pool tonight."

* * *

The Model-T pulled up in front of the pool hall at dusk that evening. It was a damp night following a late afternoon shower that had driven both Graham and his nephew from the river. Marshall stepped out onto the sidewalk and Graham crossed over to the passenger seat to do the same. He didn't fancy soiling his new shoes in the mud of the streets. The horses tied off in front of the building sniffed the car suspiciously.

"I'm going over to the pharmacy, if Doctor Eden's working late maybe I can rope him into a few games." Graham met Marshall's comment with an incredulous look. "Don't even joke about such things, I came out her to have fun, but I couldn't possibly get that drunk." Marshall laughed, "Just you wait here, I'll be back in a few minutes", and with that he walked up the block leaving Graham standing on the corner. From the sidewalk he could hear billiard balls colliding, and glasses tinkling. He cocked his hat and stepped into the pool hall.

Graham threw his elbows up on the bar, "I'm ready to wrack'em up, so set me up with a table, the red-felt if it's available. I also want a beer and a whiskey, hell hand over the bottle, I'm good for it." A couple of dollar bills were pounded out on the bar to accompany his demands. The proprietor gave Graham the once over. "Who'd you dig up out of the cemetery to get those duds?"

Graham straightened the carnation on his collar and said, "If you want to keep the change you'll keep your questions to yourself." The man furrowed his brow, then bent down under the bar and came up with a tray holding a racked set of billiard

160

balls along with the cue-ball and some chalk. He also gave him a tall beer, rather warm, and a bottle of whiskey with a glass turned upside down over the top. He pointed at a table in the corner then took the bills and held each one to the light as Graham walked the length of the establishment.

The room was thick with the sickly sweet smoke of cigars. Six other tables loomed in the dimly lit place, five of them currently hosting games of their own. Graham had eight dollars still in his pocket, which he hoped to double or triple before the night was through. He eyed greedily the small stacks of cash and coin riding on the edges of nearby tables, riding also on the fall of the eight ball. He racked up his table and busted. He swarmed around the table, sinking all of the striped balls in a fury. He was warming up well, tonight just might be his night. He lined the one-ball up on the eight ball and pulled the cue back to shoot. The cue met with an obstruction behind him and he could tell immediately that the impediment was of flesh.

A fellow with a full beard stood up and began to apologize for getting in the way of Graham's shot, but suddenly his eyes went wide and his lips stiffened beneath his bristling facial hair. He turned away from Graham and threw his knuckles on the pool table as he began to breath heavily. Graham thought he was having some sort of attack.

Graham put his hand on the stranger's shoulder to see if he was alright and the stranger spun around with a cue ball in his hand and hit him square in the jaw. Graham's back collided with his pool table and he slumped to the floor. His gold tooth slid down his throat and blood ran down his chin. Numbness rang through his head and he saw sparks of light appear in his field of vision.

He felt himself hoisted up by several hands and pushed into a corner of the room. His senses were as dull as in a dream. The bearded man threatened him with a hawk's-bill knife and cut long tears in his new clothes. He put away the knife and Graham felt other tormentors pin his arms behind him. The bearded man said something about Julia, and then struck him in the gut. Searing pain shot through

Graham's body and he struggled to get his hands free, but he was helpless. A few more blows came and Graham thought that some of his innards were being torn from their rightful place.

"I wondered when I might see you again", the bearded man said. Graham tried to make sense of the words. "You have to be the stupidest son-of-a-bitch to ever live, coming back here after what you done."

Through his blurred vision and torturous pain, Graham saw the bearded man reach behind his back and retrieve a pistol. He stuck the barrel of the gun in Graham's left nostril and tried to pick him up off the floor with it. Graham could feel the flesh starting to rip.

"You think you can get away with just anything, huh? Is that right?" The man asked venomously. "You'll never see the sun come up on this night, but before it's all over you'll have learned one last thing: there's some sins that a man'll make you pay for, even if the law'll see him at the end of a noose for it." Graham could feel the hammer being pulled back on the pistol through the flesh on his face, "Your death matters more to me than my life, that's the one thing you never counted on."

"What in the hell is going on in here?" A voice roared from the entrance.

The bearded man turned toward the doorway, taking the gun from Graham's head. Graham tried to break free with a jerk but didn't quite have the strength. The man with the beard said, "Doc, you just keep walkin', this don't concern you none." Doctor Eden started walking, but toward, and not away, from the gunman. The man took aim on the doctor and ordered him to stop, but Dr. Eden had the same grim, determined look on his face that the gunman had sported only a few seconds before.

A look of panic now spread over the gunman's countenance, he fired in the air once, half deafening the frightened patrons of the pool hall who cowered under the tables. He then fired a shot wildly at Dr. Eden with his eyes closed, a huge picture window that looked out onto the street collapse into a million pieces.

The Doctor pulled the gun out of the assailant's hand. The bearded man started to say something, but Dr. Eden shot him in the foot before he could. The man grabbed his foot and started rolling around the floor on his back, screaming. Dr. Eden held the gun on the two men holding Graham up. "You gentlemen will help me take Graham to his car."

As they walked toward the door, a man lying in the floor shouted, "Is there a Doctor in the house?" All eyes watched as the Doctor walked out the door with a gun in his hands.

Marshall was outside leaning against the brick wall. His face was as white as chalk. After the two men loaded Graham into the car at gunpoint, Dr. Eden ordered them back into the pool hall. He then roused Marshall who drove them to the Doctor's home just outside of town.

"Who was that?" Graham slurred through his busted lip.

"That was Julia's husband," Marshall said.

"Well, I guess it's a small world after all," said Graham.

The car's headlights snaked there way over a few rutted out dirt roads and then up the drive of the Doctor's fine old home. The two older men carried Graham in on their shoulders and placed him on a couch. The Doctor put a little salve on his lip and felt his abdomen to determine if there were any ruptures or hemorrhages.

Marshall sat morosely in a stuffed chair with his face in his hands. Dr. Eden finally determined that his stepson was merely battered and bruised; his injuries would have no lingering effect. The two men carried him off to bed, where he awoke the next morning in considerable pain. He turned away from the sunlight and cradled his aching guts in his arms. A few minutes later the Doctor came bustling in.

"Good morning son, I brought you some hot cocoa. There's some painkiller mixed in with it, so I do suggest you drink it," he said as he sat a steaming mug on the nightstand ten inches from Graham's nose. "It seems that none of those involved in the scuffle last night were very interested in dragging the sheriff into it. We should be thankful we've avoided such complications."

"Where's Marshall?" Graham asked.

"Oh, he left shortly after we put you to bed," the Doctor replied.

"He didn't stay?" Graham pressed.

"I told him that you'd be fine. He can't stay here, he's got Gene to look after," the Doctor concluded.

Soon Graham was on his way back to Walkertown, wearing a bloody pin striped suit and sitting in a bloody seat. It was already a hot day and he decided to stop off at the general store for a cold drink. He walked in and took a chilly Coca-cola from the icebox and paid his nickel. He took a cracker from the half-empty barrel. As he walked out of the store he met the same black man from the train platform.

"Howdy there feller, how's the world treating you?" He asked.

"Cayn't complain Mistah Walkah, sir. No sir, not one bit," the man said jovially.

"Listen don't take Dale the wrong way, I mean… with what happened back at the platform. He was just upset that the fish-fry had been canceled," Graham said.

"What fish-fry is that?" the man asked.

"You didn't tell him anything about a fish-fry?"

"Not a bit," the man said.

Graham took a breath and thought for a moment. "If there were going to be one," he asked, "how would a man find out."

"I wouldn't know sir," said the black man, "but they might serve notice in the newspaper."

Graham paid his respects and went over to the Model-T to find Dale's newspaper. It had been thrown in the floorboard and collected some mud over the past couple of days. Graham picked it up and as he did a revolver spilled out and fell to the floorboard with a clunk.

At first he thought it was the pistol that he had been threatened with the night before. That pistol had been sitting on a table in the entrance hall of Dr. Eden's house as he left, and the pistol he now held was a much heavier, longer barreled affair than the one that menaced him the previous evening. He sat the gun in the passenger seat and flipped through the paper. There was no mention of a fish fry, either by the river or else where. He lowered the paper and something caught his eye. The barrel Dale had unloaded from the rumble seat of the car was sitting out in the sun next to the general store. He got out of the car and went over to the barrel. He took the securing hoop from the top of the barrel to find that the lid was also nailed securely to the body of the barrel. He disappeared into the general store for a moment, re-appearing with a pry-bar. The nails gave a strange moan as he peeled the top off the barrel. Sunlight spilled inside, and Graham could see that the barrel was empty except for the very bottom where rusted, bent railroad spikes had been poured in, about a foot deep.

"Down by the river, huh?"

* * *

It had been a long night for Marshall; his son-in-law had almost bled to death from a gunshot wound to the foot. After making the trek to the nearest available Doctor, the bleeding was curtailed. The physician hoped to save the foot. Most of Marshall's immediate family had congregated at his home, a situation that filled him with anxiety. It was only on those occasions when his privacy was robbed of him, that he realized how much he depended on it.

It had been a hot morning, but now there was a cooling breeze coming out of the north, bending the uppermost branches of the pines with its caressing touch. Marshall snuck out of his home in hopes of a peaceful afternoon walk down the lane. With his home now out of sight, Marshall was suddenly breathing easy. Soon Gene came running up the road in an out of breath attempt to catch up with the Grandfather that had been such a father to him. Marshall couldn't have been more pleased.

"When you're seeking solitude, it's nice to have company," he told his grandson as he threw an affectionate arm around his shoulder.

They continued down the dusty avenue until the old Walker home came into view. Caleb was sitting on the front porch starring out into the field next to his old shack. Marshall waved, but his uncle seemed distracted. As they got closer, he thought he could detect a specific place out in the field that had Caleb's undivided attention. He marched out to the area of such interest while Gene tried to engage the old man in conversion.

"Howdy mister," he said.

"Now Gene, I wouldn't bother too much trying to talk to uncle Caleb. He's gone senile many a year," Marshall said as he scanned the ground.

Marshall realized that he had no idea what he was looking for and walked back over to the porch feeling a little foolish. Gene grabbed him by the arm and pointed at Caleb's face. There was a metallic green fly marching across the clammy surface of Caleb's eye.

***

When the two brothers returned from their trip to the town bank, they found a bed sheet hanging over their father's chair. A wind was rippling the white cloth. It had been tucked in under a motionless form, as to ensure it didn't fly away in the breeze. Marshall walked out from inside the home.

"Rest easy boys," Marshall said, "he's givin up the ghost. He's at peace for the first time since I was just a boy."

Dale stood there, dumbfounded. Graham began giggling in a strange, distracted way. Marshall turned and went back in the house. A handful of flies crawled over the highest point of the sheet, desiring what lay beneath.

***

The ears of corn had grown fat in Marshall's modest garden. The golden tassels hanging from the husks swayed in the breeze. A scarecrow on an eight-foot pole looked out over the crop. Marshall's house sat on a small rise, so that, from his front porch, he could also look out over every last row planted. He did so now, beaming with the pride of a man who tills the soil and enjoys the satisfaction of self-reliance. Gene sat on the edge of the porch with his feet dangling over the side. He was running a jackknife across a whetstone; a can of three-in-one oil sit beside him.

They both saw the dust of the Model-T coming up the road. It parked out beside the garden. Dale got out and started marching up toward the porch. "Hey their old-timer," Dale called out expansively as he strode up the porch steps.

"What brings you out here?" Marshall asked. "Hardly ever see you round these parts."

"I need your help," Dale said, casting a sidelong glance at Gene.

"Gene, why don't you go for a walk?" Marshall asked.

Gene dropped down off the porch and started toward the woods. He stopped at the corner of the house and said, "Hey Graham."

Graham stepped out from around the corner and mussed the boy's hair.

"How the hell did you get here so fast?" Dale exclaimed.

"Thought you might get lonely 'Wild' Bill, so's I stowed away by sitting on your back bumper," Graham said.

"Of all the low-down dirty tricks, they say old habits die hard, but I was hoping you'd shed your hobo impulses," Dale said in a swell of contempt.

Marshall watched Gene vanish into the forests beyond his yard. "Now what's got you two so riled up?" the old man asked.

"This destitute fool don't know what's good for him," Dale said indicating Graham. "That's what's wrong. Paw didn't leave no will so the courthouse wants us to settle his belongings between us. I've been living on that land my whole life, unlike this immoral transient over here. I went down to the bank and took out a loan so I can give ungrateful brother here half the value of Dad's properties in cash. He won't accept any offer."

"It's as much mine as yours!" Graham shouted with fire in his eyes. "If the money's so fair, you take it and leave me the land."

"You're just being spiteful," Dale replied, "that land don't mean nothing to you."

"You two can just come in the house and simmer down!" Marshall shouted over them.

He led them in and offered them some tea. Gene had just retrieved a big jug from the spring. They drank the cool draught and silence reigned for a few minutes. Marshall finally broke the silence to suggest that they divide the property between them.

"I mean: if your both so set on having the land, just split it between the two of you. One of you can have the plot with the house and the other can have the plot next to it and the one across the road," Marshall said feeling very satisfied with the compromise.

"Well, I'm willing to discuss it if Graham is," Dale said.

"Alright, let's talk about it outside," Graham agreed.

"That's better. Here," Marshall said handing Dale a bushel basket, "help yourself to a few ears of corn. It's the sweetest I ever raised, don't need a drop of butter."

They were crossing the front yard when Marshall followed out the front door with a double barrel shotgun. "Here Graham, take the sixteen gauge," he said, "Them crows might be back." Graham took the gun and they both walked down to the garden. Marshall strode back into his house. He drank a little more tea. Sunlight was streaming through the kitchen window behind him. He wondered if he should let the field lay fallow the next season.

The soil had been so good to him he thought perhaps he should let it rest... like the Israelites in the days of old giving the land its due Sabbath. He then wondered how many more years he would have the strength to get behind the plow. Perhaps too many winters had passed him by to worry about leaving a field fallow now. He resolved then and there to make hay while the sun shines. He took out his pocket watch and started winding it while he sat at the kitchen table. The gold gleamed in the sunlight and dazzled his eyes. He heard the report of his shotgun, one blast, then two, in quick succession. More gunfire followed and Marshall jumped to his feet, upsetting his chair. It fell to the floor.

1932

The rains poured down over the tin roof of the old brick home Marshall had built in his youth. The chorus of the raindrops induced a peaceful tranquility strangely appropriate for his final hours. A bearded man sat beside his bed, with a pretty, but weathered lady at his side. A half-dozen of their children stood around the bedside, most of them fully grown now.

A black woman rapped softly on the door before opening it a crack and announcing in hushed tones the arrival of Gene. "If you'll excuse us Daddy, we'll take our leave out the back door," Julia said. "I'll be back around supper time to check in on you." Her face was red with sobbing as she ushered her brood out the chamber door. Her husband pulled back the curtain discreetly and stared at Gene for a moment. The young man was standing in the yard, drenched to the skin. He let the curtain fall back into place before limping across the room and out the door.

Gene walked in and looked down at the old man. Marshall was wrapped in quilts as a squaw might have been. He was sitting up in bed with pillows behind his back for support. The young man pulled a chair up at the head of the bed and took his grandfather's hand.

"They tell me you're doing a might poorly these days old man," he said brightly.

"I've seen better days," the old man agreed. "It's been said that you've been back more than a week now, yet this is the first you've come to see me. I've missed you my boy. It's been a long year without you around. 'Thought perhaps I might not see you again, least ways not on this side of the veil."

"I'm sorry. I couldn't be more tore up about it, but I was too ashamed to look you in the eye," said Gene, even now avoiding the old man's gaze. "The farm's enough to shatter any man's pride and I'm not above confessing to it. There's a lot of questions I've always meant to ask you. Now hardly seems like the time to press you, but if I'm ever to have any answers..."

"I think son, that the questions you have are better left without reply," he tightened his grip on Gene's hand and pointed with his free hand, "know that before you ask them. Having warned you, I won't deny you the answers, at least in as far as it's in my power to provide them."

"One thing I don't need to ask, is about my father, who he was, what happened to him. You've been the truest of fathers to me," Gene said solemnly.

"And don't think I don't mean to do right by you, Gene. I can't leave you the house for obvious reasons, but I've still got a parcel of land my uncle left me and it's all yours to build on, sell, or what ever it's fit for."

"Caleb's parcel?" Gene asked.

"No son, the tract I've got belonged to his brother J.D., a good man who died long before you were born. That land's fell into my hands now, and though it ain't much, it'll fall into your's when I'm in the ground," the old man said soulfully.

"I'm grateful Grandpa, I really am, but that's not what I wanted to ask you about," Gene began.

"Is it not?" the old man asked.

"No," said Gene taking a deep breath, "You see, I know that in the summer of 1920 we never did see a single crow. I'm not sure if it was because of the scarecrow you put up, or if the crows just never took a liking to our crops. So I was wondering if you actually handed Marshall that shotgun because of the gold." The old man furrowed his brow. The word 'gold' hit him like a blow.

"What gold might that be?" he said looking away to the curtains.

"The gold that Graham and Dale killed each other over, what other gold would it be?" Gene asked insistently.

A change came over Marshall's face, he looked worried, terrified. "Don't even speak of it," he said. "It'll be the end of you, as it's been the end of every soul whose known it, or even heard it rumored. It was the end of those who brought it here. It was the end of those who took it from them and it was the end of those who were destined to inherit it." The old man took a glass of water from his nightstand and took a few sips that his voice not break.

"Now I ask you son, let it be. It'll never do you any good, for if anything in this world is cursed it must be that gold. I thought I would dig it up. You see, I saw it once with my own eyes, and though it would be the better part of a lifetime before I ever had any clue what befell it, I never escaped the memory. I was never able to rid myself of the strange craving that sight wrought in me."

"So it is real," Gene whispered urgently, "how can I lay hands on it?."

"I thought I knew," Marshall groaned, "I went to dig it up, thought I knew exactly where to look. In the back of my mind a voice of reason called out, 'Don't, it'll end as it has for one and all,' but I paid it no heed." The old man turned and looked his grandson dead in the eye. "What could it harm me, I reckoned. There wouldn't nobody competing with me for it. So I ignored the voice and I took a shovel, and walked out to…" he paused when he saw the anticipation on Gene's face. He thought better of it. "I digged down about three inches and hit a web of tiny roots. So I took out my pocketknife to cut through the big woven mess. Oily resin from the roots drenched my hands, but after about fifteen minutes I made it through the layer. I worked a lather up, digging with the shovel until the ground got too hard, then coming back here for a mattock so I could dig deeper yet."

He took another drink of water before continuing, "It was a hot and muggy night, as I worked by the light of a full moon like some animal digging its burrow. I was sweating like an Eskimo in the Sahara, wiping the sweat off my forehead and the back of my neck. Feeling the salty sting of it in my eyes. I didn't give up until the hole was so deep I nearly couldn't climb out of it."

The old man lay back on his pillows now, gazing at the ceiling. "I went home determined to try again the next night, and every other night, until I found it. When I woke up early the following afternoon. I felt like my skin was festering, it itched like damnation. I was sure I must be coming down with something. My skin started knotting up into tiny, red hives. My hands, my forearms, my forehead, and my neck became so inflamed that I had to go to the hospital. From there it spread to the inside of my throat and other places I won't mention."

"I have never endured anything worse. I was in hell," he said matter-of-factly. They finally had to put bandages over my eyes and lash my hands to the side of the bed to keep me from scratching them out. The Doctors said it was the worst damage they ever see'd from poison Ivy. After weeks of torment, I came home. I've not concerned myself with the gold since, and I've lived a life of complete contentment right down to this day. Now I lay before you, nearing the end of my journey, begging you not to make the same mistake as those who came before you. Leave the gold be. If ever anything bore the devil's mark, it's that gold."

Marshall ended his speech with a fit of coughing so extreme, it sent Gene in search of the black lady who was caring for him. He waited for his grandfather to hold court yet again, but after the travail of his coughing fit, the aged man drifted off to sleep.

Gene would never see the man who raised him again.

Ghosts of the Soon Departed

Gene

Ghosts of the Soon Departed

1920

That bastard of a stepfather wanted Gene out. Julia, Gene's mother, disagreed. So the great bearded son-of-a-bitch decided to beat the disagreement out of her. He was a great, hateful beast, filled with a fool's pride. On his mother's account, Gene requested to live with his grandfather.

It was only on days like today, when his mother brought her family together to visit with Marshall, that he spent any time with them. He avoided his stepfather at all cost. His half-siblings were neither dear to him, nor loathed, but he certainly missed his mother's devotion and envied his brothers and sisters their good fortune. Julia, Gene's mother, had developed a Judas complex and seemed unable to look her son in the eye, much less offer him the support he longed for.

Gene's grandfather Marshall couldn't have been kinder to his charge, and the boy looked up to him. In the absence of Gene's real father, who ever that might have been, Marshall took on all the attributes of fatherly pride and devotion.

The family had assembled for Marshall's sixty-seventh birthday, but the real talk was all about Marshall's crazy uncle who had just been released from the insane asylum, his aunt who had recently passed away, and his cousin who had recently returned to town after a long exile. Gene's stepfather seemed agitated about the man's return to town. The young boy didn't attach any special significance to this; his stepfather was always agitated about something, one thing as much as the next.

"He just better steer clear of me, that's all I'm saying. You don't return like a dog to your filth," he said, giving his wife a meaningful glance. Julia blanched and put her hand over her forehead. "There's some folks who should just be shot like a dog," he continued. Gene glared at him across the dining room table and silently agreed. He asked to be excused from dinner and went out on the porch to try and quell the rage that now threatened to explode behind his eyes. Just as he was calming down, out walked his stepfather and Marshall.

"You need to relax. You're carrying too much around on your shoulders," Marshall said. "Go play some cards, shoot some pool, get your mind off things for a spell."

"Might just do that," the bearded hulk replied.

Gene was fed up with his stepfather, and with Marshall's permission, he took leave to go fishing. It had been a wet summer and the river was red with the mud washed from a thousand gullies. Graham, Gene's first cousin, thrice removed, had met him along the way to the river. They took turns casting with Gene's cane fishing pole. The sun was hot, but they found a large elm under which to take refuge. Gene was surprised by Graham's good humor and easy manner.

"You know cousin," Gene said, "there's some that don't like it- you've come back to town. Why's people so dead set against you?"

"Maybe they mistook me for Dale," Graham said with a sly grin.

"I doubt that," Gene said earnestly, "everybody loves Dale, what with him being a war hero and all."

"Oh, so he's Sergeant York now," Graham laughed.

"You didn't know he fought in the Great War?" Gene asked.

"Fought?" Graham said incredulously, "No I didn't know he *fought* in the war. Is that what he's been telling everyone?"

"Where's the shame in that?" Gene asked.

"Let me tell you a thing or two about Dale and his exploits during the war, my young friend," Graham handed Gene the fishing rod and leaned back in the cool grass with his hands behind his head. "First of all, he couldn't have found the front lines on a map, that's how far he was from the trenches. He worked in the office of the postmaster delivering the mail of dead men to their orphans and widows. He does know a lot of intimate stories regarding heroism, they just never happened to him. He would separate the nastiest envelopes, the ones where the addresses were impossible to decipher, being covered with dried, blackened blood as they were. He was just supposed to look for an indication in the actual body of the letter so it could either be sent on or sent back. Be that as it may, I don't think he ever opened one he didn't read."

A cool wind blew over the river and Graham closed his eyes as the breeze washed over him. "You see Gene, there was a lot more money to be made in the postmaster's office than in no-man's-land. A lot of officers and well-to-do enlisted men wanted to send home items they... recovered during the war. Of course there were regulations against some of these goings on, but if you knew the right people, and made it worth their while, they could make sure whatever you wanted to ship back home made it safe and sound. My brother was the right people. Those that couldn't pay him in cash, paid him in favors."

"What kind of favors?" Gene asked as his floater bobbed up and down unnoticed.

"Well there's Dale's job, his car, the train tickets he can always get without so much as a by-your-leave," Graham continued.

"Somebody's got to do his job, right?" Gene pressed.

"What job?" Graham countered. "Have you ever seen him do anything? Somebody else delivers the mail and if you ever go down to the post office who's at the service window? I couldn't tell you who it is, but I know who it ain't".

"But cousin," Gene went on, "how do you know about what happened to Dale during the war?"

"Well, he sent plenty of valuables back to the States from Europe for himself. I know the feller in town who fenced his goods for him. He's the only one in town knows the truth about our local war hero and he told me every little dirty detail,"

Graham told him.

"Ought'n I to speak up?" Gene asked with a concerned look.

"I wouldn't", Graham answered. "People will believe what they want to believe."

* * *

Somebody shot Gene's stepfather. Unfortunately he was shot in the foot, and though there was some talk of removing it, he would eventually come away from the episode with a pronounced limp only. There was the consolation that the wound would register pain in direct proportion to the readings of the barometer. Gene was hoping for years of high-humidity.

Gene had also witnessed a fly walk across the open eye of one of his distant relations in Walker town. The man had died while sitting on his front porch, much to the shock of his two sons. The town Doctor declared the old man a stroke victim and, oddly enough, paid for his funeral. Older folks were always doing things Gene just couldn't make sense of.

Gene and his cousin Graham made a regular routine out of their fishing trips. Almost every late afternoon found them on the riverbanks. His cousin seemed to take a shine to him, but he certainly didn't have anything too flattering to say about any of the town's other residents. There was no love lost between Graham and the county of his birth. Sometimes when Gene wandered down to the shack where the old man had died, he would find his cousin acting peculiar. Gene would be carrying his fishing rod, scratching around for Graham, when suddenly he would climb out from under the floor boards of the house with spider webs all in his hair. Other times he would be found digging holes out in the middle of a small meadow in sight of the cabin for no apparent reason. Gene never asked about such goings on and Graham never commented, in way of explanation, on his strange behavior.

At other times Gene would find Graham's twin brother Dale engaged in the same peculiar diversions when he arrived, though they never acted out in such a way if the other was there to witness it. Both brothers were preoccupied with some kind of suspicion; as they would each, in private, ask Gene if he had seen his brother "doing anything out of the ordinary." The young boy's reply was always the same, "nope" he would lie.

One day when Gene arrived looking for Graham he happened upon the two brothers on their porch with a third man in a fancy suit. Dale and the man in the suit sat facing Graham who was also seated. Between them was a small table with papers, arranged in stacks covering its surface. Small river rocks were being used as paperweights. They seemed to be arguing rather heatedly.

Gene caught Graham's eye and he got up to leave. This seemed to antagonize the man in the suit who immediately began shouting and poking holes in the air with his finger. Graham answered by turning the table over. Freed from the rocks, all of the papers took flight in the stiff summer breeze and Gene resisted the urge to laugh as Dale and the loud man frantically poured off the porch and chased down as many of the documents as they could. Graham and Gene walked toward the river as the paper chasers blasphemed loudly.

* * *

The next day the twin brothers showed up on Marshall's doorstep hoping he would settle their disagreement. Each one seemed to expect the old man to take their part and Gene was anxious to see on which side of the fence his grandfather would pitch his tent. While Marshall was mulling it over, he exiled Gene to the woods. It was not unusual for him to be sent away while the adults talked about adult things, and he had, up till now, considered it a blessing. This time, however, his curiosity was undeniable. He walked into the forest at a jaunty pace as though he was off on a lark, then he doubled around and stole back in sight of the house.

The three men had disappeared. He waited. Soon enough, Graham and Dale walked out of the house. Dale was carrying a bushel basket, presumably to gather some corn from the garden. Marshall called Graham back to him and gave him the double-barreled shotgun he kept over the mantle. It was a puzzling thing for his grandfather to do.

Gene thought if they were headed for the garden maybe he should pay a visit to the outhouse. The outhouse stood on the edge of a small gully across the road from the garden. The door faced the garden and stood not very many feet from the nearest stalks of corn. He wondered if anyone could begrudge him a trip to the outhouse. He circled down to the gully, following the tree line, and then he dipped down into the hollow and crept up beside the outhouse. With a quick, silent movement, he was safely inside.

1932

The Woolworth wasn't very crowded. Most people couldn't afford anything that wasn't home-sown or hand-grown. Gene had grown into a stout young man, with fierce blue eyes and a long face with a prominent jaw. He offered a toy bow and arrow set, along with a sign on a chain that said "OPEN" to the cashier. She looked at him rather dubiously and rang up the total.

He walked across the street and into the barbershop. It was the first shave and haircut he had ever paid for. The barber was the brother of his best friend, Rube Norville. His name was Jesse and they got on pretty well. Gene sat down afterwards and started reading the paper. When business slowed down Jesse asked if Gene would look after the place while he went to flirt with the cashier across the street.

"Alright if I use the phone?" he asked.

"Sure thing buddy, just ask for it and if anybody comes in for a haircut, holler."

"Take your time," Gene said.

"Good of you," Jesse said as he was leaving, "no long distance now."

Gene gave him a thumbs-up through the glass. He walked over by the mirrors where a hole the size of a man's head had been knocked in the brick wall. "Jesse needs the phone," he shouted into the pharmacy next door. A hand appeared through the wall with a phone in it. He took the phone and walked as far away from the hole in the wall as the cord would allow. He wrapped on the receiver a few times.

"Denise, this is Mr. Helm, the're letting me use the phone over here at the Pharmacy. Get me the Cash'N'Carry," said Gene.

"Cash'N'Carry…" a voice said.

"Hello, Mr. Helm here. I need twenty-five hundred pounds of sugar delivered to my store right away."

"I'm sorry sir, but all of our trucks have already went out for today," said the voice apologetically.

"Listen son, that ain't going to do at all. I've *got* to have that sugar ready before Monday morning," Gene commanded.

"What if we brought it tomorrow morning?"

"No, I can't have that. There's nobody I trust minding the store on Saturdays. How about Sunday?"

"I thought you were closed on Sundays," the man asked.

"Can't afford to be closed these days, not if there's a chance we might make a penny. It's only the most vigilant that'll survive these trying times. Remember that and you might go far son."

"Yes sir," the voice said obediently, "we'll have a truck by. Expect it around eleven O'clock Sunday morning."

"Don't be late," Gene said and hung up.

* * *

Gene walked up to the door of Helm's General Store Sunday morning. There was a picture window to either side of the door. In the window on the right hung a sign on a chain with the message, "Closed" on it. He peeked in through the window and saw no one. The young man walked around to the back of the building carrying a sack in his right hand. He stopped in front of a small shed with a padlock securing its door. Gene produced a pair of bolt cutters from the sack and cut the lock. He opened the door and moved the debris inside to the back of the room. He then locked the door with a padlock he retrieved from his bag.

He stopped on the way back around to the front of the store, and inspected a barrel where they burned the refuse from the store. He took a toy arrow, with a suc-tion cup for an arrowhead, out of the bag, along with a wooden sign on a chain. He broke the arrow about three inches from the suction cup. He tossed the tail-end of the arrow in the barrel. The bag and all it contained followed. He went back to the picture window, spit on the suction cup and stuck it to the glass. He hung a sign on it that read, "OPEN". The sign hung directly on the opposite side of the glass as the "CLOSED" sign, thereby obstructing its appearance.

He waited. It was well past eleven when he heard three pistol shots ring out in loud succession. He watched the road while he walked out to the gas pump. As a two and a half ton truck came into view on the dusty highway, Gene was hoisting a large, heavy, metal trashcan. He walked out toward the barrel as the truck pulled up. A greasy driver stepped out of the cab with a clipboard in his hand.

"You a new man?" the driver asked.

"Yes sir, I was just taking the trash out," Gene replied.

"Well I got a load of sugar for you, just make your mark right here," the driver instructed as he indicated a dotted yellow line. "Where do you want it?" he asked.

"The old man wants it in the outbuilding," Gene replied, pointing to the shed.

The driver backed the truck up to within ten feet of the shed door. He got out and opened the doors on the back of the truck. Twenty-five huge bags sat in the back of the truck. The driver got out and waited by the door while Gene fumbled with a huge ring of numbered keys. At last selecting "#7" he opened the padlock and the driver began unloading the truck. With the sugar securely locked away in the shed, the driver started walking around to the front of the store.

"Where you going?" Gene asked.

"Are you kidding? I'm hot as blazes. I want to buy me a cold drink," the driver said.

"Well you ain't going to do that here. We got hit pretty hard yesterday and everybody and their brother wanted a drink as they walked by on their way to church this morning. We're plum cleaned out."

"I'll be damned," the driver exclaimed.

"Not necessarily, you might find salvation at the store about a mile and a half closer to town. It's called Westall's and you might want to try'em. I got a notion the're open."

"I'll do that. You take care now," and with that, the driver climbed back into the cab and the truck lumbered out of sight.

Gene walked over to the barrel, reached down into it, and into the paper bag. He took out a baby food jar and poured the gasoline it contained into the barrel. He dropped a match in the barrel and soon a plume of smoke was rising above. He waited a couple of minutes and another truck pulled into the lot. The man at the wheel looked four-thirds Irish with his red hair, freckled skin, and emerald eyes. When he said, "How'd it go?" however, it was with the same strange drawl as Gene.

"Zactly as I prophesied," Gene replied as he tossed the key ring up through the open window of the truck.

The man in the truck fumbled with the keys. "Which one is it?" he asked.

"They all are," Gene said, "twelve exact copies."

"Well take the sign down and give me a hand," the man said.

"Nothing doing," said Gene as he turned to walk away, "I took all the risk. It's my face he saw, not yours, and I'm going to keep a look out while you do all the heavy lifting." The man leaned far out the window and shouted after Gene, "You're a real son-of-a-bitch, you know that?"

He could faintly hear Gene reply, "and you're another."

The man sweating over the hundred pounds sacks of sugar was Rube Norville. He had borrowed the truck from a lumberyard and hoped he could get it back before anyone found out. He had been Gene's most loyal cohort for years. Though he never had any schemes of his own, Rube was always game for any enterprise Gene could dream up. In their young lives the two of them had gotten to know the County

Sheriff all too well. They dared not move about town together of late, as it always drew the suspicion of the townsfolk and the Sheriff rode in on the heels of that suspicion.

Rube pulled the truck around to the front of the store and picked up Gene. They headed back toward the mountains with the ill-gotten sweets weighing the shocks down to an all time low. Every wallow, rut, and mud hole seemed hell-bent to turn the top-heavy vehicle onto its side. A dozen times Gene cursed Rube and threatened to break his neck if he didn't slow down. Just as often Rube caused Gene's face to go a pasty white as he jerked the truck around a curve where the roadside fell away at a sheer ninety-degrees for more than a hundred yards. All Gene could do is stare down at the treetops below and try to swallow his heart back down into his chest.

Finally they reached the side road they were destined for. It was actually little more than a dear run, but Rube took the truck down it as if it were a landing strip. Leaves and twigs beat the windshield without mercy, obscuring all vision. The wheels seemed on the verge of ripping out from under the truck as they ran over what felt like huge logs. The large upper boughs of the trees they were passing were crashing into the cargo box of the truck. The sound of their impacts had a very destructive quality, as if the truck were being demolished with them in it.

They were both being thrown around the cab in every possible direction. Rube's grip on the steering wheel was the only thing keeping him on the driver's side. While Gene screamed and casted about for an anchor, Rube laughed hysterically. At one turn he was thrown into Rube's lap on the driver's side. He seized the moment and the steering wheel, standing up with both feet on the brake.

The truck shuddered and slid to a halt. "What's the big idea?" Rube belowed. As he opened the door to step down out of the truck, Gene gave him a shove that left him falling on his backside down below. As Gene dismounted, he trod on Rube's knuckles. He jerked his hand away from the truck where he'd been trying to pull himself back up onto his feet. Gene stepped lightly around to the tailgate.

"Damn you, you hard-hearted son-of-a-bitch!" Rube shouted through the painful digits he held to his lips.

"You're the one was trying to get us killed. Let that be a lesson to you." He walked back to the truck and opened the roll top door. Sacks of sugar were strewn everywhere and sunlight streamed in through holes recently tore in the cargo box. Gene climbed in and started dragging the sacks toward the tailgate. Rube joined him with his face and hands scratched to a bloody mess, "You've ruined my humor, Gene."

"Good, maybe I'll live to see the sun set on me!" Gene shouted. "I swear you've got the most dangerous sense of humor I've ever seen."

"Just having a little fun. No harm done," Rube said apologetically.

"Listen to me now you dirty old cobb, there's plenty of harm been done, and there's going to be no denying it when we try to get this rig back up to the road. We'll be lucky if we ever do get it back to that lumber yard."

Gene threw a sack of sugar over his shoulder and marched down the path. He never looked back, but he could sense Rube toting a sack about thirty feet behind him. Soon the path had dwindled into nothing and they were wandering through a thick wilderness. The land sloped off gradually in a saddle between two ridgelines and at it's lowest a deeply rutted rivulet of water barred their way. Gene skirted it until he found a felled tree that would serve as a bridge across the small chasm.

"Take care, she's awful slick and I ain't about to drag you out of the mud." The hardwoods slowly thinned out as they ascended the slope on the other side and soon they came to an outcropping of rock dominated by a grove of scrub pines. The ground was level and where it butted up against the steep slope of the mountain a few mammoth white pines towered over them.

Between the trunks of the white pines there was a contraption covered with burlap. Gene dropped his sack and removed the burlap from the object. A kettle and a coil fashioned out of copper gleamed in the slanting rays of the sun. They were connected to an old washing tub suspended over a fire pit. Gene smiled proudly at it. "Our fortune's made," he said. Rube dropped his sack of sugar while Gene covered the apparatus. A dozen trips later found them toting the last sacks up to the ledge while the sun set behind a ridge on the other side of the valley that spread out beneath them.

"There's a copperhead coiled up here. Give him a wide berth," Gene said as they both veered around a snake as shiny as their still. They dropped the final sacks of sugar and Gene covered the pile with a tarp and some burlap. It was a good location. They were invisible to the valley below, but they could look out over the edge whenever they wished and see any cars winding their way up the mountain. When there was little or no wind the boughs of the white pines dispersed the smoke from their fires into a wispy inconspicuous mist.

Gene took a few minutes to rest. He was pleased with himself. He knew there was still a lot of work ahead of them this night. Getting the truck back up to the main road would mean practically building a road back to it, in the dark, with shovel and axe. When they finally got back to Rube's house, they were both exhausted. The roosters had been crowing for over an hour and most of the family was already out in the fields, which meant a rare luxury, as each of the men got a bed to themselves, where they slept the day away.

He awoke in the late afternoon knowing there was little chance of him getting any sleep that night. The only thing for it, he thought, would be to grab a horse, collect Rube and sweep into town for a big raging drunk. Rube was certainly enthusiastic regarding a night's mischief and told Gene he had a line on some corn crops he could bring up the mountain for a certain number of gallons in return. "I told the man corn's better from the jar and damn if he didn't fall right in line!" Rube bellowed at the pool hall what seemed to Gene like one too many times. Most of the patrons who overheard just laughed and gave Rube a good natured smack on the back, but you never really know who's listening in a room when it's spinning like that.

Gene wondered if the sheriff knew they were in town. He had probably heard about the sugar heist by now, and any fool would have known what the sugar was for.

Gene awoke in the alley behind the pool hall the next morning. He was terribly sore and his head was pounding maniacally. The horse was gone from where it had been tethered the evening before. Rube must have ridden it back to Walkertown already. This meant a long walk for Gene. He wandered out of the alley and onto the Morganton sidewalks. He walked by the Courthouse, pausing to inspect a corner of the grounds where he had brought flowers with his uncle every week since Marshall had been his guardian, God knows why.

A thick blanket of innocent looking clouds hid the sun, but seeing all the papers on the doorsteps of town, with none yet collected, convinced Gene it was nearly seven AM. He picked up one of the newspapers, and as he walked he took a look at the front page.

SUGAR SWINDLED!

At approximately four in the afternoon, this past Friday, an order was placed with the local Cash & Carry. The order was presumably phoned in by the owner of Helm's General Store for the delivery of 2,500 lbs of sugar to be delivered to his business on highway 18. A man posing as an employee of said establishment took delivery of the shipment and then transported it off the premises. The sheriff thinks the purloining of this sugar may be related to the short-term theft of a two and a half-ton truck owned by the J. Mills Lumber Yard. The truck went missing during the hours necessary to transport the sugar from the scene of the crime. It was then returned, by persons unknown, to the lumberyard in the dead of night. The truck was vandalized slightly and the cargo area contained traces of sugar. Anyone with any information regarding either crime should report it immediately to the sheriff's office in the Courthouse. A reward for the return of the sugar is being offered.

As he walked with his nose buried in the paper he collided into a couple of men walking the opposite direction on the sidewalk. "Excuse me," he slurred. He took another few steps and looked back at the men he had crashed between. One was wearing a khaki police uniform and the other turned to look hatefully back at the clumsy oaf who had blundered into them. Gene felt a sudden sensation of vertigo. He recognized the offendedman as the truck driver who had delivered the sugar. The man's look of outrage changed instantly to a look of puzzlement. He turned his head to the front again, but his brisk pace began to falter.

Gene took the moment of uncertainty to duck down a narrow alley. He hadn't realized until now that he was still extremely drunk from the night before. He crashed into some trash a sober man might easily have avoided. As he came around a corner beside the building he noticed a wrought iron ladder leading to the roof and wasted no time mounting it. He climbed over the edge as the sound of hurried footsteps from the alley below met his ears. "You check down that way, I'll take a look on the roof," he heard a man say. He looked for a place to hide but saw none.

The sheriff's head popped up over the side. He saw nothing but an empty roof and slid down the side rails of the ladder to the ground below. Gene was lying on his side, pressed against the three-foot wall surrounding the roof, just under the ladder itself.

The sounds of the men below died away after a few minutes and he began to wonder when it would be safe to come down from the roof. If he stayed till nightfall it would be a long, hot day on that roof with no food or water. His stomach was already lurching as it begged for something to wash the alcohol from it. He decided to bide his time as long as possible. Ten minutes passed and half-a-dozen voices could be heard, making a thorough search of the grounds below. Though he feared it, none mounted the ladder.

The men dispersed and minutes spread into hours without any provocation. The old timers with nothing better to do than sit on a porch and swat at flies had probably been alerted by now. They would be watching the roads going out of town, waiting for a chance at the reward. Gene arose and spied the rooftops around him. It was coming up on midday then and he saw the movie house a couple of blocks away. The matinees would be starting soon. It seemed a likely place for the police to come looking for him, but what the hell, he thought. He crept down the ladder and walked nonchalantly over to the ticket window.

Inside he bought candy, popcorn, and several coca-colas. His grandfather allowed him some money for the month. It was now the third and he had just spent the last of it. The sugar had to pay off. Even though it was early, and a weekday, the theatre was half filled with people out of work who had managed somehow to escape the dreadful world outside and spend a little time in the fantasy world within. He wondered how many had snuck in. During the cartoons the sheriff walked in and shined a flashlight around in peoples faces. Gene didn't show his alarm as he hoped only the driver could identify him. After a painful glare the official disappeared and the feature started.

The picture was about a very poor man (as Gene knew most men were) who fell in love with a blind flower girl and ended up going to prison financing the operation that would allow her to see again. It was the most wonderful thing Gene had ever seen and he had no idea why. He sat through the film four times and slowly began to wonder if it was dark outside yet. He crept to the rear exit. When he cracked the door open someone flung it open wildly from the outside. Gene staggered back and tried to turn and run, but he just fell over himself. As he picked himself up off the floor, a half dozen snot-nosed kids ran by him and separated through the dark theater. As he left he heard an usher shouting threats at the crashers.

It was a moonless night and it looked as if the young man might make it back to Walkertown after all. He slinked through some back streets as he tried to avoid the barking dogs of the darkened town. As he passed a narrow side street he heard a voice ring out, "Hey, hold up there," he walked on as though he had heard nothing.

As soon as he was out of the man's line of sight he broke into a sprint. He heard the man behind him shouting for help and asking everyone in earshot to "stop that man." It was difficult to know how much of it was enhanced by his own hysteria, but Gene seemed to hear a few, then many people join in the pursuit, all shouting war cries of their own. The ruckus they raised upset every last dog in town with each one trying to outdo the other on all fronts, growling, barking, and howling. Gene ran between a few houses, across somebody's yard, back onto the street, and then jumped what looked like a fence in the pitch of night.

He floated through the blackness of space for what seemed far too long. His right foot hit a rough, rocky, and pitched surface. The rest of his body crashed to earth. He felt as if he had been ran through a cheese grater. He tried to suppress the inclination to cry and moan over his injuries. He heard voices above him and saw the lights of lanterns and flashlight beams. He could tell now that what he had thought was a fence had actually been the guardrail of a bridge some forty feet above. His head was still ringing from his impact with the ground when he noticed a light coming closer. It was a locomotive illuminating the slope on which he sat. He had landed on the railway, not directly on the crossties, but on the built up sloping gravel that supported them.

He heard cries from above as the light of the train engine revealed his location. Members of the small mob thus assembled on the bridge began to descend into the ravine, but the barbs of a dense thicket of blackberry bushes barred their progress. Gene staggered to his feet and realized one was damaged far too badly to flee upon. The sound of the train now penetrated the buzzing in his head and the boxcars slowly lurched past. He hobbled a bit closer and caught hold of a ladder. The lights of his pursuers began to ebb off into the distance as he struggled painfully up the side of the car.

It was an open topped car and when he came over the lip of it, he found that it was filled with coal. He stretched out in the middle of the coal and wallowed out a little nest where he could lie back. The train picked up speed and he could feel the cool night air whip over him as the locomotive beneath him shimmied and clanked. His wounds kept him awake for the better part of an hour as they slowly settled into a numb throbbing sensation. He stared up into the night sky with his hands beneath his head, shortly before dozing off, there was a flurry of shooting stars in the night sky, then he was adrift.

* * *

Gene was alone in the outhouse. The boards of the small building were assembled with little care, allowing long lines of sunlight to penetrate between them. The boy aligned an eye with one such crack and watched his cousin Dale gather ears of corn. Graham walked along behind him in the row, arguing heatedly with his brother.

"I'll tell you what I'll do, Dale: I'll let you have everything else, and I'll just take that small plot of land out beside the house."

Dale turned and shook an ear of corn in Graham's face, "Not as long as God's my witness will you have that land, nor the cookin' pot full of gold what's buried in it," he said.

Graham snatched the ear away and slammed it into the bushel basket contemptuously, "You just better hope God's not been a witness to the things you've done, dear brother of mine."

"Just see here now," Dale said, "I'm not the one who skipped out of town and lived like an animal these past how many years. I've been here taking care of business while you've been off gallivanting to who knows where, doing who knows what."

Graham's voice took on a murderous tone, "I'll only tell you this once: sell your soap to somebody who'll buy, because I'm the one person knows that don't wash."

"Just what are you getting..." Dale began to say, but his question was interrupted with a violent slap that turned the left side of his face a brilliant scarlet.

"I never intended to repeat myself, and don't look for me to," Graham said as he seemed to tower over his brother.

Dale cradled his face with his hand and gave Graham a scared look. "What in the hell did you do that for?" he asked. He was answered with the impact of Graham's palm on the side of his skull. The basket tumbled out of his hands, and his face turned a fiery hue. Graham grabbed him by the collar. Tears of rage were in his eyes as he screamed in Dale's face from only inches away. "You raped her!" He let go and said slowly, with desperation, "You met me after she walked away. You slipped me a Mickey. You locked me up in the pig sty." He paused and looked down at the shotgun in his hands. He felt like his grip might squeeze it in two. He looked into Dale's eyes and spoke deliberately, saying, "Then you cut your hair to look like me, and you met Julia at the appointed time," he gave a side long glance in contemplation, "I suppose you eavesdropped on us before you knocked me out. You gave her some of that drugged gin, and then you had your fun. When I woke up in the morning, you were long gone on the first train to an enlistment station. I was damn near lynched; had to leave town, and when you call me back, it's so's you can blow my brains out and leave me at the bottom of the river."

Dale interjected nervously, "Now look here Graham, you've got some crazy ideas and I don't know how they got in your head, but..."

"You'll not be having that gold... nor another breath of air." Graham said as he pulled one of the hammers back on the shotgun and spun the barrel up toward Dale. His brother caught the end of the barrel with his palm and pushed it away from his body before it went off, ripping off two of his fingers, along with the knuckles. He felt a dull throbbing sensation coming down the length of his left arm, as he held tight to the shotgun.

The door of the outhouse slammed open and Gene ran toward the Garden screaming, "Daddy!" Graham turned toward the child, and while he was distracted Dale reached behind his back, producing a revolver from inside his shirttail. Graham saw the pistol as it was being brought to bear and in one quick motion he jerked the shotgun out of Dale's injured hand, back pedaled a few feet, pulled back the hammer and pulled the trigger, with the gun leveled at his brother. It made a loud click and Graham realized he had tried to fire the same barrel a second time. Dale's pistol fired. A bullet tore through Graham's liver and came out his back. The searing pain shot up his torso like a freight train, but he managed to pull the hammer back on the right barrel this time, and he and his brother traded lead one more time. Graham fell through a couple of rows of corn, laying some stalks to rest under his body. Dale took two steps backward, on his heels, with the impact of the buckshot. He came to rest hanging in the twine brace where the string beans climbed. Gene stood between the two of them and looked back and forth at them. A scarecrow looked down on the scene judiciously. Gene looked up in the sky as it filled with crows until they blotted out the sun.

* * *

Gene jerked out of his troubled sleep with a great jolt, sitting bolt upright in bed. He looked around; he was back at the work farm. His best friend since he went up the river was sitting at the end of the pallet beside him. As his friend examined a hole in his boot, he said, "Cows are in the corn."

"What?" Gene asked in dismay.

The man put his boot on and pointed to the cage where a boss was going through the convicts' mail, taking most of the food or tobacco for himself and leaving just enough for the prisoner to keep him from writing and telling his family not to send anymore. "Oh that", said Gene, "what else is new?" With a since of relief that only he knew the nature of his dreams, Gene got out of bed and started wrapping his feet in worn, dirty cloth. It was freezing in the bunkhouse and there was a foot of snow on the ground outside. He was told that the work detail for the day was clearing snow from the main thoroughfare in town. He pulled his shoes over his now bandaged feet. They felt like ice.

Gene and the other men in his crew were shackled and loaded into the back of a truck. His friend's name was Jimmy, he was from Burke County as well. They were now both part of a chain gang some hundred and fifty miles away. Gene couldn't have picked a better friend; Jimmy was well respected amongst all of the prisoners. He was a bank robber with a two-year sentence and a hundred stories about blowing up safes, blowing all the cash in a speak-easy, and blowing into the next town to look for the next safe. Dale had a ten-month sentence for the theft of the sugar. Such a crime seemed wishy-washy to the other convicts. Then Jimmy found out they grew up in the same area. Jimmy took up for Gene's cause, and it made a world of difference.

As the truck slogged along through the snow, Gene's feet felt the cold like a thousand needles. He looked at the pile of shovels lying piled up in the floor. "I don't feel like I can take a day of shoveling snow," he said. "Well you can just tell the road-boss that when we stop," an old timer sneered back at him. "What if we's to throw all the shovels out the back of the truck now?" Gene watched every eye turn toward him as he spoke, "I mean: we can't shovel snow without shovels, and they won't find them till the snow melts."

Everyone looked at the mound shovels as if it were a great knot of rattlesnakes. Finally Jimmy picked up one and, with a glance at the cab of the truck, he pitched it out toward the ditch-line. Their fate was now sealed. Each man took a shovel, each one in turn, and followed suit.

When they returned to the bunkhouse that evening, their hands were covered in blisters and blood, they were also a sickly shade of blue. They stood in line waiting for dinner. It was some kind of watery gravy with great clumps of hardened flour, and something that looked suspiciously like grass clippings mixed in. The bowls at least warmed their hands. Gene was still reeling from the shock of how much snow and ice can be moved with the bare hands of a dozen men... at the point of a rifle.

Had it not been for the other men's fear of Jimmy, Gene would certainly have been the victim of a brutal beating. As it was, he only received contemptuous glares from the other men in the bunkhouse. The house-boss felt he knew who was behind the roadwork sabotage. Gene and Jimmy found themselves outside that night with hoes, trying to break the frozen ground of the yard-garden. They were chained to an iron piton at the edge of the garden. The house-boss watched the half-frozen men toil, as he sat beside a pot-bellied stove inside the bunkhouse.

The ground was hard as iron. As the men's hoes chipped away at the soil, they watched the warm red glow from the pot-bellied stove with jealous eyes. To get his mind off the cold, Gene asked Jimmy to tell him about the last bank he knocked over; the one he got sent up for. Gene had heard the story a hundred times, the knocked out security guard, the high speed chase, the tommy-guns blowing out Jimmy's tires, and the bloodhounds tracking him down; all the details were fresh in his memory. None-the-less, he wanted to hear the story.

Jimmy looked around the yard. "Alright," he said, "I'll tell you how I got sent up for robbing a bank." Gene could tell that this would not be the story he was so familiar with. Jimmy's manner and choice of words lacked the bravado he was known for.

"I got a job working at the Connelly Springs Savings and Loan," he said. "I was an accountant. Every day I watched the money come in and go out. There wasn't very much of it. In fact, I had to do everything that the owner couldn't. I was a teller, I negotiated loans, and I foreclosed on mortgages. I did whatever had to be done. One Friday the boss left early and told me he wouldn't be back until Tuesday. I closed up that afternoon and took all of the cash out of the bank. With the money in a satchel I got a train ticket for Atlanta. I made away with less than five hundred dollars.

"I ran through the money lickity-split down yonder. I got me an apartment and I found a place where I could get gin, women, and poker six nights t'week. When the money ran out I really ended up in a pinch. My bills kept piling up til' one day I got stopped in the street. Some small-timers dragged me into the alley and beat me to a bloody pulp. I just stayed in the garbage where they dropped me for an hour or so, and then I dragged myself back up to my room.

"The door to my place had a bunch of notices on it, little scraps of paper of ever color. The electric company gave notice they were shutting the power off, ma bell cut the phone service, the latest one was from the landlord who wanted me to clear out by the next morning. I looked at all the bills and notices, all the carpet tacks, and all the colorful scraps of paper, and then I went in and closed the door. I was trapped. I had no where to stay, not a friend in the world, I couldn't go back to my family where I was wanted for robbing a bank, and the goons working for that speak-easy had it in for me, I was ever'body's favorite dead-beat.

"I opened the oven. I turned on every gas fixture in the place and I stuffed a towel under the door. Then I flopped down on the mattress and waited for those nasty fumes to take me away from all my troubles. I woke up the next morning with the worst headache of my life. I got to my feet somehow and checked the gas fixtures, but they were still wide open, though no gas was coming through. I opened the door, and sure enough there was a pink slip from the gas company. 'Due to your failure in paying last month's balance, you're account has been suspended. Service will resume only when the balance is paid and a deposit of five dollars is rendered.'"

"Well sir, I walked right out of there and down to the police station. I told them who I was and what I'd done. So here I stand, blistered, malnourished, frostbitten, and exhausted, but I'm alive by-god, and I'll be staying that way until this place is just a memory. That's what you got to do Gene. Don't ever get so obsessed with something that you give up everything. Just think about that kind of a trade, ' something for everything', which would you rather have, something or everything?"

* * *

Marshall passed in the night and entered into the sleep of the just. Gene forewent the funeral service and paid his respects at the corner of the courthouse lawn instead. He stood over the soil where he and Marshall had deposited so many bouquets over so many years, Gene never knowing why. Without the money to leave a bouquet, Gene left only two red carnations, dropping one for the sake of tradition, and the other, some minutes later, in honor of his fallen patriarch. Marshall had lived to the ripe old age of seventy-nine, Gene was now twenty-two, and he wondered if he would see as many years.

He walked from the dead man's grave to the dead man's chimney. Along the way he thought of Marshall's advice, he thought also of what had happened to his father and uncle. He had a copy of the deed in his pocket, the acres were three, and they were his, but the gold could, and might very well, be buried across Walker Street as the dirt road was now called. The parcels of land on the other side of the lane had been left to relatives none-too friendly to an ex-convict. He was the bastard-son in his family and none of them would ever let him forget it. They would be particularly distrustful and contemptuous now that Marshall couldn't protect him. He would have to dig for the gold at night, when opportunity afforded it.

Arriving at his new property, he took a look around. The chimney growing out of the poke-salad appeared to be the only remnant of what was once a small cabin. Caleb's small ramshackle house sat next to a field across the street. Gene gazed about at all the real estate before him. "An iron cooking pot," he mumbled to himself. It would take him a lifetime to find it. He'd be working on the sly, in the dark, at only the safest moments, and he'd have to cover every trace of his attempts. He couldn't even dig up his own land without raising the suspicions of his neighbors. He couldn't even say how deep it was buried. Was it three feet down? Six feet? Or was the prize waiting for just one more year of erosion before it surfaced in a ditch somewhere?

"I knew it!" someone shouted behind Gene.

His reverie ended with a tremendous jolt. Rube had crept up on him from behind.

"What the hell are you trying to do, give me a heart-attack? And me not a month off the farm." As he spoke, he shoved Rube into the polk-salad where he fell on his rear. "I could have got five months instead of ten if I'd told them about you and that truck you stole."

Rube was laughing as he got to his feet. His clothes had purple splotches from the polk-salad berries. "I just came to welcome you home. I owed the county thirty days myself. Just got out yesterday when I heard you were back." Rube took a look around and asked what Gene was doing in the middle of the briars and weeds. "Marshall left this bit of land to me; reckon I'll try to throw some kind of house together on it."

Rube clapped his hand on Gene's shoulder and said, "What the hell's that got to do with an iron cooking pot?" Gene was frightened on the inside, but he never let it show.

"Yeah, I guess I should worry about some lumber first, huh?" Rube handed him a small bottle and replied, "Don't fret none. I know the feller runs the sawmill a few hollers off. If I get you a job down there he'll let you buy some old yeller pine real cheap." He gave Gene a nudge and said, "Keep in mind it ain't nothin' but knots, though I reckon that's why it's so cheap. Still yet, it'll make a house."

"What about the still?" Gene asked.

Rube took the bottle out of Gene's hand and emptied the last few swallows. "Don't worry," he said, "if we can only sell as much as we drink, we might scrape by."

1943

Working for the lumber mill was a torturous affair. Gene's hands were blistered into calloused skin tough as pig-iron. This however didn't keep the splinters out of his palms. The embedded slivers of wood turned green when not found and removed early. The green puss made them easy to find when it rose a few days after they entered the flesh. Even after the material was removed, the infection could lead to blood poisoning, and more than once Gene had to go to the Doctor with the veins running down his arms inflamed and swollen.

Doc Eden had died of grief shortly after the twins had gunned each other down, and the new, young Doctor in town owed Gene no favors. Any trip to his office set him back a few weeks pay. Between Rube and his other accomplices the still wasn't even keeping their own throats wet, much less providing an income. Prices had dropped tremendously with the end of prohibition, so that now Gene had to buy corn liquor from his competitors just to keep sobriety at bay.

Working at the mill was what he hated most. At any chance he would rather drive a team of mules than handle the old rough lumber at the mill. A sweltering day in July found him with a team pulling a few thirty-foot logs from a clear-cut back toward the mill, which lay a couple of miles off. As he drove the team and tried to keep the load dragging freely he came upon a Yellow Jacket's nest on the path they were to follow.

Rube and three other drivers were working their way along behind him. All things came to a stop and a moment later Gene heard Rube's voice shouting, "Get the lead out of your ass up there Gene!" He did as he was told, making sure the mules were carefully guided around the nest, as not to disturb it. Once they were clear, he dragged the logs roughshod over the nest entrance as brazenly as he could.

When the tips of the logs cleared the nest some thirty-odd feet behind, he could see that the insects had worked themselves into a small raging cloud. Then Rube's team reached the nest and his mules went into a frenzy of bucking and hawing. They broke harness and crashed into the woods as Rube ran in the opposite direction cursing and trying to beat the demonic little hornets off of him.

Gene made it back to the mill long before the other teams. He set his mules out and put away his harness and gear. Dark clouds had been on the rise and thunder resounded violently in the valley. He leaned up against the side of the mill. The work crew had already went home and the building was locked up, but he put his back against the wall and hoped the overhang of the eaves would protect him from the impending storm. Just as the clouds were ready to open up, the rest of the teams came in. Rube had murder in his eyes, but as he cracked his knuckles the clouds opened up and a torrential downpour descended.

Rube and the other three muleskinners went scrambling about for cover. There was a giant steel saw blade from the mill leaning against a nearby tree. It was so large that all four men were able to take refuge beneath it. As they cowered there and tried to stop up the hole in the middle of the blade with whatever was at hand, Gene walked over through the storm and leaned in to say, "You'uns better get yer asses out from under there. Lightnin' is liable'sta strike it and kill the whole mess of ya'."

Rube responded by giving Gene a shove with both hands. He sprawled back on the forest floor and when he rose to his feet he was covered over with the leaves, pine needles, and black earth that carpeted the area. He went running back to the mill and held his head over the water barrel so the run-off would wash the debris from his hair and the back of his neck. The thunder and lightning had increased to a pitch one rarely sees in a lifetime. It resounded from all directions indicating that the heart of the storm lay directly overhead.

Gene calmly walked over to the tool shed and removed a fifteen-pound sledge-hammer. He snuck out to the saw blade and stood behind it. They had stuffed the center hole in the giant metal disc with handkerchiefs. He brought back the heavy maul and swung into the blade with all his might. A moment before the head of the hammer reached its destination a flash of lightning and peel of thunder broke the atmosphere so close by, that it made Gene's heart flutter. With no delay whatsoever, the hammer then crashed into the blade. The metal vibrated and produced a ca-cophonous sound that completely enveloped its residents.

It took a few moments for Gene to notice any reaction at all from the blade's inhabitants. Then, one by one, they came out stumbling blindly, half bent over with their hands on their stomachs. Each in turn, walked awkwardly a few steps and fell over in the now standing water. Gene walked over to Rube. He was pale and his eyes were dilated to an astounding diameter.

Before he could investigate further, hail started to rain down and Gene was forced to take cover. One of the other muleskinners was on his hands and knees vomiting into a puddle. Mothball size hail bounced off his back. Gene looked at the sledgehammer in his hands and decided to return it to the tool shed. He then took cover on the opposite side of the mill and while he listened to the deafening sound of the hail striking the roof, he watched the hail stones pile up and waited for the violence of the storm to recede.

After a couple of hours, when Gene knew that the storm would outlast the daylight, he was forced to go home. The hail had long ago transformed itself back to rain. He fought the dying of the light as he walked the twisting path back to his house. He had built a one-room shack onto the original chimney and hearth that adorned his small plot of land.

He turned the key in the padlock and removed the chain on his Z-frame door. The room was mostly empty, with just a few crates used as storage and a mattress on the floor. He started a fire in the hearth and adjusted the flu. He examined the ceiling and saw that it was indeed all shored up, without the slightest dampness to betray a leak. He lay down on the mattress and blew out the kerosene lamp. He thought about his foolish colleagues and laughed. He wondered if they knew he had been behind their trauma at the saw blade. As Rube lived not far down the dirt road, he supposed all would be revealed in the morning.

"A morning without work, a Sunday morning," he murmured as he dozed off.

* * *

His feet advanced down the dirt road that next morning. The sunlight played off the water in the mud holes. Though not yet midday, the heat was numbing. As he approached Rubes home, he could see a dozen or so children in the yard. They all had June bugs spinning a few feet above their heads at the end of colorful little strings. They were dressed in their Sunday best and overlooked by a young woman on the porch steps. She was wearing a large white hat and a book sat in her lap.

Gene recognized her as Rube's sister Francis, whom everyone called Frankie. Upon seeing Gene, she entered the small house and after a few moments reappeared. "He'll be about in a jiffy, Gene," she called to him as he entered the yard. A little girl ran up to Gene with a length of string and a struggling June bug. By the time he'd tied the tether to the metallic green beetle, Rube had joined him in the yard. Gene noticed Frankie eyeing him over the edge of the book held before her face. She quickly darted her eyes back to the text.

"We're going fishing, Frankie. I'll be back for supper," Rube exclaimed.

"Fishing without poles," his sister questioned sarcastically.

"We hide the poles down by the river so we don't have to carry them back and forth each time," Gene explained with a wink.

She looked back at the opened book and said, "Listen to this: '___ ____ ___ ___ ___ ___ ___. ___ ____ ___ _____ ___ ____ ____ ___ ____ ___ ___ ____ ____ ___

____ _____.'" After reading the passage aloud, she laughed and said, "Sounds like some of the stuff folks around here make."

"Oh really, who?" Gene asked.

"Certain people I could mention," she said.

The children had stopped paying attention to the insects circling their heads and were now looking at the two men. A single June bug pulled the string free from a distracted child and took to the sky with its thin blue streamer trailing behind. The little boy ran after the escapee shouting, and all the other children laughed and pointed. Rube grabbed Gene by the arm and pulled him along as they went down the road. Frankie gave a small wave, and smiling, went back to her book.

"You're sister's pretty," Gene said.

"No she isn't," Rube retorted, "but she'll make a damn fine wife and mother."

"Does she read a lot?"

"Hell yes, all the damn time, even when she's watching every brat in the neighborhood."

"Whose young'uns were those?"

"Well one was the Sheriff's, if you're so damn interested. Which is why the two of you should stop shooting off your mouth." Rube pulled out a twist of plug tobacco and took a bite off it. "What's wrong with you anyhow? Miss the farm already?"

"In one ear and out the other, them kids ain't gonna remember a word of that."

"That's easy for you to say, but I think my number's come up, Gene."

"You do seem nervous as a dog shitting razorblades. What the hell's got into you?" Rube stopped and, grabbing Gene by the shoulder, gave him a twist, so that they were facing. His voice broke with uncharacteristic inflection when he said, "I got struck by lightning yesterday." Gene could see Rube waiting for the surprise to register in his face.

"After you lit out for home," he said trying to clinch it and get the desired effect. Gene, with an effort, said, "Are you shitting me?"

"Hell no I ain't shitting you, Gene. It's just like you said, after you left, a bolt of lightning crashed down right on that saw blade we were under. My heart seized up and I was damn near done for."

Gene started walking again, saying, "You're pretty damn lucky. I'd say you've been picked out special to live through anything."

"Sure as hell ain't the way I see it," Rube replied, "The axe is falling right on my neck. I've got the mark. There's a big chalk 'X' written on my side, just like at the slaughterhouse."

"Well where the hell are we going, anyway?"

"How often you need to be told?"

"This is ridiculous", Gene complained, "If that gold mine had any promise there'd be no sense in them leaving it idle all these years."

"If they thought that, they would have collapsed the mine, but they didn't. They're planning on coming back to it one of these days."

"So in the meantime we're going to clean the place out?" Gene asked incredulously.

"What if we did find a big load of it, Rube? Is there even anybody that'd give us money for it? Ain't they gonna wonder where we got it?"

"Let's worry about getting it first. It ain't like we got any better prospects."

* * *

The mine was located on the side of a dirt highway. The road was cut into the side of a small rise of land, leaving a rough wall of rock on the shoulder. Into this wall of rock persons unknown had tunneled, seeking a yellow metal and not finding it. Abandoned for years, it was rumored to be the den of a panther, as well as a common place for fugitives to hide out from the law.

The two men made their way across a beautiful field littered with daisies. Here the June-bugs wheeled about unfettered, and the sunlight poured down through the boughs of yellow pine bordering the small meadow. The daisies seemed a million little fried eggs on stalks to Gene. They came to a ten foot embankment at the edge of the road and ducked down as a sputtering tractor lumbered by, leaving the taste of fine dust in their mouths. Then the conspirators scurried across the lane and pried loose the boarded up entrance to the mine.

Countless warnings of perilous danger and criminal prosecution were plastered across the boarded up mouth of the mine. Heedlessly, they shouldered their way in. Rube dropped a canvas duffle bag to the ground and assisted Gene in putting the barrier back in order. Soon only a few blades of sunlight were peeking in at the edges. Gene struck a wooden match on a loose rock that came up to their knees. In the light he could see that the rock had a healthy coating of guano. He lit a small lantern and dim light, along with the faint smell of kerosene, filled the entry-way.

"Let's get to it," Rube said as he took a bite of plug tobacco.

"After you," replied Gene, handing him the lantern.

Rube had hidden digging implements under the loose dirt at their feet, Gene took up an armful and followed him down the tunnel. It was roughly five feet wide by eight feet tall, though in a certain place large rocks had fallen from the ceiling. The rock pile blocked off half of the passage. In other places the excavation had taken a turn so that it skirted around a boulder, or inclined steeply for a few yards to bring the mine over the obstacle only to descend a roughly equal distance again. The tunnel was reinforced with timbers in some places, but they were old and many had crumbled to the ground to be partially covered with loose dirt from above.

In some places the walls crawled with primitive crickets. The creatures had long antenna that whipped around overhead like a sea of twitching hair. Whenever Rube brought the lantern to close, a myriad of the insects would leap away from it, many of which would land in his hair or fall down the neck of his shirt. Each time, Rube would calmly place the lantern on the ground, take a couple of steps back, and begin swatting, smacking, and shaking the loose ends of his shirt. Once the cursing and convulsing was over, and he felt that he was free of the vermin, they continued their slow advance.

The passage ended abruptly. There was a small stack of timbers on the floor of the tunnel, along with a broken lantern, a rusted out five gallon barrel, an enamel dipper, and some other artifacts. The last fifteen feet seemed to be bedrock. Gene couldn't believe any worthwhile machinery could have been brought this far, or that anyone had ever been crazy enough to blast in such an environment, yet here they were.

"Well, it was worth a try," Gene said with relief.

"We haven't tried yet," said Rube.

Gene indicated the solid rock wall before them, "We can't get through that with picks, and shovels."

"We can," Rube said, as he felt the bedrock with his right palm, "We can do it with sledgehammers, and with picks, and with mattocks, and with shovels, and with whatever it takes. More than all else, it'll take the will to do it."

"Rube, eight hours of going at this wall, might not give us more than a few inches. What's the point in it?"

"Can't you see that the fools give it up as they were just getting at the heart of it. You don't find no gold in loose dirt. It's in the bedrock. You've got to find a vein that's shot right through a crack in the granite."

"I don't think this is granite."

"You know what I mean."

"Maybe I do, but you ain't no prospector. The only gold you ever seen was in a whore's smile."

"You don't need to be a veteran if you've got the nose for it. My instincts are sharp, that's what counts."

"Didn't you set down on a rattlesnake once?" Rube hoisted the fifteen pound sledgehammer he'd been carrying, and shook it in Gene's face. "Are you gonna help me, or ain't ya?"

It was grueling work, pounding on the rock at the end of the mine shaft, but slowly the two men wore away the stone. Every Sunday they snuck out to the mine and hoped for something more than sweat and blisters. Gene gave up digging at night, and concentrated on Rube's scheme. It seemed just as unlikely, but at least he had a partner and an enthusiastic one at that. Every flicker of mica seemed like the uncovering of the motherload to Rube, and no matter how excited he was when he thought they had made their strike, he was only more fired up to find the real thing afterward. "It'll be just like that. Just you wait," he would say. "One little glimmer, then we bring the light close, and it'll be easy living, I'm telling you."

Gene rarely had to pitch in. He only took over when he thought Rube might be on the verge of working himself to death. Monday morning trips to the sawmill were becoming an ordeal. Rube could hardly be roused for work, and when he got to his team of mules, they drove him.

The summer months passed and, by late September, Gene had given up on finding anything but bat-shit in the mine. He went out of routine and seldom worked half as hard as Rube. He started thinking of it as a chance to get away from everyone and everything, instead of hunting deer, like his neighbors, he was after gold. He kept a bucket of fresh spring water handy, and usually had some potted beef sandwiches packed away in wax paper.

Gene held an old tin pocket watch up to the light. Inside the lid an engraving read, "To M.W., with love from J.W.". "You know it's seven-o-clock out there," Gene said. Rube continued to pound on the rock, slowly chipping it away. "We're gonna be late as hell getting' back." The slow, steady, sound of the hammer falling was Rube's only reply. "Fine, but I'm done. Ya hear me? No more for me." Gene grabbed a tin cup that hung on a string and dipped it in the water pail. He emptied the cup a few times and felt the cool water inside his hot stomach. He sat with his back against the wall of the tunnel. The duffle bag was empty and rolled up, serving Gene as a pillow.

He dozed while Rube doggedly assailed the stone between him and his dream. Gene woke with water soaking his trousers below the knee. He rolled to one side and repositioned the canvas under his head. "You've kicked the bucket, ya asshole." He murmured as he drifted back into his dreams. When he roused himself once again, the dull sound of the hammer had been replaced by the sharp strike of the pick. He slowly realized that he was wet all down the side of his body. He had been sleeping in a couple of inches of standing water.

Gene turned at once toward the pail of water. It was still standing upright and nearly full. He looked up at Rube. His neighbor was chipping away at the dry stone two feet in front of him, oblivious to the water lapping at his feet. A gasp of air filled Gene's lungs as he prepared to shout words he had not yet formulated in his mind. He never would.

* * *

The tractor lumbered along the road at the pace of a brisk walk. Monroe had done the work of twenty share croppers that day. The first cut in the hay was all taken care of now. His satisfaction was at it's zenith. The tractor was old, and it had been through a few hands, but none of them could have appreciated it as much as Monroe did that evening. The back of his neck itched, and there was a horsefly bound and determined to follow him all the way back to his house, but the tough old-timer didn't care one whit for those trifles. He followed the winding dirt road past a beautiful pond and down into the low country where he lived. The sun had already set, but the sky was still bright with it's last rays.

He rounded a corner. A small meadow was below him on the left. He saw some stones and dirt run down the embankment on his right. He shut down the tractor and started to step off of it. As his left foot touched the earth, he heard a dull roar.

A second later the old abandoned mine shaft exploded with water. The barrier that boarded it up turned into toothpicks and nails instantly. A huge geyser shot across the road in front of him and fifty feet into the meadow before it touched the ground. The sound of a crashing waterfall engulfed the area. The reverse gear on the tractor didn't work, so Monroe left it as it sat. At first he simply tried to put some distance between himself and the giant cataract of white water before him. Then he headed toward the closest farmhouse with a truck. He talked the farmer into driving to the nearest phone and calling the fire department.

* * *

Gene woke up choking and trying hard not to drown. When he finally stopped choking, he vomited a small amount of water. He felt as though he had been beaten half to death. When he tried to get to his feet, he decided that he *had* been beaten half to death. He was on his hands and knees with water up to his stomach. He appeared to be in some kind of shallow pond. Dead June bugs were floating in the water and a rabbit swam by. He turned over and sat in the water for a minute, trying to figure out where he was. There was a tractor parked on a road about a hundred feet away. The road just ahead of it was completely washed away, leaving a gap of twelve foot or so. Above the missing expanse of road was a hole pouring a torrent of water down into the gully. He slowly realized the water was coming from Rube's mine, and he was sitting in the meadow it faces.

He scanned the water for Rube, but he was nowhere in sight. Gene heard a siren approaching. He got to his feet and ran, but he was in pain and the water was tough going. He nestled up behind a brush pile where the water was less than a foot deep. He hid behind the brush and watched, as a moment later, the fire trucks and police cars arrived.

Old Monroe swarmed all over the scene as if he was King Saul and the authorities were lucky to have him coordinating their efforts. There wasn't very much for anyone to do for a while. It was a moonlit night, and the only thing they had really accomplished was to tow Monroe's tractor out of the way. The water in the field was down to a few swampy puddles now and Gene knew he could easily slip away in the dark. Something made him stay. It wasn't curiosity, he knew what had happened, much better even than those he spied on. Yet something made him linger. Finally, after a lot of arguing amongst the firemen, and with only a trickle of water coming out of the tunnel, the chief went in. He was gone for a few long minutes.

At long last, Gene could see the dim electric light that was perched on the front of the chiefs helmet. It floated in the mouth of the tunnel a few moments, then he stepped out into the arc of light cast from nearby headlights. Rube was in his arms. He was naked, and his body was twisted. The flesh on his right shoulder was broken and all the meat had been peeled from that arm down to the elbow, where it hung from him as if it were on a hook in a butcher's window. The sheriff helped get him into the back of a pickup truck where they rolled him up in a tarp. They sat with his body as all the other taillights disappeared around the corner. Finally the sheriff banged on the roof of the truck and the driver slipped away into the night.

Gene sat for a long time in the dark. He blamed himself for allowing Rube to pursue such a foolish cause. He knew of no way to dissuade him, none that worked. He had tried everything to talk him out of his scheme, but to no avail. The only thing he felt he could do was to be there in case anything went wrong. He thought if he was there to intercede when disaster struck, that Rube would come back to his senses and realize it wasn't worth it. Now Gene had to deliver the news to Frankie and hope she didn't tell anyone else about his involvement. He hated having to face her. If only he would have stayed awake. He'd never slept while they worked before, never. If he had grabbed Rube by the sleeve when he woke up wet the first time he could have got him out. He would have had time, he was sure of it. Softly, to none but himself, he said, "I thought he kicked the bucket."

1953

Gene sat on his screened in front porch. He was eased back in his rocking chair, with his feet resting on a milk crate. It was a hot August day and he aimed to do as little as possible in the midday sun. He heard the screen door slam open and his eyelids rolled back in his head to reveal a young boy screaming, "They're all over me; they're all over me!" The boy flailed his arms around his crew cut scalp, and Gene realized there were dozens of little yellow jacket hornets swarming all over the child. He jumped out of his seat and screamed, "Well don't bring them in the house!" Having said that he opened the screen door, gave the boy a shove and sent him tumbling backwards down the front steps.

A few minutes later the boy was back. One of his eyes was swollen shut and his lip was getting bigger by the second. He was soaking wet, as he came back in through the screen door. Gene was still swatting at a yellow jacket with his metal screen flyswat. He smacked the last hornet to the ground and stepped on it with his work boot. "How'd ya get shed of 'em?" he asked the boy.

"I jumped in the rain barrel."

Gene looked him over, and said, "Well that's a hell of a lot smarter than dragging a hundred of them into the house where we'll be trapped with them all night."

"Yes sir," the boy said.

Gene took his handkerchief out and dipped the edge of it in a coffee can near the chair. He rubbed some dark colored syrup on the boy's lip and then stuck the cloth to his eye. "R.C., if you can't stay out of bee's nests, you best get use to getting' stung. You hear me boy?" His son nodded. "Now you go on in and your momma will get you fixed up."

Gene went outside and walked around to the rain barrel. It had a few dead hornets floating in it, with one still alive, spinning in lazy circles under the power of one wing. Gene watched the soft ripples coming from the injured insect for a few minutes. The cicadas were loud in the trees and Gene wandered lazily to the edge of the woods. He walked out through the forest and crossed a small stream. When he reached the base of a ridge nearby he began to follow a small path worn in the ground.

There were dead pine boughs lining a steep section of the hillside, he pushed one to the side and stepped into a small hollow beneath a rock jutting out of the hill side. His still was nestled inside. It was the same basic apparatus he and Rube had put together so many years ago. A little mending and cleaning took place from time to time, but many of the components, most notably the copper coil, were exactly as they were twenty years before. He crept around, behind the still, and retrieved a two-by-one foot wooden crate. The crate was wet and mildewed.

* * *

Frankie seemed worried. "Are you sure you'll be okay?" she asked.

"I'll be fine. I know what I'm doing," Gene assured here.

Frankie led their children out the back door of the small shack and across the weed infested back yard to the edge of the woods. R.C. was the youngest. He was ten-years-old, with a crew cut and a lazy eye. His twelve-year-old sister Dana followed him. She had wispy blonde hair that came down to her shoulders. She carried a baby doll with sleepy time eyelids in her arms. Frankie and her two children stood at the edge of the woods. Gene disappeared back into the house. Less than a minute later there was a loud explosion that sent everyone's hands over their ears.

The house seemed to come up off the ground a good foot and crashed back down again. Dirt and debris blasted the doors and shutters open. Red clouds of dust streamed out of every egress and formed huge columns of exhaust, as it escaped the shuttering building. A minute later Gene stumbled out the back door coughing into his hand. He fell back and sat in the yard ringing his ears with the heels of his hands. The rock under the house was hardly scorched. Gene walked up to the wood line.

"Are you okay Daddy?" Dana asked.

He kneeled down and took the lid off the crate. R.C. caught his sister's eye and pointed to his ear. She nodded in agreement. Gene took a couple of blasting caps in his right hand and a couple of sticks of dynamite in his left. When he came back he was trailing a couple of wires. As he walked he spooled them off of a piece of broom handle. He stuck the sharpened end of the broom handle into the ground and went back to the house. Ten minutes of preparation, and he was ready. He sat next to his family and clamped one of the wires to a terminal on a car battery. Then he touched the other wire to the other terminal.

* * *

The additions to the house took weeks. Everyone helped digging out the base-ment. If the kids weren't at school, they were put to work. At night Gene ran his still and snuck around abandoned buildings and poorly guarded lumber yards, looking for materials. Dana had a bucket of rusty, bent nails that she beat back into shape with the back of hatchet, then deposited into a wooden box where her father got the nails to do his work. He threatened her with his belt if he ever reached in the box to find it empty. There was little to fear there; the box stayed full.

R.C. was the official digger. Everyone would dig in turn, but R.C. worked on it full time. When a huge rock was discovered and everyone was perplexed as to what to do with it, all work stopped. Dana had been sent to the store for flour. The rest of the family sat in the yard looking down into the partially dug basement where the boulder sat, some six feet tall and four feet wide.

"I could get more dynamite," Gene suggested.

"The house won't stand it," said Frankie.

"Can't it just be dragged out?" asked R.C.

"I can't see it," said Gene, "That thing probably weighs more'n a car."

They sat in silence for another twenty minutes just staring at the obstacle. Dana walked up the lane. She lingered at the old shack across the street where a distant relative was said to have lived. The windows were boarded up, but there were still two heavily worn grooves in the plank floor of the porch. They pointed out on a vacant lot not far from her own front yard. She skipped across the street and saw her family sitting and looking under the house. She walked down into the basement and came back out.

"What are we looking at?" she asked.

"A problem," her Father said, "How to get shed of that rock."

"Dig a hole beside it and slide it off into it," she said.

They all stopped staring at the rock and started staring at her. Gene took the shovel from his lap and held it out to R.C. The boy took the shovel and as he passed Dana, he muttered, "Thanks." Gene walked Dana into the house with the flour. As Frankie started rolling out biscuits, Gene sat Dana on the kitchen table and asked her what she wanted to be when she grew up.

"A Doctor," she said with conviction.

"Have you got the grades for it?" Gene asked.

"My Teacher says I do."

"Well you still got a long way to go."

"She'll do it," Frankie said, "no doubt in my mind, she'll be the one to do it."

"Doctors spend half their life in school," Gene said, "Whose gonna pay for that?"

"My Teacher says the smartest people don't have to pay for school."

"You might be the prettiest, but are you suppose to be the smartest too?" Gene asked.

"The smartest in my school, least that's what the teacher says. Only she says I ain't suppose to tell anybody she said that or it might cause trouble."

"I thought girls were suppose to be nurses."

"You don't get to do any operating if you're a nurse. I want to save lives, not take temperatures. There was a woman surgeon on 'Trauma Ward'."

"That's a radio show, little darlin," Gene said.

"Well I'll do it for real," she said confidently.

"I bet you will," Frankie said with a big grin as she wiped her hands on her apron.

Gene patted her on the head as he got up, put on a hat, and headed out the door. He walked out to the street and started winding his way toward the sawmill. He hadn't worked there in years, but he knew those that did. He arrived just at quitting time, and he met two of the young crew that did all of the most physical work, mostly moving materials.

"Remember me boys? Gene?"

The tall lanky one showed a spark of recognition before clasping Gene's shoulder and shaking his hand.

"Damned if I'll ever forget you," he said, nudging his friend, "I tell everybody, 'The best corn I ever had came out of a jar'."

"What's your name again?" Gene asked.

"I'm Jimmy and this here," he pointed to his co-worker, "is Mike."

"Nice to see you boys again," said Gene.

"Hell it's always a pleasure running into the candy-man," Jimmy said, "Have you got something for us?"

They sauntered around as they talked. Mike played the mute and chewed on a toothpick. Jimmy wore a big floppy "News-boy" cap. He reached back with his right hand and slipped the hat forward so the short brim came down over his eyes. They seemed to be walking toward an old Dodge sedan sitting at some distance from the mill.

"I might have something for you, but I need you to help me out," Gene said. "How much do you want?" asked Jimmy

"If you boys will help me set a few trusses I can part with a gallon," Gene said as they reached the car.

Mike opened the passenger door and said, "Get in."

As they made their way down the dusty road, Gene talked over his left shoulder to Jimmy who was in the backseat. "It ain't gonna be a half day's work," he told him.

"And we get a whole gallon; that's mighty white of you," Jimmy said dryly.

"Look, if your aiming to squeeze more than that out…"

"I ain't planning no such thing," Jimmy interrupted.

"It's a deal then?"

Jimmy nodded, then pointed with the butt of his cigarette at the back of Mike's head. "If you ever need somebody to run some for you, this here's the man to get."

Gene looked over at Mike and back at Jimmy, "Is that so?"

"That's so," Jimmy said, "Can't nobody outrun him, at least not on these kindsa roads."

"Nobody?" asked Gene.

"This car run's white-lightning' like greased-lightning, nothing can outrun it."

Gene looked over at Jimmy. "This is the car, is it?"

Mike rolled the toothpick in his mouth around for a few seconds, then said, "It's fast." Outside the window, a dozen black men on a chain gang were chopping away at kudzu as the car passed.

* * *

That Sunday the heat was stifling. The two young men helped Gene get the trusses up on the top of the addition. Dana sat in the grass with her doll. She was trying to sow a dress for the doll between errands that her Father called out to her. R.C. was walking around and around the black Dodge in the yard. When Jimmy and Mike were too busy to notice, he stuck his head in the rolled down window to give the wheel a turn back and forth.

"Dana-girl?" Gene shouted.

"Yes sir?" she shouted back.

"Get me an eight inch piece of two-by-four."

"I ain't got no ruler."

"Holy hell, when I was your age we didn't need no ruler. We'd use a goddamn stick."

She started digging through the sawdust and scrap at the saw-bucks, "Will this do?"

He looked down the ladder at the piece of board she was holding up. "How long is it?"

"A Goddamn stick-and-a-half," she said.

"Don't give me none of that back-sass," he shouted through everyone's laughter. "I'm too busy to stop what I'm doing right now, but I'm gonna bust that ass later!"

She went up a few rungs of the ladder and he snatched the piece of two-by-four out of her hand. Jimmy and Mike watched as she went and sat down under the shade tree.

Jimmy met Mike's eyes and gave him a wink.

"Looks like you've got your hands full with that one," Jimmy said.

"She thinks she's smart," Gene said, "but I think maybe she's a little too smart."

"Wait a while, it'll get worse," Jimmy said.

"Not if I can help it," Gene replied.

"You give them enough time, and girls'll bring a whole different kind of trouble down on your weary head."

"They do grow up fast," Gene said.

"Faster than you think," Mike said, with a wink to Jimmy.

* * *

Jo-Jo was the family dog. It was some kind of collie mix. Everyone liked the dog, but R.C. spent the most time with the creature. When the weather was hospitable R.C. would spend all of his time outside, even nights. Jo-Jo was always right by his side, but a couple of weeks before the work on the basement began, Jo-Jo disappeared. Then, just when the boy was burying that infernal rock beneath the basement floor, Jo-Jo came trotting down under the house for an emotional reunion.

She had been away to have her puppies and had just now came back. She whined and begged for R.C. to follow her and he did. He brought a giant, sealed mason jar of chicken bones he had been saving for her. They followed the highway for quite a while then went through the woods to an old wallowed out area beneath a big rock. There were six puppies and they squeaked and tottered around when their mother returned. R.C. promised Dana he would take her to see the puppies as soon as their father would agree to give them the time. He worked hard, and by the Wednesday after the trusses went up, he was finished with the digging. They left that morning.

* * *

Gene dragged a biscuit through the gravy of a Wednesday Supper, saying, "What's holding up those kids."

Frankie laid a couple of squares of wax paper over the children's plates. "I don't know what could be keeping them," she said.

"Did Jo-Jo have her puppies out-of-State?" he asked.

"I packed them some saltines and cheese for lunch, but here it is supper and they ain't no where in sight," she said as she held back the curtain.

"Knew if they came back before dark I'd put'em to work. That's what's…"

"Wait, here comes R.C. now," she said interrupting.

"What did I tell you?" Gene said with satisfaction, "probably been waiting just out of sight, for it to get dark, before he come dragging in."

R.C. busted in through the door and descended on his food, whipping the wax paper to one side. He had shoveled three big spoonfuls of pinto beans into his mouth before he looked up and saw his parents staring a hole through him.

"Guess it's too late for me to help out with the roof," he said.

Gene gave a wave of his hand, saying, "See. What did I tell you."

"Nothing surprises me anymore," Frankie replied as she cleared away Gene's plate.

"Well 'little-man's' gonna be surprised when I take him up on the roof after dinner."

R.C. looked up in disbelief, saying, "But it's too dark to…"

"There's a full moon tonight, and I ain't a bit tired," Gene interrupted.

Frankie met R.C.'s glance and said, "Don't look to me for help. Serves you right. Not only were you trying to sneak one by on us, but you let your sister fall behind. How many times' I told you to walk right with her."

"But momma, she's slow as molasses, besides, she got here before I did."

Gene and Frankie looked at R.C.. Gene cleared his throat and said, "She ain't got here yet."

"But them boys dropped her off, they wouldn't even stop for me but…"

"What boys?" Frankie interrupted.

"The ones that was helping daddy out on Sunday."

"You sure it was them?" Gene asked.

"Well, she was lagging behind and a car stopped and gave her a ride. They wouldn't stop for me, but it looked like their car."

Gene grabbed his hat and ran out the door. By the time he caught a ride and made it to the sheriff's office it was eleven-o-clock and the deputy didn't want to call the sheriff and wake him up.

"This is an emergency!" Gene shouted.

"How do you know she ain't out on a lark?" the man asked.

"She ain't never slept anywhere but her room; if she's sleeping somewhere else tonight, it's because someone is making her."

He finally got the sheriff on the phone. He told him all the details and the sheriff called the owner of the sawmill and soon the two of them were headed to Jimmy's house. When they arrived, Jimmy's mother told them that he hadn't been home and usually stayed out all night if he wasn't home by ten.

"Even on a Wednesday night?" the sheriff asked.

"Sometimes," said the woman

Mike wasn't home either. His car was gone and his neighbor said it had been gone all day. The sheriff tried to reassure Gene, telling him that if he gave her time, she would come back on her own.

"What if it was your daughter?" Gene asked.

"How do you mean?" the sheriff replied.

"Would that explanation be good enough?"

* * *

The next few days were pure hell. R.C. watched as his parents aged before his eyes. They had neither phone, nor car. The police said they would send someone over as soon as they knew anything. So Frankie and Gene waited, watching out the front windows for a car to pull up into their yard, and hopefully let their little girl out.

Finally it happened. That Saturday morning the sheriff's car stopped on the road and Gene ran out to the car. Dana didn't seem to recognize him. She acted feverish and looked pale, with sticks, leaves, and black earth polluting her matted hair. The sheriff got a tip that Jimmy and Mike had taken her out to where they went deer hunting. When they finally found the Dodge, and the hounds followed the scent to where they were hid out, Jimmy and Mike were passed out drunk. Dana had her arms around a tree with her hands tied together. She was naked and at first she was thought to be dead. "They had this with them," the sheriff said as he held up an empty gallon bottle Gene had given them full.

* * *

For three days Dana stayed in bed. The doctor came to see her, and told them how lucky they were that she was alive. He told them that she would never have children. No one could get her to talk. All she did was eat, sleep, listen to the radio, and play with her doll. After two weeks they sent her back to school. She did nothing the teacher asked her to do. She brushed her dolls hair until there wasn't hair left. They took her out of school and she would sit on the front steps of the house running a brush across her bald doll's head.

* * *

The courthouse was packed when the trial finally came up. The two defendants had not been able to raise their bail. Gene would have killed them if they had raised it. News of the crime had carried all over the county. It was the kind of crime everyone warned their children with. Dana had become a watch-word in the rural community. Although the girl couldn't testify against Jimmy and Mike, the jury was determined to condemn them after the overwhelming wealth of evidence had been brought to bear.

They were found guilty, but received only two-year sentences. Gene had to be restrained when the term was declared. No one knew who was in greater danger of Gene's wrath, the defendants, or the judge. Gene swore vengeance as the two men were led out of the courtroom. A deputy dragged Gene out onto the landing of the courthouse and made everyone else exit on the other side. When the crowds had dispersed, Gene went down the steps and pulled every flower out of the courthouse flower garden. The judge watched from a window above, but sent no one to interfere. Gene took the flowers to the corner of the courthouse lawn where Marshall had brought him when he was Dana's age.

Gene placed the flowers gently on the grass and got down on his knees. He prayed to God for vengeance, and for his daughter to come back to the person she once was, and for him to wake-up and discover it was all a nightmare. He prayed for anything that might take away the pain. Then he went through his pockets and found a five dollar bill that was suppose to buy sugar, lard, and salt, among other things. He held the bill out and looked at it. Suddenly a voice distracted him.

"Mr. Lackey?", a man asked.

"Yes?" Gene said numbly.

"I'm from the paper, sir, and I'd just like to get a few words from you about what happened today."

Another man held up a camera, saying, "Would you mind?"

"If you don't put that camera down I'll cave your skull in with it!"

The other man stepped between Gene and the camera. "Sir, the paper's on your side. We're ready to give you a platform where you can speak out against this travesty of justice."

"What the hell are you talking about?" Gene asked.

"Those bastards deserve life!" the reporter said trying to sound tough.

"I want them out as soon as possible," Gene replied.

The reporter looked puzzled. "Why?" he asked.

"So I can kill them."

"But…"

"You're wrong about them two," Gene told the reporter, "they don't deserve life, they deserve death." He then brushed between them and walked away.

"I'll just say, 'no comment', then?"

Gene walked with the five dollar bill wadded into a tight little ball in his right hand. He walked all the way across town without saying one word to anyone. He walked into the liquor store and up to the counter. Carefully, he flattened out the bill for the attendant.

1963

It was dark and the roads were muddy. A full moon reflected in the red puddles of standing water. Gene turned up the mason jar, but his lips felt nothing. He cast the jar into the ditch. He did not hear the sound of breaking glass which would have strangely satisfied him. It was raining. A cold, steady drizzle poured down and he felt the weight of his saturated clothes pulling at him.

Gene began to unburden himself. His boots were left behind. Soon his shirt and his trousers were gone as well. The numbness in his body encouraged him. Before he had gone much farther, he could feel the water pouring over his naked flesh. The world around him seemed to be kicking and bucking. Walking was a labor, and the terrain was hazy and alien. He concentrated all of his efforts on picking his porch light out of the darkness.

Like a moth he honed in on the dim light visible from the road. Mounting the porch, he felt around for the doorknob. As he tried to force his key into the deadbolt, the snarl of a dog could be heard to his left. Gene turned just as a large mongrel reared up and snapped at him. He caught the dog by the throat and they both fell on the slippery floor. The beast kicked, writhed, twisted, and jerked as Gene squeezed the breath out of him.

He could feel the windpipe collapsing under his thumbs. The entire world was spinning out of control and Gene pressed his grip all the tighter as if to anchor his position in the hell where he found himself.

* * *

Gene sat up in bed. Light was streaming through the window before him. His head seemed to be in a vise. When he drank, his dreams were vivid to the point of madness. Frankie walked into the room with a cup of steaming coffee. Age had not been kind to her, but her loyalty was unquestioned and unique.

"I thought I heard you stir," she said.

"I usually wait until I have my coffee, before I stir it," he said.

"These drunks you go on sure don't make you any funnier," she replied as she sat the coffee down.

He threw his legs off one side of the bed and rubbed his head. "Am I gonna be late?" he asked.

"You can't possibly be," she said, "the ice company's shut down."

"Hell, that's right. Slipped my mind," he said as he sipped the coffee.

He thought of all the times he had delivered ice to the ingrates of the area. They always wanted you to chip down the block so it would fit in non-standard ice-boxes. Many was the time he was cursed for leaving a trail of water through some-one's living room as if he could change the melting point to ninety-five degrees, just to spare them a little dribble of water on their floor.

"I won't miss it," he said.

"Well they just ain't no call for it anymore," said Frankie, "most folks have got them new 'lectric ice boxes now."

Gene made a gesture of futility with his raised hand while Frankie opened the drawer on the night stand and took out part of a newspaper. She placed it on the bed beside Gene. He picked it up. The want ads held little promise, though he poured over them nearly a dozen times. He put his overalls on and walked outside. The brick path in his yard felt warm and gentle on the soles of his bare feet. Next door, R.C. slid a can shaped portion of dog food from a dog food can. Jo-Jo ate it greedily.

Gene's son had built a house next door to his own. It was less ramshackle than the house Gene had built. R.C. was a foreman at "Southern Container," a pasteboard packaging company where he had been working for a couple of years. Most people liked R.C., but there were some who resented him for getting the foreman's job. There were many people who had worked at the factory for thirty years and didn't even get an interview. Most of those who did get an interview were College graduates. R.C. had not even been to High School.

Gene could get a job at "Southern Container" and, then again, he couldn't. How could he work under his own son? It was an impossible situation. He watched as R.C. cleared out of the drive way in his Pontiac. The only answer for Gene was to go back to the hosiery mill with the lint-heads. He was an experienced fixer and they needed people who could repair the troublesome machines associated with that industry.

* * *

The aging fellow couldn't remember what he'd been locked up for. He did remember drinking quite a bit of liquor with a friend of his the night before. It seemed like the two of them got into some kind of disagreement, but it was the vaguest of remembrances, without form or character. He sat in a holding cell at the County Jailhouse and watched a fierce-eyed, black rat, the largest he had ever seen, flit along the edge of the bars. There was a tin cup in the floor, he drank the luke-warm water from it and threw it with all his might at the rodent.

The cup missed the rat's head by an inch and bounced off the bars loudly. A few moments later a Deputy came in carrying a breakfast tray. He retrieved the cup and refilled it. He slid the tray under the bars in the cell door. The rat waddled over to the food and began sniffing it immediately.

"Can't anything be done about the rats," Gene shouted.

"What rats?" the jailer asked.

"The one eating my grits… right there at your feet," Gene implored, pointing at the creature.

"Oh, *that* rat. No, there's nothing to be done about him. He's your cell-mate. Do right by him and he'll do right by you," he said as he disappeared down the corridor.

Gene snatched the tray away from his cellmate and started eating. The rat stood his ground, never taking his beady, red eyes off of Gene. As he sat his empty tray on his bunk he heard indistinct voices coming down the corridor. R.C. entered the room with the jailer in tow. He whispered something in R.C.'s ear, unlocked the cell door and left.

"You see it?" Gene asked, pointing at the rat.

R.C. stomped at the bars where the rodent was skulking. R.C. watched as it ran and disappeared behind the toilet. "That got rid of him," he said. The young man swung the door open. "They said I could give you a ride back to the house, Pop." Gene stood up and pulled his overalls up to his chest. He took a gallous and clasped it over one shoulder, but batted at the other for a minute or two, cursing softly to himself. R.C. finally stepped in and helped him buckle it up. When Gene sat down in the Pontiac R.C. asked him to wait. He left, only to come back a minute later with a small, brown, paper bag.

R.C. sat behind the wheel and passed the bag to his father. "Take a drink," he said.

Gene took a drink from the small bottle wrapped in the bag. "Thanks," he said.

"You anxious to get home?" R.C. asked.

"Only as anxious as you are to get me there."

"Then we'll take our time," R.C. said as he dropped the car into gear.

"Can I ask you a question?"

"As many as you want."

"Why'd you give me a nearly empty bottle." Gene gave the article in question a shake.

"I was opening it for you and I spilled some."

"Don't lie to me boy."

A minute of silence crawled by before R.C. asked, "You mind if we pick up Doug?"

"Not a damn bit."

They stopped at the pawn shop where Doug worked. Doug had an odd, pudgy face on a tall thin body. He was wearing black pin-striped trousers that didn't reach his ankles while he held the matching jacket over a shoulder with one finger. It was a hot day and the t-shirt he was wearing had soaked through at the armpits. He lit his cigarette, pitched the match, and began rolling the pack up in his sleeve as they pulled up to the curb. His smile faded as he met Gene's gaze in the passenger side.

"Damn boy, you look like a hoodlum. Am I gonna have to hold you down and cut your hair for you? You look like a big dummy out here on the sidewalk." Doug tipped his hat in greeting and climbed into the back seat. "Hell, it's even worse up close! You look like a God Damned lopsided scarecrow."

"You doin' alright Mister Walker?" Gene turned around in his seat and looked Doug in the eye contemptuously. After a few seconds he replied, saying, "What kind of fool question is that?"

Doug addressed R.C. now. "Are we still heading to the County Fair later tonight?" Suddenly R.C. gave the wheel a sharp jerk and the car hit the curb with a loud pop and an impact that brought everyone up off of their seats. With the car stopped, Gene was the first one out, giving the door a vengeful slam as his feet hit the sidewalk.

R.C. got out and walked around the car to examine the flat tire. Doug was busy looking under the drivers seat for the smoldering cigarette he'd lost during the impact. He dragged it out with a complete lack of finesse, burning one hand then the other. As the cigarette sailed out the window, trailing smoke, R.C. and his father argued heatedly.

Gene asked, "What the Hell did you do that for?"

"A cat ran out in the road," R.C. replied.

Gene pointed to a black mark that led from the flat tire to a crushed cat in the gutter.

R.C. could only say blankly, "Yeah."

"Well at least you got the little shit, but was it really worth all of this?"

"I swerved to try to miss him."

"What, in the hell for?", Gene screamed as he gestured wildly.

"To keep from hitting him."

"That damn thing wouldn't have hurt your car…," Gene wrestled with words fit to describe his indignation, finally mumbling, "…just a little bump," as he dragged his hands through his hair.

Doug silently held his hand out, palm up. R.C. dropped the keys in his hands. All the people had emptied out onto the streets to see what was going on and as Doug took the spare tire out of the trunk, Gene could feel the eyes of the gawkers resting upon them. Suddenly he grabbed his son by the arm and dragged him up a small alley and out of view. They turned a corner and Gene pushed R.C. away from him. R.C. backed into a dumpster before he knew it was there. His father's face was red with anger.

"This ain't the way it's suppose to be. I should have found it by now."

R.C. was genuinely puzzled. "Found what?", he asked.

"The gold," Gene replied with a choking simplicity.

R.C.'s face shown with a flush of inspiration. "So it was you…," he said.

Gene turned back toward his son in a paranoid panic, asking frantically, "Where did you hear anything about the gold? Who knows? What have people been saying?" His eyes begged for answers.

"Nobody's talking, but ever'body wondered if uncle Rube was alone in that scheme to find a vein in that old mine. Lots of folks thought you was in on that. Hell, you two was thick as thieves."

Gene was relieved. "Oh… the mine. I didn't think you were that simple."

"So you wouldn't in on that?"

"Sure as hell I was, but that was a pipe dream, it wasn't real."

"And what is?"

Gene wove a fantastic story to R.C. as the young man stood in the shade of the florists back door with an incredulous look on his face. Amazed at every detail, but obviously skeptical, R.C. felt completely absorbed in what his father related with such conviction. When Gene reached the end of his tale, he looked his son in the eye and said soberly, "If you've never believed a word I've told you, believe me now." At that moment the florist abruptly emerged from the back door between them, dissecting father and son. He was wearing a white apron and had an armful of wilted flowers.

The florist looked at the two men in turn. Not seeming to understand what he was seeing, he threw last week's blooms into the dumpster, and with the same puzzled looks at the two men, he disappeared back into the shop. The door closed and the bolt could be heard locking. Gene dug through the dumpster and retrieved a large bouquet of assorted flowers.

R.C. followed as his father passed Doug putting the lug nuts on the spare tire. He walked to a corner of the courthouse lawn, placed the flowers on the grass, knelt down and prayed. R.C. stood and watched. When his father rose the young man asked, "Why do you do that?" Gene gave one of the few smiles he ever saw on his father's face (in fact, the only one he would remember in time), and said, "Some things you can only take on trust."

1969

It was hot out in the liquor store parking lot. The smell of a neighboring chicken processing plant was nauseating. Vaporous distortions emanated from the nearby highway as cars and trucks sped by. There was a storm front massing in the west with ominous black clouds. There seemed to be something hellish about this day, something as yet undetermined. A promise of perdition flitted in the back of Gene's mind. It was vague, but it made him uneasy.

He left R.C. waiting in the car and walked into the building. He was still unaccustomed to the cool, dry atmosphere that existed inside air-conditioned buildings. The sudden change in temperature and humidity only magnified his foreboding. The sweat on his body cooled quickly, and he felt as though he had entered a fever dream.

He wandered through the aisles of whiskey, comparing price, proof, and quantity, until he found what he felt could keep him drunk the longest amount of time, for the least amount of money. When he looked up from the bottle he saw a man with dark hair and a beard that covered his throat, as well as his face, in an even layer of fur.

The man asked, "Hot enough for you?" Gene paused for one moment. The bottle was then no longer suspended by his hands. Before the whiskey could begin its descent toward the floor. Gene's grasp was already at the man's throat. The man gasped and tried to back away. Gene squeezed and felt the Adam's apple under his thumbs start to give way, but he was in one aisle and his victim in another. The shelf he had to reach across to grab the bearded man was now an obstacle and the whiskey bottle on the floor was soon being joined with others as the two men struggled.

The bearded man broke free and his back collided with the shelves behind him as he back peddled under the force of his own momentum. The sounds of breaking glass were filling the air, along with the smell of liquor. It took but a second for the man to break for the door, but that's all the time Gene needed to head him off at the end of the aisle that, until then, had separated them. He tackled the panicked man, but as they fell he turned to the side and Gene's scalp struck a beam. The other man struggled out of Gene's arms and bounced off the wall once before hitting the door.

Gene got to his feet and with one hand nursing his wound, he passed the man behind the register. The attendant was on the phone, talking frantically to the police. Outside, Gene picked up speed as he headed to the Pontiac parked nearby. Before he could reach the car, R.C. heard the screech of tires on the other side of the building.

R.C. was shouting, "What the hell's going on." as his father clambered in, behind the wheel. They tore out of the parking lot and spilled out onto the highway amid the hornblowing consternation of other drivers. Gene swerved in and out of his lane, passing cars whose drivers shouted their abuses, their heads hung out rolled down windows. Gene's eyes were wet and his face was red with rage, but for all his determination, he couldn't even tell his son what kind of car they were looking for. After they passed at least six roads their quarry could have turned off on, they hung it up and headed back toward Walker-town.

"You're 59-years-old Pop, you cayn't keep doin' this. You're getting too old to be a roughneck anymore."

"Old as I am, my neck's rough as it ever was."

"That might be true, but I ain't got no notion what it's all about."

"Don't let that worry you," Gene said as his knuckles turned white on the wheel, "Thems my troubles."

As they rolled into the small carport, R.C.'s dog ran up expectantly. The dog's owner got out with a brown paper bag in his hand. Cooking grease had stained the bottom of the bag wet and as he placed the bag on the hard-scrabble grass of the lawn, the aroma of fried chicken permeated the air. The dog sat with his head up, tongue out, looking at his master while his tail wagged.

"Look at him Pop, just as loyal as his mother was. He wouldn't rip that bag open if he was starving. He knows… until I dump the bones out of the bag, they belong to me. He'd wait forever."

Gene came around the car and watched the saliva drip from the dog's tongue for a moment, then said, "Yes sir, if people only had the same ethics. I've heard it said that if you die locked in a house with your cat, that it won't waste no time in eating you. Though a dog, if he's your'n, will starve to death right there beside your body."

The opening theme of "Bonanza" could be heard as the two men walked up the front steps. Dana was sitting in the wooden floor at the foot of the couch with a baby-doll in her lap. She watched the television in front of her as she combed the doll's blond hair with a small toy brush. Dana was now 28-years-old. "Hey brother," she said in her garbled way, "You bring your sis' anything?" He reached in his shirt pocket and produced a Mars Bar. She quickly jumped up, the baby-doll coming to rest on the coffee table. She jerked the candy bar out of R.C.'s hand, bit a corner off the wrapper and spit it into the air. "Got to thank you for the television brother."

"It ain't nothing," R.C. said.

"I know, but momma said 'I got to.'"

Frankie walked in from the kitchen saying, "That ain't the way to thank nobody Dana."

Dana took no notice; picking up the doll and holding it out to R.C., she asked, "Ain't my baby perty?"

R.C. said, "…awful perty," as he reached out to stroke the doll's hair.

She jerked the doll away, "Don't hurt her. You're going to hurt her!" she said in a plaintive tone.

236

"Now I wouldn't going to do no such thing Dana…"

"Shouldn't owt'ta be allowed to hurt her," she said miserably as she cradled the doll protectively.

R.C. opened his mouth to say something, but hesitated when he noticed Dana looking past him. He turned his head toward his mother and saw that she too was looking behind him with a concerned look on her face. He looked over his shoulder to see his father standing just inside the threshold. He was to one side of the door-way with his back against the wall. The fingertips of Gene's left hand were touching the split in his scalp where his head was injured. He had a ghastly look on his face. An audible breath entered his nostrils and exited. He walked across the room and closed a door behind him.

R.C. watched the door for a few moments while his mother turned and went back into the kitchen. He heard the click of the television's knob and looked down at Dana on her knees in front of it, turning the channels. She looked up at R.C. with chocolate on her face, "D'ya think 'the Little Rascals' are on?"

* * *

The man in the tweed jacket smacked at the dust on his trousers. They gave up great clouds of the dust he had picked up on the roads. As he stood in his tracks on the dirt road, a sickly smell reached his nostrils. He walked off into the ditch-line and found a twig. Placing one hand atop a sign, he steadied himself, all the while digging dog feces from between the cleats of his shoe with the twig. The strains of a guitar awoke him to the presence of a rather hard scrabble looking man on his porch. The man in the tweed jacket quit his flamingo-like stance, tossed his twig, and walked across the yard to the man with the guitar.

"Good day to you, brother," said the dusty man.

"Wish it was," Gene replied.

"What could make it better?" asked the dusty man.

"You don't think it's hot as Hell?"

"It's my hope that we never find out."

"So you're one of those," Gene said dismissively.

"I might be, I just might be, but I still wonder what it is you're wishing for."

"A pot of gold."

"Well, the good news is that we can all have our share."

"Some sooner than others."

"But, we must all ask ourselves if we want a fleeting wealth, or everlasting wealth."

"I don't want either. I want a pot of gold. If it's mine for one minute, and I fall into the pit of hell the next. Then so be it."

Before the dusty man could respond, a young man in jeans and a sleeveless t-shirt brushed past him. He was carrying a laundry basket. He sat the laundry on the porch and placed a dollar on top of the dirty clothes. "Pop could you make sure that mom gets a hold of this, I'm heading' back out to the house." The young man walked passed the dusty man and muttered, "Don't bother stopping by," before pacing back across the yard and into the house next-door.

The dusty man took a black book from inside his jacket, and said, "It is my firm belief that you'll find all the wealth any man could desire between the pages of this book."

"You think that now, but you're not dead yet. This morning when there was dew on the ground and a chill in the air, you thought you needed a jacket, now it's noon."

Sweat dripped off the tip of his nose as he said, "I feel no heat for I've been washed in the waters."

"Then why do you smell like dog shit?"

"Now wait just one minute…"

"Did you step in it on the road to Damascus?"

A severe look took hold of the dusty man and he pointed his finger at Gene saying, "Do not blaspheme our Lord, do not dare to…"

"Is that your sign at the end of this road?" Gene interrupted, pointing.

The dusty man turned and looked at the sign, "It belongs to my church," he said.

"So you've erected a church to yourself, have you?"

"It's not "my church" in the sense you mean. I belong to the church."

"Damned if that church ain't got a lot of belongings, you, that sign, who knows what all else," the dusty man opened his mouth, but Gene cut him off, "I don't own no shitty smelling dust balls, but I do got a sign, you were leaning on it just a minute ago." The dusty man looked back at the sign. "Go on over there and take a look. Tell me what it says."

The man walked back out onto the road. The sign read "**NO SALESMEN**".

"But I'm not selling anything," the dusty man shouted.

"Are you not?" Gene shouted back.

The man knocked some more dust off of his pants and resumed his march. As he passed R.C.'s house he saw a hand written note on the mailbox that read "No saving souls allowed on the premises." As the dusty man sidled up to the sign belonging to his church, he looked up at its depiction of the lake of fire and the final judgment. He then looked back at the two houses and said aloud, "Pride precedeth a fall."

* * *

Gene took his guitar back up and began tuning. As he repeatedly plucked a string and turned a knob his eyes fell on R.C.'s house. He looked down at the laundry basket, then back at the house. Finally he got up, stuck the guitar pick between the strings, and walked over to it.

As he passed a window he noticed his son working on something in the floor.

Wiring and various electrician's odds and ends were scattered about him in the floor. In R.C.'s lap was a large stewing pot. Gene saw him reach down and pick up what appeared to be several sticks of TNT all bound together with the guts of a clock attached to the bundle. He placed this into the stewing pot, picked up an R.C. cola and took a long swig. Gene walked around to the front door with his guitar. He listened quietly for a few moments. Then he knocked.

R.C. could be heard closing his bedroom door and walking toward the front of the house. The front door opened. Gene asked if he could come in, but R.C. suggested they sit on the porch because of the heat. R.C. went back in and reemerged a minute later with iced tea.

"That feller had a hell of a lot of nerve walking up to the porch, when I've got a sign that says I don't want to be bothered."

R.C. drank a little tea and said, "Folks like that usually think they're doing you a favor."

"Yeah people can be awful generous," Gene paused and took a sip; then said, "I mean just look at that monstrosity of a sign they're sharing with us."

"...And you will see many strange and wondrous signs."

"Wondrous to behold?"

"So they say."

"What have you been up to?" Gene asked as he resumed tuning his guitar.

"Just getting something ready for work."

"Work been steady?"

"Steady enough."

Gene ran through the tune for "The Wild Wood Flower" a couple of times, while R.C. finished his tea. When he stopped he held his guitar close to his chest and cleared his throat. He looked out at the harbinger of the coming apocalypse. He seemed to look through it, beyond it. "Remember when I took you and Dana to the County Fair?" If R.C. replied, Gene didn't hear it.

"You were just a little shaver then. It all seems so close. The years, they just fly away. You work your fingers to the bone and it never stops. If you get a Saturday or a Sunday to relax and take stock… Well, it's just a flicker, just a breath you take before you wade right back into the tide that's running up again you, trying to take your feet out from under you.

"I never thought I would spend my whole life trying to keep my head above the rising waters. I thought I would have something different, truly, I did. Do you remember riding on that carousel?" Gene was again deaf to any response. "You waved to me as you came around. Then you watched me over your shoulder until I disappeared. You would whip your head back around and there I would be again. Your hand would be waving at me again.

"That's the way my weeks, months, and years have been. No sooner does one pass, than another falls on it's heels. I watch them pass in a big blurry whirl, always too distracted to reach out for the brass ring. It sits there without ever being re-trieved, not because I couldn't reach it, but because I never tried to reach it. I was too busy going in circles. Never gaining any ground."

"Pop, I'm reaching out. And when I get that brass ring, I'll give it to you."

"Then stop waving. Stop your fucking waving and reach for it."

Gene got up, dragged his guitar to the edge of the porch with a scraping sound, and hoisted it into the air. He walked across the road and out into the old barren field that haunted his dreams. He paced the ground. He stopped from time to time and dropped to his knees to examine the dirt, feel it with his hands. He walked out to the half demolished cabin where Graham and Dale had grown up. He stared back across the dirt road to where Caleb's cabin had once stood. R.C.'s house now stood there, with R.C. on the porch staring back at his father.

He looked at his own house, standing where J.D.'s house had been burned to the ground by Federal troops. He looked up the dirt road. Beyond his view, at the end of the road, was the house he grew up in, with the rows of corn in which so much happened in so little time.

He crossed the street, passed between the two houses, and walked by the ruins of an old pig pen. He crossed a field, for many years fallow, and now being conquered by the underbrush. There was no sign of the barn which once stood there. He climbed a steep ridge, and stumbled down the other side and down into a valley. He walked a worn path, now with dirt bike tracks scoring it. He walked, unbeknownst to him, past the single shallow grave of two soldiers. He wound his way through the forest. Finally the path forded a stream. He began to walk across the creek, the cold water soothing his feet, when he noticed some ripe, plump blackberries. He took off his hat and gathered a few.

* * *

Gene's eyesight wasn't what it used to be. In the night, standing on his porch, he could no longer see more than the dull, blank, dark before his eyes. Even on a night illuminated by the full face of the moon, he was just as well as blind. Thus it was, when the tapping began.

Every night, for an hour or two, the tapping could be heard. The sound came from the field across the street where Gene knew the gold to be buried. It wasn't the sound of digging. It didn't sound like an object striking the earth. It sounded like the dulled sound of metal striking metal. It was a hollow dampened sound, as if the earth resisted its reverberation.

On nights when Gene would stand on his porch and attempt to pierce the blanket of darkness with his eyes, he could almost imagine a gold ingot, weary of waiting, striking itself against the inside of the iron cauldron. It was calling out to him. It knew he was there. It woke him in the night. He would be tormented by the sound for an hour, maybe two hours. Then it would mysteriously cease, only to resume again the next night.

Month after month the sound persisted like a maddening siren's song. As the winter came on, the tapping grew louder. Gene couldn't sleep. The tapping woke him and sent him into a terror. When it ceased he tossed and turned expecting it to resume at any time, though he knew it would wait until after the next nightfall.

The next morning he would go out into the field to find no trace of what had caused the sound. The only reprieve came with the first snow. A calm fell over Walker town just as the snow fell to earth. The tranquility continued until the snow had melted away a week later. When the tapping resumed, Gene's nerves were shattered. The peace of the preceding nights only served to emphasize the return of his torment.

The next morning, Gene left home while it was still dark. When he found himself walking into Morganton the pre-dawn light was just beginning to materialize. He marched to the Courthouse lawn. He knelt down on his hands and knees. Tears came into his eyes. The grave he knelt over was under a shade tree, and the snow clung to it stubbornly. Gene felt the cold moisture against his knees.

"Is this your doing?" he whispered. "Are you J.D.? Does it belong to you? Did you die for it? Are you damned to crave it still? I lay my head where you laid your head. Marshal loved you like a father, though you weren't. He loved me like a son, though I wasn't. I have tried to honor you. I tried to claim what our family has suffered for all these many years. Now I'm tormented. Am I to be damned before the grave? What justice can I offer you?

"Alright by God, I'll end it. I'll make my peace with it. I swear never to lift a finger to find that cursed vessel, that seed from hell planted deep in the ground. May it never sprout, may it smother. May I drop dead if I ever seek out that venomous hunk of iron again. May I never more walk the earth if I break my vow."

A number of people had paused on the sidewalk to hear what this man was on about. As he became aware of them he wasted no time returning their incredulous stares. He jumped up onto his feet with such intensity that some onlookers stepped back in fear that they might be attacked. "Go," he shrieked, "Get the sheriff. There's a man buried here. A man that needs to be planted in the church yard." The people did run. For Gene, at that moment, looked very much like a person who might put a man in the ground.

* * *

That December night, after a long day at the sheriff's office, Gene waited in the dark. He sat on his porch, breathed into his hands, rubbed his ears for warmth, and he waited. An hour passed, then two hours, then "TAP…TAP…TAP." It began again. Gene rubbed his forehead roughly with his knuckles. He pulled at his hair. Suddenly there was an off-key tap.

Gene held his breath. He had never heard a tap quite like it. All was quiet for a moment, then a much louder, again off-key, tap. It reverberated throughout Walker town and when it died away, a silence reigned. Gene laughed, he smiled uncontrollably and he laughed. He walked into the house, laid down on the bed, and slept the sleep of the just.

He awoke in the morning, slipped his boots over his bare feet, and walked across the road. There, in the field, was a patch of red earth about three feet wide. Something had dug down into the ground, or perhaps, as Gene suspected, something had erupted from up out of the ground. Gene looked around. Nothing else seemed unusual for a winter's morning. He looked back down at the ground. Slowly, he backed away from the scarred earth, not quite knowing how to feel.

1973

Gene wasn't happy with his new neighbor. Doug may have been the best friend of his son, but Gene had never trusted him. For as long as he could remember, Doug had been involving R.C. in one scheme or another and left him holding the bag each time. The boy (regardless of age, Doug would always seem a boy to Gene) had always reminded Gene a bit too much of his own best friend from days gone by. Just like Rube, to Gene's sensibilities, Doug had the makings of a traitor.

It was in the late Spring a few years before that Doug had enjoyed a generous inheritance from an obscure relative. Immediately R.C. began to pressure his father. He asked if Gene might not sell the acre beside his house for Doug to build on. Eventually Gene caved in. He sold not only to please R.C., but so that he might finally have something to put in the bank.

Gene would gladly have sold the property to anyone else, but sold reluctantly, and at an extortionist's price, to Doug. Not long afterward the house began to go up. It seemed way too extravagant, modest as it was, sitting beside Gene's house. There was even a pool around back, wafting the smell of chlorine across the lawn and directly on to Gene's porch. Gene blamed the smell on his chronic headaches and scowled when ever R.C. crossed his yard in cut off blue jean shorts, with a towel in his hands.

"Where the hell do you think you're going with that towel in your hand?"

"Take a guess."

"Well when you get there, tell his lordship, if I see his dog in my yard again I'll pepper his ass with a ten gauge."

"You wouldn't shoot a man's dog."

"His ass, not his dog."

"You'll do no such thing. His dog don't even get in your yard."

"You just tell him for me."

"Why don't you come along. You're welcome to come you know."

"I suppose you're in cahoots with him to murder me."

"He ain't out to murder you."

"It's only a wonder he ain't finished me off with that chlorine yet."

"I'll tell him you said, 'hey'."

"Now you want me to swim in it."

It had been in February when the accident occurred. It seemed Dana had been watching something on television about a Doctor, Pharmacist, Nurse; no one could be sure. Whatever the inspiration, she decided to reenact the characters' actions herself, as she often did. She crept into the bathroom and took all of the medication out of the medicine cabinet.

She emptied all of the pills onto a plate. They shined before her with a candy colored beauty as she counted them out. She sorted them by color, then by size, and finally by shape. She tried to get her doll to take a red and white capsule, then scolded the doll for not cooperating. She held the pill up so that it could plainly be seen by the doll. She raised her eyebrows and tilted her head, as if teasing a young child for its childishness. She put the pill to her lips, and as she did, she heard the front door open.

Dana leaped up off the toilet seat. When she did the plate flew from her lap. She reacted by snatching the plate before it could crash to the floor. The pills tumbled to the floor, bouncing and skidding in every direction. Dana got on her hands and knees and began scooping up handfuls of pills and slipping them into which ever bottles she could. When she heard steps coming toward the bathroom she grew frantic, quickly putting the pill bottles back in the medicine cabinet. The knob twisted on the door, followed by loud knocks. Dana stuffed the remaining pills into her pockets.

Dana unlocked the door and Frankie burst in fuming. She scolded her daughter, who was never allowed to lock herself behind doors, and sent her outside to play. Gene gleaned these details from Dana much later. At the time he only noticed, unremarkably, that Dana had been corrected. She ran out the front door and into the yard, looking back nervously as he continued to apply shoe polish to a pair of oxfords. They looked overdue for a shine, and as he rubbed the polish in with small circular motions, Frankie reappeared on the porch.

"You all right?" he asked.

"Surely," she replied, "I just needed some Aspirin."

"What was Dana up to?"

"Only the good Lord knows. She was locked up in the commode again."

"Didn't clog up the toilet this time did she?"

"No,… had a kitchen plate in there though."

"Odd. It ain't the kiwi giving you that headache is it?"

"Smell don't bother me none."

An hour later Frankie was in a cold sweat. She was trembling and felt weak. She sent Gene to the medicine cabinet. The cabinet had at least fifteen years of prescriptions in it. Each bottle contained the last day's dosage. On the label they had scribbled what it had been prescribed to treat, and who in the family had been taking it. Gene found a bottle with the words, "fainting spells, Frankie, dec. 71". He brought Frankie the pill and a glass of water. She slept, and four hours later he woke her and gave her another. She went back to sleep and sweated through her clothes. Four more hours passed and he had to shake her awake for another pill.

She mumbled incoherently, never opening her eyes, yet she swallowed the pill and drank a little water. He went back and read the label on the bottle one more time. He searched in vain for a drowsiness warning, wondering all the time why a drug that treats fainting would cause a person to want to sleep. He determined to make her get up when he brought in the next pill. He thought, if nothing else, she could at least sit up in bed and read a book. This time when he shook her, she did not wake. He shook her harder. A tremor of fear shot through him. He felt the cold electricity of terror seize him.

He threw the glass of water on her face. Her nose made a weak wet hiss when the water hit her nostrils, but she neither awoke or coughed. He looked at her incredulously. He then looked down at the pill in his hand. It was orange. He was sure the last one he brought had been white.

He flew back into the bathroom and picked up the pill bottle. It was heavy. It had more than one day's dosage in it. How could he have failed to notice before. The bottle was almost full. He cursed himself and fumbled with the lid. He pulled the stopper on the sink closed and dumped the bottles contents into the sink. He grabbed the porcelain with both hands as he watched the pills slide down to the shiny metal stopper. There were pills of every shape, size, and hue.

He ran for the phone. As he did, he forgot about a step up into the living room. He fell hard to the wooden floor and was back up just as fast. He misdialed the rotary phone three times, before he gave up and dialed the operator.

The ride in the ambulance was frantic, but for Gene all things had slowed and as he watched his wife expire, as he watched the paramedics perform CPR he felt unattached to any world. As her life ebbed away, his life was mystified. He was a ghost not yet beyond the grave, not yet at it's threshold. His body was rendered useless, he only haunted it as a spirit haunts a house. He could no more blink than a phantom could close the window. He seemed to see everything, while hearing nothing of what went on before him. His blood was vapor.

* * *

Now he sat on his porch. The smell of kiwi was long absent. He smelled only the chlorine, and wondered if formaldehyde carried the same scent. How many times had he thought about that day in the months since then. Dana came up on the porch and looked through the front door.

"Is momma making super yet?" she asked.

He was quiet for a moment, he was a ghost for a moment, then he said, "no."

She wrinkled her forehead and said, "Well I'm hungry."

"We'll fix you up in a spell."

She squinted, smiled, and returned back to the lawn.

When it had happened, when Frankie died, they thought Gene had killed her. They went so far as to make a trip out to Walkertown to collect him and gather evidence. The police came in with their search warrant, but not long after the cuffs were on his wrists, they found a robe hanging from a nail on Dana's bedroom door. The pockets were stuffed with pills. The detective came out just as they were putting Gene in the back of a squad car. They knew then that it hadn't been murder.

When they found out an arrest was impossible they seemed to become even more hateful. They threatened to take Dana away, and put her in a home. When the ghost couldn't respond, they thought perhaps he wanted her in an institution. So they made sure she didn't go to one. They wanted Dana to be a constant reminder. Everyone seemed to blame him; not R.C., but everyone else.

Clouds began to gather that afternoon, dark clouds. In the distance a soft glow of unseen staccato lightning cast its glow near the horizon. The gray shroud grew to a density that brought on the night an hour early. Gene put Dana to bed as a cold wind slid mysteriously across the field on the other side of the road. As he tucked her in, he watched the tall grass ebb and flow, transfixed. He imagined it was the wind that blew out of Eden. A wind that chilled Adam's back as he walked away. It had never stopped blowing. It spent all of history blowing, traveling until it arrived here, at this place, at this time. It was an ill wind.

When he sat back down on the porch the wind had ended its journey. It had reached its destination and rested upon the land. Gene could no longer see the field through the darkness. The air felt heavy with the anticipation of the first, few, fat, drops of rain. A porch light came on at Doug's house. Doug passed beneath it and approached Gene.

"R.C. said Smokey's been messing around in your yard."

Gene looked down on Doug without inviting him up on the porch, "He misheard me."

Doug grinned, "I hoped it was something along that line. Why, that dog wouldn't…"

"Tell me something," Gene interrupted, "Where do you get off?"

"I think maybe I misheard…"

"Not this time."

"Well, just what do you mean by it?"

Gene leaned forward and put his elbows on his knees. "Up until I sold you that land, I worked hard all my life. If I wasn't laboring hard on a works project, chain gang, in a mill, factory, mine shaft, or field, I was busting my ass to try to find a way to keep from working." He pointed down at Doug, "After all that, here comes this peckerwood back from over seas, and it seems no sooner do you sit your duffle bag down, than you're set up in a fine house with a swimming pool. What's more, you build it on the only thing I've ever had of value in my life. A lifetime of hard labor, barely making enough to pay the property taxes on that parcel, and I have to sell it outright to a snot-nosed brat. It ain't proper, it's an insult."

"I just got lucky. There's no need to dog me out," Doug pleaded.

"Where's my luck then," Gene asked, "I've been waiting for it my whole life."

"We can't all be lucky."

"I reckon not."

"For some of us, a pot of gold just falls into our laps. When it happens we're despised." Enraged, Doug started to walk away when Gene shouted after him, "What about the rest of us?"

"If it ain't in your lap, you're going to have to go out there and take it," he screamed.

As he said this he pointed. Perhaps he pointed to the world at large, but Gene saw his finger leveled with the terrain that had humiliated him for so long. The enigma that had been his family's curse for generations. Doug disappeared into his house and doused his porch light. As Gene gathered a few things: a lantern, an umbrella, a shovel, and a mattock, the storm finally broke. Lightning flashed over head, thunder shook the house, and rain poured off the eaves of the roof in great torrents. He walked out into the freezing rain and crossed the street. There he planted his open umbrella and sat the lantern beneath it. The cold water pouring down his back, he began to dig.

* * *

The sun was again shining when R.C. came to visit his father in the hospital. Gene lay on the bed with his lungs again filled with fluid. He was pale, he was weak, but most of all he was grim. R.C. talked to Gene, but Gene didn't respond. He was tired, just as Frankie had been tired. He had told his son all that there was to tell him. He couldn't be sure how long he'd been in the hospital, maybe a week. His son looked sad, and he looked like he was trying to hide it. That was all the communication he could endure. Gene wasn't sad, he was no longer angry, and he wasn't bitter. He was a ghost. His eyelids came between him and his son.

* * *

...Gene threw a sack of sugar over his shoulder and marched down the path. He never looked back, but he could sense Rube toting a sack about thirty feet behind him. Soon the path had dwindled

into nothing and they were wandering through a thick wilderness. The land sloped off gradually in a saddle between two ridgelines and at it's lowest a deeply rutted rivulet of water barred their way. Gene skirted it until he found a felled tree that would serve as a bridge across the small chasm...

1st R.C.

Ghosts of the Soon Departed

1953

Doug thrust his hand into his pant's pocket as the other boys stood waiting. They were all between the ages of nine and thirteen. The six of them stood in a circle around a short stump erupting from the forest floor. Small, yellow and black hornets wove a highway in the air. They lined up to enter a small hole at the foot of the stump. Those returning from their exploits lined up to climb back down into the ground, while those leaving filed in behind one another as they flew the first few feet from the nest, only to veer off as they left one another to forage.

Doug pulled his hand from his pocket. He deposited a penny and a nickel on top of the stump. His change joined a modest collection of coinage already waiting atop the stump. R.C. looked around at his competitors. "Alright, so we're all in. Choose your weapons," he said. They all then turned and walked into the forest a few paces, but never out of sight of the stump.

When they resumed their previous positions, each was holding a small pine bough. They closed within arm's reach of the stump. Every bough was nervously pointed skyward. In the hole, where the yellow jackets went in and out, stood a few sentries. They seemed to tense up, as R.C. watched them, almost as if bracing for an impact. A moment passed and then the pine branches came crashing down.

What followed was as chaotic as the D-day invasion. The beating immediately kicked up a cloud of dry dust from the foot of the stump. As R.C. felt the pine rosin against his sweaty palms, he saw the small dust cloud begin filling with the angry hornets. He had tucked his pant legs into his boots and his shirt into his pants in preparation of the event, but somehow the stings came regardless.

Three of their number abandoned the yellow jacket nest and their money as soon as they fully realized what they were in for. Another left his post not long after with more than a dozen stings. It was then between R.C. and Doug. With less antagonists the hornets concentrated their attack. R.C. saw the determined look in Doug's eyes. He looked down at the money glittering on top of the stump, and then back up at Doug, as he beat the ground ever more relentlessly, ever more chaotically.

He felt the endless stings as some kind decentralized sharp pain, while at the same time the warmth of the swelling tissue already began to waft through his body. He could feel the breeze from tiny wings on his exposed skin, the crawling of tiny creatures on his crew-cut, their legs scrambling onto the flesh of his cheeks. He could see Doug suffering the same torments, when finally a yellow jacket climbed out of his hairline, across his forehead, and stung him between eyebrow and eyelid.

Doug screamed, dropping his pine bough, and running away blindly, he knocked himself against trees, tripping, rolling, stumbling, and tearing at his clothes as hornets trailed after him. R.C. looked down at the money, reached out, and grabbed it.

* * *

Doug lived off the highway that led to Walker town. It was about a five minute walk and he and R.C. walked it often. Doug was tall and gaunt as a child, always following R.C.'s lead. They both helped out down at the sawmill in any capacity that might bring in enough money for a trip down to Denton's store. The work (whatever work there was for them) was hot, exhausting, and rough.

They would drag themselves into Denton's store after sundown with their hands cut up, clothes sweated through, and sawdust in their hair. R.C. would hit the shelves and then deposit on the counter a Moon Pie and an ice-cold bottle of R.C. cola. Old man Benton would always say when he saw the two come in, "There's young R.C. and his friend." Anytime Mr. Benton had some work to be done around the store, such as shoveling the snow from out front, he would pay the boy in R.C. colas to have the chores done.

Soon he was known to all and sundry as R.C. and his given name became forgotten with the passage of time. R.C. became a notable story teller, not only for the kids at school and in and about Walker town, but at local fiddler's conventions. If he wasn't telling an Archie Campbell story, he was spinning one of his own yarns. His relation of personal anecdotes were full of local color, and this is what pleased his audience.

He told stories about taking a bicycle he found in the junkyard off a hill, how it had no brakes and drove one of the handlebars through the meaty part of his chin to emerge under his tongue. He told how he was cornered by dogs on the way to school and threw a liver mush sandwich one way while he ran the other, escaping while the dogs fought over the morsel. He told them how he went camping in the winter, carrying a pillow which he accidentally dropped in the creek. When he awoke after a frigid night in the woods, he found the pillow frozen solid except where his head had been lying.

Soon he wove all of these and many other elements into one long, complicated narrative, some of the details were true, others invented, all were exaggerated. Folks began to recognize him wherever he went. They would stop him and beg him to tell his stories, bribing him with R.C. cola. He was slowly coming to realize that he had a powerful tool at his disposal: charm. What once cost him endless time and effort, not to mention no small amount of blood, was now given freely to him, based only on his power to make himself liked. It was a strange awakening to find that he only had to exert the force of his personality to get what he wanted in life. He planned to do so, for the rest of his days. From that time forward he never approached anything without a plan that would put him ahead of the masses, a plan that took clear advantage of his reputation and abilities.

It was decided early on by R.C. that he would excel, that he was now at his poorest, and with the passing of each year, he would prosper, increasing his influence, standing, and assets. It seems a lot to say of someone so young, but to struggle, to lead the hard scrabble life his father had, was something R.C. ruled out before he was caught in its very first entanglements.

* * *

It was an early autumn morning when R.C. and his sister Dana set out on foot to see their dog's new litter of puppies. Gene swore a number of inflammatory oaths after them as they left the mud and weed yard of the half constructed house.

The indictments were aimed at the matter of having both the children back in time to do some work on the roof. With the house already out of sight, a last few of their father's words found some isolated trick of acoustics to reach them... "...a storm might descend when least expected..." Hansel and Gretel turned back in the direction of their skeletal home. They stood dead in their tracks as a sudden wind bent the wispy tops of a few saplings, sucking the seasonal leaves into a sky that suddenly seemed all the more portentous for it's vivid blue hue. "When you least expect it," R.C. mumbled.

It was a long and not altogether unpleasant walk. The sunlight remained steady and gold, but not so intense as to fatigue the two wayfarers. They caught bits and pieces of roads, paths, and railroad tracks here and there, while at other times they walked between rows of crops, through weed filled meadows, or through the underbrush of dense forests.

When they finally reached the hollowed out shelter beneath the great rock at the edge of the field, Jo-Jo was nowhere in sight. Her puppies were whining softly and Dana scooped up a couple of them. She caressed and adored the frisky little creatures. R.C. lay back in the cool grass. It was a field of what the children called broom-straw. With his head resting snugly on the ground he could see the rising gold stalks of the plant, which seemed to tower above him. With the stalks in his periphery, he wondered how small he really was. The perspective made him feel peculiar.

After a few minutes rest, he eased himself to his feet. Dana was trying to curb the puppies' clumsy attempts at exploration beyond their resting-place. She talked with a bit of straw between her teeth, "R.C. you got to help me. They won't stay put." Her brother walked up to her and took the piece of straw from her, tossing it over the rock like a tiny javelin. "Don't gnaw on that stuff. People are going to think you belong in Broughton Hospital."

"Everybody knows I'm smart as a whip. It ain't the hayseed makes a hayseed."

"Now Dana, that just ain't so. Most people are just foolish enough to make up their mind with one look."

Arms akimbo, she asked, "How so?"

"Well, take them niggers they had working on the road this past Sunday."

"What about them?"

"I heard that feller, what wore the 'Jimmy-brown' and helped daddy with them trusses on Sunday,... he told his friend when he heard them boys on the road-crew singing: just what got them there.

"The feller in the hat said...

* * *

~WHAT THE FELLER IN THE HAT SAID~

"Here's one way for it to happen: There wasn't any work at the mill and I was hurtin' for a jar of corn. So I went to dig some ginseng up by old Joe Tomkin's place. I had me a stick sharpened up and ready, but there weren't no sign of what I was after; not a sprig of 'seng to be found. It was damn-hot, you remember... a couple of months ago?

259

"Anyways: I spied Joe's watermelon patch from up on the ridge, and I thought I'd help myself to a runty old cannonball. Well, I dragged me one into the woods, with his old hounds just bellerin' to beat the band. That's when I reckoned he was out-and-about somewhere. I nestled up on an old stump and commenced to chomping'. It was warm from the sun, but that didn't stop me. Bout that time this nigger, older than the family bible, comes up on me. Don't know how he was even on two legs, looked like Lincoln freed him personally.

"He says, 'Scuze ol' Merle, didn't see you their.' Now this old dark blue savage, he's hawling a sack of ginseng, and the roots are just hanging over the edges of the burlap. 'Diggin' 'seng are ya?', says I. 'Look's like you've found more than a scrimp,' To which he says, 'Naw'sa', which just goes to show that they're not only born liars, but they never get over it.

"So he's lookin' down his nose, and over his lips somehow, ha-ha, at me eatin' the red of'n the rind. I tried to be friendly and make a little joke, 'Yeah, white folks eat it too', says I. Funny right? Not a chuckle do I get from this old sambo. So I try to be generous and offer him a piece. Now I ain't never give a nigger nothing but a hard time my whole life, but I didn't know what else to say. He just gives this old thick-skulled look of his and says, 'naw'sa' right then he just hobbled off, still lookin like Methuselah dipped in tar. I just cayn't help but look after him till he's carried himself out of sight, using his ginseng stick, like a crutch, the whole way.

"I just think, 'Uppity Nigger' and go back to eatin'. My mind starts to wander as I look at the back of Joe's house. You might not remember, but Joe sold me that car sittin yonder. You'd think we'd be thick as thieves, but here's the rub: a week later I found out what the sumbitch paid for it his self, not two days before I took it off his hands. He fucked me like a pig caught in the fence, and the more I turned it over in my mind, the hotter I got.

"Finally I got so mad I swept down into his melon patch like a plague into Egypt. I stabbed and thrashed with my 'seng-diggin' stick until there wouldn't ah melon to be had… and I was about to do the devil's work with his cantaloupes, when up comes the sheriff's car in a cloud of dust. I lit out, but when I hit the edge of the woods I ran my shin up against a fallen tree; damn near broke it. Of course the dogs are all raising cane, and I can barely get up and over the ridge before I hear the dogs on my trail.

"Well, I lay down on my back, grab my shin and start rolling around on the ground. Here comes Joe with the dogs on a lead and the sheriff bringing up the rear. I didn't let them get a word out; told them how this nigger was up to mischief in Joes garden and how he hit me in the shin, took my ginseng and runned off. They caught up with him not far away, he acted like he didn't know what they were talking about. Finally when the old fool said, *he didn't even like watermelon*, the sheriff called him a liar to his face and knocked the spit out of his mouth.

"Before they led him back down towards Joe's, the sheriff shook my hand; did you ever think you'd live to hear tell of the sheriff shaking *my* hand, and he thanked me and gave me back my big sack of ginseng. I took it in and cashed it out. Helped set me up for a little while, and I bought this honey of a 'Jimmy-brown'. That's one way it can happen. If you walk down there towards the sound of 'Swing Low, Sweet Chariot' and you see a darky older than Africa itself, that'll be him. I wouldn't bother checking though, a nigger that old would have died after a week on one of those road crews. Probably couldn't sing no how."

* * *

"That ain't nothing' but hogwash," Dana said.

"He swore up and down that's exactly what happened."

Dana sat down with her legs crossed and tumbled a couple of puppies back down into their dug-out. She looked up at her brother in anger, "That's an awful story, and there just ain't no truth in it. It would have been way too early in the season to dig ginseng and expect to get anything worth your trouble. Then again, what was the sheriff doing up at old Joe Tomkins's place for not a reason under the sun? On top of all that: if there's ever a time that Joe Tomkins growed any watermelons in his garden- I ain't heard tell of it. He just told some foolishness is all."

"Well, the whole point of the story is this: the sheriff knows a nigger when he sees one. It don't matter any thing but what he looks like. That's what I'm on about, one look is all it takes for most folks, and if you don't want to look like a fool then you'll take care to listen to your brother.

"Any body what has a weed hanging off their lip, or a chewed up tooth-pick while we're at it… Well they might as well be lightin' matches just to watch 'em flare and smolder. You ever seen that?" R.C. holds an imaginary match up before his eyes.

"They'll take a whole pack of matches and just light 'em one after the other, until they're all gone. I've seen folks stare into the flame until it disappears and a little trickle of smoke rises. It takes them another couple of seconds yet to look away. They're dazzled, almost hypnotized, then they shake it off and light another. I've even seen it burn right down to their fingers. It burns 'em and they snap out of it, suck their fingers and curse the fact that fire's hot."

"What you tryin' to say?"

"What I'm tryin' to tell you sis', is that there's folks around just ain't got no commonsense, and you don't want to go lookin' like that bunch of stupid idiots."

"You sure talk mean about folks."

"Yeah, but I talk nice about you."

"Well all I can tell you about that story, is that it ain't nothing' but a pack ah lies, start to finish. Worst thing about it is how hateful it is. I don't care if somebody's dark as midnight, that ain't no reason to pick on 'em, people don't do it out of being ignorant, they do it on acount of pure meanness, and you know that to be a fact R.C."

At this point Jo-Jo came running up with a half eaten raccoon she'd found on the shoulder of a state highway. Both the children greeted her with loving praise and affection. R.C. gave her the chicken bones and she spent a few minutes burying all her victuals in several nearby locations before she settled into her little wallow to nurse the hungry pups.

Dana caressed Jo-Jo as she spoke softly, yet sternly to her brother. "The other day when them colored folks was down near the house working in that ditch, me and you snuck off to sit on the bank opposite them and listened to them sing. It was beautiful, God was speaking through their voices. He was speaking true and sweet. I ain't never been happier. I ain't never felt so content. We listened to them for quite a while. Then it sort of dawned on me that they were wearing chains. All folks got to work, sweat under the sun, get blisters, get covered in sticky, itchy bits of old honeysuckle. What bothered me was the chains. Then you got an idea to start bringing them some water from the creek, and we brought them some muskedines as well.

"At first I thought the work-bosses might run us off, but they didn't pay us much mind. I ain't never been looked on with so much kindness as them folks on that chain gang showed. I just want to have a fit: to think that anybody could end up in chains just because somebody thought they looked like trouble. I want you to promise me you'll stop thinking of folks like that R.C." Having said that, she finally turned to look at her brother, who looked away, at nothing at all.

"I can't change my ways like that."

"But you wouldn't think ill of somebody just on account of their skin?" R.C. half lifted his knees, put his hands around them and stared into them, as if the answer was there. At last he said, "No. No, I don't think I would. Them folks didn't seem..."

"...But if you'd been there with the feller in the cap?" she interrupted.

"No, not no more. You're right. The only thing worse than a fool, is a wise man that agrees with one."

"I'm glad you're my brother."

"Yeah," R.C. grins, "it coulda been worse."

They both lay back in the cool grass with the soft, warm sunlight sending the shadows of broom straw shoots dancing across their faces. A soft breeze was sending pulsating waves of motion through the meadow as small puffy clouds crossed before the sun. With his eyes closed, R.C. could hear the call of a mourning dove somewhere nearby, and he could see the color of the inside of his eyelid change from black to soft pink as the clouds approached and retreated in their endless revue.

* * *

R.C. awoke with a wet tongue slithering across his face. He pushed a wet snout away and saw Jo-Jo's face looming above him. Evening was fast approaching and his heart raced with the knowledge. He quickly got to his feet and shook his sister awake. The situation seemed dire. They both knew they were in for it. R.C. took his sister by the hand and they took flight with Jo-Jo barking a farewell.

Through the brambles and across shallow creeks they ran, R.C. shouting at his sister to hurry, while she begged him to slow down. As her breathing grew quicker and her legs heavier, he was forced to let go her hand. He quickly outpaced her and lost complete sight of his sister. He hurled himself in the vague direction of the dirt road that would finally lead him home. With a final effort and some stinging pain, he flung himself through a small thicket of thorn filled blackberry bushes and tripped in a small ditch to fall in the road. A horn blasted in his ear as a flat-bed truck, loaded down with a couple of tractor tires, slid to a halt just a few feet from where he lay.

As a cloud of red dust past over him, staining him the color of the road as the particles stuck to his skin, a man stuck his head out the window of the truck. "Damn boy," the man shouted, "raised by possums were you?" R.C. looked up at him blankly. "You damn near made me spill this R.C.," the motorist continued. The young boy slowly got to his feet.

"Well, are you going to get your ass out of my way or do I have to come down there and kick it into the ditch?" R.C. stepped down into the ditch. He could no longer see the driver, but, as the passenger side window passed him by, a brown globule came flying out and landed in his hair. He ran his fingers through it and they came back with tobacco spit. He saw the man's hand come out the driver's side window as the truck rumbled away, the man giving him one back-handed wave before dwindling down the road and out of sight around a curve.

The boy walked a good fifty yards down the road toward home and then looked over his shoulder. He saw nothing. He walked another fifty yards and turned around to see nothing. He walked a final leg of fifty yards and stared back in the direction from where he came. He watched the lane for five minutes, then ten minutes, finally he began to retrace his steps. He walked about a halfway to where the truck tires had furrowed the road, and finally saw Dana emerge another hundred yards beyond. "It's about damn time," he mumbled to himself, and turned back toward home.

His sister continued to fall back, never quite keeping the pace her brother was setting. It seemed strange to see her from so far away, completely out of reach, yet never out of sight, remote and obscure. For some reason it made him feel nervous to see her from such a vantage. He turned more often to witness her progress than he might have if she were nearby. Finally his unease got the better of him and he stopped to wait on his sister. He leaned against a mail box beside a shotgun-shack that had burned down a couple of years before. Angry little paper wasps began to swarm out the rusted seams of the mail box and R.C. quickly backed away from it. The world seemed so hostile to him, and as Dana might say, "hateful."

He sat beside the ditch and waited for his sister to catch up. The weeds were cut away neatly and he perched himself up on the bank beside the road. He recognized the work of the chain-gang he and his sister had tried to show kindness the previous week. Their footprints had been obscured by the leg irons they dragged along. He looked back down the road and could see a dark sedan kicking up a dust cloud some distance behind his sister.

Not far away: a coal black stud tried to mount a mare that wasn't in season. She started bucking and a hoof connected soundly between the eyes of the stud. The victim of the kick tottered backwards a few paces and stood, it's legs canted away from it's body at an unnatural distance. The nostrils of the horse flared with quick breaths. The whites of the animal's eyes growing pink, then deep blood red as the pupils began to dilate until the eyes seemed to bulge from their sockets. The lips of the horse then curled back exposing the teeth and gums to an extent almost unimaginable without surgery. The horse stood as such, the transformation taking less than a minute, a paradigm of demonic pain and sinister fate. The horse began a senseless and pitched rampage, rearing, running, rolling, thrashing, and sending all and sundry on the farm, man and beast, into panicked alarm. The episode ended with three fence posts and twenty-five feet of barbed wire splayed on the ground, and the horse, with it's two front legs broken, receiving a rifle bullet to end it's miseries. The slug form the thirty-ought-six left a neat hole in the horses forehead, right in the middle of the horse-shoe shaped welt that began the trouble.

Not far away: A small boy, aged six, lit up with joy when his cousin told him he could have a quarter. All he had to do is lick a clean path from one corner of the concrete floor in the living room of their house to the other corner. The floor was covered with cigarette ash, mud, dirt, grime, and the filth of mice and rats that scurry about when they think themselves unobserved. Over the next forty-five minutes the child gagged his way across the floor with eyes watering and stomach convulsing. More than one pass was necessary before the concrete could be seen in a neat, three-inch narrow swath from corner to corner. The child went outside to wretch. When the last of the dry-heaves subsided and he felt the soft, warm faced swoon that follows a prolonged period in tears, he turned to find his cousin outside, watching. He walked up to the older cousin with his hand outstretched, palm up. His cousin gave him an incredulous look, "Now where in the hell would I get a quarter?" he asked.

Not far away: R.C. watched as a dark sedan stopped beside his sister. The rear passenger door opened. He could see his sister holding the open door in one hand, she seemed to be talking to someone inside. She got in the car. R.C.'s face lit up, "a ride," he thought to himself. He stepped forward into the ditch as the car approached. The car didn't slow down. In the ditch he was once again unable to see anyone in the car as it passed. He stepped into the road as the car drove away. The sun, low on the horizon, reflected off the back windshield. For some reason R.C. stared into the blinding light, trying to penetrate it and see into the car, but he was only left sightless, in the middle of the road. He had no choice but to stand there for a moment with his eyes closed, trying to dispel the awful phantom suns that had burned into his retinas, like a stupid idiot who stared long into a flaring match head.

1963

As R.C. grew into a young man he never forgot the many lessons he learned at so early an age. He apprenticed a cabinet maker some few years after Dana's ordeal. He sought to learn all he could from the old dullard that instructed him. R.C. often told his friends that a mouse couldn't be kept alive on what the cabinet maker paid. To add insult to injury, by the time he was fifteen-years-old his employer began assigning him cabinets to build on his own.

The finished quality of these cabinets was to such a degree that the old man could sell them as his own work. Not long after this the old man ceased to build cabinets at all, simply giving R.C. all of the work. The man lived so cheaply, so meanly, that R.C. thought little about being duped in any way, the old man complained of many ailments and it was imagined that he was staying out of the workshop because of ill-health.

Then one morning R.C. arrived to find the work shop locked up. He tried his key, but it no longer fit. It was a frigid morning, and seemed to grow only colder in the few hours R.C. passed sitting by the door on a chopping block, waiting for his boss. As lunch drew closer R.C. decided to direct his numb toes toward the shack where the old man lived. The old man's truck was missing and no one responded to his knocks. He stood outside and peered through the window. The room he could see looked even more barren than he expected.

A Plymouth pulled up to the house behind R.C.. A sign on the door of the car said, "Windlass Realty". A man in an expensive hat stepped out of the car. "You're trespassing, son," the man said. R.C. was dumbfounded; he just stared at the man as if he were an apparition. "You hear me, boy?" the man asked. He pursed his lips and examined the teenager in the tool belt for a minute. "Oh, did you help him in the shop?"

R.C. nodded and asked about the old man's health, half expecting to be informed of his death. "He ain't never been better," said the man, smiling broadly. "We should all have it so good. Not just everybody retires to Florida at the age of fifty-five." In the midst of the shock, R.C. remembered betting a friend of his that the old man was seventy-five if he was a day. "Sold the whole spread, lock, stock, and barrel to Mr. Deenes, owns Bellum Container in town."

R.C. took off his tool belt and hung it on a nail in the front door. He walked past the man, out the drive, to the state road, and turned toward town. A few miles later, when he walked into town, he asked a stranger where Bellum Container was. He finally found the building, with it's chain link fence, parking lot, and factory. He walked on to the factory floor where everything was covered in a fine brown dust. A man repairing a conveyer belt directed him to the offices and after insisting a half-dozen times and waiting over an hour, he was allowed to see Mr. Deenes. They talked for ten minutes and R.C. had a new job. He shook his new employer's hand and on the way out asked, "What do we make here anyway? I saw a lot of boxes out there, but nothing to put in them."

"We make boxes," Mr. Deenes said with a smile.

"Well, that explains it," laughed R.C.

* * *

Now it was five years later, and a lot had changed. When he found out how much the cabinet maker had actually been selling those cabinets for, he swore he'd never fall into a trap like that again. He now made every effort to ensure he was paid a salary worth his efforts. During the intervening years he had also purchased part of the land on which his father's house sat. He built a modest, but sound little A-frame house on the land and paid his mother a weekly fee for meals and laundry.

So it was, late one night, that his mother knocked on R.C.'s door to complain that Gene had "went on a drunk" due to his dismissal from the ice company. She had no way to know where his journey might take him, or what state he would be left in when it was over. R.C. left on foot that night to scour the general vicinity in hopes that by some stroke of luck he should stumble upon his father and either coral or carry him back to his worried wife.

The clouds had threatened rain all day; they now made good on their promise. Cascading sheets of cold, angry rain fell in torrents. Gutters bent under the deluge and the dirt roads R.C. walked upon became streaks of mud cutting through the countryside, with red water standing six inches deep in areas where the ditches were overflowing. Thunder peeled and lightning strobed in staccato flashes that gave an instant of unimpeachable clarity, while leaving you completely blind the next.

For the first time, R.C. felt genuine concern. It was common for his father to disappear on 'a drunk' from time to time. Eventually he would wake up somewhere, often in a ditch, decide he had had enough (until the next time) and wander home to recuperate. As R.C. eyed the ditches to his left and right, he began to worry that Gene might drown in a foot of water on this very night, unless found.

The thought then occurred to him, that if Gene had been caught out in this down pour, he may have tried to take shelter with a neighbor. Reluctantly at first, but then calcifying into stern determination, he marched in turn from one front porch to the next. The people who came to their doors were angry, never concerned, a hard-hearted lot to be sure. Most complained that they had their own family drunk(s) to look after. R.C., however, was not to be dissuaded. In fact, he resolved to ascend the front porch steps of the most short-tempered coot he had ever met, one Lloyd Fisher, even though no one in his right mind would look to him for the milk of human kind-ness that is: shelter from a storm.

R.C. climbed over the old man's gate and carefully crept across his lawn, some-where in the darkness was Lloyd's dog. This dog was known and feared by everyone within a five mile radius and Lloyd Fisher, ogre that he was, loved that dog, oh, not as you or I love a dog. He loved the fact that he possessed the most dangerous beast known in those parts. It was the type of dog that might chew the head off a rabid moose, when more formidable prey wasn't available, yet Lloyd could kick the damn thing right in the chin and it tuck its tail between it's legs, whimper, curl up in a ball and piss on itself.

We can suppose that it made Lloyd feel more formidable than his malnour-ished, gout ridden, and chigger bitten little body generally allowed for. If that dog was the biggest bad-ass in the county, and he could kick the dog's ass, then what did that make him? The old misanthrope claimed that the animal was a wolf, most everyone else who saw it (usually from a treetop) agreed that it must have some wolf blood in it. R.C. took more peace-of-mind from imagining a pedigree along the lines of a German shepherd on stilts. It didn't even have a name, unless what the old man called it sufficed, "Come and eat, you sumbitch," he would say, and he always seasoned the beast's food with a generous amount of gunpowder. He bought black-powder at Denton's Store hand in hand with the canned dog food.

The gunpowder was said to cause the animal's stomach to bleed and keep the varmint in constant ulcerous pain, which accounted for the dog's foul, almost psy-chotic temper. So as R.C. walked towards the front steps, he kept an eye peeled for the sumbitch. Suddenly lightning struck so close by, that the flash, and peel of thun-der were simultaneous. In that blazing instant, R.C. saw his father on Lloyd's porch, bare-ass naked, with his arms extended forward, and his elbows locked. He had the sumbitch by the throat. The creature stood on its hind legs, taller than Gene, its lips curled in a cruel snarl, all foam and fang. Its eyes bulged out of its head abnormally.

R.C. was witness to this spectacle for only a second, and then he was plunged back into the pitch-blackness of night, with thunder reporting like ten thousand tons of T.N.T. going off in his vest pocket. Suddenly, the rain dissipated, and aside from the trickle of water off eaves, all was still and silent.

"Pop... Pop, are you up there?" Gene asked with more of a hiss than a whisper.

He felt his way forward with his hands, half wondering if he hadn't imagined the whole thing. He crept up the steps on cat paws and reached out. His hand bumped into a rocking chair, which, in turn, bumped into the wall of the house with a meek hollow "thump". R.C. nervously yanked the chair back towards himself. An imitation sheepskin jacket, stiff as parchment, brushed his knuckles. He dug through the pockets of the coat until he produced a venerable Zippo lighter.

A flick of the flint gave him a flash of two prostrate forms lying on the porch nearby. With another flick a tongue of flame rose from the wick of the lighter and he could see the overthrown beast resting on its side, motionless. Beyond the mongrel, his father was curled up in the fetal position, his back against the house. He examined the dog. There was a puddle of foam under its snout and its eyes continued to bulge out of its skull in the most unsettling way. When he lifted the dogs head, its long pink tongue lolled out the side of its mouth and a single drop of blood trickled to the tongues tip before dripping on to the raw cement of the porch in a small starburst pattern.

R.C. now concerned himself with getting his father away before Lloyd came out the front door with his trusty ten-gauge shotgun. To his consternation, when he tried to revive his father, Gene moaned like the ghost of Jacob Marley. R.C. covered the patriarch's mouth until the wail trailed off into a soft gurgling snore. He looked around: no lights were on. With his father cradled in his arms, R.C. made his way down the treacherous, cement block, front steps and absconded Lloyd's property. R.C. struggled with the burden of his family the half mile back home and deposited his father in his bed to the great relief of his mother, who never even asked what happened to his wardrobe.

* * *

When R.C. began work at the plant, they put him to work with a man every-body called "Yank" as he was originally from Massachusetts. That is: they called him "Yank" to his face, and "Dickless" behind his back. He had moved south in 1953 and was a ten year veteran of the cardboard container facility. Yank had always been given a lot of grief by the rest of the crew who accused him of being a carpet bagger.

R.C. came to understand that Yank was often referred to as Dickless because he wouldn't join in with the roughneck behavior of the rest of the crew. He also set a slow pace. The foreman despised Yank, but couldn't fire him, for the fact that he was the only person at the plant who could run every machine the company owned. In addition to operating the machinery, he also sidelined as a "fixer". Fixer's were usu-ally hired, to do just that: fix any of the industrial equipment in the plant. Yank saved the company a 40 hour wage by doing all of the repairs and maintenance himself.

As training was considered a "bitch-job", the crew always passed it on to Yank, and in R.C., he found an apt pupil. By the twentieth year of his life, the young man had surpassed his teacher in his knowledge of the cardboard container plant and its processes and equipment. R.C. was beginning to think he had achieved all that he could. He had learned a lot about the business, quitting school at the age of fourteen to concentrate on earning a living, but it seemed the opportunities weren't there. One day that changed.

* * *

Out at the loading and shipping docks, behind the plant, a railroad spur trailed along beside the building, and giant rolling doors allowed trucks to back their trailers right up into the plant. On rainy days they could load and unload with out getting any of the pasteboard products wet, and thereby ruining them. It was on a warm summer day however, that R.C. found himself outside eating a potted meat sandwich and drinking what else, but an R.C. Cola.

He was sitting on a small stack of pallets, the warm pine sent of which was thick in the air. Past the empty concrete pad a green field stretched out beneath some high tension power lines. On the other side was a large textile mill and a private runway where small, personal planes, mostly little two seaters, were housed in a couple of tiny prefab hangers. R.C. was glad to be out of the stifling atmosphere of the plant for his lunch. He wiped the sweat from his forehead and looked at the cardboard dust collected in the palm of his hand.

"Need a fortune teller," the foreman asked. R.C. wasn't looking at him, but he certainly knew that smart-ass voice well enough. Past his hand he could see the foreman throwing his dark shadow across the bright concrete. The task-master had his arms in their normal tea-pot configuration, as if whatever met his eyes, just wasn't going to suit him. "I need you to get the lead out of your ass, and get back on the clock, we just had a shitload of orders come through for a furniture plant across town."

R.C. took another bite out of his sandwich and watched the shadow take its hands off his hips and look at its wristwatch. "Where's Dickless at anyway? This ain't no commie crew like they got up North, down here we bust ass to get this shit out, or we get the shit busted out of us and we're out on our ass."

"Read that on a billboard, did you?" R.C. rejoined dryly, before taking a drink of his soda.

"Just wipe the snot off your nose and tell me where he is."

"He's in the toilet."

The shadow mounted a quick withdrawal with the click of brogues on cement, but stopped cold as R.C. made a cold and distinct pronouncement. "If you ever talk to me like I'm some kind of dog again, I'll break your god damned nose. If you do it where other people can hear, I'll break your neck." Silence followed for a few sec-

274

onds, then the steps could be heard to resume, as they trailed back into the building.

R.C. showed no signs of rushing back to work. He drank the rest of his soda and watched as a 50's model Chevy pick-up pulled on to the tarmac next to the small landing strip across the way. A well dressed, grey haired man got out and walked back to one of the small hangers. He unlocked a door and disappeared inside. A moment later the rolling door came up and a small plane sputtered to life and crawled out to the runway. The man cut the engine, and when he did, R.C. could hear the distinct, hesitant steps of Yank coming around the pallets behind him.

Yank sat down as R.C. watched the pilot walk back to the hanger and lock it up. Yank began unwrapping a honey bun. The young man saw an uncontrollable tremor pass up Yank's left arm and rattle through his fingers for what seemed like a couple of minutes. He whipped his hand a few times as if he was shaking water off of it. Then he took up a fistful of fabric from his pants leg. The fit finally subsided. Yank gave R.C. the slightest sidelong glance and continued to eat his pastry with his right hand.

R.C. noticed another single-engine plane in the distance. It was passing the landing field so it could bank and come in on the strip. He looked back down at the tarmac and watched the pilot load some luggage from the bed of his truck, into the back of the plane. As the man got back in the plane, R.C. watched a plume of smoky exhaust appear and the propeller jerk to life a second or two before the roar of the engine reached across the field to him.

The landing strip faced the plant directly, and beyond it he could see the small plane that had circled, lined up for a landing. R.C. knitted his eyebrows. He looked down at the plane on the ground. It leaned forward as the whine of the engine changed pitch, then it throttled down rather quickly. The man got out and removed the chock blocks from the wheels where he had forgotten them.

The plane on the ground would have to cross the landing strip to get onto the runway. The plane in the air was closing in, but as the pilot on the ground collected the chocks he faced the container plant the whole time, enveloped in the roar of his own plane's engine, he never looked over his shoulder, where now, R.C. could see straight down the propeller shaft of the landing plane.

The pilot climbed in and closed the cockpit door, as the landing plane's nose tipped up, ever so slightly. As the one plane's landing gear made contact with the asphalt, R.C. could hear the idle change on the plane on the ground. Instinctively R.C. came to his feet. Yank stole a quick glance at R.C. and followed the young man's eye-line, then took a quick look over his shoulder to see if anyone else from the plant was watching. He could barely make out the foreman coming down the steps inside, with the Plant Manager hot on his heels.

R.C. watched as the plane on the ground started to taxi across the landing strip. The landing plane had already throttled down and decelerated, when the pilot saw the other plane blunder into its path. A deep ditch on either side of the runway prevented it from going around the obstacle, and there was not enough room to stop before an impact. The engine of the landing plane suddenly whined as the r.p.m.s went into the red. Gunning the engine, the plane suddenly got some lift and barely cleared the other plane, as it climbed into the air once again.

R.C. caught his breath just long enough to realize the pilot was still gunning the engine. Planes never took off or landed from this direction, and the pilot of this plane was trying madly to climb high enough to avoid all of the obstructions in his path. As the plane got closer and closer to the plant, it looked like the pilot just might make it. Suddenly the front landing gear hit an upper cable on the high tension power lines. Giant balls of phosphorescent light went up in plumes at the two metal towers the plane was passing between.

R.C. was now sprinting in the direction of the nearest roll-up door in the plant, quickly enough in fact, to see the lights flicker and go off, while the deafening machinery inside was silenced. Yank, on the other hand, was planted in his spot, completely unable to move. It was he, who saw the plane flip nose down as the electric cable tripped it. The great weight of the aircraft's engine however, owing to certain physical laws of motion, was not to be stopped so easily. It was wrenched out of the plane by the impact. R.C. passed the foreman and the plant manager as he fled toward the door. A forklift driver with a pallet of banded cardboard, eight feet tall, took his cue from R.C. and abandoned his still idling vehicle. The forklift and its load blocked a full three quarters of the doorway. R.C. ran around the obstacle and into the pitch-black interior of the plant. Behind him he could hear incomprehensible shouts and as he ran through the darkness a loud crashing noise followed behind him as if a dumpster had been dropped on asphalt from a 100 feet in the air.

He didn't look back. Sunlight streamed through a small doorway on the other end of the plant and he flew toward it as a dart towards the bulls eye. He suddenly collided with someone in the dark, it was a violent, clumsy collision that left both men tossed on the concrete floor. R.C. didn't feel a thing, and in fact, didn't even come to rest. His knees and elbows took some impacts with the unforgiving floor and he was back on his feet, running as fast as ever.

He finally shot through the doorway like a cannonball out of it's muzzle. He went to a trot, then a walk, and finally stood bent over with his hands on his busted knees, panting. A profound weakness coursed through his body, as he realized he seemed to be safe now. He stared down into the blinding white glare of the reflected sunlight on the concrete. He closed his eyes and saw stars in the stigma left by the dazzling sidewalk. He wondered if he might faint for a moment before he realized that Yank had been left to face the music. A sudden fear came with the realization, and R.C. caught a second wind.

As R.C. made his way toward the dock he could see the forklift on its side in the doorway. The pallet of cardboard was splayed all over the floor and the forklift was still idling. He walked up to the vehicle. The key was somehow broken off in the ignition. He closed the tap on the propane fuel tank and slowly the motor sputtered out. On the other side of the forklift a small crowd had gathered in a semicircle. They were looking at the ground.

He walked outside and found the mangled body of the foreman on the concrete just outside the door. The motor of the plane was a few feet away. Blood was pooled up beside the body, its leading edge mixing with a pool of oil oozing from beneath the engine. The black and red fluids swirled together as they mingled without mixing. One of the black workers, Bulldog they called him, was standing nearby with a bloodstained handkerchief to his nose.

"Did you get hurt, Bulldog?"

"Huh? Oh, somebody ran into me in the dark."

"What happened here?"

Bulldog dabbed his nose a couple of times and, convinced that the bleeding had stopped, put the handkerchief away, saying, "Well, the plant manager was just telling us that the boss-man come to him, telling him he needed to fire somebody for being a lazy smartass, and as he was taking him right out here to him, like he was a bird-dog, this here plane up and hit the power lines and the engine comes flying out." Bulldog put his hand back on his own shoulder and stretched his neck to the left, as if gawking at the chewed up form on the ground was giving him a crick.

"Well", he continued, "the engine come barreling down this way and the boss-man, he tried to scuttle on back inside, but he got caught up between the engine and this forklift as he was trying to get round it. It crushed the hell out of him. Hell, you can see it came in hard enough to knock it over, bail and all."

The body was still in one piece, but nothing inside of it looked intact. It was a ghastly apparition, looking like road kill that's been left in the street to get repeatedly squashed. R.C. walked over to the engine. The propeller was long gone, but the shaft still protruded from the front, where the bit of the fuselage to the fore of the engine had been peeled away and brought to rest here with the motor. He could still feel the heat radiating from the murderous object.

The soft breeze shifted, and R.C. could smell the distinct odor of ozone in the air. He turned and could see the plane, crushed in the green grass. Behind it a cable smoldered, popped, hissed, shot sparks up into the air, and hopped up a few feet sending undulations through the end that trailed back up into the tower. It seemed a living thing: some great terrestrial electric eel, gloating over the mischief it had caused.

The plane seemed to have tumble head over heels until it crashed, tail first into the grass. R.C. looked back at the forklift, Bulldog was running his hand over the contours of a huge dent in the side of it. R.C. turned and walked out toward the plane. He passed a couple of large busted up patterns on the concrete pad where the engine must have bounced, like a stone skipping on water, as it traveled towards its deadly destination. He could hear sirens in the air as he broke into a run. He passed a shed, and as he got closer, he noticed that the cockpit windshield had come cleanly out of the plane and was lying in the grass before him.

A couple of people from the crew were at the wreckage with their arms and heads inside the plane, but Yank wasn't among them. A man was in the grass near the plane. He was down on his knees, bleach white, with his face in his hands. R.C. recognized him by his suit, as the pilot of the plane that caused the accident. R.C. looked down at the windshield. The blades of grass pressing against the glass from the other side looked wet. He picked the glass up at one end and rubbed his palm across it.

It was blood on the glass. He looked behind him. There was a small crowd behind one of the sheds he had passed. They were just at the edge of the plant property lines. He picked Yank out of the group and ran up asking if he was okay. Yank was, but the 10-year-old boy they were gathered around wasn't. His legs looked like they were broken in a thousand places, with the feet now pointed in the wrong direction. Little trickles of blood were at his ears and nose, and his eyes bulged. Yank told him that the father, who was still in the pilot's seat didn't look much better.

Suddenly, police, firemen, and paramedics swarmed the place, and dispersed everyone. They separated all the witnesses, and took long detailed statements. By the time R.C. got home, he was exhausted. Just the same, he knew that the day's disaster would allow him a chance to rise above his station.

* * *

It was Saturday morning, and R.C. had just turned over in bed. The beating on the door had been going on for a couple of minutes already. He opened his front door and found a friend of his father's on his front porch. "That's one hell of a shiner you got there," R.C. said. The man with the black eye related the fact that he and Gene had been drinking in town the night before. R.C. lost his glib expression.

The man with the black eye told him that they had been shooting pool, when an argument found them out in the street. After a few blows, Gene lifted his shirt and showed his friend a pistol he was carrying in his belt. The man with the black eye had then decided to try his luck back in the pool hall. He left Gene out in the street. Gene shouted a couple of times for him to come back out.

When he didn't, Gene fired his pistol in the air. A Deputy Sherriff came up behind him, and now he's in the lock up for discharging his weapon in the city limits. Fifteen minutes later R.C. was handing some cash over to the sheriff, and being lead back to the holding cells, which had become so familiar to him in the past ten years.

When they got to the cell, R.C. could see his father sitting on a bunk in his cell, with an empty food tray sitting beside him. He was wearing only his white, long, thermal underwear. A pair of brown work boots were on the floor next to his bunk. The jailer who unlocked the cell, leaned in and whispered in R.C.'s ear, "He's got the D.T.s pretty bad, you get him out to your car, and come back in. I'll give you a bottle to snap him out." The jailer then walked back to the offices.

Gene was gulping air through his mouth and he had a wild-eyed look. He was staring down at the bottom of the cell door. Gene pointed at the ground and asked if his son could see it. R.C. gave the door a ferocious kick, and guided his father's eyes with his own, along the path that the phantom rat used to scurry away. He told Gene that he was there to take him home.

His father stood up and reached down with both hands to his waist. He pressed his thumbs to his fingers as if he were grabbing something around his waist and pulling it up to his chest. He held, whatever it was suppose to be, with one hand and reached over his left shoulder with his right hand. R.C. didn't know what to make of it.

He made motions of pulling something over the shoulder, and then made a fastening gesture over his heart. Now R.C. understood that Gene thought he was putting on some overalls. Gene tried to reach over his right shoulder with his left hand, but couldn't seem to reach the shoulder strap. He tried to reach up behind his back with his right hand, mumbling, "Well, where the hell is it." Then he started to turn in slow, irregular revolutions, like a puppy chasing its tail.

R.C. walked over to him, "Let me give you a hand, there." He reached behind his fathers shoulder and pulled the ethereal strap over. With a snapping motion he connected the non-existent gallous to the bib of the garment. Gene started to walk toward the open cell door. "Ain't you going to put on your shoes, pop?" Gene looked back at his boots on the floor. "I've got shoes?" he asked.

Back at the car, Gene squinted at the bright daylight, while R.C. ran back in the building. He emerged a moment later, and got in the driver's side with a bottle of bourbon. It contained just a swallow, all that should be needed to bring his father out of his delirium.

A flat tire, a revelation about some gold, and a passenger, in the person of Doug, R.C.'s best friend, and the car found itself winding the last quarter of a mile home. Gene turned around in the front seat to eyeball Doug with open hostility. "You going to get a man's job, now that your buddy here is foreman at the cardboard plant?"

"Pop, I hadn't told him about that."

"I can't blame you," Gene said as he turned his face back to the windshield. "Who wants a hanger-on trying to ride your coat-tails on your way to success."

The car stopped in front of Gene's house. Gene stepped out into the cloud of dust. "I'll see you boys soon, he said. With that, he walked into the yard, toward the front door. Doug got out of the back, and sat down in the passenger seat. He slammed the door, and they were off.

"What's this about you getting the foreman's job?"

"I'll tell you if you'll come work for me."

"Tell me then."

R.C. smiled. He took a pinch of tobacco out of a red and green pouch. He began chewing his tobacco as he related his story. "After that son-of-a-bitch got squished in that plane crash, I knew it was my chance to straighten that place out. I told the plant manager I was the one he needed for the job. He told me the owner would be down for the interviews, and he wouldn't consider anybody for the job that didn't have at least ten years experience, I told him I had all of the experience needed to run that plant ten times better than it had been running up to then."

He spit some tobacco juice out the window and continued, saying, "They brought us all into one room and they had a podium set up in front of a couple of dozen chairs. There was about fifteen of us, and then there was the big important people that we were trying to convince to let us have the job.

"We took turns at the podium, everybody saying why he was the hotshot most suited to be foreman. They took us in order of seniority, and guess what, I was dead last. When I got up to the podium I told them they should simply give the promotion to the employee who's made operator on the most machines, and who had the highest production scores in the plant, plain and simple. I told them that there wasn't anybody alive, except for me, that knew every process in the plant, could drive and repair every loader and tow-motor in the place, break every machine in the place down to its nuts and bolts, put them all back together, outpace any other worker on any line we've got working, and get respect from any man working in the place."

Sensing that the manager wanted R.C. for the job right from the beginning, Doug asked, "What did the owner say to that?"

"There wasn't much anybody could say. I held the production record on every job in the plant. They moved the second shift foreman up to first shift, and I took over the second shift, foreman's job this past Monday."

Doug gazed down at R.C.'s feet as he let out the clutch. "Dead man's boots," he said.

* * *

Later that night the two friends were at the county fair. As they walked between the rides and the barkers, they ate their corn dogs and scoped out the pretty girls. They were looking for the girls who got off the Ferris wheel together, a sure sign that trying to buy them a candy apple wouldn't get you a punch in the nose later on.

"Have the people in your crew given you any trouble?"

"Well, this fellow they call Bulldog came to second shift right when I did. He's use to working with me, but he ain't use to me telling him what to do. Him and a couple of other guys were smoking cigarettes in the john the other day, and their machines were just sitting idle when we had a big order we needed out. I told them they'd have to smoke on their regular breaks and gave them two minutes to get back out on the floor and get to work.

"Five minutes later, and they haven't come out. So I go back in and tell them if there not out of there, I'll punch their time card out, and they won't have to worry about how long they take in the bathroom again. The two of them went back to work, but Bulldog stayed right where he was. I punched his time out, and fifteen minutes later he finally went back to his work station.

"I told him to go on home, he was fired. Hell if he didn't have this big old hissy fit, right in front of everybody. When he finally left, his two buddies came up and said if I fired him, they were walking out with him. When I told them to get going, they looked at each other and just told me one morning they wouldn't be there, and then I could see how many orders we could get out without them.

"That night I won a pistol off of a punch card game they had at the plant. I went out to the supervisors parking lot after work. Of course it was dark, and I got in my car, and I started to put the key in the ignition. Somebody's hand shot in the car just then, and they blocked my key going in. I jabbed them right in the palm with the damn key!"

"Watch your language young man," an old lady said over her shoulder as she waited in line at a game stall. She turned back around and looked at the machine in front of her.

"See there, you distracted me and I lost my God Damned quarter!"

R.C. held up a quarter, and she snatched it away. "Rotten son-of-a-bitch, she grumbled as she stormed away. The two friends just looked at each other, and then stepped up to the machine. It was a glass fronted contraption, about chest high, with a shelf that moved back and forth on a little ledge near the bottom of the glass. Quarters were piled up on the ledge. Many were dangling off the precipice, seemingly ready to fall into the trap door below with the slightest nudge. R.C. readied a coin in the slot at the top of the machine and aimed the little shoot the coin was to pass through towards the biggest pile of change he could see below.

When the shelf retracted, he launched his quarter. It landed on the ledge, and the shelf moved forward like the tide. It pushed the coin into the great pile of quarters awaiting a push off the edge. Nothing moved. The quarter just buried itself beneath the pile. R.C. picked another quarter out of his left hand and kept trying.

"Where was I? Oh, Bulldog had his two friends out there in the parking lot and he was trying to drag me out of the car. They thought they were going to teach me some kind of lesson. I got hold of his head and dragged it in the car. I took my right hand and got that pistol out of the shoe box in the passenger's seat. I stuck it to his head and cussed him up one way and down the other. His two friends were smart enough to run off, and when I let him go, Bulldog just set down in the parking lot and cried.

"I just drove on home," he said as three quarters finally fell down into the trap-door. "The next morning Bulldog shows up at the door. I didn't know what he was up to, and was suspicious as hell. He apologized and asked me if I could give him his job back. I told him I could fire people, but I couldn't hire them. I reckon I'll tell the plant manager that I fired him for taking too long in the john, and then found out later that he had a stomach flu or something."

As R.C. took his winnings out of the trap door, Doug asked, "Was that the pistol you pawned on Tuesday."

"Yeah that's the same one. I thought that with you working at the pawn shop, you might do me a little better."

"No, my uncle keeps strict tabs on that stuff."

"Look here Doug: I won three dollars."

"Yeah, but didn't you put five dollars worth of quarters in there?"

"Well, I gave that old bitch one."

"I think I could come up with something better to do with my money, than burying it."

"Oh hell, come here I've got to tell you something." R.C. led his friend into the animal exhibit, where a prize winning Brahma bull was the only one who could over hear him. He told Doug how Gene was becoming delusional. He told him about the rat he hallucinated, he told him about his father praying and leaving flowers on the corner of the courthouse lawn, and he told him that on the way home from jail, while Doug was putting a spare tire on the car, his father had told him some cock-and-bull story, he obviously believed in, about gold being buried near his house. He'd been sworn to secrecy, and had humored Gene's paranoid delusions.

1969

Dust, originated by man, as man originated in dust, rolled down the lane, in Walker Town. The car slid abruptly to a stop next to the two lane blacktop. A sign painter jumped up off his chair in the ditch-line. He covered the lower part of the sign he was painting with a sheet, as a giant cloud of dust poured over him. He coughed with his eyes clamped shut, and tried to breath through the shoulder of his flannel shirt. R.C. and Doug laughed like hyenas in the car.

"Doing' some painting there, are you pilgrim?" R.C. asked.

The painter looked over his shoulder. "What do you think?" he asked.

R.C. was leaning his head down so he could see across Doug and out the passenger window. "Oh Hell, you want to know what I think? You should have asked me that before you started painting this giant eyesore right at the edge of my yard." The painting depicted a faceless deity on a floating throne. Below the figure was some kind of inferno. The figure was pointing down toward the section of the sign the painter was protecting. The sign was about eight foot tall and sixteen feet wide.

"That is the ugliest thing I've ever seen," Doug said.

"It's our Lord sitting in judgment," the painter replied.

"Hell, I should have recognized him," R.C. said while he elbowed Doug. He continued, while pointing up at the blank area where the character's face should have been, "I'm pretty good with faces."

"So what's he suppose to be doing?" Doug asked.

"He's standing in judgment."

"Listen pal, I don't mean to tell you your business, but it don't look that way to me."

The painter looked at the throned figure and then back at R.C. He walked up closer to the passenger window of the car, mixing a small pail of red paint, and asking, "Well, what's he doin' then?"

"*Sitting* in judgment," the painter looked over his shoulder at his work.

R.C. slammed his foot down on the gas, leaving both painter and painting in a shower of dirt, dust, and gravel. The back tires touched asphalt with a screech and the car fishtailed into it's lane and sped away. R.C. looked in the rearview mirror to see the victim of his ill humor straddling the double yellow line and throwing gravel at his trunk while he shouted words R.C. couldn't possibly hear. He adjusted the mirror and said to Doug, "The spirit is upon him."

* * *

The sedan pulled along the rutted out road as best it could. The trees curved over the single, twisting, lane, shielding the two passengers from the midday sun. Finally they pulled off under a copse of pine trees. Out of the trunk they gathered some fishing poles, a couple of wicker satchels, and a couple of small wire hutches with grasshoppers crawling, one over the other, inside.

The two men marched along a small winding path. They walked silently up and down a few hollows until they finally broke through a small stand of bamboo and scurried up a gravel railroad bed. The sun could finally look down on them as they walked down the tracks and made conversation.

"So when do you report for Basic Training?" R.C. asked Doug.

"I've got about two weeks."

"A couple of weeks, huh? You still going to be able to help me tear down the old Caleb house?"

Doug slung his satchel so it would hang behind his hip. "I don't see why not," he replied. The two men passed a remote house with green clapboard siding as

R.C. asked if his friend was scared. He was assured by his friend that he was very scared indeed. They walked by a large mound of rocks, each football-size or larger, that formed a freestanding wall, about four foot high and eight foot thick. It was a mound of some kind, and covered the tracks opposite the two friends. They walked on, without interruption.

"If I were you, I would be half way to Canada by now," R.C. suggested.

"How could you do that?"

R.C. replied, "Just by putting one foot in front of the other, same as we're doing right now, only in a northerly direction, and for much longer duration." While R.C. made this point, the two men saw a snot nosed little brat trying to pick up a rock about twice the size of a watermelon. He lifted one side with a strain then dropped it with an exhalation. His clothes were soaked through with sweat.

"You need a hand there, little man?" Doug asked.

"Nope, I can handle it," the boy said as he went through the same struggle with the same result.

The two men looked at each other for a couple of seconds, then simultaneously, they began divesting themselves of their fishing gear. They got down in the ditch line with the kid. Doug gave him a soft shove out of the way, and with a grunt, they picked the rock up.

"Where are you going with it?" Doug asked.

"It's right up here," said the boy, leading them back up to the tracks.

"What the hell have you got against a bunch of foreigners anyway?" R.C. asked.

"I ain't never met no foreigner," the boy said.

"Not you, you stupid idiot."

"Listen, I ain't got any choice in the matter," Doug said as he took baby steps backwards with an occasional glance behind him.

"Like hell, as not," R.C. retorted as they carried the rock like a couple of pall bearers face-to-face.

"Right here," the boy said, pointing at the mound of rocks. "See if you can get it on top."

They swung the rock like a hammock, and it landed on top causing some of it's neighbors to spill and roll down the sides. The two men walked slowly back to their gear, arguing the whole time. They gathered the equipment and continued on their trek. Before they had walked long, they saw a rabbit between the tracks. It half-hopped, then wobbled to the side a couple of times.

"That damn thing must have rabies. Looks drunk," R.C. surmised.

Doug walked up until the tip of his shoe was almost touching it. He reached down to pick it up as R.C. warned him that the creature would eat him alive. Doug grabbed it by the scruff of the neck and picked it up. Its lungs were rapidly cycling the air. He put the varmint in his wicker satchel and they walked on.

"Mayhap rabies is good for a medical discharge," R.C. mused.

The wind blew soft in their faces, relieving some of the midday heat. As they walked on, Doug lit a cigar and took a puff or two before it went out and he chewed on the tip. For his enjoyment, R.C. took a Baby Ruth candy bar out of his shirt pocket. As he bit a corner off the wrapper he saw something brown, glossy, and serpentine climb up the gravel ahead and across one of the tracks. It began to work it's way toward them, keeping its left side up against the steel rail.

"What the hell is that?" asked R.C., stopping short.

Doug stopped a couple of steps ahead. The creature was still coming toward them. It was some kind of fur-bearing creature, the length of a squirrel, but much more slender. Doug stooped down for a better look, took out a wooden match and struck it on the head of a railroad spike. He stood back up, relighting his cigar. With the puff of smoke, a change in the wind could be seen. The varmint stopped suddenly, and its snout went up in the air. After a couple of seconds, it shot back over the rail, down the embankment, and into the underbrush as fast as its under-sized legs would carry it.

"Was that a weasel, do you think?" R.C. inquired once more.

Doug took up the hike again, as R.C. came abreast of him, saying, "Yeah, a blood-sucker for certain."

"I didn't think they came out by daylight."

Doug pulled the cigar from between his teeth. "They don't usually," he said, "but he's probably been tracking this rabbit I've got in my fish basket. If they get the scent of something, just some little tingle of blood on their nostrils, they'll stay on the scent forever. They're not fast, but they've got stamina.

"He's probably been after this cottontail since late last night. That's how they win, they just won't quit. Either he would have wore this rabbit down till he was helpless, then killed him, or he might have just runned him until the critter died from exhaustion. From some things there's no escape."

"Well Doug, don't think too hard on that when you get where they're sending you."

* * *

The path through the forest had become somewhat difficult with the new growth of the spring season. Gnats were trying to get in through the ears of the intrepid fisherman, as they wound their way closer and closer to the sound of flowing water. As they neared the creek, the sound of running water was replaced by the sound of roaring water.

The trail ended at the top of a waterfall. It was 75 feet tall and nearly impassable from down river. All of the best fishing was in the remote area above the falls. Serious fisherman would take this trail to the top of the falls, and work their way upstream. The object was to hit as many "holes" as you could, on your way toward the mouth of the river. Here the trout were of the tenacious "native" variety, as opposed to the supposedly inferior fish that had been introduced by government agencies downstream.

R.C. could finally see the sunlight dappled water at the top of the falls through the few remaining trees. He stepped out of the wood line with the roar of falling water below him. The rocks under his feet were dry in the sun. Following rainy weather they were often slick with algae, but the sun was high and bearing its might on the river bed. The water was white, tumultuous, and beautiful as it cascaded in its mad rush for lower altitudes. R.C. held on to a grapevine as he leaned over the cliff for a quick glimpse at the bottom of the falls.

Doug and R.C. worked their way upriver until they reached some rocks that offered a crossing. They hopped from one to the other on their way to the far bank. The water was fast and the river narrow in most places, but they knew where a restive patch lay, and soon R.C.'s line touched water for the first time, in the shade of a great boulder. Doug let the rabbit out of his trout hutch, and it bolted into the wilderness. Doug then worked his way around the great rock.

"I wonder if bugs bunny believes in divine intervention," R.C. called out as Doug struggled through the brush.

* * *

They caught a half dozen trout between them, on their journey up the river. It was treacherous going, with cliffs, rapids, and basking snakes all to be avoided. Eventually, good fishing, coupled with unforgiving terrain convinced them that working their way back down river might not be a bad idea. "Let's try our luck at those same holes, one more time," R.C. suggested, as if it was the fishing, and not the fatigue that dictated their decision.

They stopped at a pool of water backed up behind two great rocks near one of the river banks. R.C. pulled in a couple of bottles of soda he had the forethought to leave in the water on the end of some twine earlier in the day. They were nice and cold now. He took a draught from one of the bottles as he sat on a rock with a bologna sandwich in his other hand.

"Boy, that water must be cold as a glacier. I'm tempted to jump in here where the water's quiet."

"Don't you do it," Doug replied, "I'm not going in after you."

"I can dog paddle," R.C. said, sensing a hint of insult.

"I know you can swim, R.C., but they call this pool 'Dead Man's Hole', on account of the current."

R.C. craned his neck up a notch, looking at the water. "What current? I've seen water move faster sitting in a bird bath."

"You can't see it move," Doug said as he reeled his line in, "that's why they say so many people have drown in this spot. Those two rocks that are butted up against each other right there, they're what's holding this water back from shooting straight on down stream like a slue. Only, down underneath they pull apart about four foot wide.

I don't know how far down that is below the surface, but I'd guess a good seven or eight feet at least, because the water's just shooting through there without leaving the slightest eddy on the surface. That hole only starts out four foot wide, by the time it comes out the other side, it's just a crack about six inches wide.

If you fall in right here, it'll pull you in, you won't be able to fit out the other side, and you'll have damn near the whole force of the river," Doug pointed upriver as he said this, and despite himself, R.C. looked in that direction, "keeping you right there in that hole, crushing the air out of you, and leaving you there until the sheriff pulls you out on the end of a hook, or the crawdads get fat on you.

They collected their gear and made ready to depart. R.C. smirked, and said, "Well, if this hole's killed so many folks, name one of them." Doug just looked at him, pursed his lips, gave his head a half turn, and began to walk down stream. R.C. fell in behind him, but before they'd gone very far, Doug stopped him.

"Wait a minute. What the hell is that?" he asked himself as he stared at a mud bank on the edge of the water. R.C. tried to pick something out of the rocks, mud, water, and roots that Doug was examining, but he spied nothing unusual. Doug stuck the tip of his rod in through the hanging roots, and suddenly, with a snap, something jutted out of the rock and broke off the end of the fiberglass pole with a sharp beak.

The snapping turtle pulled its head back, while its tongue undulated trying to expel the painful fibers from its mouth. "Did, you see that?" R.C. exclaimed, "You've got eyes like a hawk Doug, I thought that was nothing but a muddy rock. Doug was already unscrewing his reel from the rod with a key. He tied the key to the fishing line, reeled it up until the slack was all gone, and threw it into his trout hutch, on top of his catch. He put the rest of his keys back in his pocket, tossed his broken rod on the ground and proclaimed, "fishing's over."

* * *

The sun was setting directly behind the two men as they made their way along the railroad tracks. R.C. talked Doug's ears off about everything he could think of. Consciously avoiding the subject of the draft. He hadn't been kidding about Canada. He got one of those letters himself, but poor eyesight had kept him out. When he got back from taking his physical he was relieved to unpack the trunk of his car, knowing that a trip north wouldn't be necessary.

"So you'll be helping me tear down that house?" he asked.

"I said as much… You know I'll be there," Doug replied.

R.C. tripped over a big rock in the middle of the tracks, "Ow, damn!"

Doug weaved between a few others. "You all right?" he asked.

"Hell no," he said as he limped past a fireman who had a kid by the collar, giving him a good shake. "That rock didn't do my in-grown toenail a whole hell of a lot of good."

293

"What's that?" Doug shouted over the blare of a siren, as they walked around a fire truck parked on the tracks.

The boy ran past them in the same direction and took hold of a woman's hip, his face full of tears. She was wearing a ratty old robe, and laid into him with a strap as she pulled him out to arms length by the hair of his head. Never letting up, she began marching him toward a nearby house. A sheriff's deputy ran to catch up with the pair, one arm extended to take the woman by the shoulder.

R.C. took Doug by the arm and pulled his ear close. As they walked past a man sitting on a crate, with gloves in his lap and an engineer's hat on his head, R.C. said, "It's this damn toe of mine. It's killing me." They passed a couple of diesel locomotive engines lying on their sides in the ditch, as Doug pondered his friend's toe.

They began climbing over a big mound of coal, half in, and half out, of a pile of lumber and axles that must have been a freight car at one time. R.C. nearly fell and had to apologize when he whipped his arm around for balance and inadvertently lashed his friend across the shins with the fishing rod in his hands. As they waded through a crowd of pigs being herded by men in grey coveralls Doug asked, "Have you ever tried Epsom salts?"

"A hundred times, and it does sooth the pain, but after a day on my feet like this, I still end up limping, with blood in my sock." As they skirted their way around a police cruiser, the passenger stepped out. He was a tall deputy with a C.B. handset still in his hand. He cocked his elbow on top of the open car door.

"Not so fast, boys," he half shouted at their backs. "Come here, the both of you." They looked at each other, then at him. Without any eagerness they stepped up within arm's reach. The man in the uniform put the handset back in its cradle, and stood back up, arching his back a bit in a half-stretch, he rested the heel of his right hand on his revolver.

"You think I was born yesterday?" he asks.

"No sir," Doug answered clumsily, as if it were a sincere question.

The deputy gave them a come-here motion with his left hand, saying, "Let's see them."

The two men just stood there.

"I knew it," the police officer said with satisfaction, "Fishing with out a license. And it's going to cost you twenty dollars each."

As he whipped out his ticket-pad, R.C. said, "I was just carrying my friend's rod, I've got nothing to fish with." The deputy sized him up as he stuck the lead of a stubby pencil to his tongue.

* * *

The next twenty freight cars weren't derailed, and they walked almost all of them before Doug said, "Thanks a lot buddy, letting me take the fall." In the caboose a man was sitting in a doorway drinking a soda, with his feet dangling over the tracks. Doug's friend haggled with the man until he retrieved an R.C. cola from a bucket of ice and gave it to him.

As they left the scene of the train wreck, R.C. snatched the ticket out of Doug's shirt pocket, wadded it up, and pitched it in the weeds, saying, "Don't worry, by the time that twenty dollars comes due, you'll be well out of his reach."

* * *

It was yet another hot day, when the two friends met again to tear down the old dilapidated house across the street from Gene's property. The place was leaning away from its foundation and looked on the verge of tearing itself down.

R.C. had already been at work long enough to have the front porch completely dismantled. As Doug pulled up in a pick up truck, a twelve year old girl was pulling nails out of boards and sorting out the cast off materials into different piles. Doug put his cap on and approached the house.

"Howdy there, missy. What's old R.C. paying you with?"

"He's given me the best of these scrimps to make me a treehouse with," she replied.

"Where's the boss man hiding?"

"He's in yonder taking down them windows," she answered back.

"Well, I'll just go in and see that you get one of them to boot."

Inside, R.C. was just sitting a window, still framed, to the floor. Within a few minutes all of the windows were lying in the ragweed outside, and the little girl was appraising each in turn before she laid claim to her tithe. Now that all of the glass was safely outside, the two men could see to bringing down the remnants of an old chimney.

Built of field rock and brittle mortar, the stove or hearth that had fed it in bygone days was long gone. The trunk of the vessel now came down through the ceiling about one foot and rested its weight on a platform supported by two braces cut from sourwood and nailed deep into the framing of the wall with huge nails forged by some long dead blacksmith.

After some debate, Doug was behind the wheel of the pickup, with a chain running from his tailgate, between the window joists, and wrapping the two lengths of sourwood. The engine revved, the tires spun, got traction, and with a crash the top of the chimney disappeared through the roof and launched clouds of dust out every crack in the house. As the little girl went home for some mid-day cornbread and greens, the two men began to toss the stones outside.

"A lot of corn husks in this mess," Doug commented.

"Yeah, they filled it up and then sealed off the top," R.C. said.

"What's this?" He held in his hand a small leather-bound book. At one time it must have been black, but now shown a chalky grey, with mildew stains casting crazy patterns on its cover. A corner of the tome broke off and hit the floor and the stiff, brittle scraps of paper were carried up off the floor by a sudden gust. Both men watched the bits of paper evacuate through an open door. There was a short pause, which seemed somehow outside their stream of time.

The door behind them slammed shut from the sudden wind, ending their reverie with a startled jolt. They took the book into another room and found it to be a bible of great vintage. The inside of the front cover bore an inscription in blue ink. It read: "No matter where your road lead you, let this be your map." The dedication was signed, "Your Loving Mother, Christmas Day 1860." R.C. tried thumbing through the book. Some pages broke in two, others were stuck, twenty together, and seemingly petrified. Toward the middle of the book a few folded pages of stationary fell out. Doug quickly cupped his hands and arms together and caught them as one might try to catch a hollow, dried eggshell.

As they attempted to unfold the pages they broke evenly at the folds. Doug went outside wordlessly and a few minutes later, brought in some panes of glass from the windows outside. They pieced the pages back together, and sandwiched them between the glass. The pages constituted a couple of letters.

Ghosts of the Soon Departed

William
1st Epistle

Ghosts of the Soon Departed

1864

Beloved Mother,

    To relate to you all of the incidents I have been witness to in our struggle would require much more of my time than my duties will allow. Rest assured when the artillery is some day silenced, there will be time enough for all things. Whither I meet you next under the elm, or beneath the canopies of the hereafter I know not. With the Almighty's help I know you will persevere, whatever my fate.

    A great deal depends on our leaders, and forgive me if some hard earned lessons have soured me on this account. It is my belief that this war is bound for futility, unless we act as true patriots and cease the quibbling that reduces us all to a poorly allied collection of provincial interests determined to undermine each other in the pursuit of our own selfish interests.

    If we cannot unite our young nation in purpose, it will surely be reunited with the nation we have sacrificed so much to free ourselves from. With God's help, we may still rally our country, quench it of unionist sympathies, and grant our inheritors a bold new nation.

~

    I have no doubt that Catherine has kept you informed since I last had a moment to write to you personally. She and I have no secrets from you or Father, and she shares, I am sure, all of our epistles with the whole of the family. Regardless, I will now render to you a few personal observations, as to my recent experiences. I know that I can trust you to hold fast these pages I now impart. One day they may be of value, if ever I decide to publish a full account of my struggles in the second American Revolution.

As you know, when I heard of the construction of an ironclad, shallow draft vessel, being built in Tarboro, with the purpose of freeing Plymouth and the surrounding areas from the Yankees, I would not rest until I received orders to join her crew. It was never my intention to sit in a Naval yard in Charleston directing work crews for the duration of the war. After an ordeal in the regard of requests, demands, and false promises, I found myself boarding the Cora in mid April, which was to rendezvous with the ironclad, now christened Albemarle, as she steamed down the Roanoke River, bound for a clash with federal warships.

My first sight of the vessel was a sad one. The fore deck as she came into view, was very close to the waterline, and I immediately worried about the ease with which another vessel might swamp her. An ironclad is very nearly wrapped in anvils, and one can only imagine the tonnage, buoyancy being sacrificed for the sake of durability under fire.

To add to my dismay she was negotiating the river stern first, dragging chains from her bow. Naturally this gave rise to a tremendous concern on the part of maneuverability. If this were not enough to sink my morale, as I boarded I took note of the six gun shutters, and thought six cannon a feeble armament with which to threaten federal boats. Imagine my surprise when I climbed down into the casemate and discovered only two Brooke's Rifled cannon on board. These two weapons, though well made pieces, seem a joke made in the poorest taste.

Though hours must have passed as we steamed downriver avoiding obstacles our opponent had placed in our path, my next vivid memory is of our ram engorged in the sinking wreck of the U.S.S. Southfield. Having rammed her, she was surely sinking, but seemed to be taking us with her. To my back was the boiler, and beyond that the fire room. I heard the commotion of many men straining to their work, in an attempt to raise enough steam to pull our bow from the other ship before we accompanied her to the bottom.

Being the least senior of the officers, I was in charge of all on board who were not needed at a battle station. To prevent them being under the foot of men with a job to do, I quartered my command in the crews apartments, just forward and beneath the pilot house.

My bones did turn to molasses when I saw the river water collected at our feet pour to the foremost part of the compartment. My eyes went directly to the iron grate above us, I wondered what chance I had to get out alive whence the bow dipped further, and the river started pouring in from that portal. To be trampled or drowned seemed my likely fate at that moment.

All the while this was happening, above us loomed the U.S.S. Miami, raining down all manner of abuse upon us. It was stunning to be inside a vessel taking constant fire at point black range, from weapons as powerful as any on the open seas, and yet take no discernable damage. At one point the Captain of the vessel assaulting us, became so impassioned that he took personal charge of one of his most powerful pieces, and firing the cannon onto our sloped armor, was killed by the explosion of his own ordinance.

I knew nothing of this at the time of course, but apparently, the Captain of the Southfield, stepped from the deck of his sinking vessel, directly on board the Miami, at the exact moment that the Captain of the

Miami was killed. Immediately, he took command of the vessel. Here, one must assume, is a man with a destiny. Fate has ordained that he command a warship, and may the pity of angels fall on the smoldering body of the man who stood in his way.

It looked to me as if my goose were cooked. I stood fast between the crew and their passage above decks. There, I stood with cutlass in hand, hoping to keep them calm and stay ahead of them when the order to abandon ship was given. Suddenly an order came down from above, "All free hands on deck, prepare to board!"

It was later told to me by the First Officer, that The Captain feared that men would not dare to venture above decks, for fright of being caught in the open, with no cover, and exposed to all manner of cannon fire and musketry. Furthermore, would any Officer be brave enough to lead them? No sooner was the order given, than we poured out on to the foredeck, in a veritable geyser. From over the pilot's shoulder, our good Captain Cooke, watched me deliver all available hands to the fray.

I had pistol and cutlass in hand, and gave the order to fire, wherein a couple of sailors at the rails of the Miami fell with wounds. The rest, shocked and surprised at our audacity, took cover and returned fire. The Captain stood astounded as he watched me on the deck commanding the men with a calm hand, and total authority. Armageddon seemed to be raining down on us, as even more fire descended to our decks, and I heard the call from the Miami above, "Prepare to repel boarders!"

What Captain Cooke took to be bravery, was actually only a symptom of our collective cowardice. As each man, to the last, knew he could face any danger in the open morning air, before facing the cold killing waters that would collect in the belly of our iron beast. What is more, not one of the men operating under my orders suffered death or injury from the fusillade bearing down on them.

In fact our only casualty was a lever man on the aft gun who wanted to get a peek at the battle from inside the casemate. Here we were, naked, as it were, before all; with enemy fire raining down on us like a storm of hail in July. Not one of us scratched, yet this poor soul below us shows his face at one of the small canon shutters, and an officer on board the Miami ends the man's career on earth with a single pistol shot.

Any Calvinist Preacher worth his salt could argue a theology of predestination, based on the two instances I have herein submitted and convert the Pope in Rome! At about this time, many of us on the foredeck, were up to our ankles in the river, but before the rising waters reached the grate of which I have spoken, the Southfield came to rest on the riverbed. As the sunken vessel settled, the Albemarle was suddenly released, which proved more than a match for some of our sea legs, as our vessel stuck its nose to the air like a plantation widow, and made a crawfish maneuver toward the far bank.

As the Miami retreated, cheers drown out the sounds of our engines. The Brookes guns then fired, more in a salute, than in any hope of striking our fleeing enemy. It was then that it occurred to me that our cannon had not been fired at all… during the entire battle. I was put in charge of collecting the survivors of the Southfield that had not clambered aboard the Miami, as prisoners of war.

The purpose of our endeavors aboard ship on this occasion was to aid General Hoke's troops in the recovery of Plymouth, by freeing the adjacent river of Federal boats and shelling both Battery Worth and Fort Williams, while he pressed the opposition to accept terms. We regained Plymouth in this way, and struck a blow that was no doubt felt in Washington itself. A handful of victories such as this could eventually disable the blockade, and renew our hope of victory.

~

There was a strange occurrence that followed these events. I was dispatched with a detail of men under my command, to march the prisoners. We were to rendevouz with the sixteen hundred prisoners General Hoke had captured during the enemy's surrender. I saw the sad product of war in all its verities during this march. I must admit that I became rather disheartened seeing what our work, which we had so heartily cheered, had wrought upon men who stand before GOD just as I do.

The Sergeant in charge of taking prisoners to the rear and escorting them to prison, had just made his mark on the paper releasing my charge into his custody, when a Yankee prisoner, in an artillery uniform, asked leave to speak a word with me. The Sergeant brandished a rusty revolver, as if to pistol whip the man, but I ordered him to stand down.

The Yankee stood with a man he said to be his brother. He asked me a number of curiosities and had me quite puzzled as to what he was getting at. He then told me he was a Southerner, and felt sure to be killed by his guard as a traitor. It was a piteous plea he made, full of the worries he held for kith and kin back home, if their breadwinner did not return.

My heart has always been hardened to Southern Men who took up the Federal cause, and particularly to those who enlisted in their wretched Army. How many fellow Southerners has his cannon fire killed and maimed? On this day, after what I had seen, to judge him seemed a grievous sin.

Perhaps I was wrong. I took his name down, along with that of his brother. I then took the guard aside. I told him that I had been told of the threats he had lain upon the two prisoner's heads. I informed him, though it a lie, that I had given one of the other guards a gold dollar, and made him swear upon the bible I carry (by the generosity of my Mother) *that he would report to me under what conditions they were handed over to the command of the prison. If anything befell them along the way, the man, whom I would not name, would report all of the particulars.*

An unlawful killing could mean a Court Martial and a firing squad. This I think put the fear into him. Although I have no way of finding out, I am sure they made it to the prison safely. What befell them then, I know not. They have their fate just as I have my own.

~

With a fresh provision of coal, ham, lard, bacon, tobacco, and all other sundries captured at Plymouth, we found ourselves, early May, steaming into the Sound from which the Albemarle took her name. The flotilla we led included two other ships, neither of which very formidable. One of our escorts carried troops, the other fuel and provisions. We went forth directly, and resolutely into the midst of seven Federal Warships, the weakest of these carrying far more cannon than we could muster.

One of our escorts had the good sense to stay behind when they saw the opposition amassed before us. The other was commanded by a fool, by the time we were in the worst of it, this ally of ours had struck her colors. As I write this letter she stands in the enemy's hands. No doubt she is undergoing repairs and will soon be arrayed against. Once again, our weakness becomes our opponent's strength.

We were here, in the Albemarle Sound, to assist with the attack on New Bern, but we came up, it seems, against a brick wall. After a few well placed shots with our aft gun, she was hit. Breaking off a couple of feet of the barrel around the bottom of the muzzle. The Brooks is a reinforced banded gun and therefore, less prone to misfire when damaged,

thus she remained in use, but her effectiveness was irretrievably compro-
mised. Soon we found ourselves in a familiar position: hull to hull with
an enemy craft.

It was the enemy who decided to ram us this inning, to little effect.
It knocked many of us around, submerged the aft beam, and as long as
they held steam, kept it under. As I have told you, the sight of water
rushing into a 300 ton ironclad vessel can turn anyone's blood cold. The
sure leadership of Captain Cooke managed to keep our morale up during
this test of nerve, nothing less could have.

Just as we were being rammed, and again, just after being rammed,
we fired our lone undamaged cannon at the looming bow of our enemy, a
scant few yards away. The force of these shots pierced not only the ves-
sel, but also her boiler. The screams and cacophony of Hell, were heard
on that day, in the roar of escaping steam, and the tortured screams of
men being scalded to death. Forgive me dear Mother if I speak plainly,
those who spare the cult of womanhood the truth of this conflict are in
error, though I know only you who would agree. I can not even speak
thusly to my gracious bride. Catherine disagrees, but I say, wherever
truth is hidden, ignorance is in plain sight.

Again I attempted to lead a boarding party, but the order to board
was soon rescinded, and wisely so, for it would have been our doom to
attempt it. Of course, by then our fighting spirit was so roused that we
would follow any order, no matter how fool-hearty, as long as it was is-
sued from our noble captain.

Soon the ship retreated, firing her stern chasers, so as to hit us below
the waterline, which would surely have meant our sinking. More than
once, I watched a shell strike the water to starboard. Looking through
the starboard gun shutter which was the death of our former leverman,
I turned my head quickly, trying to brace for the impact. Through a port

shutter what do I see? The same shell rebound after passing beneath our keel and breaching a mere twenty yards to port. The angel of death, passed under.

With this ship cleared of our vicinity, the six remaining vessels poured the terror down upon us. Although I'm told this part of the engagement lasted a mere thirty minutes, I scarcely believe it. I do not know if the enemy carried fifty guns, or a hundred, but they expended all they could bear, for as long as our escape remained blocked. This was an endless moment, the membranes within the nose and ear were soon ruptured from the impacts, and the remorseless noise and concussion they created.

We all knew a fear, an animal fear beyond reason or sense, and the only thing that held us together was the knowledge that we shared a common fate, and sink or swim, if you'll forgive me, we must remain loyal to one another.

When we at last had opportunity to escape back up river, our funnel was so damaged that we had no draft. Our fires smoldered, the pressure bottomed out in the boiler, and capture seemed inevitable. Someone suddenly shouted, "Grease the pig and scald the sow." We stepped to it, loading all of our bacon, lard, and fatback into the furnace. This fuel burned hot as blazes without draft, taking us as far as Plymouth, where we have been licking our wounds ever since. And this they called a victory.

~

It is now early July and Captain Cooke has been relieved of duty due to ill health. With his departure, so departs my love for the vessel he commanded. They have handed The Albemarle over to Commander John Newland Maffitt, the famed blockade runner, and he can have her.

Commander Maffitt has no doubt contributed greatly to our cause, but blockade runners are little better than pirates in my opinion, and it is hard for me to place the same confidence in him as I did Captain Cooke, let alone my admiration. All things coincide, and I, as well, have been relieved.

I have orders to report directly to Secretary of the Navy Gideon Welles, for what reason a man of his distinction would call me to Richmond, I know not, but to Richmond I will go, and it is my hope that I will carry your blessing.

Your Devoted Son,
William Roberts

William
2nd Epistle

Ghosts of the Soon Departed

1864

Dearest Catherine,

Though I continue to write you from time to time, when the good Lord allows, I have not been able to touch on the subject of my current duties or the circumstances under which they were assigned to me. It has been a fortnight since I was called to the Capitol. I met immediately with Secretary Welles who commended me on my service aboard the Albemarle. As the accolades rained down upon me, I became somewhat suspicious as to my reasons for being in his office.

This, however, was just the beginning, as the Secretary of The Treasury was then called in. The chore of buttering me up was then handed over to him and he launched into it with appetite. In fact, Mr. Welles had very little to say, after making the introductions. I responded with apparent modesty, though what I actually experienced was shame, knowing that there were true heroes in the field as well as on the sea, who aren't even commended by their Sergeant Major, much less these men of esteem.

Eventually the man got around to the subject of my father's business, and my chores therein. It seems the treasury was looking for a man, an officer, who had a spotless record, believed in the cause, was God-fearing, had seen the tiger smile, and had experience escorting large amounts of moneys across country.

It seemed to them that I fit the bill exceedingly well. They asked if, before secession, any moneys in my charge had been lost or come up short upon receipt. For my part, I answered truthfully, and they seemed all the more impressed when they pressed me to know the amounts, and the frequency of such sojourns.

"You're my man," the gentleman said, and with that I was fully vested by a man from England whom they brought in, and promoted to Captain on that very spot. They introduced me to a blond haired youth whom they called in from the vestibule. His name is Lieutenant James Marion, and he is in my charge at this very moment.

As I wondered to myself who would be produced next from just outside the office door. They sent the insurer out to see to it the vestibule was cleared. They then locked the door going out into the main hallway, and he came back into the office closing and locking that door. He sat the back of a kitchen chair to the door and sat down in it, leaving his head to rest right next to the keyhole.

I was astounded as to the purpose of our privacy. As soldiers turned away anyone with an interest in entering the vestibule, a map was lain on the Secretary's desk. He pointed and said, "This is Haynesville, in the State of Tennessee. For purposes that needn't bother you, moneys were delivered there in the form of Mexican Double-eagles."

"Gold," James whispered, unintentionally.

"Yes, Mr. Marion, gold," the man said with barely restrained hostility.

"You are to dress as civilians, traveling by rail whenever possible. You will reach this location by the most expedient means necessary. Once you have found lodgings return to the station. At the station you will post a handwritten bill beside the ticket office window, requesting the hire of a boot black who's to enquire at your lodgings. A man will respond to your bill who wears a jacket with one sleeve torn from it.

"You will retain him under this pretense. He will offer to take you where the fishing is good in those parts. All of this subterfuge is necessary because the Yanks are in and out of there from time to time, they attempt to make use of our rails there, and even when they're not about, Union sympathies run high in that region.

"This man will equip you with a wagon which contains the goods we spoke about earlier. You'll also get fresh uniforms and he'll outfit you with the best of everything for your journey. Papers and maps hidden with the cache will guide you on the rest of your journey. What I can tell you now is that you are to travel overland to Florida and then via ship, through the blockade, to a Southern Isle.

"Originally these moneys were to be taken a southwesterly course, but with Chattanooga and Charleston in question, they were halted on their original journey. We see now that Sherman is meant for Atlanta and we will yet hold Charleston, at least certainly long enough for you to complete your mission. Pass between these two cities, hugging near the port town, but not too near, mind you.

"We can't afford for you to fall in to too heavily populated areas. Avoid the people you meet. Avoid enlisted men. Talk only to other Confederate Officers, and tell them only what your orders say. These orders contain no delicate information and will be included with the wagon. Know those orders. Know them by rote."

~

We now know our orders by rote, and not much else. We have collected the goods and drove our fine, heavily muscled mules into the mountains of North Carolina. The word of "the bootblack" is that the gold is to be used by Jefferson Davis, should the worst happen and he need legal council when charged with treason by the Federals, but James speaks at our campfire of the two Secretaries reading the writing on the wall and doling out some well protected security for their dotage.

I say posh on his tales of conspiracy, but inside I feel a rogue's heart beating, wondering if they're more afraid of our being caught by the Union troops or our own. When I tell him orders are orders, he holds up our fictitious documents, telling me his orders are to report to a Battery in Southern Florida that's been abandoned for these six months.

What has me even more on edge is that we are known. The bootblack warned that while on route to Haynesville, he received word that our mission was known to the Federals and details of it, along with a description of ourselves and what little we brought from Richmond, was now circulating among the Union brass. He told us to be wary of those Union officers looking for quick promotion upon our capture, and to fear those looking for quick riches upon our disappearance.

James is a curious creature. He seemed eloquent and professional when first we met, but as soon as we left the offices of government his true colors were on display. He wanted to know what hardware I packed for the ride. The Navy revolvers we carry are of a piece, however, he was beside himself with envy when he examined the fine English carbine I won, I'm embarrassed to confess, from Commander Maffitt at cards.

He first laid eyes on the gun in our hotel lobby in Richmond. Then and there, before all and sundry, he threatened to win it, out from under me, in the very same fashion I acquired it. From then until now, he has continuously bragged, boasted, and brayed in the most low and course fashion. The man suffers a devastating physical impediment, in that he seems physically unable to shut his mouth. He never tires of his own voice, and although he can be an amusement, there will come a time when, need be, I will have to shut his mouth for him, gladly curing him.

As a result of the bootblack's report, we are both clean shaven for the first time since we were in knee britches. We may be the only two commissioned officers in the whole of the Confederate Military to go about with no whiskers of any kind.

I am afraid that the words I write here will have to remain pressed in my Bible, well hidden with our cache until this mission is over. We can take no chance of anyone discovering our true purpose. I also carry a letter for Mother, I will post it when I am nearest Summerville, though I dare not get as close as I desire.

~

We are now leaving the most mountainous portions of North Carolina. The people who inhabit these parts are Unionist for the most part, and those who aren't fear their neighbors to such an extent that they dare not offer hospitality to passing troops. We are bound for a place called Morgan Town if I recall correctly. We've decided to suspend our mandate to avoid settlements in order to resupply, having lost some of our store down a ravine on a treacherous mountainside.

The heat has become almost unbearable. James shed his jacket earlier this morning. Unfortunately our jackets are the only Confederate issue we possess. We brought them with us from Richmond. Imagine our chagrin when the bootblack handed over the new uniforms we were promised, and we found them to be captured Union garments. I told my companion, when he put away his jacket, "Lieutenant, some yokel here abouts will certainly put the lead to you, thinking you a Yank, with that blue belly." He denied the resemblance vehemently. "Twere it so, these woods is thick with traitors," said he, "I'd probably be all the safer."

~

It is my belief that we have today passed the town we sought to resupply in. All we met on the road today was a slave mending a fence. I hailed him saying, "Hand, tell me where lies Morgan Town." He removed his hat before addressing me. "If it's Morganton yous afta, I'm afraid you've put your back to it already, sir." James sat up from his nap just then and piped in saying, "Listen here, we don't need no back sass from you."

The slave's eyes grew wide, and he looked back to me saying, "You done got yourself a Yankee prisoner!" Well I laughed until I thought I might cry, and James was raging with anger. He swears if we continue to travel south, passing a local peak, name of Ironmonger, on our left we'll surely hit Morganton before nightfall. He took the field hand's word at nothing, and even argues with the map, claiming the surveyor drunk when he charted these regions. Devil his due, he did get the last laugh when he woke from his next nap to find the infernal heat had driven me to the same wardrobe.

Now I sit here on a stump, having eaten my cold Johnny-cakes for lunch, watching James with his charts and maps spread out on a bed of moss. He keeps looking over my shoulder at Ironmonger, then back at the position of the sun. Perhaps this task was better suited for army officers, navigation on land being so different from that at sea. We'll push on in a moment, until then, my thoughts are of home.

Lost Without You,
William Roberts

2nd R.C.

Ghosts of the Soon Departed

1969

Doug and R.C. quietly put the letters away in the Bible. Then they took the book with them out the door. They stepped down, a couple of feet, out of the open doorway where the front porch once stood. The little girl was back from lunch, "Well... tarnation, what's went with the glass in my windows?"

They said nothing to her. They walked mutely into the adjacent vacant lot, and halted when they were in the shade of the great tree there. Doug put his hands on his hips and turned about where he stood, surveying the real estate. R.C. squatted, and resting on the heels of his feet, he appraised the slope and contour of the turf spreading away from the hardwood.

"So they thought they were Yankees," Doug said quietly.

"If they'd ah known what they're cargo was, would it ah mattered?"

Doug pulled up some grass by the roots and examined the earth beneath. "I suppose, with a bulldozer, we could have that money in our laps by this afternoon."

"Can't do no such thing."

"Why not?"

"This passel belongs to the bank now."

"So what can we do?"

R.C. stood back up. "Here's what we'll do: we dig by night. We'll carefully re-move the grass, roots and all. We'll dig straight down... no that's too messy.... we'll drive a rod down, and if we strike something worth pursuing, we'll dig. When we collect, we'll dig a whole in my yard and claim we found it over yonder. This here cabin sat right over there during civil war times anyways." He fanned his downward spread palms as if caressing the grass at his feet, saying, "We split this ground up with a grid, we work by the square foot, circling the tree, and spiraling out until we find it."

"What about Gene?"

R.C. looked across the street. He panicked for a second when he thought his father held them in his stern gaze, but the old man merely slept in the easy chair facing them, a ragged fly-swat still clutched in his left hand."

"He's superstitious, when it comes down to something like this. Best to pursue it without him, although we share equals with him, whatever we uproot." He looked down at the scriptures in his hand. "Touching on that subject," he said, "we should split these letters up so we both have a claim against each other."

"That seems fitting," said Doug, "though there's no lack of trust."

"Hell, I know that, but I'll feel better about the whole thing. You can take the one to his mother, as well as the bible. The letter to the wife makes mention of yours, and they both have the same signature. I want to have the one that references them goods. I'll examine it thoroughly while you're away. There may be some signposts in it that could be of some benefit."

* * *

The partnership sent the little girl home, and left the structure half demolished. They drove the pick-up to an antique store and found the oldest iron cauldron they could. They went to the hardware store. They bought a six foot metal rod and a 25 pound sledge hammer. They went to a machine shop. They had the rod milled to a point on one end, and a plate welded to the other. Then they returned to R.C.'s house.

Back at his house, they buried a small log of wood, a large rock, and the cauldron. They first drove the rod into the dirt. They tried to pry it out, but mired five foot into the ground, it wouldn't budge. Doug placed a tire jack under the metal plate and began jacking it up. He nodded to R.C. and R.C. put both hands on the plate. The rod easily glided back out of the hole.

They next pounded the shaft over the log. At a depth of four foot, the spike struck the wood with a flat thud. They tried the rock. Striking it, the rod made a sharper report than usual. Lastly they probed for the cauldron, which they had filled with a hundred dollars worth of pennies from the bank. When the metal of the rod, struck the metal of the cauldron, it rang out like a muted bell.

They dug the cauldron up, lest it be found when they made claim to the actual pot of gold, and raise suspicion. They removed the pennies and carried the cooking implement out to a ravine nearby, where junk (everything from failed water heaters to the rusted frames of Volkswagens) had been deposited for years.

"Well, at least we'll know what to listen for," said Doug. R.C. looked down at the antique. "Seems a waste to discard a fine relic like this. There must be some purpose we could put it to."

"Don't be foolish. You've got your mom to do your wash. This wretched thing can only bring trouble. Mark my words: for one t'the other of us to possess it would be our undoing."

And they pitched it down the gully.

* * *

It was an awkward farewell. To be forced to depart, never knowing if he would return was troubling enough, but to do so on the dawning of their new enterprise was nearly more than Doug could bear.

Soon R.C. began his nocturnal quest. He was troubled at first by just how well the sound carried at night. The "tap, tap, tap" seemed eminently louder than he ever could have expected it. The chorus of crickets couldn't hope to overcome his staccato report, and he waited minute by minute for his father to investigate. He prepared in advance a million explanations, each more ludicrous than the last. Strangely his father never made an appearance beneath the tree.

Gene watched out his window. He sometimes came out onto his porch, R.C. holding his breath, but never ceasing in his rhythmic strike of metal on metal. He would hold one hand over his eyes and stare in the direction of the sound. He would go back in, turn the porch light on. And come back out to look again. R.C. knew his father's eyesight had dimmed over the years, and the grizzled coot was too stubborn to get a prescription. He couldn't see more than a few feet into the darkness and R.C. knew the only way he would be discovered would be if Gene walked right up to him while he was in the act. He fully expected it, but it never transpired.

* * *

Back at Bellum Container work went on as usual. There were quiet rumblings. Unsubstantiated rumors went about. There was a dissatisfied faction amongst the workers, particularly the black workers. Occasionally R.C. would have to clean the word, "Strike," scrawled in chalk, off a cinderblock. The Plant Manager, Mr. Deenes, had already organized a few crises meetings for the management. The point being to put down any talk of Unionizing, and make it as hard on what he termed "the corrupting element", as they could legally get away with. It seemed to work over the short term.

The latest challenge R.C. faced, was helping Mr. Deenes win a big government contract they were planning to bid on. The contract was for a cardboard box without a bottom, it was to be a large, shallow box, longer than it was wide. The real problem in designing it, so that it could be shipped in bails, and folded into an assembled box by workers at the destination, lay in the lack of right angles. The two long side panels angled out to a shallow point approximately two-thirds of the way from one end.

The plant contained no equipment designed to crease the cardboard in just such a way as this. R.C. spent a number of hours fiddling with the problem. He finally changed out the blades on one machine, removed the guide bars, and had a special sabot fabricated, in which the cardboard would trundle through the apparatus.

He placed a sample on the belt and watched the maw of the deafening machine consume his offering. He walked past the hood that covered the operation deck, and waited suspensefully for his experiment to emerge. When it appeared, he hit the kill-switch and removed the cardboard. He folded it into the exact configuration required by the contract.

All that remained was to send the item to a dye shop where the exterior of the box would be tinted to match the customer's expectations. He unfolded the container and turned the interior side up. He rubbed a stamp on an ink pad, stamping the cardboard in bold red letters: "R.C.'s CREW."

When he wasn't engaged with his nightly search, or working, he often found himself bored and lonely. He tried having Yank over to play checkers and drink iced tea, he tried learning the guitar, but the only thing that gave him any real pleasure, now that his friend was away, was working on chores around the house.

He built a fence for his father, he put a back porch, with a hammock, on his house, he even invented projects with no rhyme or reason. One day after hours of perspiration he looked down at his latest preoccupation. The face of an alarm clock with wires, transistors, and various arcane apparatus of the electricians trade hanging from it, found itself connected to two six volt flashlight batteries, daisy-chained together, and at the end of this conglomeration eight red rods, banded together, with leads coming out of one end, shown menacingly.

On each heavy stick the words:

"HIGH EXPLOSIVES!

T.N.T., net weight 2 pounds"

were written, R.C. sat back to admire the creation of his hands. "Now what in the hell do I do with it?" he mumbled to himself, but before he could conjure up an answer, a knock came at the door.

* * *

In Vietnam, the clay under Doug's feet was strange to him. He had only been in country a couple of months. He never knew how different things would be on the other side of the world. When the mud is different, when the very air you breathe tastes of the upcoming, or fast retreating monsoons, when the water you drink tastes like nothing you could have predicted, you begin to understand that even the very basis for life in this alien world is something outside of what you deemed all your life to be natural.

It wasn't the culture that seemed remote, exotic, and impenetrable, it was the world itself. He had seen shacks, half starved dogs, and flea-bitten children chasing roosters, in the world he came from. What he hadn't seen were the dense jungles, flooding river basins, and giant termite mounds.

He had requested the most dangerous duty available to a soldier, or so it was said: mine detection and removal. He was taking the gamble that he could learn to use the equipment, and then, with the skills he acquired finding explosives hidden beneath the dirt, he could find hidden gold likewise.

His insistence seemed suicidal to his fellow soldiers. An unusually conscientious Platoon Leader even required him to speak with the Chaplain before he would consider assigning him to the duty. Finally, he was put under the apprenticeship of an engineer hailing from California.

The military was the first time Doug had been around anyone raised in an environment other than his own. The engineer's name was Phil Ostrosky. He was a Buck Sergeant, and took Doug under his wing. They got along really well, everyone called

Phil "Pole" and Doug "Yokel."

Pole's biggest obsession was the music scene in Los Angeles. He had a collection of L.P.s that he kept in the screened in shack the two of them shared. They had a jeep and a radio. Calls came in, they hopped in the jeep, or a helicopter, and soon the airstrip and quartermaster buildings were far behind them and they were on their way to confront another collection of hair-trigger, home made, half-assed, ordinance, guaranteed not to match up with anything in the field manual.

When they eventually made it back to the rear, Pole would drop the needle on a record. He'd say, "A little aural stimulation is the only thing that can relax me after a hard day shitting razorblades." At first Doug hated it, but finally Pole sat him down, and said, "Listen Yokel, you're looking at this all wrong, these musicians have a lot more in common with you than you think. Let me play you this record by "The Byrds." Doug protested, telling him that he had heard him play that cosmic, trip-out bullshit a dozen times and hated it a little more with every repetition.

Then the needle hit the groove and he heard a fine Georgia accent singing a country tune in the high-lonesome style, complete with steel guitar and honky-tonk piano, he was sold. Soon he looked forward to getting back to the record collection as much as his mentor. In time he even began to like the cosmic, tripped-out bullshit he had so recently denigrated. When he finally accepted the fiftieth joint held out to him, late one raining night, he liked it even more.

One morning the sound of incoming rockets woke Doug and Phil from the recovery phase of a previous nights debauch. A copy of Sgt. Pepper's was still spinning on the turntable. Borrowed from the mess Sergeant, the disc was spitting out an indecipherable incantation. As they grabbed their M-16s, flack jackets, and helmets, a round hit near enough their small shack that the needle jumped clear onto the paper label at the center of the platter. As the arm tried to peel the slowly revolving apple off the decal, it emitted a thick, low pitched, roar of frustration.

They ran out their screen door, with one hand holding their helmets down on top of their heads, and the other carrying their weapons by the rear sight assembly. They fled through the blossoming explosions and falling dust, as they tried to reach their trench. Doug over shot, when he jumped into the trench, hitting the opposite wall with his chest. His helmet skittered off the top of his head and sat on the sandbags, top side. He fell back on his ass, and nervously tried to lock and load.

He watched as an unspent round came out his weapons breach, realizing his rifle had already been readied for firing. Pole was already behind an M-60 blasting away at the horizon. Stakes were driven into the ground to limit the machine gun's field of fire. He saw Pole traverse until he hit the left limit, then traverse clear to the right limit, never relaxing his fire. This either meant the entire N.V.C. army was arrayed before them, or there were no visible targets, and Pole was just trying to lay down suppressing fire.

The incoming rounds were no longer falling, and the order to cease fire was coming down the line. All was now silent. A Huey-Cobra helicopter was returning to base. The troops in the trench watched as it swung around, over the tree line a couple of hundred yards distant. Doug imagined that the pilot must have seen their aggressors. Without peaking over the edge of the trench, he could see the nose of the chopper dip earthward, as the bird of prey fired it's rockets through the tree tops.

The enemy on the ground threw some small arms fire up at the bird, but when the pilot answered back with some cannon fire, the silence resumed. The helicopter circled a couple of times, then returned to base, the hollow thump of its rotors the only sound to be heard. For two minutes after the chopper landed, all was tranquil.

Doug could see his helmet balanced on top of the fortifications before him. He looked down the trench, up the trench. Everyone else was looking over the berm. Exposed from their chest up. Some had field glasses. Some were talking into radios. Some were looking through the sights of their weapons.

Carefully, Doug reached his hand up out of the declivity. He kept his head well inside the safety of his trench. The helmet wobbled at the tips of his fingers. It rolled a few inches farther away. He felt for the chin strap. He made contact with the nylon webbing.

He retrieved the helmet and as it was being pulled over the sandbags, dangling by the chin strap, a short burst of machinegun fire, maybe ten rounds, kicked up dust in front of his position.

Everyone hunkered down, or hit the floor of the trench. Oddly enough, no one returned fire. As the sound of the shots echoed, Doug was looking down at his feet. The helmet hit the floor of the trench with a hollow thump, chin strap frayed in two. A drop of blood landed on its dome, three drops followed, them a trickle formed.

Doug felt like a robot manipulating a senseless mechanical limb. He looked dead ahead and slowly lowered his left arm through his static field of view. He couldn't see the blood running through his armpit, but he could see it dripping off of his elbow, his wrist was fully saturated, finally his hand was before his face. His pinky and its neighbor were hanging off the back of his knuckles by a sliver of flesh.

"I'm hit."

* * *

While he was in hospital, he heard that Pole had bought it. Oddly enough, he was killed by a "Bouncing Betty" that was laid by U.S. Marines, not the enemy. Usually they "bounced" up just high enough to blow your genitals out your rectum, but this one had more spring in its step and, at head-level, it killed Sergeant Ostrosky instantly. He was bringing in friendly mines when it happened, but this one had been forgotten when the maps were drawn up. He left Doug all of his records, and his pot.

Doug walked out of the hospital with nerve damage and eight fingers. He had a couple of days of light duty before they put him on a plane for the states. He was lead by a Lieutenant to the tail-ramp of a gigantic plane on a tarmac. Body bags were laid out on the plywood floor inside. The cadavers were assembled in evenly spaced out rows. Lined up in completely parallel ranks. It looked like a platoon formation of K.I.A.s, all flat on their backs, very military.

The officer handed Doug a staple gun. He cut the metal band on a pallet of cardboard. He took the top sheaf off the stack and folded it along the creases. The exterior was jet black, the raw cardboard inside was still khaki in color. A cardboard box was assembled before his eyes. It had the unmistakable angles that gave it the shape of a coffin.

He put it over the nearest corpse. Cardboard flaps, a discreet tan color, extended around the bottom of the corrugated casket. The flaps lay flat on the plywood floor. The Lieutenant took the staple gun from Doug and stapled the coffin to the floor. He gave it back to Doug. "Now, when you've finished with this, report back to me and I'll find something else for you to do."

Doug walked over to the pallet. He looked back at the glossy black coffin stapled over the dead man's body, surprised by how hard it was to tell it from the real thing. He picked up the next sheaf, on the khaki interior of the box was a brand, stamped in red, block letters: "R.C.'s CREW."

* * *

It was late November, and R.C. was driving his Pontiac in to work. A smooth blanket of snow rested on the ground. It was impossible for him to search for the gold without leaving tracks behind in the snow. This was his first taste of winter, when the ground froze, his quest would become much more taxing, and he would have to sit out all future snow storms as well. No man ever wins back time lost. He was in a foul mood. Bulldog tried to give him a flyer at the main gate. Mr. Deenes asked him as he punched the clock, if he had heard anything about a strike.

Mr. Deenes took him by the shoulder, whispering, "All of the colored workers are ready to up and join. They've done got some of the good white folks, people that have been working here for years, stirred up. I don't hardly know what to do."

R.C. told him not to worry and followed his boss into his second floor office. They poured some coffee and R.C. sat down facing him. Mr. Deenes paced behind his desk a minute. He rifled through his desk. He opened a cabinet on the wall. He opened another, reaching deep within and feeling around. He pulled his arm out. He opened a metal locker, finally finding a carton of cigarettes within. He opened the carton and produced a pack. He opened the pack and produced a cigarette. He rifled through his desk again. He found some matches and lit his cigarette.

He now paced behind his desk, smoking the cigarette. Finally he leaned over the back of his chair, with his hands resting on it, and the cigarette bouncing around on his lip as he mumbled, "You and Di... you and, Yank, you've always gotten along really well haven't you?"

R.C. tensed, though he tried to hide it. "Fairly well," he said.

"The reason I ask, and this is hard, I mean hard for everybody, is that I think he may have been a contributing factor in the turmoil we're facing."

"A what?"

"Now I don't mean to say that he's done it out of contempt. I'm sure he had the best motives in the world, but these northerners, they're all pro-union, it's just the way they're put together. A fish is built to swim and a Yankee's built to organize. I'm not casting dispersions, that's just the way it is. Hell, it might even be for the better in some of them places up yonder, but for this industry, in this climate, it just won't wash, I'm sorry.

"Now the owner is looking to me, to take some action on this problem. I've got his papers all in order here. Let him work his full Friday night shift, and in the morning, call him into the foreman's office and give him his walking papers. There's no need to sight the reason. If you have to, just tell him he's not been cutting the mustard, and we've took on too many people lately. The numbers will back you up, and if they don't we'll make them."

The ash had fallen off Mr. Deenes cigarette twice during the speech. R.C. was trying desperately to keep calm. He tried to speak distinctly, and without sarcasm, when he replied, saying, "Mr. Deenes, would it make any difference if I told you that Yank's been anti-union ever since this whole thing started? He's shot his mouth off about it more than a few times. He wasn't so popular before all this, but now he's downright despised. Bulldog and the rest of those fellers consider him the biggest stumbling block out of all the workers. If we fire him, you'll be doing them all about as big a favor as they could ask for."

"It's admirable to look out for your friends R.C., but I don't want you coming in my office and feeding me a load of bullshit just to protect one of your buddies. You'll play ball and help me with this problem, or maybe I'll reconsider and hold your soft touch to blame for this insurrection. Now get the hell out of my office and do your job. It might be dirty, but it's still your job."

* * *

As the night wore on, the workers became more and more rowdy, increasingly insubordinate, and turned the volume of their unionizing ever higher. It was a Friday, and they had been asked to work a double in order to get out an important order. It was just before dawn when R.C. invited Yank into his office.

"Look here, Yank, there's something I've been meaning to talk to you about."

"If it's about these rabble-rousers out here, you've got nothing to worry with me. I'll back you up any way I can. For every pinko, a pink-slip, I say."

R.C.'s voice squeaked out, "Oh no, it's nothing to do with that," in pathetic reply.

"Out with the old tyrant, in with the new," Yank declared.

R.C. bent forward, resting his elbows on his desk, "How do you mean?" he asked.

Rhetorically, Yank asked, "Did I ever tell you about this Indian tribe I heard tell of?" He paused only a second before continuing. "They believed that a pregnant woman who ate a lot of rabbit before giving birth would rear a fast son. Eating bear: a strong son. Eating fox: a cunning son. They had a taboo against eating human flesh for obvious reasons. Then one day someone thought, if a great man rises up, we could feed him to a pregnant wolf. The wolf would bear cubs, who would inherit his greatness, then all of our pregnant women could eat the flesh of the wolf cubs. We would then have an entire generation of great men!"

R.C. looked puzzled, "Is there a moral?" he asked.

"Sometimes greatness can be a curse, not that I have anything to worry about there."

A quiet followed. It went on for a minute, then two. Yank must have sensed the axe about to fall, his face grew long, his eyes went hollow. "I've tried to do good, sonny, but I've got the shakes, and the shrapnel in mah legs hurts so bad I got to take the morphine. If I do I can't concentrate worth a damn, and I'm slow as hell. If I don't, I'm in so much pain I can't hardly walk, my eyes water, my head starts aching, and the craving for that damned stuff starts putting me in a bad way."

R.C. stared down at the calendar on his desk, he couldn't look up. Yank was sobbing now, and seemed on the verge of hyperventilating. "Everybody here is just a torture to me. It's only you that's taken a fair hand to me, they would have fired me... Them boys drew a big dick on the hood of my car the same week my momma come down, it snowed that night, just like it is now. Mom was staying at my house, hadn't seen her in ten years. There was a big hairy dick on the hood of my car, under the snow, I drove it home. Parked it out front. The engine was hot. I was sitting in front of my little T.V. The snow melted off, I didn't know it was there."

Yank was practically shrieking the words. "She asked if I had any Goody Powders. I said go out to the car and see what you can see. She went outside. It was taking a long time. A car cranked. I went outside, her car was gone. I tried to call her back home. She wouldn't answer. I stopped calling. I never called. Heard she died. It was years later.

"A big dick!" he shrieked. There was a pause as he gasped for breath. "I don't even have one!" R.C. looked up, "That's right, I don't. Don't nobody know. It's just that nobody likes me, and when somebody called me that one time, they could tell I didn't like that. So they kept it up. They've always kept it up. I was a prisoner, in Korea, they smothered a glass phial with grease… stuck it down… they beat it with a hammer… broken glass… I don't even have one!"

R.C. thought Yank might have to be carried out, but slowly he coaxed him back into a rational state, told him to go home, he would see him Monday. He helped him out of the office and swore to punch his card at quitting time, which was fast approaching.

As he went back out on the production floor, he saw that the work stations were empty. The doorway beside the time clock wasn't empty however. He heard loud voices and saw people, black and white, congregated at the door, a crowd so large, in fact, it spilled outside. Tater, Roho, Jap, Sonny, Bud, Hoss, Bimbo, Bulldog, Rubberneck, Little Man, Spud, Mousy, Gunny, Chigger, Gramps, and dozens more crowded around the exit, all speaking simultaneously in a great din of noise and restrained activity. He looked up at the scaffolding outside Mr. Deenes office. There he stood looking down at the goings on, palms resting on the hand rail.

R.C. fought his way toward the door. "You men get back to work right now! There's five minutes still left on the clock!" He couldn't even hear himself over the din of the assembled workers. Then he heard the roar falter. Suddenly it was deathly quiet. He could see the men at the doorway gaping at something outside. He brushed his way through them and stepped onto the stoop back steps.

The snow lay in a sheet, reflecting the bright sunlight of the morning. He was dazzled and saw only white before him. The folks outside were staring at something out there, but nothing presented itself. Not a thing to see but snow. Slowly, R.C. began to see something more: little red crosses, they were floating over the snow. Above the crosses he began to see eyes, floating without bodies. The sun went behind the clouds. Forms coalesced around the floating objects, were part of the images. People… clad in white.

The Ku Klux Klan, there was no question, they were here. R.C. started to open his mouth, but Mr. Deenes pushed him aside and walked out to meet them. "You boys are trespassing, I just called the sheriff's office. They're sending somebody down here right now."

The Klansman at the head of the formation spoke, at least R.C. thought he did, it was hard to tell which one since none of them stirred, and he couldn't see their mouths. "How do you know the sheriff ain't here already?"

"Listen folks, if you'll just go home right now, we won't press charges."

"We're just outside your property line. We're standing on the power company's land. Ain't no law against that."

"What can I do for you? What do you want?"

"We heard about these uppity niggers down here. We're good law abiding people. If there's people causing trouble for a local business, we just want to know who's the bad apples in town."

"Bad apples? There ain't no bad apples here."

"Well, we heard different. Thought maybe we'd just make a list as your shift let out, license plate numbers, that kind of thing."

"There ain't no call for that. You just skedaddle and we'll do our own house-keeping."

"Listen here, it ain't nothing to fret over. Just some of these boys, is misguided. Later, when we've got our list together, we'll just send somebody round to the house of each of your lost sheep."

"I don't think so."

"We'll just let them know what it is we don't like about unions down this way. If they ain't home, sometimes a word with the wife can have the desired effect."

"I'm responsible for every man working here," Mr. Deekes shouted, pointing back at the plant, "white, black, purple, union, or otherwise, and if we've got any problems we'll fix them, in-house. You're not going to congregate here, and you're not going to put pen to paper. You're going to turn and walk away, or I'm going go get in my Chevy truck and run your ass down, right here in the snow."

The hooded figures looked at each other uncertainly. "Alright nigger-lover," their spokesman said, "I'll give you a chance to weed them outside agitators out. You just gets rid of them, you hear? We don't cotton to loud mouth niggers in this town."

"Since when does this town cotton to the Klan," R.C. mumbled to himself.

The cloaked apparitions turned and followed their tracks back from whence they came. The ringleader assuring them that they could get all the names they needed when the strike commenced. Mr. Deenes came back up the steps, as he entered the building all eyes were on him. Bulldog stopped him on the way back to his office.

"Mr. Deenes, I just wanted to say that… that's a brave thing you did. We appreciate you sticking your neck out for us."

Mr. Deenes shook his hand, pulling him closer to say, "Listen Bulldog, the men trust you. Maybe between the two of us we can work this out, diffuse the situation."

"We can give it a try," Bulldog said weakly.

Everybody went home.

* * *

R.C. slept through Saturday. The Sunday morning paper carried a story about the body of a Civil war Home Guardsman, whose body was found on the grounds of the courthouse. The authorities were tipped off by a man who asked that his name not be publicized.

He knew that it must have been his father who told them. Who else could have known. He thought about the gold. The snow was melting, soon he could try again. He wondered if the body, now exhumed, might not carry a clue, might not put others on the scent somehow. "I'll feel a damn sight better when the goods are in my hands," he said to himself.

That afternoon he went to see Mr. Deenes at his home. His wife let him in. Mr. Deenes greeted him in the living room. He apologized for the coat and tie, explaining that he'd caught him in his Sunday-go-to-meetings. He offered R.C. a chair. A sheet was hanging over the back of it.

R.C. picked up the sheet to move it and a pillow case hit the floor. Then he saw that it was no pillowcase, and the sheet was no sheet. He picked the article up. Mr. Deenes had his back to him, lighting a cigarette with a table lighter. "What are these?" R.C. asked.

He turned, puffing on his cigarette. He laughed. "Them's my Friday-go-to-meetings."

R.C. turned and started walking back toward the front door. "Where are you going son? I thought you were all fired up to talk to me about something."

R.C. turned in the doorway, "I was going to try to talk you into changing your mind about something. I knew better, but I came anyhow. You're not going to change your mind about anything, so I might as well head on home." Mr. Deenes watched him with a puzzled look as he went out the door, got in his car and drove away. He flicked his ash into the slush outside his door, then he went back inside.

* * *

The next morning Mr. Deenes came in early. It was his birthday and all of his worshippers had turned out for the event. He blew out his candles, and opened a few gifts. The last one he came to had been brought up by R.C. "You say Bulldog sent it up?"

It was ticking. He let everybody listen to it. "Last week I would have been afraid to open this one," he joked. He opened the top. There was a starburst pattern made of cardboard, beneath it, a metal lid with a handle shown. He reached through the vortex shaped aperture and clutched the handle. Every head in the room was huddled around the gift. The ticking was louder now.

Slowly he lifted the lid off the top of the heavy container. He held it a few inches above the cavity beneath. A dozen strings ran from the lid down into the cylindrical metal container below. A few seconds of acknowledgement passed as the assembled witnesses took in the sight of, timer, wiring, and dynamite. Somebody shouted, "It's a bomb!"

Mr. Deenes let go of the handle, but the cardboard aperture held to his wrist firmly. As he tried to draw his hand away, the strings trailing down went taught, and there was an explosion. Everyone in the room, saving R.C., collapsed on their stomachs and with spasmodic movements began to try to crawl away from the smoking gift. They were all in shock, pale white, gasping for air. A few tumbled to one side while their blood pressure bottomed out and their lips turned blue.

The confetti from the party-poppers hung from the lip of the pot. The bits of broomstick lay, with their new paint job, in the gift, along with R.C.'s dismantled alarm clock, ticking strong as ever.

"Bulldog my ass," R.C. said, "that one's from me, and remember: it's the thought that counts!"

The cardboard container plant across town hired him one hour later.

* * *

The week passed and Saturday morning a knock at the front door woke R.C. up. He found Doug on his front porch. He was in his dress uniform, and there was a duffle bag by his feet. A heartfelt reunion followed. As they caught each other up on what had been going on.

When Doug asked him about the gold, R.C. let out a sigh. He led his friend out to the field of lost dreams. There was an eruption of red earth under the tree. R.C. told Doug what had recently caused this scar in the meadow.

With the snow gone he had resumed his tap, tap, tapping, when he heard the bell toll. The same ring of metal on metal he had heard during the test run. Quickly he fetched digging utensils and began his excavation. At a depth of four foot, his shovel struck metal. With his blood pulsing in his ears, he cleared the red mud off the top of a rusted metal lid at his feet.

The lid looked exactly like the one they had tested with. He lit a kerosene lamp down in the hole, and removed the lid. Doug couldn't stand it. "AND…" he demanded. And nothing, just dirt. There was no cauldron, only a lid. He lifted the lid, and there was only dirt, no treasure, just red mud. There was no treasure. He didn't doubt that there had been. Where did it go? The only evidence that it was under that patch of ground was purely circumstantial. As flimsy as could be. It was time to face facts. It was a pipe dream. There's no such thing as buried treasure. The mere thought of it is reserved for children, because they don't yet understand how the world really works. The quest was over.

They would never possess the gold.

1973

The fishing was poor. They were on their way back down stream and R.C. had nothing to show for all of his troubles. The fish weren't biting, but a storm was riding up on them. Sometimes, fishing at a good hole, a man could bring in a whole mess of trout at the first dimpling of the water as the clouds broke.

Doug was just bringing in his line down at Dead Man's Hole. R.C. rushed to catch up with him, the perfect spot to take advantage of the first drops of rain. They might come home wet, but they would come home with fish.

A great rock butted its way up to the edge of the fishing hole. The water was high, almost up to the lip of the stone. He stepped to the edge. There was something floating about two feet from his toes. It was the bible, open to some page in the New Testament, the text facing the sunlit sky. "You've dropped your Bible... the letter!" R.C. exclaimed.

Doug got behind R.C. and grabbed him by the belt and the collar. R.C. reached out over the water, hung over the water with Doug supporting most of his weight. His boots strained against the stone as his fingertips nervously prodded the edge of the book. It slipped farther away, and he paddled the cold water toward shore until the book slowly floated back toward him.

The sunlight disappeared, the sky darkened, thunder rolled loudly up the canyon, and R.C. thought he could see the shadows of great hungry fish, darting about, deep beneath him, as the first drops of water sent undulating ripples around the edges of the book's black cover.

As he tried to gain a purchase on the tome, his finger tips barely brushing its edge, he couldn't help but read what was written at the bottom of the page. "An end is come, the end is come: it watcheth for thee; behold it is come."

The darkness intensified suddenly, and a flash of lightning followed. The raindrops had ceased and he could see the glaring bolt reflected in the water, it pulsed behind him. Doug loomed over him in the reflection, a huge faceless shadow silhouetted for barely a moment.

Doug threw him in the ice cold water with all his might. He felt an unseen force, a powerful current pull him under with its deadly gravity. He cast about grabbing the edge of the book before it fell out of his grasp at a depth of three feet. He was pulled down farther as he watched it float back to the surface in a cloud of bubbles.

Beyond the surface he could see the shadowy form of Doug leaning over the pool, watching. R.C. was pulled down into a crevice. A tremendous force pushed against his chest, he taxed his constitution, not to exhale. Lightning strobed, illuminating the pit that trapped him, but no thunder could be heard.

He could finally resist no longer. He exhaled to his fullest capacity, in a great vapor of bubbles before his face. He had a split second to watch them rise in the flashing light, before he filled his lungs with water.

* * *

R.C. pushed himself up on both hands and gasped a huge breath of the morning air. The sun was shining, and flashes reflecting off the wind chimes outside dazzled his eyes. Shielding his face with one hand, he wondered how long he had held his breath before he woke up.

His mother's funeral had been a hard time. He blamed his recent bout of nightmares on the circumstances of her passing. For a while suspicion had fallen on Gene, but anybody with any sense knew what Dana must have done, accidentally of course. The wrong prescription in the wrong bottle, and Franky's stubbornness when it came to seeing about the doctor.

Doug's luck had turned for the best. His uncle, the pawnbroker, had died a few years before. He was hush mouthed about it, and the will was contested, but eventually he collected on all the wealth that lifelong miser had accumulated. He had his own house now, on the other side of Gene's property. Selling the lot was his father's only chance at security for his impending dotage.

R.C. rang the doorbell at Doug's back door. The pool was behind him. Clean, blue, and sparkling in the summer sun. The smell of chlorine was strong in the air. Doug opened the door and leaned against the frame, the three fingers of his left hand wrapped around the jamb. He waved his friend in and they shot a game of pool. It was Saturday after all.

"Going to see your dad?"

"I'll head on up to the hospital after this game."

"You're not worried?"

"It's just pneumonia."

"What possessed him to be out in the rain at night anyway?"

"Borrow your car?"

"Don't see why as not."

"Distributor's off mine."

"Need help with it?"

"Tomorrow, I reckon."

"Just as well, I got to cut the grass."

Doug loaned R.C. his second car, an old Volkswagen beetle.

"You ain't got no sunglasses?" Doug asked.

"I'll be alright."

Doug opened the glove compartment and fished around in it. "Here, wear these."

"Thanks."

Doug started to close the glove compartment, then opened it again. "Best not leave this in the dash," he said as he pulled a pistol out and stuck it down the back of his pants. "I'll take it in the house and lock it up. Now you'll have to double-clutch it, or you'll never get it out of second gear."

"I'll put you some gas in it."

"Ain't no need."

"I'll do it anyhow."

They waved as R.C. backed out of the driveway.

* * *

The doctor told R.C. the worst. Gene's body couldn't cope with the strain, not after a life of chronic alcoholism. His system was weak, his organs worn out, it wouldn't be long now. He couldn't believe it. R.C. thought about Gene's song, Wildwood Flower, about all the times he had heard it and hated it, been sick to death of it, and how he would spend the rest of his life always wanting to hear his father play it for him, just one more time.

"Come on in," Gene said, waving his son in from the hallway.

"I allowed you might be a sleep."

"So you was reduced to peepin' around corners?"

"I reckon so."

"Do I sound weak and flimsy."

"Not a bit."

"I do so, and there ain't nothing to be done."

"Hush that."

"I won't neither."

"What made you want to spend the night out in the rain, was you on a drunk."

"It's that gold, boy. It finally, just did, do me in."

"Pop, there ain't no gold, and before you waste your breath arguing, I've got something to tell you." R.C. sat down in a chair and continued, "I thought there was, not at first, but I found some letters, only I didn't want to get you all riled up. Me and Doug, we found some papers in that old cabin we tore down.

"So yeah, I know there was some gold at one time. Me and Doug, we set out to find it. He went to the Army, trying to learn how to operate a metal detector, and I set to driving up a stob in the ground, you had to hear me pounding on that thing, you're half blind, but you ain't half deaf. Anyway, I went over every square foot of that tract. One time I thought I found it though.

"I hit some metal about four foot down. I dug down and found the lid to an old cast iron pot, just the kind you suspected. I lifted that lid up, and what did I find? Nothing, but more old red dirt. That's because that's all there is under there: old red dirt.

"Did you dig any deeper?"

"Deeper?"

"Damn it, I've done raised a stupid idgit, what in the hell's wrong with you?" Gene was turning blue, as he shouted with a weak, phlegm filled voice. "That lid don't weigh nothing, and the pot heavy as hell. Ever think that pot might have settled down a little further? That the lid, nothing but gravity holding the damn thing on top, might not have? Damn red dirt, you call it, all up under the handle. Pot sinks two inches, lid don't. Then dirt and roots just works it's way in between…

He paused for a second, long enough to finish a thought, but not nearly long enough to catch his shallow breath. ""You didn't tell anybody did you? Did you tell that fool Doug? By God, I knew it! He's got that money! Uncle my ass! You showed him right where it was. What in the hell would he want to share it with you… He's the God Damned son-of-a-bitch that put me up to it. Go get it he says, go get your treasure, it's right yonder. He's killed me, now he'll have it all… my whole fucking life… never… can't…"

The Doctors and nurses were swarming, Gene had turned three shades of blue, and R.C. didn't even have the strength to get on his feet and out of their way. An orderly leaned his chair back on two legs and started dragging him away. Gene was seized up in a fit of coughing. The people in scrubs held him down and someone gave him a shot in the arm.

R.C. sat in the hallway, still in the same chair. He waited for the people to file out of the room. The Doctor lingered last. R.C. got to his feet and walked in timidly. The doctor was writing something on the chart.

"He'll sleep now. The Doctor ventured a look into R.C.'s eyes, I hope you settled whatever business you had between you. He's… does he have a preacher… or somebody he would want to be here?"

"Damn boy, says fifty pounds, feels like a hundred." Gene mumbled.

The two men turned and looked at Gene, still unconscious.

"Lookout, that bank's slick as bat shit." Gene said, weak but distinct.

"Rube, you's a slow son-of-a-bitch, keep up."

They listened to half of a conversation, for a couple of more minutes. R.C. explained that it sounded like his father was reliving an old lark he must have went on moon shining.

"Sounds like he's went back thirty years or more… some old adventure."

"Here's a tree fell over, we can cross."

The Doctor left.

R.C. lingered until Gene's adventure was at an end.

* * *

It had been a long night, but he told Doug a fishing trip Sunday morning was the only thing to calm his nerves. He was about early, fixing the distributor cap on his Pontiac. He told Doug they would just go as far as "Dead Man's Hole".

The mosquitoes were thick, and a heavy dew meant that it was hard to keep your footing as the trail led down to the stream. Doug seemed nervous for some reason, he said he thought the excursion peculiar, timing wise, but he didn't argue. R.C. had never been more calm, determined even. This set Doug's nerves on edge for some reason. R.C. confessed to a fear of spider webs in their path, insisting that Doug walk ahead. First Doug had heard of it. As they stepped out on to the stone shelf, Doug's feet came out from under him on the slimy rocks. With his hands full of fishing implements, his body hit the ground with a hollow thud. He seemed to almost bounce over the side of the waterfall. There he hung from a sapling, it's shallow roots cracking and popping. R.C. saw Doug's tackle tumbling down to the rocks below. The small ice cooler burst into a million pieces, sending ice, like shrapnel, flying in every direction.

R.C. quickly pulled the sapling up out of the ground by it's roots. He stood there for a clear, stark moment, his friend dangling from the other end of the green sapling, the water cascading below, the rocks glistening in the morning sun, so far beneath them. He pulled Doug back up to the top, hand over hand. They both sprawled out and tried to catch their breath. Finally, Doug spoke up nervously, saying, "Cliffhangers always last longer in the movies." They laughed deliriously for a few minutes, then began their long walk back to the Pontiac.

* * *

The waitress brought R.C. his plate of fried chicken livers and filled his ice tea. Doug was eating his fried okra. The chicken bones on his plate were already picked clean. R.C. shook his head.

"What are you snickering about?" Doug asked.

"You're so damned peculiar, you know that? Eating one thing until it's all gone, then you move on to the next, I swear to God."

"Yeah? Well, it takes all kinds I reckon."

There was a momentary silence before R.C. said, "You know, Pop never did trust you."

"Oh yeah? How about you?"

"Hell... he trusted me, I'm his damned son."

"What I mean to say..."

The waitress came between them to clear some dishes.

"Can I get you boys anything else?"

"Just the check, and a polk for them bones."

* * *

R.C. pulled the Pontiac into Doug's driveway so they could load the gear back into his shed. They unloaded the trunk and Doug invited him in for a game of snooker. R.C. stretched, but then he said, "Ah, what the hell."

The light above the billiard table swung slightly from the pull on the cord, turning it on. There was another light, a lamp lit on a desktop at the far end of the room. An upholstered chair sat behind the desk, and mounted fish were on display all over the walls.

There was a large window on the wall opposite the desk. Outside it was darkening. There were framed photos from Doug's scant time in the service. Uniformed men sitting on ammo boxes with German shepherds at their feet. A few guys with beers in their hands, crew cuts on their heads, and Hawaiian shirts on their backs, standing beneath a neon sign written in a foreign language, a rickshaw barely visible in the background.

On the desk, Doug's purple heart sat in a small display box. There was a hi-fi against one wall and a rubber tree plant against the other. Doug started racking the balls. R.C. chose a cue.

"Is they any chalk?"

"I think there should be some in the desk."

R.C. walked around the desk at the other end of the room and sat down in the chair. Doug's keys were hanging out of a lock on the top drawer. R.C. opened the drawer and began digging through the accumulated brick-a-brack therein.

"How the hell can you ever find anything in here?"

Doug drank a little more water out of the Styrofoam cup he'd been nursing since the diner. He put a 45 on the record player and pushed a button. The needle arm came to life, pivoted over the spinning vinyl and dropped itself into a groove. There was a moment of hiss, then the music began to play. Doug spent a minute or two rolling cues on the table, looking for the straightest of the lot.

R.C. searched, the music played, Doug gave up on the house cues, produced a leather case from beside the stereo, and began to screw together a two-piece cue it contained. He walked around the table and emptied the rest of his water on the trunk of the rubber tree plant. He saw some lightning bugs outside the window.

"Where did you get that pot.?"

Doug heard his friends voice from the back of the room. He looked down. The rubber tree's roots were nestled inside a cast iron cauldron. "Well, I..." the statement was interrupted, during its pause, by a bullet that passed through the back of Doug's head, and out the front of his skull, just below the hairline.

The bullet exited the room through the corner of one of the panes of glass. The pistol's report followed thereafter. Acrid smoke hung over the desk. Doug was stiff on his legs, the bumper of the cue in his hands rested on the flagstone flooring at his feet. Just for a moment, it kept him upright, long enough for the final strains of the music to fade. His body now fell, the tip of his cue striking his chin as he slumped.

He fell awkwardly, in such a way that can only be described as ugly. Crumpled in the floor, his life's blood poured out of his wounds in a puddle. The room was completely quiet, until the hum and buzz of tiny electric motors could be heard. They lifted the needle from the record, spun the arm away from the disk, and with ostentatious clicks and snaps, dropped the arm into it's resting place.

R.C. got up. His face was flushed red, his jaw cramping with the clench of his teeth. He placed the smoking 45 automatic on top of the desk, beside the purple heart. A mess, a big mess, it could have been so simple. He began suddenly as if he had planned it this way all along. He went outside, nobody in the neighborhood but Dana, with her head in the T.V. no doubt.

He laid a towel under Doug's head and let it soak up the blood, then he wrapped it around the head and tied a garbage bag over it. He cleaned the bloody spot on the floor with comet. There was a little blood on the walls and the window glass as well.

When he was satisfied that the blood was all gone, he found the canvas cover to the billiard table and wrapped the body up with it, securing it tightly around his victim with the drop cord from the stereo. He put the body in the trunk of his car. He took the rubber tree plant outside and removed it from the cauldron, and left it laying in the yard. The lid had been in the desk. He poured the dirt out in a small pile and sat pot and lid in the passenger seat.

He scrounged up a cinderblock from amongst the weeds at the edge of the yard. From outside, he hurled the cinderblock through the window, aiming for the small bullet hole in the glass. The cinderblock came to rest on the gaming table's one-spot. He came in through the busted window, went through the living room and opened the front door.

He went back, put the pistol in his pocket, collected the spent brass, and came out the front door carrying a television set. The T.V. rode alongside Doug in the trunk, as R.C. slowly backed out of the driveway, and put the house behind him, front door standing wide open.

He drove the car into a small forgotten barn nearby, never shining a headlight. He got the body and cauldron out of the car and then went back to his trunk, where he knew there was a hatchet. When he got back in his car, he didn't stop driving until he was clear across town.

They were constructing a new bridge across the Catawba River. He moved a few cones and barricades, and drove out onto the expanse. The river flowed, dark and pungent, thirty feet below the span. He took the body out of the trunk and tied the television cord around its ankles. He gave the cord a stiff jerk. It popped right out of the television. Shit, what to do now? Not enough cord to wrap it around the T.V. and then secure it.

He rifled around in the trunk. Nothing. Damned if Doug didn't set that doggy bag full of chicken livers, and bones in here while he was getting the tackle out of the trunk, and just plain forgot it. He picked up the brown paper bag, soaked clean through in dark glistening patches of chicken grease.

Rope… not rope, twine, sitting there the whole time in a little bundle. That paper sack had it covered up, I'll be damned. He tossed the bag aside and wrapped a couples of good twists around his victim's ankles. He tied the other end of the cord around the television, until the body would be soundly anchored to it. Two or three feet of loose cord led between the two burdens.

He picked up everything he intended to leave with and put it all back in the trunk, and closed it. He sat the T.V. in Doug's lap and picked him up. He cradled the body in his arms, with the T.V. balanced on top. He took a few strenuous steps toward the guardrail, and hurled the body, at a running go or something near to it.

The body and its anchor cleared the bridge without touching, just barely. As they fell in tandem, they parted a little. For a second the cord between them could be seen in the bright moonlight. They struck the water loudly, and the body floated for a second, before the appliance dragged it under, and out of sight.

* * *

The Star Spangled Banner had just ended, and the American Flag was replaced by an Indian Chief's head, his bonnet every color imaginable. A monotone buzz came out of the television. Dana turned it off and went out on the porch yawning. All the lights were out. She hated the glare on the screen. R.C.'s car pulled up into his driveway with the headlights off.

He got out and went around the back of his house, he came back with a shovel. He opened his trunk. He put an old black pot on the ground right at his tail gate. He dropped something the size of a cantaloupe, maybe bigger, into it. What next, did he pulled out of the trunk, but a couple of stiff old gloves, probably work gloves, been left out in the rain. In they went, then he turned, putting his body between Dana and her view of the pot. He took something out of his pocket, and put this last thing into the vessel at his feet.

He closed the trunk and put a lid on that old pot. Across the street he went, carrying the pot by it's handle, and hefting the shovel over his right shoulder. He stopped under the old hardwood and looked up into it. Dana looked up into it as well, but couldn't make out what he was seeing.

About five minutes into digging a hole, Dana got bored of watching her brother and quietly retired for the night. R.C. went back into his house when his chore was done, feeling that he done all he could, in good order. Tomorrow was Monday. He had a second funeral to manage, but first he would need to go into work and make sure whoever was subbing for him knew which end was up, and what he expected to find when he got back.

* * *

Early in the morning, light ventured down to the bottom of the riverbed. A television was mired up into the mud near one of the piles for the new bridge. Above it, tethered like a balloon, hung a body by a length of twine. The air inside the tarp it was wrapped in, had all floated into the top most portion of the container, affecting a head beneath the canvas, where there was none.

An invisible nectar floated downstream. It originated in tiny wisps from the cord. The smell set a small crustacean's antennae to twitching, and nervously it crept out from under a small rock along the muddy floor. It was a brilliant blue in hue, and shown vividly in the diffuse sunlight.

The creature began its march toward the great obelisk half immersed in the sediment before it. Never had the creature smelled fried chicken fat before, and it marched toward the scent's source as a hypnotist's victim might.

As it climbed up the console, it could smell a subtle aftertaste in the current, a faint hint of lard, though the crayfish only knew it as different from the first un-named secretion. Its prickly legs carried it up the cord to the place of greatest satura-tion, and its complex ingesting instrument began its manipulations.

Upstream, the great leviathan strained its eyes at the subtle movement ahead. It brought its mass up off the riverbed and let the current carry it toward its prey, with-out sound or movement. The great turtle floated, its head tucked in, and its fierce eyes piercing the murky water. It could see its breakfast just on the other side of the cord, claws pointed toward the surface, the twine bisecting the length of it carapace.

Just as the great beast shot forward its muscular neck, the crayfish fanned its tail in an almost preternatural instinct. This carried the small creature just outside the death zone of the snapping maw. It fanned itself back to the safety of the rocks below, one of its claws sacrificed. Appetite is a torment.

* * *

The foreman walked down the length of the bridge. A cement mixer idled near-by, and a couple of engineers were already on the expanse, looking at blueprints and drinking black coffee. The foreman stopped near the sawhorse table where the other two men debated.

He gazed down river. There was a sheet of fog like a blanket. It nestled on the tops of the pine trees at either bank, and ran about a mile down stream, below this cottony layer of steam, looking as solid as milk, the air was as clear as crystal.

The river ran east. He looked down what seemed a hallway, a mile long. The floor: water, the walls: yellow pine, the ceiling, only seventy feet above their heads, was cloud. At the end of this cavern the sun was rising in the tiny patch of horizon visible. The glare made it seem that the sun was rising out of the river, maybe even the river Styx. It illuminated the tenuous scenery in a golden unearthly light. "Come here boys, you have to see this."

They all gazed in silence for a moment. "What in the hell's that?" one of the engineers asked. He pointed down at something wrapped in a tarp that had just surfaced in the river. A tan work boot had erupted from one end of the canvas. Doug floated toward the light at the end of the tunnel.

* * *

R.C. hustled at the plant that morning. It had only taken him six months at his new job to ascend to the position of plant foreman, and now, a few years later he held that title on first shift. He was making sure his sub knew the proper way to rotate operators at meal times, when the plant manager called his name on the intercom.

As he walked in and saw the grim countenance of his superior, he worried that he was going to get another lecture on the subject of bereavement, the sympathies of the company, allotment of time off, etc. His boss bid him sit down, then he sat on the edge of his desk.

In a paternal tone he began, "R.C., I know that things have been tough on you lately, but I'm afraid it might be true, what they say about bad news coming in threes. I just got off the phone with the sheriff's office. They're saying they pulled a body out of the river this morning. They think it might be your neighbor."

R.C. put his forehead into his left hand and started coughing into his right. "I can see this comes as a big shock, and it might take you quite a few minutes to get back on your feet, but they want you to go down to the morgue as soon as you can manage it. I took the directions down for you. They need someone to identify the body."

* * *

On his way across town, he couldn't stop wondering what had went wrong. How could this have happened, the signs of burglary should have thrown them off, and how could they have found a body tied to a twenty-seven inch console TV at the bottom of a river. Wait, that was it, he covered up in two opposing conceits.

If he just got rid of the body, then Doug would have been on the missing person's list. If he had created the signs of a burglary, and left the body and gun right where they were, it would have looked like he surprised a thief. He tried to convince himself that it was better this way, that the muddled evidence would leave them scratching their heads for the next twenty years.

Shit, where was he? He must have passed the morgue a mile back. He did a u-turn. How could they pin it on him? What was his motive? He was only fooling himself, they could always trump up something, a falling out amongst friends, an argument between neighbors, the malicious coveting of Doug's comfortable existence, or maybe a young man, unable to cope with the death of his parents, goes on a violent spree. Wait, there it was, time to face the music.

He got out of the car reassuring himself that they just wanted someone to identify the remains. But he's got no head! It was a pretext. Were they going to jump him and put the cuffs on him as soon as he walked through the door? The door right in front of him. The door he's passing through right now.

354

The room was air conditioned, but he guessed that made sense, if you think about it. A woman in a white uniform sat behind a desk, and there was a couch against one wall. She wasn't bad looking, so how in the hell did she end up working here? She looked up from a ledger book where she was scribbling.

"Mr. Walker?"

R.C. nodded.

There was a door behind her, and one to her left. She pointed to the one on her left. "Right through there… Take your time, and be sure, I'll be right here if you need me." He opened the door to reveal a room, not bigger than some folk's living room. It was lit by long, industrial, fluorescent bulbs. One of these bulbs wasn't lighting properly, it sputtered and flickered with a crackling buzz that sat R.C. on edge.

"Please shut the door behind you." He did. It seemed odd: he was in here alone. What if he tampered with the body? The walls and floor were tile with mildewed grout. The ceiling was asbestos. The floor tapered to a grate in the center of the room. The smell of formaldehyde filled the air. A faucet near the floor dripped. Against the wall on his right was a stainless steel cart with esoteric instruments laid out on top. Beneath the instruments, and hanging off handles on either end of the cart, were thin starched white towels.

A U-shaped curtain rod was suspended from the ceiling against the left wall. From it hung a dingy rubber curtain. The curtain was closed. He approached it. He reached toward the wall on his left, grabbing the curtain with his right hand, near the top. He prepared himself. He opened the curtain.

His breathing was measured, and he stood his ground, but all the power of his will could not extinguish the terror in his eyes. On the gurney before him was a khaki colored coffin with a huge stamp on it reading "R.C.'s CREW". The words bore themselves deep into his slithering soul. Was there a body beneath it? He began to reach out slowly with his free hand. The curtain on the other side of the gurney was suddenly flung open to reveal a man in a police uniform shouting, "I caught you!"

* * *

He woke up with a harsh smell in his nose. A pretty woman was looking down at him. "Are you okay?" A rotating fan spun through molasses on the ceiling. He hadn't noticed that when he came in. He sat up on the couch. The woman helped him to his feet. "Right this way," she said. Sounded good, he was ready to leave. She lead him through a door behind her desk.

She went out and closed the door. He was in a small office, not outside. Nothing here but a desk, a couple of chairs, a single metal file cabinet, and a cop with a clipboard. He wore a light brown shirt and dark pants. He had a long grey mustache down to his chin, although he couldn't have been more than fifty at the outside.

He helped R.C. into a chair that faced the desk. He went behind the desk and adjust his tie. "I'm glad I caught you," he said. "Viewing the remains in a gruesome case like this one can be… well, troubling. We only make the request if it's absolutely necessary. I'm just sorry I gave you such a start."

"You scared me," R.C. said weakly.

"And I apologize, but if you had looked under that box… I don't know, it's one memory you shouldn't have to live with."

"The uh…"

"What's that Mr. Walker, or would you rather I call you Reginald? Spose your friends call you Reggie?"

"Oh, uh… Reggie's fine."

"Pleased to make your acquaintance, despite the circumstances. I'm Sheriff Kinsley."

R.C. managed to shake hands. "Pleased to meet you," he lied.

"Now, you had a question?"

"The uh… box…"

"Oh, the cardboard casket. Army surplus. It's a little more dignified that way.

We have them in body bags of course but, keep them covered up, I say. At least do so when you can."

"But it was inside-out."

The sheriff looked at the wall as if he could see the room beyond, musing. "You noticed that?" R.C. could feel his color change. "Well, yes the black side should go out, but you see, we got a new man. I'll give him a talking to."

"A friend of mine was in the army, he told about…" the sentence dried up.

The sheriff lifted a towel off the top of a tape recorder on the desk. He took a reel out of a drawer and started feeding the tape through some sprockets. "Mr. Walker… Reggie, I'm going to need to take a statement from you. I can use the clipboard if you prefer, but we'll both be a lot longer if I do." Before I get started I just wanted to do a little background." The recorder prepared, he stood up.

He produced an electric shaver from the drawer and a small round mirror which he hung on a nail behind the desk. "I hope you don't mind Reggie. I wasn't coming in until noon. They rousted me out of bed and I was out and on the job in five minutes." He rubbed the stubble on one cheek. "I've got an election coming up, and it won't do for me to look like no hobo as I go my rounds."

He turned to the mirror and talked over the buzzing apparatus in his hand. "I know you and the deceased were very close, close in proximity, and close in comradery…"

"You don't need me to view the body?"

"Nope we already got a positive I.D.," he said mildly.

"A positive I.D.?"

"The family," as he buzzed a cheekbone.

"But how the hell could they…?" Too loud R.C. thought.

The shaver clicked off. Two eyes stared back at him in the mirror. The Sherriff turned around, finally lowering the electric razor from his face. "Come again? What makes you think his own family wouldn't know him, Mr. Walker?"

"Please, Reggie."

The sheriff pushed a red key on the tape recorder. "Mr. Walker, I'm going to ask you a few questions."

* * *

R.C pounded his palms on the steering wheel of his Pontiac as he drove back toward Walker Town. He couldn't have been more angry about the betrayals he was subjected to during his interview. He kept looking in the mirror to see if anyone was following him. He wouldn't know an unmarked car if he saw one, but it was a compulsion he couldn't deny. Denton's store was coming up on the right.

He pulled into the bottle cap lined parking lot. The traffic behind him drove by with out heed. Mr. Denton was outside, with an apron on, weighing tomatoes for an old lady. He saw his favorite customer coming from a mile away. By the time he got there, old Denton was holding out an ice cold R.C. cola, already opened.

"How's R.C. today?"

"Call me Reggie."

'Huh?"

"Never mind, what's good for exhaustion?"

"Bananas."

R.C. rummaged through the yellow fruits. "I'm only one guy. The smallest bunch you've got is eight."

Denton came around the stand with a butcher knife and split the bunch in half.

"That's better. Ring these four up."

* * *

When he pulled into his driveway, he could see a number of police cars parked on the side of the road in front of Doug's house. He just gritted his teeth and went inside. He was completely exhausted. He sat the bananas on his kitchen table, and went out the backdoor. He emptied the soda bottle. He looked at the transparent, empty vessel in his hand, the initials "R.C." embossed in the glass. It was drained and hollow, a cool breeze blew across his back porch, nudging his hammock and producing a dull droning hum over the lip of the bottle. He tossed it into the tall unkempt grass in his backyard. Discarded amongst the weeds, it caught a glimmer of sunlight. The reflection from the glass was a brilliant corona in the young man's eyes. The wind dissipated, the blades of grass stood upright once again, the reflected light diminished and disappeared. The empty vessel was lost to sight. It was discarded, its light extinguished. The spell was broken and the young man rediscovered his exhaustion. The hammock looked inviting. He feel asleep swinging in the warm morning air.

* * *

He woke from his napping to the sound of a screen door slamming. Dana dumped a bucket of soapy water off the porch next door. She noticed R.C. and tossed him a wave, which he returned. He went back in the house, not sure how long he had been asleep. He doubled back in the kitchen.

Three bananas. He rubbed his finger over the fibrous rupture where the fourth banana had been. "Mr. Walker?" He turned around to see two men in sports jackets. One of them was eating a banana. The other one had his jacket unbuttoned and pulled away from his belly. A thumb was in his pocket, and a holstered revolver in his belt. "The sheriff wants a word with you."

One of them walked over to the front door, tossed the banana skin outside and said something out the door R.C. couldn't make out. The sheriff came in off the front porch.

"There he is," he grinned broadly, "sleeping beauty. Ain't you a prize?" He motioned at the couch in the living room and one of the detectives took R.C. by the upper arm and shoulder, sitting him down on the sofa.

"Listen here, Mr. Walker, or should I call you R.C.? I'm going to give you a chance right now, though I only stand to lose by doing so... Do you have something you need to tell me? Something I need to know? Something you might have forgot to disclose this morning?"

"No? Alright boys, read him his rights." The detectives charged him formally, and read the Miranda to him. "Alright you heard your new friends here, you ain't got to say shit if you don't want to, and hell, that's just fine by me. In fact, I wouldn't mind having the floor for a minute or two, if you don't mind?"

"I'll just take that as a 'no, you don't mind.' Let me take right off, by telling you how much I appreciate you getting me re-elected, mighty kind of you. You don't know what's out front do you?" He pulled the curtains back from the window. "Them there that's being held back like bulls at a gate, them's reporters. Eight newspapers and three network affiliates!"

He cast a proud look over his shoulder at his prisoner. "The hungriest of the bunch is channel three. Told me they'd go to a live feed quick as I snap my fingers. I told them not to fret, I'd be snapping them soon.

"You think you're pretty damn slick don't you?" he sat back down. "Thought you could get away with murder, easy as Crisco's greasy. Well, let me tell you, you ain't worth a damn at covering your tracks, you ain't worth two dead flies.

"Phone drug me out of bed this morning. Body in the river, come on down. Hands are gone, head with them. Who the hell could it be? What the hell's this laying beside him? Tarpaulin, George says." One of the detectives tried to avoid eye contact with his superior when this was said. "Didn't fly, not on my airline. I say's damned if it is. So what then?"

"I call dispatch, give me a run down I say. Not much I'm told, household dispute, three drunk and disorderly, a hostile stray dog put down, a few piddly citations, and a burglary. I call the Deputies what called in the burglary, at home, they were already off duty, sleep during the day.

"Come in through the window, left through the front door. Walker Town's at the end of their beat. Patrol was over, they were just turning the car around, to head back, sun was up, shift was over. Saw the door standing wide open.

"Owner home I asked them. Nope. Did the feller have a pool table? Now how in the hell did you know that, he asks. Listen here Mr. Pepsi-cola, I got me a nine foot table at home. You're dumber than owl shit. We've got you everway from Sunday. There's police from all over out there, even some national. Not so's I need them. No, that's not the point at all.

"Here's the rub: This is the most gruesome crime to happen around here since Franky Silver stepped off her broomstick, and you know what happened to her. You're in for it now sonny, they're gonna strap you in a chair and goose your cook. In the meantime, this here's publicity I couldn't buy for a million dollars. The circus is in town! I'm the ringmaster, and you're in the center ring, you're the main attraction."

"You ain't got no evidence," R.C. managed to growl.

"Hear that boys? It speaks. I got it all son. Got it all." He motioned one of the detectives out the door. The man came back with a cardboard box, probably had a red stamp on it somewhere. "Christmas came early! Looky here," he took out a plastic bag with a hatchet in it.

Shit! In the trunk, thought R.C.

"Look familiar don't it?" He took out a tape recorder that also looked familiar. The men plugged it in and the Sherriff pushed a green button on the contraption. The sheriff's voice began to erupt from the machine.

"Ms. Walker, what did your brother do when he came back to his car with the shovel?"

"He took some stuff out of the trunk and toted it across the street," R.C. heard his sister's simple voice say.

"What did he convey the articles in?"

"Huh?"

"Did he carry them in a sack?"

"Oh! Naw, he toted 'em in an old iron pot."

"What was in the pot?"

"Some gloves and a cantaloupe I think."

"Could the cantaloupe have been a head."

"In a cartoon maybe."

"No, I mean could you have mistaken someone's head for a cantaloupe… in the darkness?"

"What in the Sam hill would somebody be doing without their head?"

One of the detectives giggled, then looked like he was ready to climb down his own hole.

"What did he do with the iron pot?"

"He planted that canteloupe under that tree yonder."

The sheriff hit the red button, and the hiss of the tape ceased. This is just for starters. I'd hate to bore you with every little shred we're using to put you under the jail. People's mad as hell. A good country boy, decorated veteran, killed, mutilated, and dumped in the river.

"Shouldn't surprise me none though, you Walkers has always been trash. Your Daddy was the biggest drunk in Burke County, and that's saying something, spent a year on the farm, and they's been many said he had plenty to do with his own friends death, old Rube…" He snapped his finger a few rhythmic times, before giving up. "…what's-his-name.

"Don't even think I don't know about that bomb scare down at the Bellum plant. Didn't nobody want to press charges on account of the embarrassment. If I'd been Mr. Deenes, I would ah took a personal interest in skinning your hide. Damned people worked for you said you kept order with a pistol.

"It's all over the TV, worst villain since Lee Harvey Oswald. Haynus crime…" he said this last phrase distractedly, then came back to himself, "and I'm going to solve this murder in 24 hours. That'll set everybody's head to spinning!"

"You ain't got shit!" R.C. shouted. "My sister's word ain't worth a fart in the wind. She thinks that baby doll's real, claims it's got a special disease keeps it from growing up, she's crazy as hell! Where the hell were you when…"

"Shut your fucking craw, you cringing dog! I got your fucking murder weapon right here in this bag, and you being as stupid as a sack of hammers, it's probably got your fingerprints all over it!" He took a breath, "And what about your late night planting?"

"What about it?"

"Let's just go see. Come on boys, help the gardener to his feet. Let's stretch our gams on down to the melon patch shall we? Lettuce comes in heads, what about cantaloupe?"

* * *

Dana was watching "Captain Kangaroo", when it was interrupted with a news bulletin, and it was just getting good. She slumped her chin into her hands in disappointment. A reporter was talking, but she couldn't be seen. The TV screen was taken up by the upper body of a man. He was standing there with cartoon flames surrounding him, this interested her, maybe it was one of those cartoons with real people in them, like "Mary Poppins"

It was kind of hard for her to tell if it was really a man, because his head was covered with a white towel that hung loosely. His arms were behind him, and some-one was holding him under the armpit, but they were off screen. The voice of the reporter described the scene.

"…Now he stands accused, and this could be his hour of judgment. Authorities believe that he has hid some of his victim's grizzly remains nearby, in an area they've roped off."

The man walked out of frame suddenly. Now visible, behind where he stood was a small white figure without detail, it cringed in the flames, shielding its head with it's wispy forearms.

The camera made a jerky pull-back, revealing that the figure was in a lake of fire. Vague shapes of goblin-like creatures writhed about in the background. Above it, a faceless giant of some kind sat on a throne in white robes. Rays crowned the head of the giant, and his left hand was pointing down at the helpless figure. Written beneath the throne were the words, "Depart from me, ye cursed, into everlasting fire, prepared for the devil and his angels."

The camera jerked to the right and went out of focus before it reframed and followed the towel headed figure up a ditch lined with policemen. Dana had gotten up, disappointed, and was just getting ready to change the channel when the woman's voice said, "We will continue to keep you posted on the latest developments. We now return you to your regularly scheduled program, already in progress." Mr. Green Jeans suddenly filled the screen and Dana ran back to her seat, saying, "Oh goody."

* * *

"How was the speech boys?" The boys told the sheriff it was pretty good. All except one boy who kept his mouth shut. Doug's head, his hands, and the real murder weapon were out there in that field somewhere. Soon those idiots in the green fatigues would find it with the mine detector they were scouring the field with.

When their divining rod located it, they would have everything they needed. This grinning jackass with the sheriff's badge was going to win. R.C. hadn't thought him so shrewd. He could break loose maybe, but his hands were tied behind his back, there was no cover until the woods, people with trained dogs stood everywhere ready, and all of these men were armed.

A Chevy van sat in the driveway of Gene's old house. The two social workers debated whether or not Dana's file indicated a better fit for her at Broughton's Hospital, or at Western Carolina Center. One thing they knew for sure: without R.C. nearby, she couldn't stay here.

They waited for R.C. to be taken away in the back of one of the squad cars, a mere formality really. So they twisted cigarettes out under the souls of their shoes, right there on Dana's front steps, waiting for the inevitable. There was little chance he could exonerate himself now.

The soldiers in the field seemed to have found a spot they liked under the tree. R.C. was surprised to feel the cuffs behind him being unlocked. The sheriff marched him up beside the jeep where the soldiers spit tobacco and talked about baseball. The sheriff took a shovel off the jeep and tossed it into R.C.'s hands.

"They've marked it there, see the X? Get to work."

"Excuse me sheriff? A word?" asked a reporter held back at the road.

The sheriff straightened his tie and walked down to meet them. R.C. spit in his hands and set to work. Nothing to do now, but take it like a man. He looked around as he dug his own hole. The two soldiers weren't paying too much attention to him, neither were the cops, and they were farther away. The jeep was actually cranked. It idled only a few feet away.

The gun. The pistol, it was in the cauldron. It was a bare two feet under his shovel. Get the gun, jump in the jeep and take off. There was a trail on the other end of the adjacent field. He followed the twists and turns in his mind.

The squad cars he saw around him might not make it through the trail, and he saw no other jeeps. He new where the trail came out too. August, when Mr. Deenes goes on vacation. He should be starting a week in Myrtle Beach. He would have took the car. R.C. knew where the spare key to the garage was, and the key to the truck was above the visor. Replace it with the jeep.

Stash the jeep, take the truck... if he drove straight through, he could ditch it near the Mexican border, and walk across at some desolate stretch, or maybe Canada, like he tried to tell Doug... He looked down at the tip of his shovel... Doug.

The sudden sound of metal striking metal. He looked around, everyone was bored or preoccupied. The jeep's engine purred innocently. He got down and started pulling the dirt away from the iron lid with his fingers. He could almost feel the gun in his hands.

* * *

Dana watched as the ping-pong balls rained down on Captain Kangaroo, he said something, but there was blood-curdling screaming coming from across the road. She got up, what a commotion, she thought. She closed the front door, muffling the distracting noise.

She headed back to the couch, never lifting her eyes from the screen. Before she got there, they interrupted the show for another "Breaking News Bulletin." Dana sighed incredulously. "Again," she muttered. The camera was battling with police, guardsman, and other journalists to get some footage. The tumult was drowning out whatever the correspondent was suppose to be saying.

R.C. was kicking and flailing wildly. He screamed and cried and cussed, not trying to escape the arms that were subduing him, but merely suffering a hysterical fit. The camera finally got the shot it was groping for: a look down the maw of an old rusty iron cauldron filled with gold double eagles and a little red dirt.

Dana went over to the television. She was mildly aggrieved at this interruption of her viewing pleasure. She turned from channel three to nine. "Oh shoot," The Wild, Wild West was just going off. She turned it to U, and started turning the bottom knob. Channel eighteen wasn't coming in very well, it was a grainy Dick Van

Dyke she saw, flipping with the vertical hold.

She turned the dial to thirty-six, where some politicians sat behind a table with microphones, on stands, pointing at their mouths. Her face turned sour. "Just PBS left," she said as she turned the dial farther. Suddenly the screen was clear, as well as the tone.

"People talking," she said, as soon as she realized Sesame Street wasn't on.

She sat back down on the couch. Half an hour until the programs change. She pulled an old family album out of a drawer in the coffee table, and sat her doll up to take notice.

"Now looky here baby, at these old pictures."

The man on the TV with the microphone was sitting in front of a wooden stage cluttered with musical instruments and equipment. To his right were seated five men. "… first, I thought we might have a little chat with the members of the group, then they're going to perform one of their songs. We'll be talking with Robbie Robertson, Levon Helm, Richard Manuel, Garth Hudson, and Rick Danko. So gentlemen, how long have you all known each other?"

Dana was flipping through the pictures. There was a photo of an old man with bushy eyebrows in a field, half a dozen folks were gathered around him. Another picture was of two young men, who looked a great deal alike, except one had a lot more hair than the other. She flipped from page to page. The hollow eyes of the men and women entombed in the book stared out at her, beseeching, but for what?

Outside the two social workers mounted the front porch as the crowd was dispersing. Inside, Dana turned another page. There was a young boy, and a young girl sitting on either side of a mutt with a kind face. They each had one arm thrown over the dog's shoulder, and they were both smiling broadly. "These here folks looks familiar, baby, but I can't quite recollect them."

She tried to remember, as The Band played, "The Night They Drove Old Dixie Down."

The End

Revelation 9:12

www.ingramcontent.com/pod-product-compliance
Lightning Source LLC
Chambersburg PA
CBHW072111250626
47159CB00007B/2397